A SHORT TIME TO STAY HERE

A SHORT TIME TO STAY HERE

Terry Roberts

A NOVEL

INGALLS
PUBLISHING GROUP INC

INGALLS PUBLISHING GROUP, INC

PO Box 2500
Banner Elk, NC 28604
www.ingallspublishinggroup.com

Copyright © 2012 by Terry Roberts
Cover concept by meh with Robert Dickens
Book design by Luci Mott

Library of Congress Cataloging-in-Publication Data

Roberts, Terry, 1956-
A short time to stay here : a novel / Terry Roberts.
p. cm.
ISBN 978-1-932158-99-1 (trade pbk. : alk. paper)
1. World War, 1914-1918--United States--Fiction. 2. Hotelkeepers--North Carolina--Hot Springs--Fiction. 3. Concentration camps--North Carolina--Hot Springs--Fiction. 4. Prisoners of war--Fiction. 5. Women photographers--Fiction. I. Title.
PS3618.O3164S36 2012
813'.6--dc22
2012006557

IN MEMORY OF MY FATHER

Lee Roberts
1913-1982

HOT SPRINGS
AND SURROUNDING AREA
WESTERN NORTH CAROLINA
1917

Little birdy, little birdy,
Come and sing to me your song—
Got a short time to stay here,
And a long time to be gone.

—Traditional

A SHORT TIME TO STAY HERE

CHAPTER ONE

OF course I couldn't sleep.

I am a barren, haunted sleeper under the best of circumstances, and these circumstances were contrary—even for me, a man made of contradictions.

That was the first night that we had all two thousand, three-hundred and seventy aliens behind the wire, some six hundred of them under the roof of the Mountain Park itself. I was comatose by nine o'clock, collapsed in my own sweaty clothes across my bed, but clear-headed by the dark middle watch. At two, I gave up sleep entirely, stripped, took a brief, cold sponge bath, and put on my dressing gown over trousers.

Then I did what I was accustomed to do in earlier, finer days. I walked the dark halls. All but invisible myself, I strolled back and forth on each long hallway, nodding to the guards at each lamp-lit end, stopping to listen and to watch. How were they different? I kept asking myself. These Germans: how different from the rich patrons we had served before the war? And how were we to serve them now, encaged as they were behind our newly-constructed fences?

I lived then on the top floor of the Mountain Park Hotel and had done so for the seven years since Major Jack Rumbough installed me as manager. Lived by myself in a double suite of rooms, 305-306, up under the beautiful, steep Mansard roof. Meaning that I dressed and bathed, slept and drank there. I actually *lived* my life across three floors, through all three-hundred-plus guest rooms, the offices, the cavernous ballroom, the gracious dining room. The lobby with its potted palms and rich, leather-bound chairs. The deep-delved basements, the high, narrow attics under the groaning roofs. The mile or so of porches, both glassed and open. The several more miles of hallways, with their chestnut chair rail and fine Scottish Rose details. When it breathed, the Mountain Park, I breathed; when I talked, it talked.

For seven years, I had grown into the old hotel, plank by plank, chair by chair, monogrammed linen napkin by monogrammed linen napkin, and it had grown into me. It so became me, so obsessed me, that every cook knew my favorite dishes, every bellhop knew to disguise how much wine I carried up to 305-306, and every flower girl knew to sell her leftover blooms to me.

So when I walked the halls at night, it was often in a kind of half-waking dream, most like when you roll over in your own bed, barely floating into some awareness of your body, touch yourself tentatively, pull at your twisted bed clothes, and slip again without murmur beneath the blanket of sleep.

I had walked those halls so many winter nights when the great hotel was all but empty, suspended high in Western North Carolina snow and ice: walked in an overcoat and boots, past the long rows of locked doors, stopping to listen at only a few—the rooms with winter guests—who would be comfortably asleep while I roamed in lonely guardianship.

I had walked the halls in hundreds of spring, summer, autumn nights as well, when many rooms were still flush with lamplight, and the halls themselves ferrying ever so many lost souls: drunk many of them, often desperate, even predatory men and women. The majority with more money stuffed into a pocket or beaded, glittering purse than any of my employees would see in a year.

That night, however, June 15, 1917, was different. The hotel was full, yes, with at least two German merchant marine officers in every available room except for the few that contained only one very senior officer. And I walked, knowing that every door would be shut, every hallway carefully watched over by our newly hired guards. The hotel was as quiet as I'd ever known it, even in winter, so quiet that I could hear the spring wind scrubbing tree branches together outside on the lower lawn. The muted pink colors of each Scottish Rose painted in geometric precision at regular intervals above the chair rail seemed almost restful, as if each angular blossom invited me to return to bed. But what had wakened me that night was something too intense for any flower.

A dream had pushed me up through the billows of sleep into swarming anxiety. Not a dream that had anything to do with German aliens or the high wire fences surrounding the lawn or the army orders I'd spent the day studying. A dream of my own flesh-and-blood cousin: a man I'd known off-and-on since we were both boys, who had grown up into his own cold maturity and become the sheriff of our Madison County, North Carolina. Several years before, Cousin Roy Robbins had pistol whipped a man nearly to death on the side porch of the Mountain Park, and I'd been unable to stop him. A harmless man really, who worked for me in the hotel bathhouse, who'd been accused by several guests of theft—stealing small amounts of money from their clothes as they floated in the medicinal hot springs the hotel was famous for.

Roy had been sitting at table in the dining room—his wife Pauline cooked for us—when the report circulated among the guests. He had dragged the man out of my office and beaten him senseless, ignoring the pleas, shouts, even screams of several guests. Left him cut and bleeding, face down on the side steps and gone back into his dinner—his appetite, if anything, keener than before. I arrived just as he was judiciously kicking the man's senseless body down the steps. It was as calm an act of violence as I'd ever witnessed, and it was morning before we were sure our little thief would survive it.

The dream? A dark wash of color, with Roy's drawn revolver whipping through the air and striking flesh and bone with the dull, sickening crunch of a hammer smashing a pumpkin. I heard, saw, felt it all as if under half-frozen water. On the night in question several years before, Pauline and I had struggled to save the thief's life. But in the dream, the little man was me. The face being shattered by Roy's offhand fury was mine. For Roy Robbins had a very real and very personal reason to hate me.

So I stumbled as I walked along that first night of the German invasion: staggered in stiff-legged reaction to the nausea that swarmed through my stomach, left over from the depth and intensity of a nightmare beating, wondering what it meant. I, the Inspector General of the Hot Springs Internment Camp, the man entrusted with over two thousand German sailors who'd been stranded in America when the war started. Stephen Baird Robbins: hunter, hotel manager, drunk.

The Mountain Park was a four story masterpiece—or so she seemed to me from the very first day I saw her. She'd been built in 1886 by Major James Henry Rumbough, after the original hotel that had stood on the site burned one mid-winter night. She stood in a great U-shape with the base of the U containing the kitchen and offices on the lobby floor. The two wings stretched south across what we called the lower lawn, over two-hundred feet each, parallel to the French Broad River and to each other. One housed the dining room and ballroom on the first floor; the other the lobby and a row of rooms for staff.

The little town of Hot Springs, adjacent to the hotel, would never have existed at all except for the healing waters that drew people to the valley. Spring Creek came down out of the mountains and cut the town in half before curving behind the Mountain Park and spilling into the river below the springs. The most we could claim in those days was a post office, the railroad station, a few churches, and a block or so of brick businesses along Bridge Street. We had the Dorland Boarding School and perhaps five hundred residents year round, many of whom worked for the hotel before the war and for the internment camp once it started.

With the exception of Asheville, you could fly on a crow's wing two hundred miles in any direction you chose and you'd find nothing. Rather, you'd find no structure as large, no hotel as prestigious, no ballroom. ... Hell, you wouldn't find anything you'd recognize except hard-scrabble farms, pastures, hard-use barns and smoke houses and corn cribs; steep fields of corn, wheat, burley tobacco. Western North Carolina and eastern Tennessee in 1917 wasn't the "rural, undeveloped South" of northern newspaper articles; it was a land far beyond. It was a place of the steepest mountains, the wildest river gorges, the meanest lives, and shortest winter rations in the country. It was deep, hard, lonesome, and—if you weren't starving to death—beautiful.

Somehow, magically, just in the middle of it, was a luxury hotel: a phenomenon that I couldn't explain. I could understand it when I was with Jack Rumbough, the Civil War veteran who had become something of a surrogate father to me. I understood it then because of his constantly roving eye, his restless energy, his unnerving habit of saying "why the hell not?" in the face of any challenge addressed to him. I could accept that the Mountain Park Hotel existed, but I couldn't begin to explain it.

That night, the first night of our Germans, I walked every hall of every wing. Restless. unsure of what and why, but far more comfortable on my feet than standing or lying still.

The top three floors were of sleepless interest to me because of what I didn't know. The strange men who slept there. Men who spoke a harsh, guttural language that I couldn't penetrate. Men who had sailed a million sea miles to every corner of the globe, now brought here by the oddest trick of history. I realized as I walked that I was almost tiptoeing in my loose boots, tiptoeing so that I could hear. I was listening intently but for what? Here and there the faintest snore, the whistle of breath, and from outside a few of the rooms, the barest, whispered conversation. Once a laugh, high and snorting, that startled me because it sounded so strangely familiar even though its owner was, in all likelihood, from the Black Forest.

On the bottom floor, I ducked into the main office to be certain we'd posted a guard there. We had; he was sound asleep, and I had to kick his chair leg to wake him.

On the desk, pushed against the outside window, were the carefully stacked ledgers and Department of Labor manuals left there by the Reverend Walter McBride. Former Presbyterian missionary and chaplain to the Dorland Institute for Girls, a small boarding school established in Hot Springs by the Presbyterian Mission Board at the turn of the century. The Right Reverend, as we called him, was careful, precise, reflective, and quiet. The man, perhaps, that I should have been had my father lived and my mother held sway over my childhood.

As I passed on up the hallway, I stifled a yawn. Perhaps, God willing, there was sleep in the night for me yet. Some rest for my straining heart.

At the foot of the stairs, I paused with my hand on the banister, feeling the old hotel breathe in its calm, deep rhythm, settling down with the accustomed summer weight of six hundred human bodies. Even though it was only the first night, I could feel a pattern beginning to form: a future that just might shape into something stable, perhaps even peaceful—over against a world frantic with blood lust.

Then, before I began the slow climb up the steps to the third floor, I had a sudden visceral recall of Sheriff Roy Robbins, felt the creep of flesh across my own face as it was struck by an imaginary gun barrel.

And I remembered that we had our own war in Madison County. Just here in Hot Springs, folded away in our mountains—often a vicious, blood-stained place long before the German invasion.

Who was that lost man who climbed up and up those stairs on that dark night? Who was I then—in my own eyes and in the eyes of those who watched over me? Was I warden or prisoner?

When the door to 305 closed behind me, I peeled off my old, worn dressing gown even before I lit the kerosene lamp with the candle stub I'd carried on my walk. I turned without thought to my standard refuge, the last strategic step in my dance toward sleep. Two bottles of wine stood on the dresser, a third in a bucket of ice on the floor. I wrapped the bottle in the towel Bird left with it and poured a glass of the clear, dry white I'd tried to drink myself to sleep with earlier in the evening. I swirled it before the globe of the oil lamp, gazing at the pale wash of light without really seeing it.

After a moment, I walked out onto the sitting-room porch to let the cool hemlock-scented night air wash over my body, bare from the waist up. Bird had learned to save back the best of the summer wines that we served despite prohibition and to bury each bottle of white wine in ice for me, so that the wine was cold, clear, pungent like the air. I let it pool on my tongue, while my taste buds dulled into a stupor, and then I let it trickle down my throat a drop at a time. Wine was the only solace to me then, barely afloat in the ocean of my own life, without even the surety of a star by which to navigate.

Thus I stood that first night: high over my river valley, at the confluence of the French Broad River with mist-borne Spring Creek. Suspended in the chill air over a river gorge as lush and deep and beautiful as any in North America. Half naked in the moon-drunk air. Rich with wine. Full in the middle powers of my life in what I knew to be the most gorgeous place on earth.

And yet ... no man more isolated within the stern walls of himself. No man more the prisoner of his own cold thoughts.

CHAPTER TWO

In the weeks that followed the first arrival of our German sailors, camp life settled into a pattern.

Even the ramrod stiff Robert Snyder, the regular army officer who'd been sent to ensure we followed procedure, found a niche when I walked him out to the river and showed him the stone pillars that were all that was left of the French Broad Bridge, our primary contact—other than by railroad—with the outside world. I explained to him that because of the war effort, the county commissioners couldn't get the steel they needed to repair it. A small, mule-drawn ferry operated there at the foot of Bridge Street, but we were still cut off from the main road on the far side, and we still needed a way to connect with the main water reservoir high on the opposite mountain. The bridge immediately became Snyder's obsession, the one structure in the continental United States central to his own personal war effort.

Of course it wouldn't be long before he found the steel he needed, sitting lost on a railroad siding near the Army base in Chattanooga, Tennessee. And it wouldn't be long before he requested what he called "prison labor" from Camp B to help in the construction.

John Sanders was sworn in formally as the Captain of the Guard. John was the longtime mayor of Hot Springs and easily its most dependable citizen. Sober, taciturn, always present for duty. John was an engineer of sorts, and it was he who came up with the plan to march the entire twenty-three hundred prisoners into one camp or the other on alternating days. Camp A contained the Mountain Park and its various pre-war outbuildings, including the bathhouse and its hot springs; there we kept the officers, segregated from the sailors. The sailors were housed in Camp B, directly across Bridge Street from Camp A. They were quartered in hundred foot-long bunkhouses lined up on what we had called the upper lawn before it became a prison camp. John was convinced that we could lessen the pressure on the two water and sewage systems if we alternated days in each camp. The result? After a few days, there was a marked reduction in the tension between the two groups, as the Germans themselves began to organize athletic teams and classes in English.

John had released the Right Reverend Walter McBride from guard duty early on, and in addition to his duties as bookkeeper, Walter had been placed in charge of the German mail. He hired several teachers from the Dorland School as part-time censors. He and his teachers passed their eyes over each piece of incoming and outgoing mail as required by the government and allowed by the Hague Convention. It would be too much to say they actually read the letters as none of them could read German, but they did have a two-page list of suspicious words to look for. In addition, Walter finished setting up the camp record system, so we could pay the German internees we hired, for the bridge construction or to do menial tasks around the camp, the required twenty dollars per month, issuing them five dollars in fresh currency and depositing the rest faithfully in accounts set up for them at the Hot Springs Post Office.

John also helped me decide what to do with D. C. Peinart, the quietly efficient cook sent to us from the Hamburg-Amerika steamship company, who was there to help us prepare food our Germans could eat. We assigned him to Pauline Robbins, Roy's estranged wife, who had lived and cooked at the Mountain Park before the war. Peinart became Pauline's right-hand man in the kitchen: working miracles with potatoes, as she explained to me, in addition to his expected magic with cabbage. Regardless of whether they spent their days in Camp A or B, the officers, or the Aristocrats as I called them to myself, always came back to Camp A and the Mountain Park for dinner; where more and more they were served meals planned by Peinart, who had spent the afternoon teaching his platoon of mountain women how to cook the German food. He never ceased bowing, literally bowing, when and wherever he met Pauline, something that, once the shock wore off, she began to do in return. Initially, as a sort of mockery of her little man, and then out of habit, and finally, of course, out of real affection.

At the very center of all this sprawling, complex web of activity lived Siegfried Sonnach. Later, after Siegfried disappeared, it was easy to think of him as some sort of will-of-the-wisp, a ghost almost. But when he first got off the train at the Hot Springs station house, with dozens of other officers, he was strikingly real. Tall, thin, blond: he was a streak of bright yellow paint splashed across the plain gray of the others. Siegfried had been there when the confused group of officers milling on the train station platform had suddenly fallen into ranks so that their leader, Herr Commodore Hans Ruser, could emerge from the passenger car to stride slowly across the platform and be introduced formally to me. I noticed Siegfried because I saw him stick out his tongue at the old gentleman's back, for all the world like a contrary school boy.

Siegfried Mikael Sonnach was fluent, or so he claimed, in three languages and had traveled all over the world. Son of a wealthy industrialist and educated at Oxford, he was German to the core, but full of a happy irreverence that seemed to me more the product of Italy or Spain—countries that I imagined to be drenched in sun and flowing with wine. On the second day after his arrival, Siegfried sought me out to explain why he was the logical choice to become my translator, the person who could move easily among all the various groups of Germans in the camp and carry my will to the masses. I refused immediately, not trusting his open, smiling face for a moment, but in the days that followed, he flowed smoothly past my objections to make himself indispensable: to Walter, to the German officers, and to me. He had the gift of listening; everyone talked to Siegfried. And so without seeming to try, he collected information like a magnet draws metal, information that he shared with me each evening on the side porch steps or in Walter's office. Of course he only told me what he wanted me to know; but even so, what he told me was much more than I would have known otherwise of the rich, exotic, European life growing up inside the fence.

Once things settled down, I began to meet the trains from Knoxville and Asheville at the depot. Not all the trains; my schedule would never have allowed that. But once or twice a day, in the afternoon usually, when it was most likely that we would receive supplies or correspondence, or even more internees, I would take one or two of the office staff with me and escape for a few moments outside the wire. Already, I was growing claustrophobic from living almost entirely inside that high wire fence. I was having dreams of locked gates that couldn't be unlocked, mysterious guards whom I'd never seen before refusing to let me pass. So my once or twice a day strolls to the train station became my first excursions outside the wire, outside the fences that I had helped to build.

On the day that mattered, a day that would become memorable for many reasons, I took Siegfried with me to the depot, Siegfried and an off-duty guard. A Labor Department telegram had warned us cryptically of the arrival of one more train load of internees, musicians this time, so Siegfried, having taken his oath as a gentleman not to run off, was there to translate and the guard to walk our new guests the hundred yards from the depot down Bridge Street to the camp gates. Siegfried was ecstatic at being outside the fence, almost bouncing rather than walking, trying to teach the guard to pronounce German words. At the station platform, I stopped at one end and sent Siegfried and his man another fifty feet farther to the far end.

It was July the 4th, 1917; I remember in part because the German Commandant, Hans Ruser, mentioned the irony of American Independence that morning when I'd greeted him at roll call in front of the Mountain Park. July the 4th, a day we had always celebrated before the war with a huge bonfire down by the bathhouse. It was hot in the sunshine, and I'd stepped back under the shade of the train station porch while we were waiting. Imperial Germany, I thought, inserted into a sleepy, little mountain town that was not really even a town at all, just a village that had grown up around the feet of a huge hotel. And a hotel that was there only because of the springs. "A thermal phenomenon," I'd called it once in a promotional brochure, "mineral water of precisely 105 degrees Fahrenheit, bringing pleasure and blessed relief to the tired and discomfited."

Chance. Fate. Luck. And now Germany. The train pulled into the station, its brakes groaning, its own smoke and steam writhing around the great engine for a moment before dissipating in the sunlight.

No musicians. No internees of any kind. I walked halfway down the platform toward Siegfried and the guard, watching as they greeted the few local passengers who got off. I was still standing in the shadow of the platform roof, when I was startled by a voice at my side. "Excuse me."

Beside me, suddenly, all but silently it seemed, stood a thin, black-haired woman with the most penetrating blue glance. As I turned toward the voice, I caught ever so faintly the clean smell of soap—soap and perhaps vanilla. She was intense, even then, when first I saw her, and she seemed for a moment to loom over me.

"I'm sorry," I whispered. She'd caught me by surprise.

"I said excuse me." She smiled then, and it seemed as if her eyes glistened. "Do you know anything about this little village?" She glanced at the metal sign nailed to the depot wall. "Hot Springs?"

"Enough," I said.

"Where would you say, then, is the cleanest, safest boarding house? And how ..." She pointed to a pile of luggage that had been growing up behind me, stacked by the conductor and a small boy who worked the platform. "...can I get all of this to the house?" She glanced back at me. "Are you in service?"

"You mean in the army?"

She glanced down at my clothes, and involuntarily, my eyes followed. My vest and trousers were more-or-less clean but certainly not pressed, and nothing like a uniform.

"No," she almost laughed again. "I mean, may I employ you to help transport...?" Again she waved at the pile of trunks and boxes, which now included a large, bulky object shrouded in black cloth, mounted on a wooden tripod.

"Sunnybank," I said, "is the name of the house you want. Mrs. Jane Gentry, proprietor. And it would be difficult to imagine a man more in service than I am these last days." I glanced down the platform and was relieved to see the guard taking Siegfried by the arm and leading him reluctantly down the far steps and back toward camp.

"Well then...." She paused, waiting on my wandering attention. "Perhaps you have the time to help me with all this ... this mountain." We faced the mound of her belongings.

"Leave anything in New York?" I asked.

She was not amused. "How did you know I was from...?"

I gestured to the large label on the nearest box. Anna Ulmann, 1000 Fifth Avenue, NY.

"What's that?" I pointed.

"It's a camera. And I have to tell you that it's by far the most valuable thing I own." There was an edge of real irritation in her voice now. Obviously, she thought me an idiot. "Perhaps I have made an unfortunate choice." She meant me.

I looked at her again, the side of her quiet, intense face. The diamond in her small ear. The swirl of raven black hair curled just at the fluted slope of her neck. What sort of woman was this? "Perhaps you have," I said.

She suddenly turned and caught me staring at her. The look on her face eased slightly at the sight of my smile.

"You'll need a wagon, Miss Ulmann." I turned, slightly unnerved, to call out to Tad, the station boy, who would know whose rig was in town and available. "And yes, I believe I can make the arrangements for you."

When a wagon was secured, I helped Tad load her boxes and trunks, but she wouldn't let me help her with the camera itself, an awkward box fastened to its three stork legs. When it was safely stowed, she visibly relaxed and again featured me with that sudden and shocking smile. "I apologize for my earlier tone," she said. "It's been a long journey." And she reached forward one gloved hand to give me a dime.

When her back was turned, I handed the dime to Tad. "Uncle Steve?" the little barefoot boy looked up at me.

"Humm?" I was watching her even as the wagon pulled away, noticing for the first time that her dress was blue. Most like her eyes.

"What's a camera?" Tad asked.

John Sanders caught me even as I was being let back in the gate at Camp A. I had noticed his approach from the Mountain Park across the long expanse of grass because he had broken into a rambling jog, what amounted to a blind rush from someone like John. I walked to meet him, assuming that his could not possibly be good news.

"We lost two of 'em," he said breathlessly

"How *lost*?" I asked, having expected this from the beginning, only surprised it was just two and not twenty.

"We did the morning roll call of the sailors in B ..." He gestured across the street toward Camp B. "... and we were missing three. Which isn't that unusual in the morning. So we counted 'em as we brought 'em across the street, and Jimmy Gentry found the one he knew from his barracks. So we were ..."

"Down to two." It took Cap'n John forever to tell a story.

"Right, down to two. But we mustered 'em again on the lower lawn, and as far as we can tell, Theodore and Eugen Schaefer are gone."

Siegfried, of course, had walked up behind us as if he were one of the guards instead of one of the internees. And before I could respond, he interrupted. "Did you say Schaefer? Theo and Eugen?"

John nodded, still catching his breath.

"Brothers," Siegfried said. "Both under twenty. Both very homesick."

I cursed under my breath. "John, I want you to do two things. One, round up a few off-duty guards and search B. Every nook and cranny while it's empty. Make sure they aren't hiding, so they can slip out later. Two, while you're uptown finding your men, send me Uncle Bob Ramsey. He's probably ... never mind, I'll find him myself. ... Siegfried!"

"Yes, Herr Robbins?" So help me, he clicked his heels and saluted.

"Keep your mouth shut! Do not stop to talk to anyone else except McBride and bring him back here in fifteen minutes."

There followed an hour of intense, flurried activity. I found Uncle Bob in the kitchen of the Hawksbill Boarding House on Walnut Street, eating a fried-egg sandwich fixed for him by the cook. The Hawksbill was one of his regular stops. The Ramseys were moonshiners, and Uncle Bob delivered to a half-dozen places in town, carefully and quietly avoiding Roy Robbins and his deputies. I sent him off for a flock of the boys in his extended family, mountain boys who had grown up in the woods, hunting to put food on the table since they were old enough to hold a rifle. "Dogs?" he asked me, wiping the grease out of his whiskers with an old gray rag from his pocket. "You need dogs?"

"Yeah, Bob, but not more than a couple. Quiet, not mouthy. We want to find these Germans, not scare them to death. Have your boys meet me at the Deepwater Bridge in an hour. ... And Bob!"

"Huh?" He crammed the last bite of sandwich into his mouth and gave his face one more swipe with the rag.

"Keep it quiet. I want to catch 'em before the sheriff knows they're gone."

He grinned his toothless grin. "Shit on the sheriff," he mumbled around his egg and bread.

As I was walking back to the gatehouse, a little town boy fell in step behind me, a sure sign that word was starting to leak out. "Listen, son," I said to him. "You know who Prince Garner is?"

"Ev-body know Prince," he replied, wondering at such a stupid question.

"Here's a nickel then. Find Prince and bring him down to the gate-house on Bridge Street. Can you do that?"

"Faster 'an you can," he yelled and ran off.

Although we could not be more physically different, Prince Garner was my brother in spirit. He was a dark-skinned man of what he called "mostly Negro blood." He was the hotel barber, part-time preacher and singer of hymns, and the head of the small African community in Hot Springs. He'd made a point of educating himself during his time in the army. A large, muscular man, even at fifty-five, with all the jaunty charisma of a Mexican bandit. First sign of trouble, my automatic instinct was to send for Prince.

By the time I got back to the camp, John was unlocking the gate to the now empty Camp B, four off-duty guards armed with shovel handles standing beside him. I only stopped with them for a moment because one of my biggest worries had manifested itself at the main gate of Camp A. Captain Robert Snyder, our pet regular army officer, was standing at attention, noticeably armed with his service revolver.

Snyder was vibrating with excitement. "Robbins," he shouted to me from across Bridge Street, "we must make of these miserable vermin an example. We must find and—"

"Whoa," I said and held my hand out to him as if directing traffic. I knew from when we'd met that he was scared of me physically, and I didn't want to lose that advantage. I noticed Siegfried too had just come to the inside of the Camp A fence.

"Captain, do you know anything about search operations?"

"Yes sir, I am trained in formal search procedures, and I demand that you place me in charge of at least a section of the field operations in order to—"

"Whoa," I said again, immediately sorry that I'd restarted him. "Captain, I want you to take Jimmy here and his brother Jeff and go straight north up the tracks toward Tennessee. It's the logical way for them to run, and they're not likely to stray far from the river or the railroad. Oh, and take Sonnach with you as your translator."

So, after another ten minutes of dramatic rhetoric and even more dramatic posturing, Snyder's little search party set off down the tracks toward Tennessee five miles away.

"Do you really think that's wise?" Prince asked. He'd arrived at the gatehouse in company with not one but at least a dozen of the town boys, wearing a broad-brimmed sombrero that he could only have gotten from Major Rumbough.

"What? Letting Sonnach out of my sight?"

"No. Letting Snyder out of your sight. Did you see that pistol he was waving around?"

I smiled grimly. "I told Jimmy Gentry to let him pull it out if he wants. Even shoot it off in the air if it makes him happy. But if he so much as points it at anybody, to level him."

Prince bestowed his most benevolent smile on me. "You're smarter than you look, Stephen. I've always said so."

"Good, 'cause I've got something else that needs your say so. If I can't find these two German boys by dark, everyone in town'll be peering out their windows with loaded guns. Your job, Prince among men, is to keep everybody in town calm."

He shook his head. "Stevie, tell me the truth. They dangerous at all, these boys?"

I opened the note Walter McBride had sent me by Siegfried. *Two brothers, nineteen and twenty years old. Blond and blue-eyed. Theodore and Eugen.* "Truthfully, Prince, I can't imagine they're a danger to anyone except themselves. For God's sake, tell everybody not to shoot 'em."

I walked out the railroad tracks in the opposite direction from the way I'd sent Snyder and his "detachment." South: convinced that two lost boys, thousands of miles from home, would choose to go in the only direction they knew, back towards Asheville. As I walked, I could feel the breeze picking up, blowing directly into my face, and far away at the limit of my vision, I could make out what looked like a higher range of mountains to the south. Storm clouds, I realized, hanging like deep blue peaks above the mountains themselves. The summer before, the high, black clouds had come down the river valley with oceans of rain and nearly washed away everything in the world that I loved.

When I came to the end of the board fence of Camp B, where the wire fencing began, I could see John and one of his guards ahead of me at the back corner of the camp. As I approached the two, John lifted part of the fence back to reveal where the two boys must have cut through. Their tracks showed plainly in the low ground beyond; they hadn't gone ten feet before getting mired in the mud.

"Well, hell," I said to John.

"What does that mean?"

"Means you got to walk back down to the Park and get McBride to send a telegram to the High Sheriff. Inform him of the escape."

"Roy! ... You sure we got to tell him."

"If we don't, he'll string me up for concealing it. You want to be the Inspector General?"

"Hell no. I'll go tell Walter."

The guard stood where he was planted, holding back the piece of cut wire. "Lance, isn't it?"

He nodded.

"Hugh Lance?"

He nodded again.

"Well, Hugh, go back to the bunkhouse where the Schaefers slept and bring me something that belonged to them, even if it's a sheet or pillow case."

"Fer the dogs?" He finally spoke.

It was my turn to nod. "And the sooner you get it, the sooner they'll be running."

It took me the full hour I gave to Uncle Bob to get to the Deepwater Trestle, and when I arrived there, he was sitting on the rail with seven of his kin, seven mountain boys who were as different as night-and-day from the town boys. Each one thin, angular, watchful. Each one wearing overalls, so patched and faded that they looked like a soft and second skin. All but two wore shirts of the same worn description; two without shirts at all. Four of the boys cradled rifles in their arms, as natural an extension of themselves as the overalls. All wore the rough brogan shoes of mountain farmers. All could have been any age between fifteen and twenty-five or thirty. Three of the boys had a single hound each tied on a length of plowline.

The dogs eyed me even more warily than the boys: two blue-tick coon dogs and one black-as-night Plott bear hound.

"Bees get on that black dog?" I asked as I walked up.

The boys nodded in unison. The one holding his leash grinned and said, "Yessir. Sting his nose."

"That's 'cause they think he's a bear. Ain't that right, Uncle Bob?"

Bob nodded solemnly. "Pure hate to be a black dog next to a bee tree."

The ice broken, one of the boys asked the obvious. "What you want us to hunt, Mr. Robbins? Whatever it might be, we'll track it."

"Two German boys broke out of the camp at Hot Springs. Cut the wire and got away. Neither of 'em has a gun. Neither has ever set foot in the mountains ..." As I described the two German sailors to the local boys, I could see clearly what before I had only supposed. High masses of dark clouds in a solid wall, moving down the river gorge behind them. Pillars of storm the depth and color of an angry bruise.

The last thing I said to this, the real search party, was about how it would rain hard that evening, maybe even all night. That the creeks down the walls of the gorge would rise up, perhaps the river as well. But it was only a storm, not the flood out of the Bible; and the men they hunted were not convicts or soldiers. Barely even men at all, far from home. "... and so I expect that by morning, you will bring 'em back here alive, soaking wet but alive, and I expect to pay five dollars a man for only one night's work."

The shortest of the boys stood up and spit a dark, accurate spatter of tobacco juice onto the opposite rail. Even before he spoke, I realized he was the oldest and most probably the leader. "My name's Edgar Ramsey, and I'm to speak for the rest of us. You a mountain man, Mr. Robbins, and you know five dollars is a lot of money. I reckon it's more than them Germans is worth. We'd go get 'em for nothin', but if you got that much money to throw away ..." He grinned through stained teeth. "... why, then, we'll take it for you."

I gave Edgar the sheet off Theodore Schaefer's bed, passed to me through the fence by Lance. The boys rubbed it on each of the dog's noses in turn. The Plott ignored it completely as too human, too tame, as beneath him. The blue-ticks understood, however, and after casting about for a moment, led Uncle Bob and the boys up the tracks. The eight of them following in a loose group, jogging silently after, their overalls whipping around their bodies in the blustery wind.

I had done everything I could think of to do. I knew the Ramseys would find them quickly if they were to be found at all. And if they weren't found, I knew they'd simply disappear, lost in the higher mountains to starve or fall to death, eventually making a meal for buzzards. Having sent the Ramseys on their trail, I could think of not one more piece of the puzzle to adjust. So I walked back over the trestle, high over a river that suddenly seemed gray and dangerous, as if stained by pulverized granite. I walked back to the Mountain Park, feeling the rising wind take an occasional cold shove at my back.

At the Park, I collected my old hunting hat, a rain slicker, a railroad lantern, and started back up the tracks. I wanted a drink of hard liquor very, very badly to steel me against the coming night. But I knew that wasn't in order, not in this new dispensation of fence, wire, and guardhouse. It was dusk as I started back up stream, following the Ramseys into the rising storm.

The wall of wind and black cloud that met me in the gorge delivered spasms of rain and hail, some of which blew sideways in sudden intense gusts. It brought down a black dark, blasting what was left of the afternoon into Tennessee, and it dropped the temperature fifteen degrees almost as an afterthought.

Once the storm had blown the French Broad's door open, exposing the whole valley, it just rained. It fell steadily all that night in cold, miserable, soaking ropes of rain, so that the rails glistened in my weak pool of lantern light, and the trunks of even the thickly woven hemlocks were slick with black water.

As I hiked the tracks, always a staggering, gimp-legged kind of walking, I searched through my body for the flicker of thirst. It was most always there, the desire for a drink. For at least a year, I had pushed the hunger for strong drink deeper and deeper into my body and kept it there with the wine I drank at night, the wine I used to lure myself into a stupor. Still, though, even as I walked in the steady rain, the shadows of my lantern swinging eerily in the trees, I wanted that bottle of musky red wine that waited for me in my room. Wanted it enough to consider turning back to the Mountain Park even though two of my charges were lost on the mountain.

I met the Ramsey boys at mid-morning, as the storm was breaking up. I had walked the six miles up to the Runion sawmill and back and most of the way up again during the night, once hearing the frantic yelping of a bear dog on trail.

When I first saw the search party, they were far up ahead on the tracks, moving toward me like black silhouettes in the smoky blue air. There were nine upright figures in the group, and they carried one inert form on a rough litter. As I came up to them, I could make out the one strange face in the group—pale beyond belief, blue eyes sunken into his skull, stumbling along in shock—one of the Schaefers.

The face of the man on the litter was covered by his shirt. One arm twisted grotesquely despite someone's best effort at respect. The unearthly stillness of a dead body.

Uncle Bob only shook his head sorrowfully. The smallest figure in the tableau, Edgar Ramsey, stepped beside me, and we let the others pass. When they had gone far enough such that speech was respectful, he told me the story.

"Near as I can make out, them two boys, for they ain't no more than boys, must have run like hell 'til they got to Runion. Then they seen the lights from the lumber mill and no doubt heard the noise. That scared 'em and so they backtracked. Them two little blue-ticks took us straight to Runion and then back aways," he said slowly, making sure I understood. "Ashamed of themselves for missin' where them Germans gone up Pumphouse Creek to hide. So, it was after dark when we started up the creek, and then when it was most black dark, the Devil got interested and took over."

"The Devil?"

"That ol' black bear dog. He begun to talk about it and Jody let him go up the creek. We cut those two little blue bitches loose and went up after Devil."

"Could he scent them in the water?"

"Naw. He didn't even put his nose down. I think he heard that one boy yellin'. 'Cause after a few minutes, we could hear this awful strange voice a screamin' up on the mountain. Scared one or two of our boys 'til they wouldn't go on. I ain't sayin' who, but they sat down straight away, so that there was only Bob an' Jesse an' me. But we kept on, and after a little bit, you could tell it was a human voice yellin' for help. Sounded like '*Hapen me! Hapen me!*' I think the Devil was on him then.

"Directly, we found 'em. High up the Pumphouse. Near as I can tell, the one boy slipped on the rocks. It was wet as hell in the woods, and he must have fell in the creek. It washed him straight down a long, slick place and he smashed head-on into a rock. I don't know exactly how, but somehow he trapped his arm as he washed down 'cause it was tore most off.

"By the time we got to 'em, the one boy was sittin' in the creek tryin' to hold the other boy's face out'n the water. The tore up boy was still alive. I could hear him gurgle-like, tryin' to breath. But we had to make-do by feel, and it was too slick to stand up. I think he was dead afore we ever got him out of there. It was still early, Mr. Robbins, and I knew you'd be worried, but damn, it was dark in there and steep as the backside of hell."

He was nearly in tears by then, was Edgar Ramsey. It was an awful story to have to tell. He kept holding his hands up to his face, and even I could smell the blood on them. I put my arm around him then, as we stood there in the railroad gravel.

"Look," he said. "I know you wanted 'em both alive, and if what Bob says is right, you'll catch it for lettin' one of 'em get killed like that. So you don't have to pay us nothin' if you don't want to. I feel like we done let you down."

"Edgar Ramsey, it hasn't hit you yet, but you saved a man's life last night. I'm proud to know you, son, and will be as long as I live."

We stood together in the mounting blue light and stared after the party of men on the tracks ahead of us. It seemed to me just then that we all dangled by the most slender thread. And that the life contained in any human form was the merest flickering flame.

CHAPTER THREE

WE carried Eugen Schaefer's body to the post office in Hot Springs, taking turn about with the same make-shift litter the Ramseys had constructed to carry him on.

Then I led my silent procession of Ramseys through the gate of Camp A and up to the main office in the Mountain Park. All but Edgar and Uncle Bob stopped on the porch, soaking wet and exhausted. Edgar and Bob came into the office with me to collect their money. When I sent Walter for the cash box, he handed me a note: a rich, cream-colored envelope with engraved initials on the flap. The note paper within was equally heavy and vital to the touch. I was so tired that my eyes swam, but I could read the distinctive, open hand.

> *Dear Mr. Robbins,*
> *Please allow me to introduce myself. My name is Anna Ulmann, and I am a professional photographer from New York. I have come to North Carolina to take documentary photographs of native mountain people and of the German interns, and several of our mutual acquaintances in New York insisted that I seek you out as my guide.*
> *Mr. McBride explained that you "were on the mountain" dealing with an emergency and kindly suggested that I write you a note. And so you hold in your hand my brief introduction along with my hopes that I might call on you again.*
> *AU*

The same initials as on the envelope, and I confess that I was so addled from my night "on the mountain" that it took me a long moment to recall the camera at the depot. And then I remembered those piercing blue eyes.

Let her take pictures of Eugen Schaefer, I thought, awaiting burial on a plank in the post office, all blond and bleached bloodless, torn to pieces by a mountain storm. That would make an interesting image for that whore of Babylon New York City. I wadded the note into a ball and threw it at the trash basket, wondering if my own hands smelled like blood.

When I looked up from where I had collapsed in an office chair, more death was in the room. Cousin Roy Robbins was bending stiffly to sit across from me. I glanced around the office, half to see if he was only a nightmare dream. Edgar Ramsey stood watchfully at the counter, unsure what to do. His Uncle Bob had already disappeared. Walter was standing nervously by my side, the cash box forgotten in his hands. No, I wasn't dreaming. After a moment, Walter laid the cash box down on the desk in front of me.

What fooled you about Roy is that he had grown out of his rough-cut youth to look like a preacher. Thin, clean-shaven face. A hook nose, broken any number of times early in life—once by me— but softened now by a pair of eyeglasses. Thin sandy hair smelling of a barber-shop pomade combed strictly back over a high forehead. A faintly disapproving frown as if he'd just smelled something he didn't like. Since becoming sheriff, he affected a black frock coat and a string tie and started carrying his pistol under his coat rather than on the front of his belt. What fooled you is that sitting there, he looked almost like he was made of milk. But he wasn't; he was made of sin. He was as smart as a rogue fox and sneaky mean. I had fought with him as a boy, and he openly despised me for leaving my family behind and becoming Major Rumbough's "nigger." And there was more—there was Bird Shelton's husband, the one man in all my years around guns that I had actually shot.

"So, cousin, you find the two that run off on you?" Roy called most men "cousin," but I'd never liked it since in my case, it was literally true.

"The Ramsey boys found them on Pumphouse Creek." I was struggling mightily to clear my head. "One had fallen before the Ramseys got there though."

"So the score is one dead and one alive." It wasn't a question. Roy spun in his chair to inspect Edgar. "You Ramsey?"

Edgar nodded warily.

"Was he dead when you arrived on the scene?"

Edgar glanced at me and then shook his head. "No, sir."

"You see him die?"

"I guess so, though I couldn't tell you exactly when it happened."

Warning bells were going off in my mind. Somebody, I wasn't sure who, was in danger.

"I'm going to have to hold you until the coroner's inquest," Roy said to Edgar.

"Hell, you say," I said to the side of Roy's pale face, so nicely shaven that it looked like white candle wax. "You haven't got anything to hold him for."

Roy turned back to me. "When an unauthorized agent is involved in the death of an escaped prisoner, of course there has to be an investigation."

I glanced down at the cream colored envelope that lay still on the desk in front of me and began to slowly tear it into even, precise shreds. "Bullshit, Roy," I said. "Plain and unadorned. First of all, Edgar was acting as an authorized agent of the Federal Internment Camp, contracted by the Inspector General of the Camp."

He raised his eyebrows.

"That's me," I said.

"Oh, I know who it is. I just wonder how much longer it will be you, given the fact that you can't seem to keep track of your prisoners very well."

"Well, Roy. I'm it for now, and Edgar was doing exactly what he was instructed to do, which was find and return the two escaped internees. Internees, not prisoners. Plus the one who died did so from injuries that occurred ... *before Edgar arrived on the scene*." John Sanders walked into the office from the hall, behind Roy. He held in his hands one of the sawed-off shovel handles we'd distributed to the guards by way of arming them. I had no idea if he would use it on Roy.

"Be that as it may," Roy said, staring back at me calmly. "I still have the authority to hold him in custody until the coroner can convene an inquest."

I leaned forward and reached out to grasp his knee. "You're on federal property, cousin, and I'd like to see you try and take him."

He stood, as much to avoid my touch as anything else, I imagined. Offered me his thin-lipped, gray smile. "Oh, if I wanted him, I'd take him, federal property or no. Truth be told, Stevie, the catch ain't worth the bait today." He fixed his carefully brushed hat on his head. "But your boss, Mr. J. Edwin Rumbough, asked me particular to keep an eye on you and to let him know if I spied anything at all unusual that he should know about. Protect his property, so to speak." He was referring to the Major's oldest son, Ed, who despised me.

"Meaning?"

"Meaning you can expect to see me again. Least sniff of trouble, I'll be stopping by." And he turned and walked out past Cap'n John and Edgar, quickly and ever so quietly, like a snake disappears into tall grass.

"Make sure he goes out the gate," I said to John. "And make damn sure it's locked behind him."

After paying off the Ramseys and absorbing Edgar's gratitude, I could feel the weight of the past thirty-six hours pushing down on my neck and shoulders. I was surprised to see that it was afternoon. Four o'clock or even later.

I thought of my safe haven on the third floor, my 305-306 with what I hoped was a long drink and a longer sleep. But it was not to be; my work day was not over yet.

For when I turned to the door, there was Bird, twisted and plain, standing beside the photographer woman, the Anna something-or-other. And what a contrast it was. Bird Shelton was a prematurely aged and palsied mountain woman, whose life I had saved three or four years before by shooting down her rampaging husband in the dining room of the Mountain Park. After the trauma of the shooting, Bird's back and neck had become permanently twisted, so that she seemed constantly to be looking up in fear; and so far as I knew, she had become a mute. At the very least, she never spoke out loud so that you could hear what she was saying. After my trial, she became by common consent my watch guard and assistant. On the other hand, Anna Ulmann, for I had finally remembered her name, was straight and polished, a New York sophisticate.

Her gaze made me suddenly aware that I still wore the same clothes as when she'd last seen me, only now they were soaked through and my pants legs and shoes a muddy mess.

She cleared her throat and spoke directly at me. "Pardon me," she said, "I am looking for Mr. Stephen Robbins, the Inspector General of the Camp." Bird twisted from the waist to peer up at her and then motioned with one skinny arm toward me, meaning as plain as day that I was it, he was me, we were one and the same.

Other than Bird's apartment, we had no inner room, no private office. So I merely held open the wooden gate in the waist-high counter that ran the length of the office proper, and motioned her toward the overstuffed leather chair in the back corner where there was natural light from two large windows. The chair where Prince liked to sit and read Bird's Bible.

Then I handed the cash box to John, asked Bird to "please, please make some coffee" and returned to sit across from Anna Ulmann. I was so tired that I chose a stiff wooden office chair, hard enough to keep me awake if nothing else. I saw that I was leaving muddy footprints wherever I walked.

"I'm sorry," she said. "I thought you were going to get Mr. Robbins."

I tapped my chest. "Me," I said. "Not much to look at just now, but I'm all we've got to show right this minute."

I could see she was taken aback, but to her credit, she recovered quickly. "Now, I am sorry. I thought you were ..."

"The station porter?" I guessed.

"Or worse," she admitted. And smiled. And I'm sure I smiled back at her, out of pure reflex at the sense of her humor. I did not like this woman, but at least she knew how to laugh at herself.

"Why didn't you tell me who you were when I asked you to remove my luggage?" she asked.

"You snuck up on me," I admitted. "And besides, I most often do what I'm asked."

I could tell she was looking at me more critically now, reconsidering some earlier estimation. "Have you been swimming in your clothes, Mr. Robbins?" she asked suddenly.

And I confess it: I laughed out loud. Tired beyond tired and relieved no doubt to have Cousin Roy out of the room and this ... this photographer woman in his place.

"In the rain," I said. "I was out strolling in the rain."

"On the mountain," she reflected. "Dealing with an emergency."

"You see that man who was in here just before you?" I asked suddenly. She nodded. "With the string tie and that fancy hat?" She nodded again. "You see that big revolver he had strapped on under his coat?" This time she shook her head, barely, no. "I once saw him shoot a dog with that gun, just for pissing too near his boot."

There was embarrassed silence for a moment, and I was dimly aware that I was too loud, too rough. And then Bird was between us, with a steel pot and two white clay mugs. Bustling in her bent and snuff-stained way, trying to make up for my sudden rudeness.

I apologized then, for the moment at least sorry to have been so sudden with this woman, wanting to make her laugh again. "Miss ..." Her name came to me from somewhere. "Miss Ulmann," I bowed my head. "I am not normally so disgusting to look at or to speak to. I have had a long night of it, and the sheriff was just the last weight in the scale. How may I help you?"

When I took a long sip of the coffee Bird had given me, I realized gratefully that she's managed to slip a dollop of liquor into my cup. Something to calm my nerves no doubt, so I wouldn't embarrass us any further.

"Mr. Robbins, I'm sure I have no idea of the pressures you are under. I'm sorry for bursting in on you when you haven't even had time to shift your clothes. ..." She went on in what seemed a truly conciliatory way, but I missed her words while studying her face. Her hair was thick and black, swept back over her head in a glossy mane. Her face was thin and intent, her eyes a blue-gray, almost green now, in the darkening room. "... a documentary photographer records the social and cultural record of a time and place. And I have to admit that when I heard of the German internment, I was ..."

I interrupted her. "You came all this way to take documentary photographs of our Germans? What in the wide world possessed you to do such a thing?"

"I was intrigued by the collision of cultures. I have traveled to Europe and back on ships like the ones crewed by these German officers, and when I read that they had been imprisoned in the deepest ..." She paused, unsure how to finish her sentence.

"Darkest part of the South," I offered.

She smiled and nodded. "I couldn't help but believe that there would ensue the most interesting contrast between the two. European sophistication and ..."

"Mountain ignorance."

"No," she almost leaped from her chair, and then set her mug carefully on its arm so she could gesture with her hands. "No, not that. Mountain innocence."

I wondered for a moment just what in God's name she could mean by innocence. We were many, many things in the far-back coves but innocent would never have occurred to me.

"No," I said.

"What do you mean, ... *no*?" She was quizzical, not angry yet.

"I mean no, there won't be any contrast because I don't intend to allow but a few of the Germans out to work or, God forbid, the local folks in. Why do you think we built the fence?"

"Are you afraid of what might happen?"

I bit back the less than civil answer that bubbled on my tongue. "Yes, I am afraid of what might happen."

"Can I take photographs of the prisoners inside the fence?"

"No, no." I waved my hand at her as if to dismiss even the thought. She began to speak but I cut her off. Even with the liquor in my coffee, I was still cold and wet and tired of it all. "Are you a woman, Miss Ulmann?"

"Excuse me?"

"I didn't mean to insult you. Obviously you are. There are over two thousand men in these two camps. And while they are used to being at sea for extended periods of time, they are not used to being at sea deprived of female companionship. Quite probably the last thing on earth I need right now is a young, cultured, ... attractive woman prancing around inside the fence with nothing more to protect herself than a box on stilts."

"They're called *legs*."

My face must have betrayed my confusion.

"Not mine, the camera's. Legs. And rest assured that I do not prance."

"Probably not, but you take my point. The answer is no."

She stood so suddenly that the cup Bird had given her tipped heavily off the arm of the chair and landed with a solid thud on the floor. She flinched and so, unexpectedly, did I.

She stood for a moment, hesitant, and then reached down to snatch up the empty cup off the floor. I imagined her struggle to contain her temper and almost felt sorry for her. To distract her, I pointed to the object wrapped in brown paper that she clutched in her hands. "What have you got there?" I asked. Trying to gentle her down.

"Ironically enough, Mr. Robbins, this is a present for you." Her voice had an acid edge. "I was taught by my father to never pay a call without bringing a present to my host." She stepped to the counter and laid the object lightly down, still seeming to vibrate with frustration. She opened the gate and I rose. When I followed her through the opening in the counter, she bent suddenly and picked up her crumpled note where it lay on the floor beside the trash basket. I knew immediately that she recognized the paper. With obvious disdain, she threw it straight down into the basket.

"Apparently I have better aim than you do," she said. And for the second time in a half hour, I had to laugh. She glanced over her shoulder, possibly to see what I thought was so funny.

"You do have better aim than I do," I laughed again. "Walk outside with me, Miss Ulmann, and tell me why in the world you really want to take pictures of our Germans." I smiled. "If you tell me the real reason, maybe we can arrange something."

We walked through the empty lobby, ghostly now since all of the finer furniture was draped in sheets. Her shoe soles whispered over the bare floor boards, while mine squeaked wetly. We paused at the ornate front doors for her to take her gloves out of her purse and slip them on her hands. In the dusky light, I noticed for the first time how small and yet how wonderfully competent her hands seemed to me. Her fingers were stained with what I imagined might be photographic chemicals, but still quick and knowing as they burrowed into the gloves.

"I came here to escape New York," she said quietly. I glanced back up at her face, faintly gleaming in the light slanting through the stained glass laid into the front door. She looked determined and quite serious. "I have a husband there from whom I am divorced. And I find that I must make my own way in the world." The tone of her voice had changed entirely, was darker now, more direct.

"To make a living you mean?"

"Yes, make a living, earn money from my photographs. And also to think and feel for myself, which is what I try to do with the camera. Find the essence of things rather than their surfaces."

"Aren't there any essences in New York, Miss ... Mrs. Ulmann?"

She smiled grimly. "Yes, of a very different sort. But my husband casts a long shadow, Mr. Robbins. If I'm to discover my own way to the light, I think it must be far away from that shadow." She glanced sideways into my own face. "Don't you have any ghosts, Mr. Robbins?"

I met her eyes for the briefest moment, now almost gray in the darkening room. "Oh yes," I admitted. "You just saw one of them." Meaning Roy.

"Then perhaps you can appreciate my position." She smiled ruefully. She placed one gloved hand on the huge brass door knob in front of her. Following her cue, I reached out and braced myself to pull the heavy oaken door open. Rarely used these past months, it groaned deep in its hand-forged hinges.

When we stepped through to the outer air, both of us, I think, paused just to breathe. I was surprised to see that the entire day had fled, and evening was at hand. "Why don't you ask me again in a few days, Mrs. Ulmann? When I'm not ..."

"Soaking wet?" She finished the sentence for me, again with that glint of humor.

"Exactly," I said. "Give me time to see it through your eyes."

She nodded abruptly and stepped to the edge of the porch.

Dusk had slipped down the river while we talked. It was cooler, and a half-moon had risen through a sky rinsed clean by the previous night's storm. The vastness above was still a sweltering pink in the west, but the light had already faded to purple in the east, freckled by stars. I could feel the river surging in its wide curve around the camp and the town, dwarfing the hotel, the barracks, the houses, dwarfing all human intent.

She gazed outward as if stricken by the immense, brooding beauty of the place. "The fences disappear at sunset," she said.

CHAPTER FOUR

What the Germans did during the months of July and August was truly impressive. The "YMCA" building, which looked amazingly like a barn because that's what we'd known how to build, became the site of mid-afternoon musical and dramatic performances.

At night in Camp A there were classes in shorthand, geography, English, chemistry, as well as marine navigation and engineering. For a man who'd been raised in a deep mountain cove and first educated in a slapped-together one-room, eight-grade schoolhouse, it was a miraculous introduction to an alien culture, a culture of learning. They taught each other with a dogged, systematic determination that I could not have imagined.

When I first approached Commodore Hans Ruser about the possibility of paying a contingent of experienced men to help Robert Snyder rebuild the French Broad River Bridge, he assigned an engineer from his own ship, *Vaterland*, who recruited two crews of twenty men each from Camp B—experienced carpenters and ship builders all. The engineer began to work the two crews on alternate days, Monday through Saturday, and he proved to be astonishingly tactful in dealing with Snyder, while he and his men set about tearing down the old stone bridge pillars and rebuilding them from the riverbed up.

The Germans also played with the same serious, almost furious energy. They begged, borrowed, and made tennis rackets, and then reconditioned the tennis courts that had been swept clean by the great flood. Each camp organized a "football" team in order to play the other, the sailors in Camp B looking forward with great glee to the abuse of their officers.

One day, when the entire contingent was in Camp A, John Sanders took me out to see a detachment busily digging out the thousands of pounds of gravel-saturated mud that had filled in the swimming pool during the previous summer's flood. They were hauling the debris in wheelbarrows to the river's edge and dumping it into the churning, flowing water.

"I give 'em the shovels," he said, "and the wheelbarrows. Anybody who'll work as hard as they do deserves to have tools."

"Aren't you afraid they'll tunnel under the fence?" I asked, hoping against hope that they had given Cap'n John a sense of humor in return for the shovels.

"No," he said. "I ain't."

I have often been asked in years since what the Germans looked like. Especially given the nature of the propaganda that swirled around us during the war, I think people must have expected them to have horns, hooves, and tails, constantly on the lookout for babies to boil and churches to burn. Even very educated people would ask about Aryan characteristics or Nordic features. The disappointing truth is that they were profoundly varied in appearance: light juxtaposed against dark, tall and aristocratic against thick and beefy, incredibly quick and athletic versus slow and ponderous. And yet, there was some thread that seemed to run through the core of all. They were neat and economical in everything that they did; and they were always, always organized.

"Like an army of ants," John Sanders observed one bright August morning. He was tired from a night supervising his increasingly lackadaisical guards. "If you'll just spend one whole day watching, you'll see it. They all of 'em, all twenty-three hundred of 'em, move as if they had one single purpose in mind and won't tolerate any stand in their way."

"What do you think we should do about it?" I asked, suddenly convinced that he was close to the truth.

"Stay the hell out of their way, I guess," he said.

"That's just great," I replied. "What if one day they suddenly all decide to dismantle the camp and walk off to Tennessee with it?"

"They's thousands of them, Stevie; on any given day, maybe twenty of us. What do you think?"

And he was right. As stiff and high as we had built our fences, they alone wouldn't hold this small German army. My mind drifted back to Commodore Hans Ruser and his coterie of officers. Perhaps all my years of "service" had corrupted my point of view, but I began to wonder if our real job wasn't just to keep them happy.

During the period following our first interview, Anna Ulmann had sent me several notes seeking further negotiation, but I continued to put her off.

There was also something that rang false in the photograph she had given me. For that's what her square object in brown paper had proven to be. A black-and-white photo in a plain wooden frame. The image was that of a young woman sitting on the porch of a cabin, her right hand resting on a spinning wheel. At first glance, it could have been taken a hundred years before or, I knew, as recently as yesterday, in any number of tucked-away places. The woman's face was interesting, but my attention kept being drawn back to her hands, something about her hands. ...

The woman bothered me the same way her photograph did. There was something about her that I couldn't explain as well. Her eyes perhaps, now cloudy and now full of light, mostly blue but once or twice gray-green in a darkened room. I couldn't explain why she bothered me, but I did know that the summer of 1917 was not the time to be taken up with a woman. So I put the photo in a drawer and attempted for those few weeks to do the same thing with her, shove her into a drawer in my mind, and close her off to thought. She was, after all, a woman, and therefore not to be trusted.

It is difficult now to recall the exact chronology, but one night during those in-between weeks, Lillian Jamison somehow made her way past the guards at the gate and came to call at the Mountain Park, seeking whatever lean affection there was to be had in Suite 305-306. Lilly was a fairly well-to-do woman from Asheville, who had stayed at the Mountain Park before the war and conceived some minor passion for me that I nursed along in a desultory way simply for her occasional nighttime company. The kind of company that seeks the dark in a half-dressed, alcohol-soaked room. She was a college educated woman who had said more than once that I had turned her head by quoting Shakespeare to the Mountain Park flower girls.

What she learned from me I couldn't say, but what I learned from her was that stray entertainment didn't lead to love, not for someone as cold as me.

But get past the guards she did and find me on the back porch as I sat enjoying the one cigar a day I allowed myself. She'd brought a bottle, and when she bent to relight my cigar, I caught some powerful scent that wasn't really a smell but rather the closeness of her, the willingness of her.

So I let her pour us out a glass or two there on the porch, and I agreed to let her have a look at my sanctuary, the rooms high under the gables. Both of us pretending that she hadn't seen those rooms before, more than once. And I almost let that ancient, dire usury follow its accustomed course, my own spirit in a waste of shame. Her throwing herself away in my specific direction.

I wonder sometimes that a man of forty-odd, a man who'd lived through what I'd lived through up to that point in my life, could still have a conscience. But I couldn't bear the thought of her in my bed, her expensive clothes strewn across my furniture, her shoes tossed into the corner of my room. I couldn't bear the thought of talking to her. Not another day, not another night, not another moment. All I had wanted was her willing body in the shadows, nothing more human than that. And I despised myself for almost taking advantage of her yet one more time.

My only grace was that I swallowed my swarming despair and talked her up and into her clothes. Talked her down the stairs and out the door, saw her to the gate myself. And told her I would never see her again for her sake. Could never see her again because of the war. There was the deep, raw sense in me that I had to face her in order to be done with her. And so I did, saying good-bye with a vengeance, making myself speak the truth into her red and tear-stained face.

And still Anna Ulmann wrote her notes, patiently, sincerely, desiring only to take photos of the German officers at play, at work, at home in the "far mountain fastness."

Jane Gentry, the proprietor of Sunnybank, was one of several Hot Springs business owners who'd hired a German internee to work during the day. A guard would accompany each of these men, most of whom spoke at least a smattering of English, outside the gate to a home or business in town, where they could practice the gardening or craftsmanship they had brought with them from the old country. Mrs. Jane had hired Siegfried, of all people, to build for her a garden house behind Sunnybank, even though I had told her point blank that there were a hundred men in the camp with more carpentry skills. "Yes," she'd admitted, "but none to keep the boarders so entertained."

So on a Monday in late August, I replaced his usual escort and went with him up Bridge Street through town to Sunnybank—he to saw a few random planks and bend a few nails, I perhaps to visit Anna Ulmann and so lay her ghost to rest. When we arrived at Sunnybank and climbed the row of terraces in the front yard, Jane took Siegfried immediately off to the kitchen where several boarders were still at breakfast, leaving me alone on the side porch with a cup of coffee. Jane had promised to let Anna know I was there before rushing back into the house, so I assumed that I should sit and sip the scalding hot coffee and slowly let my body relax into the rocking chair. After all, I thought, how often in the past weeks had I been offered the luxury of just sitting?

After a moment, however, I realized it wasn't in me on that particular day to sit quietly. Too many thoughts were dancing in the deserted lobby of my mind. So I got up to walk out into Mrs. Jane's back yard, her "garden" she was teaching us to call it, even though there wasn't a single stalk of corn or staked up tomato plant in sight. There, I happened onto one of Mrs. Jane's prized iris blooms, the old purple and yellow variety that was just becoming common in the mountains. I gazed into the open, fleshy opulence of the bloom, turned almost inside out in offering itself to the bees that hovered nearby. How would Anna Ulmann see it, I wondered, through the optics of that huge, dark box—as an impersonal study in light and shadow or as some supremely sensuous creature flinging itself into the open air?

"My dear Mr. Robbins."

I jumped so that the coffee sloshed out of my cup.

"I'm sorry." She grinned. "I startled you."

When I wheeled around, she was only a few feet away, wearing a color like the inside of a sea shell, some pink I couldn't name.

"I'm trying to imagine how you must see it," I stammered. "When you view it through your camera."

"Often as not," she said, "what I see in the lens doesn't prepare me at all for what comes to light when I develop the plate. Things appear that I had only guessed at when I was buried under the cover. ... I'm afraid that there is one obvious way in which I don't have your gift."

"For spilling things?"

"No." She smiled. "No, I rarely see the humor. I never see what's funny until I've taken the photo, and somebody points it out to me in the print. You, on the other hand, are always laughing at something I don't even hear ... or see."

"It's just sarcasm," I said. "I can be an ironic son-of-a ..."

She pretended not to hear me, and after a moment, tried again. "Sit beside me, Mr. Robbins." She pointed at the lone bench in Jane Gentry's garden. "You know why I came to Hot Springs, North Carolina. In fair and open trade, you must tell me the story of how you got here."

I confess I hesitated before I began. I had come to tell her point blank that she would not be allowed inside the camp, and since I fully intended to deny her, I was not sure that I wanted her to know anything about me. "When I was a young man, long before I met Sarah Rumbough—"

She interrupted me to ask, "Your former wife?"

I looked up in surprise.

"Your Mr. McBride shared just a few details," she explained.

"Any of them of interest?"

"Perhaps. He told me you were from a far mountain cove. And that you came here ... as an orphan. When you were ten years old."

"More nearly twelve," I said. "And not quite an orphan, for I do have a mother. Runaway most like."

"And that you went to work at the Mountain Park, in fact that you were always there, trailing after Major Rumbough until you..."

"Were adopted?"

"He didn't say that."

"Rose up through the ranks?"

"More or less," she admitted. "Rose up through the ranks by marrying the major's daughter."

I snorted. "Not quite. The major tried to talk me out of marrying his daughter, and not because I was common."

"Then how did you rise up through the ranks?"

"I learned to read."

She seemed taken aback. "Was it that unusual? For a mountain boy to read?"

"Don't see the need, most of us," I admitted. "But in my case it wasn't read as in keep a ledger or sign a guest in and out. Mrs. Rumbough led me through the entire library up at Rutland before she died, almost page by page. So when I say read, I mean read as in Poe. Or Twain. Jane Austen."

"You read Jane Austen?"

I had to smile. "Try not to sound so surprised."

"But you said mountain boys don't see the need."

"I said most of 'em, not all." I did not like this woman. The more time I spent with her, the less I liked her.

"But why did it help for you to read *Pride and Prejudice*? I don't understand."

"Because that's what the guests read. So at first I read solely out of ambition—that and I memorized poetry. I could pretend a little bit of culture, and the Major thought that's what people like you needed."

"People like me?"

I nodded. "New York, Chicago, Charleston. People like you." I waved at her general air, her stance, her attitude. "People with a way about them. As if they were a different race before God."

"*People like me?*" An edge to her voice now.

"Sure," I said. "People like you. Maybe not you personally. ..."

"My father stayed here when I was a child. He was very much like me. And I stayed here as well, according to him."

"You personally?"

"Yes, Mr. Robbins, me personally. Although I do not claim to be a different race before God."

"You sure? You've been pretty high-handed about your pictures." I was losing the battle to keep the harshness out of my voice.

"You go to hell. I have not been high-handed about my photographs. If anything, I have been meek and proper, submissive even, just like my father taught me. Except when you have pushed me beyond reason. ... So have you decided? To let me photograph the Germans?"

Her feistiness warmed me somehow, scrubbed against me just enough to generate some heat. "I have decided," I said suddenly, surprising even myself. "Though you won't like the rules that come with the decision."

"What did you—"

"I'm going to let you inside the fence a few times during the coming weeks, but only during daylight hours and only accompanied by Bird and—"

"Thank you," she said. "I mean it, Mr. Robbins. You may be setting me free!"

"And only when I'm fully aware of when and what you're photographing."

"You mean you want to watch?"

I hesitated. I did want to watch, but damned if I was going to admit it to her. "I need to be sure that you don't capture any images that shouldn't be seen in the larger world."

"I don't take an image prisoner, Mr. Robbins," she said as she reached out to tap my hand. "I let it flow into the camera of its own accord." She pressed my hand a moment longer than absolutely necessary, and again I was struck by how self-contained she was, how little use she had for human contact. Even so, it was as if the sun suddenly shone full into her face; just for a moment it escaped the shadows. Then the light was gone again and she stood.

She stepped back from me and tripped over one of Mrs. Jane's decorative river rocks.

Not gracefully, not even prettily. She sat down hard on the ground. "Damn it!" she said, loud enough to be heard in the house, upstairs or down.

Trying not to laugh, I helped her to her feet. She brushed the garden dirt off the backside of her dress so vigorously that for the first time in her presence, I was given forcefully the sense of her body. "And you too, Stephen Robbins, for having watched me do it."

Anna Ulmann, laughing and dirt-stained, kept growing and shrinking in my eyes, but most of the time, she seemed to be perhaps two inches shorter than me, beneath her thick, thick black hair, probably five feet, six or seven inches tall. Broad shoulders for a woman who so often seemed so thin. Or maybe not thin, maybe fine-boned, with small wrists and those delicate-strong hands. Strong and yet feminine legs, or so I imagined from her ankles and calves—all that I'd seen of her legs as I watched her fall. Feet small like her hands. And I laughed back at her laughter, she continuing to brush Jane Gentry's garden off herself long after there was no more dirt to brush. She had a moving, wavering presence that was far more than the sum of the stomach she laughed with and the breasts that seemed more and more to be fully, unavoidably there. She was, when she wasn't paying attention to herself, all movement and light. At that moment, I had to remind myself not to like her, she being for the first time quite real.

Later, as I walked with her back to the house, she asked me what I thought of the photograph she had given me.

"I believe it's a fake," I said.

"What do you mean?" She stopped and reached out to pinch the sleeve of my coat.

"I mean that woman doesn't live in that cabin. Or if she does, she doesn't use that spinning wheel. Or a churn to finish her butter. Or cook on a wood stove. Or harness a mule to plow."

She glared at me in sudden irritation. But then her look softened—somewhat—into something slightly less fierce. "It was posed," she admitted, "but how do you know just by looking?"

"Her hands, Miss Ulmann. If nothing else, they're clean. No working person's hands ever come completely clean."

"Call me Anna," she said distractedly, staring at her feet. And then after a moment, "you're right of course. She was a college student home visiting her family in Georgia. But don't you see? That's why I need you—to help me understand what is real and what isn't in this hidden away, folded up country of yours."

"What makes you think I even—"

"And I hate the fake, the posed, the lie. In New York, I take posed portraits of famous men and even, sometimes, women. Actors, politicians, editors, writers. And they all want to look better than they are. Taller, stronger, smarter." She turned and faced me. "No heart, no nobility. None ..." She paused, partly just to catch her breath after the outburst. "And that is part of what I intend to leave behind."

"The lie?"

"Yes. Well, no. Sometimes a lie comes in handy. The pretentiousness and the conceit. That's why I came here—to escape my husband

and his arrogant friends. I came here, where people live simple, natural lives." She said this last bit as if reading from a tourist brochure, and like most such, it wasn't very convincing.

"I thought you came for the Germans."

"Well yes, but the Germans just make the other stand out."

"I remember. The pure, innocent mountain folks."

She nodded, staring into my face.

My own face suddenly cold under a sheen of midday sweat. "I know those people you're talking about," I said. "Truth be told, I am those people. And there's nothing pure or innocent about us."

CHAPTER FIVE

In early September, we received a special gift from the federal government; the musicians we'd heard so much about finally arrived.

A train from Richmond brought us the thirty-seven members of the German Imperial Band, complete with their instruments, banners, and uniforms. They had been in the United States for three years already, having been caught up in China during the 1914 Allied recapture of Tsingtao, a Chinese port held by Germany since before the war. To date, they had enjoyed the hospitality of the Japanese and the Italians in the Far East before they had been delivered into the care of the United States Government, which at the time of their capture in 1914 was still neutral. They had been interned at Ellis Island of all places and had made lives for themselves in New York and New Jersey until the New York musicians' unions began to complain about the competition, and they were "removed to the Federal Internment Camp at Hot Springs." They were led and conducted by the esteemed Dr. George Ballerstedt, native of Vienna, or so one telegram informed us.

They were preceded by boxes and boxes of documentation, which I had faithfully delivered to Walter McBride, from which he had culled one or two especially interesting files that he knew I would enjoy. Two of the musicians, Carl Bickenese and Arthur Koppen, had applied for release from custody so that they could join family members in the United States and so earn a living. Both had been refused after elaborate hearings because they were members of German reserve military forces as well as the German Red Cross. As Walter pointed out, however, both were now too old to serve, and neither Walter nor I could imagine exactly how the German army was going to summon them to active duty from Milwaukee and Hackensack respectively.

By the time they actually arrived, the townspeople all knew they were coming and turned out in force to watch them detrain. One young woman, a former maid at the Park, yelled from the back of the crowd for the Imperial Band to "line up and toot them damn horns!" The man I took to be Ballerstedt, given he was wearing an immaculate, if badly discolored, white suit and sported a monocle, did not appear amused. Even though their official rank was something of a mystery, we gave them choice quarters at the Mountain Park in Camp A.

It was at the same time as the arrival of the Imperial Band that I had agreed to let Anna Ulmann inside the wire to photograph our increasingly active and enterprising inmates. Walter nominated the Imperial Band as her first subject, with Bird hovering at his shoulder in such a way that I wondered if it had been her thought in the first place.

"The Labor Department keeps saying that we need to produce a carefully documented record of how the Germans are being treated," he argued, "so that we can prove to the international community that they are well cared for." I agreed with their plan, more so to get Walter and Bird off my back than to please Washington or the "international community."

"Let her start with the damn band, then," I said. "And anytime she's inside the wire, make sure that there's a guard to protect her and Bird along to protect 'em both." I had thought of Bird in the first place because I knew no German could abide Bird's crazy, crook-neck stare.

The band brought with it layers of complexity that had nothing to do with Anna Ulmann. Within a few days of its arrival, Commodore Ruser appeared in Walter's office with Siegfried and a middle-aged musician named Georg Mende, a man so seemingly insignificant that I hadn't even noticed him at the depot. After Ruser and I traded pleasantries, the stately Commodore returned to his "football" practice, taking Siegfried with him, and continued coaching his officers in their preparations to do battle with the sailors. Georg Mende then asked in a stiffly inflected English if he could "engage in a few moments of my time." I nodded and smiled, but he then looked significantly at Walter. I stopped him at that point. "Whatever it is you want, Georg, it may be Walter who can help you."

"Sir, I am not a secretive man, but I have no notion about the reception of my thoughts. I am told you are the primary man in this place and yet you are always laughing. You are smiling. I ask the officers and I ask the men, and they all point to you. They say that you are the doctor to my problems."

"But what is it, Georg? We're forty miles from a town." I waved my arm for emphasis. "Hundreds of miles from anything like civilization."

"It's not a town that I need, Mr. Robbins, and certainly it is not civilization. It is only that I want to be married." He took a deep breath. "To the American woman. To a citizen. And everywhere I have asked, they are laughing at me. Everywhere I hear only *No*. I wish this, Herr Robbins—that someone such as yourself, someone with power, would say *Yes*, and then her mother would let her come to me."

There was a moment of surprised silence that neither Walter nor I broke.

"Surely," Georg Mende went on. "Surely, Mr. Robbins, you have known the bliss of matrimony. That happy state."

"Oh, I admit I've visited the state of matrimony. Bliss, however, I'm not so sure of. But I don't signify here. In order for us to help you, Georg, you have to explain the problem. Who have you asked for help?" Even as I was speaking, Walter had walked across the storage space behind the desks and begun to rummage through the boxes of records that had arrived with the band. I knew he was searching for Georg Mende's file.

"When we were at Ellis Island, Mr. Robbins, I am part of a quartet. A quartet with the saxophone and trombone and another trumpet, and we learn to play your American jazz. Your night music. So we can earn some money in the pocket so far from home. I meet a woman one night, a waitress who becomes my friend. We dream, she and I. We dream to have a life after the war. She has taught me ..." He patted his chest with the delicate touch of a musician. "Me, Georg Mende, who am no smart man, to speak English. So I can speak her father. She say yes, oh yes, but her father only laugh. And the next time I see her, she has a dark eye." He drew a circle around the socket of his own eye to illustrate, and I knew what her father had done when he finished laughing. "It was at this time that I speak to the authorities at Ellis Island, who must have a background check. And the interview. And they call her in to interview her. In six months, I make three applications to become a citizen, Mr. Robbins, and each time I have been said No,

No, and No. Three others of whom I am aware were granted clemency. Clemency?"

It sounded right. I nodded.

"Were granted clemency. But each time I am refused."

"Georg?" Walter spoke from behind me. "Are you a member of the German armed forces, regular or reserve?" I wonder where our little Right Reverend had found such an officious tone; then I remembered he was a preacher.

"No, no. Most definitely I am not. I am a member of the German Red Cross and of the International Red Cross." He turned back to me. "They ask me this same question over and over."

"Georg," I said. "I believe you know the reason why you've been refused. If you will tell us, we will try to help you, but only if you tell us the truth."

"Mr. Robbins. The father of my friend is a powerful man. The father of my friend is an Irish, a policeman in the army of Brooklyn, New York. A captain for many years. He does not wish for me to marry his daughter."

"Because you are German?"

"Mr. Robbins. I believe you to be an honorable man, and that I must tell you the truth. He is a—"

"Catholic!" Walter spoke up suddenly and decisively.

"And ...?" I asked.

"I am of the Jewish faith."

Walter let out a surprised whistle.

"Georg, I can understand about the father. No father is rational about his daughter. But are you telling me that the U. S. Government turned down your application for residency because you're a Jew?"

"It's entirely possible that—" Walter's nagging voice behind my shoulder.

Interrupted by Georg Mende. "Mr. Robbins. May I tell you that the cousin of the man who is the father of my friend is also the immigrations officer who talked to me at Ellis Island? Talked to me as this man is talking now." He nodded at Walter.

I could sense Walter's growing discomfort, but I confess I was delighted with our German musician. For his stubbornness if nothing else. "Georg, you have managed to get cross-ways with just about every unwritten code in these United States of America. What's her name?"

"My friend?"

I nodded. And this gentle, inoffensive man, who was in most respects, so perfectly bland, blushed pink. "Her name is Colleen McManaway."

"Do you have a picture of her?"

He stood and pulled from inside his threadbare jacket a worn leather pocketbook. He opened it carefully to show me the small photograph of a woman standing beside a vine-covered gate. She had long, luxurious hair, red perhaps, and a pale complexion. A wonderfully broad and smiling face. Freckles, I imagined, though you couldn't tell from the photo.

I glanced up at the man standing over me and could see the tears in his eyes, tears that I was sure sprang just from the opportunity to speak of her.

"Put your photograph away, Georg Mende," I said. "It is a precious thing. And tell me why it is that we should take on the entire state of New York, the Department of Labor, and the United States Immigration Service for you and your Colleen."

"She has taught me to say what it is, Mr. Robbins. In a language that we Germans do not possess." He looked at me as a man does who is about to pledge his allegiance to something very personal. "She has taught me to say that I am in love with her and she with me."

There was a long pause, during which Walter shook his head nervously. I can't say what the look might have been on my own face, for I was thinking that I didn't know that language myself, had never learned what Colleen McManaway had taught her Georg.

"Yes," I said.

"Pardon?" he said politely.

"You said earlier, Georg, that you only needed someone like me to say Yes. Well, I guess I'm as much like me as anybody, and I'm saying it. Write to your Colleen; tell her she must come to us here by train. If she can't afford the ticket, I will wire her the money in New York. If you need Walter to write to her mother, he will do it. ... I cannot make you a citizen, Georg Mende, you must understand that. But you're not in New York any longer. You're in my country now. And in my country, you are free to marry whom you choose, Catholic or Jew."

After Georg left beaming, Walter McBride cleared his throat.

"What?" I asked.

"You are to just about to get the entire camp in trouble with the federal government. That man is an enemy alien. He's a Jew. He's been turned down for release and repatriation three times. He's the sworn enemy of half the Irish Catholics in New York. And to top it all off, you are not licensed to marry people."

"I had in mind that you might want to perform the ceremony, Walter. Being so righteous and all ..."

"Hell no. Not me. I would like to maintain my position here."

It was an odd thing for him to say, but just at that moment, I was too amused to pay proper attention. "Walter McBride. Since when did you take up cursing?"

Something in that interview with Georg Mende stirred in me a growing unrest. A discomfort in the pit of my stomach that was not particularly painful but still came and went in waves that were hard to ignore.

I wouldn't name it. Except to say to myself that I thought I should walk outside the wire in the late summer dusk. After the two giant contingents of Germans were safely within the wire of their separate camps. When the thousands of plain crockery dishes were washed and the great bread pans were once more stacked to dry in the kitchens. When the evening guard shift had settled into their rounds for the night. Then, as the skin of the world ruffled and settled, ruffled and settled for its dark rest, I should myself escape.

Before the war, before our German invasion, I had been in the habit of taking a cigar and two kitchen matches out the front door at dusk. Always alone so that I could savor the evening, and think, perhaps, of my father, whose habit I emulated with the cigar. I would smoke and walk down through the trees to the river. Some evenings I would sit by myself and smoke my one cigar on the bench we'd put there for lovers. But most evenings, in the times before the previous year's flood had swept away the river bridge, I would cross over and walk the old turnpike, deserted at that time of day. It was the quietest, easiest slice of my life, the one slice that no one else owned a piece of.

The first time I tried to do this after the internment, however, I ran straight into a wire fence. Distracted and tired, it hadn't occurred to me that I was caught just as much as the Germans were. I could stick my arms through the fence or even the tip of my glowing cigar, but my body and soul would have to walk all the way back to the Camp A gate to seek release.

That particular night, the evening after hearing Georg Mende describe his love, I felt the need to roam. The need to escape my own guards.

Perhaps, I thought, perhaps I should walk up to Sunnybank and take a cup of coffee with my old friend, Mrs. Jane Gentry. I would ask her to sing one of her ballads, what the mountain folks called a love song, and she would sit and rock and sing "Lord Randall." I told myself that I wouldn't even care if the photographer woman wandered through the room.

It seemed to me that in the parlor or kitchen or out on the porch at Sunnybank resided the answer to some restless question that my spirit was asking.

Robert Snyder caught me in the hallway as I was leaving, animated by some dire telegram that he had apparently received, still clutched in his fist. He waved it at me dramatically as I tried to edge past him. "Spies," he hissed. "Saboteurs!" He was whispering, but so loudly that any spy on the first floor could have heard him. "The War Department says that there are German espionage agents in the camp. That outside sympathizers will pass messages back and forth through the fence. That we must watch the international mail. We must double the security on the fence." He rose up to his full five feet, five inches. "The security of our country is at stake."

"Did you say the sky is falling?"

He didn't get it. "The Germans. Contacts in the town. Sabotage!"

"What the hell is a German saboteur going to do in Hot Springs, Robert, blow up the post office?"

He shook his head at me, obviously disappointed at my lack of concern, and hurried away down the hall, in search of someone, I imagined, who would take him seriously.

I slipped away, down the darkening halls of the Park, wondering if Robert Snyder, like Georg Mende, had ever fallen in love. It seemed inconceivable, like asking if a judge had ever been drunk or a nun naked. But then, I suppose most judges were forced by what they saw and heard to drink and most nuns ... I wasn't sure about the nuns.

I walked behind the hotel to the wagon gate. We had built a wide gate on the gravel supply road that led from Spring Creek directly to the stables and kitchens at the back of the Park. There was no guardhouse at the wagon gate and no passage of internees in and out under any circumstances, but the guard on that section of the fence kept the key secreted in a hollow tree and would let me in and out as I chose.

And so I was free of the camp, Jimmy Worley yawning as he returned the key to its hiding place.

I crossed Spring Creek where for years had stood the footbridge that led to the back of town and up the hill to Rutland. When the bridge was washed away the summer before, we had laid a chestnut log over the stone pilings. I stopped halfway over and stood silently with my eyes closed. It was an old trick of mine, so I could hear the creek, could feel it washing away beneath me. Normally it was peaceful, the water coursing away into Tennessee, but not that evening. That evening, I could feel a wave of dizziness behind my eyes, a vertigo that threatened to drop me into the water and from there into the deeper run of the river.

I walked on through the woods behind the town, aware that it was she who drew me. She who might or might not be as aware of me as I was of her. Who might know me, as I knew her, in the creep of her blood or the sigh of her breath. Damn her anyway, I thought, for having invaded my world, her and her camera.

Had Walter McBride ever been in love? With the young teacher from Dorland School that he had met and married? The chaplain and the teacher. Had John Sanders? Had he ever stopped analyzing the geometry of the world long enough to notice the curve of a woman's neck? My God, had Pauline been in love with Cousin Roy, that reptile, had she lusted after him before she married him? And how did she feel now, now that she knew him?

I found myself brought up short, standing on the corner of Spring Street and Bridge Street before it started up the gentle hill toward Sunnybank. A little girl was standing outside the corner store, busily sucking on a piece of stick candy. Dirty bare feet and a torn dress sewn out of old sacking. Except for the candy, she would have seemed a ghost, as out of place on the empty street as an apparition.

"Mister Robbins?" she said gravely.

"Yes, Ma'am?"

"What them Germanies you got over there really like?"

"What's your name, girl?"

"Dacey."

"Well, Dacey, near as I can tell, they're human."

She considered this for a moment. "Like you'n me?"

"Near as I can tell, they're so much like you'n me, they might as well be named Robbins or Fortner."

"Fortner's my name," she said.

"I know."

"You want some this candy?" she asked. "I done ate the stripes off it, but it's still good."

I crossed the street and started up the hill. My dear Pauline, married to the High Sheriff of Madison County. A few days before I had seen her pick a handful of Black-eyed Susans and give them to D. C. Peinart as they stood for a moment on the small porch off the back of the kitchen. She in the overalls she sometimes wore in the kitchen; he in his carefully preserved shirt and tie, his sleeves rolled up over his pale arms. Her hands rougher and larger than my own; his smaller, quickly dried on his apron.

He had taken the bouquet and, of course, bowed. And then ever so gently kissed the back of her hand. I was touched almost to tears; if he ever turned her hand over and kissed her palm, the secret inside of her curled, work-worn fingers, what then? Would they wake to find themselves in Tennessee? Or standing in the sun-drenched Gulf of Mexico? As I knew my Cousin Roy, they had better discover themselves far, far away.

I found myself standing at the foot of the long terraced walk up to Sunnybank. Standing alone in the early dark, wondering at myself. The air dimmed all around me, the sliver of new moon just barely peeping out over Dogged Mountain. Had Stephen Baird Robbins ever been in love? In forty-plus years of feeling and not feeling? Of running to and from his own instincts? Me? Had I ever once been swept away in the deep water of a dream. No, I thought. No, I had never given myself up, and perhaps it was not in me to do so.

I was far too harsh a man. My edges much too sharp to touch.

I confess that I turned back then, leery of the house at Sunnybank, shy of what might wait there—whether acceptance or rejection. From where I stood I could see the yellow glow of lamplight through the front door. I could smell the wood smoke from Mrs. Jane's chimneys. But I turned back again into my carefully measured world, where the fences ran straight and true, and it was clear who belonged inside and who out.

Rather than walk back through the trees to the wagon gate, I went straight down Bridge Street to the main Camp A gate, where I was let back into my prison by one of the Gentry boys, whom I interrupted gazing at a girlie magazine inside the guardhouse.

As I started across the long expanse of the lower lawn, past where the first hole of our golf course had been, I was caught by a familiar odor. Cigar smoke, good and strong, drifting from the deep shade of the one copse of trees we had left standing in the lawn. Whoever he was, I could see the tip of his cigar glowing in the shadows.

I angled toward the trees, curious to see who might be out this late. Curfew and lock up were still ahead of us, but the vast majority of the Germans did not like the black dark of mountain nights, and few ventured past the Mountain Park porches after dusk.

I was met at the edge of the trees by the last man I expected. Commodore Hans Ruser, portly, dignified, stepped politely out of the shadows so I could see him clearly.

"Welcome to my sanctuary, Herr Robbins," he said in his correct, strongly accented English, gesturing behind him at the trees. I stepped closer and stared briefly into the shadows to be sure he was alone. "You have caught me, sir," he continued, "indulging in my favorite vice."

"I've never known cigars to be a vice, Commodore," I said. "Unless they're damn bad cigars."

He bowed ever so slightly from the waist and offered me his thick, square hand.

I shook it warmly, glad to be pulled out of my own thoughts. Plus he was a man I respected—automatically, instinctively.

"Then it is my hope that you will share with me." For a blank moment, I thought he meant we should pass his cigar back and forth like a Cherokee pipe, but then he reached inside the lapel of his coat.

"Nothing could make me happier, Commodore," I said. "Before the war, I used to walk here each evening and smoke. From here to the river ..." I turned and pointed. "It was even my habit to walk as slowly as possible so that I could digest the day."

"I'm sorry ... digest?"

"Think it over. Try to make some sense of all that had happened since first light."

"I see." He took my arm then, in what might have been a feminine gesture, had he not been so obviously a man in full. "Like me, Herr Robbins, you are the commander of a large vessel. And there are times when the weight of such a responsibility must be set aside." He handed me a cigar wrapped in ornate foil.

When I tore the foil away, the odor was instantaneous and rich.

He paused for a moment while I clipped the end of the cigar with my pocket knife—my father's knife—and lit it with a kitchen match from my vest pocket. Even the first puffs were deep and sweet.

We walked on then, as two men would anywhere in the world.

"So, my young friend, how does command sit upon you today?"

"Uneasy rests the crown," I admitted, the line rising out of some inner memory.

Ruser chuckled. "Did you choose this ship, Herr Robbins? Are you by trade a man of the prison?"

"*Warden*. We would say *prison warden*. And no, I am not. I am a hotel man. A manager is what I am, and when I'm at my best and things are running smoothly, you wouldn't even know I'm here. My job is best done behind the scenes."

"So, again we are alike," Ruser mused. "I left the navy to sail the great passenger ships. I would think about time and tide rather than whether the great guns should fire. And when I did my job well, the passengers did not even know that I existed except as a name on a brass plate."

"Do you miss it then? Do you miss the sea?"

"Any sailor dreams of the ocean. But this is not so bad, eh? A safe harbor in a stupid war."

I glanced sideways at his profile to see if he was serious. "Is it stupid, then?"

"Of course it is. Death and destruction to no good end. And from what I've seen of you, Herr Robbins, you strike me as a man who might agree."

"Call me Stephen, Commodore. Of course I agree. Seems such a sad waste. ... Many of my countrymen, of course, are mad for it."

"As are mine, Stephen, as are mine. Even some of the men in this camp would add to that death and destruction if they could."

"Sailors?" I nodded across Bridge Street toward Camp B.

"No, no. Mostly they will do as they are told if fed well and given sufficient recreation. The dangerous men are among our officers, mostly young men of an aristocratic background, who believe they must find a way to fight." He drew a line on his cheek with his cigar and after a moment it struck me what he meant—a dozen of the younger officers bore saber scars on their faces, typically lean and angry faces.

"How can they fight here? There's an ocean between us and the front lines."

"You are still a young man, Stephen. In my experience, the lust for blood is like the lust for a woman; it always finds a channel. My young officers can fight each other, they can fight me, or ..." Now I could feel him glance at me. "...most likely, they can fight you. Every time a letter from home tells of a brother dead or a father wounded, the urge to fight someone, anyone, grows stronger."

"Do you think they'll try to escape?"

He shrugged. "Possibly. But then where would they go? It is more likely that they will find a way to fight the war right here inside the camp."

"What must I do?" It was only later, upon reflection, that it seemed strange to be taking direction from the senior German officer. But at that moment, Ruser's presence was too large to ignore.

In the summer darkness, he paused to consider. "Watch and wait, my friend, nothing more. Let my senior officers and me see if we might not distract the young warriors. For you see, Stephen, we have no more wish to disturb our little island of peace than do you."

We parted ways just after, and I slept easy that night, as I recall. Not the sleep of the righteous, because I don't know just what that is. But I had been strangely reassured by Ruser confiding in me—and by his own peaceful intentions.

I slept so well that I lay unconscious late into the next morning and, even when I woke, still seemed wrapped in some delicious sense from the night before.

I drank my two cups in the hotel kitchen, surrounded by Pauline, Peinart, and their troop of mountain women who were busily preparing lunch. I gulped the first cup steaming hot and then sipped the second while Walter, who had found me there, briefed me on what had happened during the night and what was to come that day. During the afternoon the Imperial Band intended to play a concert of martial music on the upper lawn, opposite the depot, for the guards and the townspeople. Their return, Walter assumed, for my encouragement of Georg Mende.

The band was to be released into Camp B for the concert, assuming that I agreed, and there would be an opportunity for Anna Ulmann to make her photos of Ballerstedt and his musicians in uniform. Bird and a guard along for good measure.

After we served out lunch, I walked alone over into Camp B while munching on a thick sandwich of coarse bread and sweet butter, chased with sips of coffee from a flask. I walked the entire perimeter of the fence in Camp B—walking, watching, breathing. Ostensibly, I wanted to be sure that it was wise to allow the concert; to test the fence and to decide just where the musicians should stand to play. Less obviously, I wanted just to breathe; I had slept so long and so well that I was stiff and needed the exercise.

I ended up finally very close to where I'd started, in an open space between tall hemlock trees, directly across from the depot platform. The ground was flat enough, the grass short enough, the line of sight to the depot straight enough. It was the place for the concert. I dropped my suit coat on the ground to mark the spot and wandered back toward the gate.

As I rounded the corner of the YMCA building, I could see Cap'n John and two or three of his guards escorting the Imperial Band through the gate. Thirty men in elaborate blue uniforms with red and yellow sashes, all carrying instruments. One man was carrying a large box with some awkward sticks attached to it; after a moment, I saw Anna among the men with Bird, and I realized that the box was her camera.

When the band walked up, I could see that their uniforms were worn and patched, their sashes faded and, in a few places, torn. The instruments, however, shone from patient care, and Ballerstedt carried himself with imperious composure.

As the musicians arranged themselves in careful rows facing the depot, Anna set up her camera just inside the fence, facing back toward the band where she could capture the entire ensemble in rank order. She had favored me with a nervous smile as she'd passed, and now I walked over to where Bird was patiently holding a box of some sort, waiting on Anna as she prepared the camera.

I suppose I was light-headed even then. Even before the blow that was coming. But after a night of dreamy sleep, I needed to see that Anna Ulmann was as impossible as I'd intended her to be, as awkward and out of place.

And so she was. As unnatural as the camera, balanced precariously on its tripod. As awkward as Bird, who handed me the box containing what looked to be large glass plates, while she fished in her apron pocket for something. After a moment, she handed me a slip of paper and took the box back. The paper was a Western Union telegraph form, folded and stapled.

I walked back into the nearby stand of hemlocks to read the telegram while I listened to the concert. As always, to see without being seen.

It originated in Asheville, at the law offices of Craven Johnson. It contained an earthquake.

```
ASHEVIL NO CAROLINA
Stephen I am sorry Major Rumbough died
last night
Sudden stroke Talk to me at funeral Monday
Be careful meantime Craven
```

I could see that there was a bench in the trees. A bench that I managed to reach in time, to sit there rather than on the ground. Somehow this was not right. Somehow I had not known. Or perhaps I had known but missed the warnings while thinking of other things.

Even Jehovah could not live forever.

I saw the musicians raise their instruments in pantomime, but I could hear no music in that gasping air, and it was as cold as I've ever known in the shadow of the trees.

CHAPTER SIX

W HAT is it about alcohol that we love? That it cuts us loose from reason, suspends the laws for a time, so that we can feel or say the truth? That it greases our emotions so that they can slip out rather than stick dryly in the hollow of the chest?

Or that it takes us outside of ourselves completely, lifts us for a moment out of the individual prison we walk around in?

Or maybe just that it dulls the everyday pain, the vicious rubbing away of ourselves day by ever-so-long day?

Times in my life, I would have said any or all of these, some of it sweet, some of it harsh, some of it in flames.

That night, that unseemly, unholy Saturday night that I first heard about Major Jack Rumbough, I bought a quart jar of pure white liquor from Uncle Bob Ramsey for one silver dollar and carried it cradled in my arms up the hill to the porch of Rutland, the high house that the Major had built for his wife, Mrs. Carrie, just after the Civil War. I sat on the porch in the old man's own rocking chair and I addressed that jar. It did not take me long to get the lid off.

This porch was where he and I had sat together ever so many times, usually after supper when I came to report on the doings at the Mountain Park, and he stared off into the far mountains, chewing tobacco or drinking apple brandy, a tin cup of which he would pour for me as well.

The very porch where he and I together drank ourselves into a stupor on the night my only child had died. The little boy who was taken off by infant cholera, and whose death had all but guaranteed that I would not live with Sarah. That night we had hurt ourselves with liquor, just as we had intended. Hurt ourselves for not being able to save him, the little boy that the Major loved as much as I.

So I took my jar of good Ramsey liquor up to the porch at Rutland and, in the old traditional way, hurt myself again, hurt but alone this time. I didn't ease the door on my mind open the way you do with a glass of wine or a cold glass of beer on a hot day. No, I shot the door off its hinges. Drinking and singing. Just the way the Major would have liked, had he been there to share.

"Where are you, old man?" I kept asking him. Shouting from time to time, in case he wasn't nearby. I knew what he would say if he could; I could even hear it in his Tennessee twang. "Halfway to hell," he would say, "and slipping downhill."

Wherever he was, he was beyond hurting, and I had to hurt for the both of us. In long, measured swallows that scalded my mouth and throat. The Ramseys knew how to put pure pain in a canning jar. The prescribed medicine for those of us who have been abandoned.

Dora Henderson Garner found me the next morning. She was sitting there on the step beside my sprawled legs as I slowly groped my way up for air. Sitting on the step reading her Bible, whistling under her breath, occasionally reaching over to pinch my leg to bring me to the surface again. Reading and pinching and whistling.

"What are you doing here?" I said. Or tried to say.

"Watching after you," she replied. "Says here in this Book I'm to watch after you."

"I don't know that I'm in that book," I said. Perhaps came closer to actually pronouncing the words this time.

"Ever-body in this Book," she said. And patted my leg where she'd been pinching me.

"I'm sorry about your father," I said, my mind beginning slowly to work again. Dora Garner, Prince's wife, had skin the color of oak leaves in the fall, the result of her sweet African blood, but Major Jack was her father nonetheless.

"I know you are, Stephen. I'm sorry myself. I been prayin' over him most of the night, while Prince has been out lookin' for you."

"Why's he looking for me?"

"Keep you from doin' yourself a harm. Keep you from drinkin' yourself to death."

I glanced around for my nice jar, but it was gone, and I knew if I ever saw it again, it would be holding pickles in Dora's kitchen.

"You reckon Jack would want to go to heaven?" I asked, hoping to get a smile out of her. "I know he was your father and all, but he could be awful hard sometimes."

"God a lot tougher than that man," she said and patted her Bible. "Say so in here."

By Sunday afternoon, we had the Asheville paper at the depot, and I knew that Jack's funeral was set for ten o'clock the next morning. Ten o'clock meant I could take the early train. And given the responsibility of the camp, I would go and come in the same day; be back in Hot Springs on the evening train, for there was nothing for me in Asheville, after they were done at the cemetery.

I tried to talk Prince and Dora into going with me. But she would not leave home, even for her father, and Prince wouldn't leave her behind, even to watch over me.

Dora's mother, Mary Henderson, had been Mrs. Carrie's maid, come up from South Carolina with her before the war, as a slave. And somehow, in the long tangle of their lives, she bore a daughter to the Major during the war, and yet stayed on after, living with Mrs. Carrie when she and the Major were apart.

Jack Rumbough had loved his black daughter, some say better than the white ones, who had scattered to Asheville and beyond. He had built her a house in Hot Springs and found Prince to marry her. Dora as quiet and shy as a spring morning. Prince as loud as a thunderstorm. And they'd been together ever since.

Thus, Prince became the closest thing to a brother I could ever have or want. Closest in understanding if not blood.

And so I missed him that Monday morning as I climbed aboard the southbound train, first upriver train of the day to Asheville. Called him a name or two as I walked the length of the dining car and into the passenger car, looking for a clean seat, as far away from other people as possible. I was wishing I had him to fuss at me, when, just as I was leaning to sit, I saw her.

Four seats away, she was sitting with her back to me, her head bowed over something in her lap. I could see the shoulders of a formal looking gray dress, buttoned up the back with small, black buttons. And a black velvet hat. There's no rational reason I should have known her from this little evidence, and for a moment I doubted the instinct, but then I realized it was her neck that I knew. Thin, bare, bowed; Anna Ulmann, quite possibly the last person on earth I would have cared to see.

Before I could stop myself I walked the ten feet up the aisle, forming in my mouth the very words I had asked Dora Garner the morning before. What are you doing here? This time with a knife edge.

And standing beside her seat, I half said them. "What are you...?" And stalled as I realized that she was bent over some papers clutched in her lap—letters perhaps—and that she was crying.

She looked away, toward the window, shaking her head ever so slightly by way of response and lifted the letters in her hands, lifted them as if they were the answer to "What are you...?"

I walked back to where I had intended to sit, confused. Not confused—why was she there, on that train. Not confused—why was she crying, even. There could be a hundred reasons for either. But why did I feel so strongly against her? What did I care if she was weeping on a train?

And then the woman herself interrupted me. By sitting down opposite me, our knees almost touching.

"Mr. Robbins," she said hoarsely, "I feel that I owe you an apology." Her face was red and pinched. "I'm not sure why, but in some obscure way, I feel as though I've invaded your world and that you don't like it."

"That's a pretty fair summary," I said, and probably smiled, like a kid who'd been caught out.

"Is it that you don't care for me personally?"

I shook my head slightly, not sure how to fend off her question. "No, I don't think that's it. There's actually been a moment or two when I liked you well enough. When you fell down in Jane Gentry's back yard..."

Her mask almost broke—whether to smile or cry it was impossible to say. "That was not my best moment."

"I don't know. Maybe it was. I know I smile when I think about it."

"Well, then, if it's not me personally, is it the place where we find ourselves that makes you—?"

"On a train?" We were jerking into motion even as I said it.

"No, I mean the prison camp. The war. The—"

"It may just be me," I said suddenly. "I'm pretty busted up in case you haven't noticed."

She leaned forward ever so slightly, staring at my face. "Physically?"

"No. Every other way, Mrs. Ulmann. Except that."

"Anna," she said. "Please." And leaned back, again ever so slightly, still staring at my face.

"Are you leaving Hot Springs? Is that why you're on this train?"

"I'm going to the funeral," she admitted, and looked down at the letters, now folded into their envelopes, still in her hands. "You remember that I told you he was a friend of my father's from many years ago."

"Jack Rumbough?" I was incredulous.

She nodded. "Major James H. Rumbough. The man who—"

"Owned the Mountain Park?"

"I was going to say, adopted you."

"He gave me a home," I admitted.

"I'm sorry for your loss," she whispered. Again, she seemed on the verge of tears.

"But why are you crying? He didn't take you in."

"Not crying," she whispered, and clenched her eyes tightly shut. "It's just that his death reminded me of my father." And then a hot tear did streak her face, that mask of self-control.

Not knowing what else to do, I reached over and patted her hands where they were clenched in her lap, and then she did the strangest thing. Perhaps because she thought I was reaching for them, she gave me the two envelopes, put them deliberately into my hands.

They were both from the Mountain Park, the standard green ink on thick, white paper that had been in use when I was a boy, herding cows and cleaning tables. They were addressed in a clear hand to Mister Reuben Ulmann of 1000 Fifth Avenue, New York City. And above the Park's engraved emblem and return address was scrawled in the same ink "Rumbough." I recognized Jack's signature immediately as he had taught me to counterfeit it when I became manager, so I could sign the dozens of items a day he had no patience for.

I glanced up at her. She was swiping the tears away with the backs of her gloved hands, as unused to crying, I thought, as she was to touching. "Go ahead and open them," she said. "You knew him ..."

I held the envelopes to the shadowy light from the train window, angling them 'til I could make out the faded postmark. Hot Springs, North Carolina, and the dates. I opened the first one.

It held a single sheet of hotel stationary and was addressed to "Dear Reuben." A short note thanking him for "the boxe of truly fine cigars" and for his kind words about the Mountain Park. Jack was glad that Reuben and his daughter had enjoyed their stay, and in his estimation, the place was "not the same without little Anna running furiously up and down the stars." You old goat, I thought. Where did you learn a word like *furiously*?

"I think he misspelled *stairs*," Anna whispered.

"He couldn't spell worth a damn," I said. "One of the reasons he didn't write many letters."

I handed her the first letter and opened the second. Still only a single sheet of stationary but this time the page was brim full.

My friend Reuben,
  I can apreciate much of what you say.
  As you know, I have a mess of daghters myself but only
a couple of them worth the trouble. The dark one, by the
way, is one of good ones. The best perhaps.
  And so I can apreciate how you fear for Anna now that
her mother is gone. I have to tell you, thogh, I think she
could do far worse than being raised up by a loving
father. Just be kind, Reuben. I don't believe that I was ever
  kind enough, except to Dora.
  I believe every word you wrote about Anna by the way.
She will be a beuty—hell, she is already. But more to the
point, she has real, god-given talent. She should trust her
talent—mare than any man. Her talent will be with her
long after we are gone.
Come on back down next summer
—and bring her with you.

He had signed it, not with a scrawled last name, as was his habit, but with his first name—*Jack*—what he had asked me to call him when I married one of his not-worth-the-trouble daughters.

It was my turn then, I confess. To fight back tears. I had known the man for nearly thirty years, seen him most every day that he was in Hot Springs, and now here was a side of him that I had never glimpsed, a friend that I had never known. And here was the evidence, handed to me on the way to his funeral.

"He must have loved you very much," I finally managed to say. "Your father I mean."

"I think that's one of the reasons why I came down here," she said. More in control of herself now than I was. "To find a way to trust my talent."

I nodded. "And to find your father's friend? Find Jack Rumbough?"

"He was not the main reason, but I assumed he would be here somewhere. Even after I learned that the Mountain Park was no longer a luxury hotel but a pri—"

"Internment camp. We try not to say prison."

A bare smile. "Even after I found out the Mountain Park had been turned into an internment camp, I still thought I might find this kindly, old gentleman who had known my father. And instead I found fences and guards and ... you."

"That must have been a disappointment," I said.

We were quiet for a long time then, or at least what felt like a long time. As the train labored upriver, past Stackhouse and Barnard, the river beside us going stone gray and then crystal again, as clouds came and went overhead. First warm, liquid light and then cool shade flooded in the window as we rounded the curves.

"Dora Garner," I said finally.

"Hmmm?"

"Dora is the dark daughter he mentions in the letter ... Prince's wife."

"Was Major Rumbough's daughter? Is she—"

"African? Yes, she is. Half anyway. And you might as well call him Jack," I said. "Since you're getting to know him. Since he and your father were friends."

"My father always talked about coming to the Mountain Park as if it was heaven on earth, trying to get me to remember it."

"But you can't?"

She shook her head. "Glimpses sometimes, but never anything solid."

"Do you remember a short, stocky man? Little bit bowlegged. Scar on his forehead. With a long mustache that hung down on either side of his mouth?"

"Is that the … is that Jack?"

I nodded. "That's him. Feisty as the devil, but charming when he wanted to be."

"I wish I did remember him." And with that one simple, forlorn statement, she became quite real to me for the second time, as in the day she fell in the garden.

We were silent again, for a space. The river kept its own peace, flowing north as we flowed south. We passed Alexander's Station, where for years before the Civil War there had been an inn and drover's station, with huge pens for cattle, horses, hogs, even geese and turkeys.

"The train track follows the old Buncombe Turnpike along the river," I said to her. "Fifty years ago, there was an inn over there in the trees and yards for farmers driving their stock to market. Imagine a couple hundred half-wild turkeys being led up the road in the fall of the year, on their way to South Carolina to be sold at market. Some barefoot country girl with a sack of corn leading the old Tom out in front of the flock, and all the rest coming along, gobbling and pecking in the dirt." She laughed quietly, whether at me or the turkeys I couldn't say.

Later, as we eased past the tobacco warehouses just north of Asheville, she in turn broke the silence. "Stephen, I know you don't care for me. Ignorant city woman that I am. But I wonder if just for today you could put up with me. Help me find the church. Help me know who's who."

"I can walk along with you," I said. "Jack would enjoy knowing you came all this way to sit beside his casket. Besides, you can be of help to me as well."

"How?"

"Keep me from picking things up and throwing them. From cussing out stray family members. Keep me from hurting anybody."

"Including yourself?"

"Including myself."

She nodded grimly.

We took the streetcar up to Pack Square from the station, noisy as
it strained to climb the hill, but neither as crowded nor as dirty as I'd
feared.

From the square, we walked down Church Street slowly, as I could
feel her curiosity about the town radiate out around us. When we
paused before crossing one street, she slipped her hand behind my elbow and, with the slightest pressure, brought me to a standstill. And I
didn't mind: either the pressure of her hand or being brought to heel.
"Tell me where I am," she requested. "What I'm seeing."

And as we had fifteen minutes before the service, I pointed out
the huge pile of dark bricks that passed for First Methodist down and
across the street. A block farther at the foot of the long, sloping hill the
Episcopal cathedral under construction.

"Cathedral?" she asked. "Really?"

I glanced at her out of the corner of my eye, and she was smiling
now in a faintly ironic, even playful way.

"Everybody calls it the *high church*," I said. "Does that make it a
cathedral?"

She looked at it critically. "I don't think it's *high* enough," she said.
"I was married in St. John's Episcopal in New York with a ceiling so
high that no one has ever seen it because of the smoke from the can-
dles. Flocks of pigeons live their entire lives inside St. John's."

"That's pretty damn high," I admitted. "What was it like getting
married in a cathedral?"

"I don't remember," she said after a moment. "All I remember is
that the dress was so tight and the groom so serious and so scary that I
almost fainted. I couldn't breathe, which was surely a sign of things to
come. Where did you get married?" And when I hesitated. "Good for
the goose is good for the gander."

"Right down there," I said, with a painful constriction in my stomach. "Same place as the funeral. First Presbyterian. Serious and rich and
very, very formal. I don't think I ever saw the bride; she was wrapped
up like a mummy." I thought back. "A mummy dragging a sail. Which
was probably also a sign of things to come. She did not like to take her

clothes off under any circumstances."

Anna leaned closer to whisper. "I'll remember that when I see her today."

Two elderly matrons frowned as they passed us, admonishing our laughter. You could tell they were on their way to the funeral.

The inside of the First Presbyterian Church of Asheville, North Carolina was all dark wood and shadowy light filtered through somber stained glass. It had the feel of deep and straight-laced seriousness. It would have been fitting for a funeral except that I knew Jack Rumbough hated the place. His wife Carrie, whom he'd loved in his rough and off-hand way, had chosen this church for her daughters when they'd set up residence at the Hopewell Mansion in Asheville. The Episcopal bishop in Biltmore hadn't suited Miss Carrie for some reason, and the old Scots minister here had paid court to her successfully. She had, in turn, used her own money to help fund the construction of this somber and high-minded edifice, in part so that her gaggle of daughters could bask in the social sun of a larger church. The daughters, chief among them Sarah Rumbough Robbins, had loved the fact that for years, First Presbyterian had been the home to Asheville's richest and most affluent people, giving them the setting and audience they craved.

But Jack had hated it. Hated its sobriety and haughtiness. Hated its lack of humor. Once, after the church had refused to open its doors to the hoboes camped in the woods during a particularly bitter winter, Jack had taken a dozen of the weakest men out of the woods back to Hopewell in protest, as a way of thumbing his nose at the church fathers. Miss Carrie hadn't minded; she herself immediately began making soup by the gallon. Three of the daughters, however, had refused to speak to their father until spring. Which was an unexpected blessing, or so he'd told me one day.

When Anna and I entered, we walked boldly halfway up the long center aisle and eased into a row opposite Craven Johnson, the Rumbough family attorney, who had taken on his portrait-in-oil aspect for the occasion. The portrait did turn its head ever so slightly toward me and wink one eye as Anna and I sat down on the hard bench.

"You didn't tell me it was so ... *cold* in here," Anna whispered. And there was a chill in the air.

"Power of suffering." I said back, enjoying leaning close to her hair to whisper. "Scots believe you can't get to heaven without suffering." And then we fell quiet as the family entered. Still, though, she did not remove her hand from my arm until the procession of the family had passed, and I retained the warmth of her touch as they marched on down the aisle.

They came in order, as the sons and daughters of a powerful man are like to do, conscious of their value and their place. J. Edwin Rumbough, the oldest son of course, came first, with his shadowy wife. My former brother-in-law, Ed, who somehow in the tangled skein of years had come so to despise me. Ed, whom I knew could not be trusted for a moment. Then Anna, or Nan, as her mother had taught us out of habit to call her, widowed and alone. Elizabeth, or Bessie, having married a sober man since the unexplained death of her first and famous husband, the son of a President. Then Henry the attorney, who had enough sense to stay away from Asheville and Ed's long shadow; and whose sickly wife must have stayed home in Columbia even for her father-in-law's funeral. Sarah, or Sadie, who'd picked me up out of the gutter for a few years, holding fast to the arm of a tall, beautifully dressed man whom I did not recognize. God help him, I thought to myself involuntarily. Then Caroline, blessed Caddie, the spiritual one, who could no doubt see her father safely now into heaven. She had the arm of Johnny, the youngest, whom I barely knew at all, but who seemed more supported by his sister than supportive of her. Taken together, they were an impressive and even intimidating crew. Pale, intelligent, over-bred, as alert as hawks, even in mourning.

As Sadie passed with her aristocratic giant, Anna stole a glance at me, and I nodded. She gave me the slightest and most secretive of smiles.

The funeral sermon was delivered by the Reverend Dr. Robert F. Campbell, the same stern Scotsman who had preached Miss Carrie's funeral four years before and who had left Jack in a rage for using the occasion to threaten us all with hell fire. Campbell was a tall, balding man with impeccable black clothes and a superbly rational approach to eternity. So cold that I had always imagined that like Shakespeare's Caesar, his piss froze before it hit the ground.

As you might expect of a Scots cleric, born and educated in the

Highlands, he praised Jack's industry. He praised his contributions to the community. He praised his gifts to his large family. But then Dr. Robert F. Campbell did something I never would have expected him to do. He told the truth.

"James Henry Rumbough had no affection for me," he admitted suddenly, laying down his prepared notes and removing his glasses. "He once ordered me out of his house when I was visiting his dying wife." I saw Ed look up suddenly, as if to head off the impropriety of what was coming. "He and I argued more than once about the very existence of God. Once ..." Campbell actually smiled, something I'd never seen him do. "Once, he even spit tobacco juice all over my shoes for telling him he might roast in hell."

"That's the Major!" shouted a strong voice from the balcony.

"He was not a Christian man in the sense of church attendance and showy prayers and his name on a prominent pew. But every year without fail, he secretly gave me a thousand dollars to spend on the poor people of the town at Christmas. And every year, without fail, he told me that he'd drag my carcass through the streets if the money didn't go straight where it was aimed.

"Six months ago, he told me one evening that he had never known his own father. That he knew him to see him, saw him often enough on the streets of Greenville, Tennessee where he grew up. Occasionally even at the dinner table. But the man had no time for him, had no time for his own son who passed him in the street. That his father was a tough man who could not speak without curses and who could not reach out without striking. And that his father had died suddenly and unexpectedly when James Henry Rumbough was still just a boy. More than anything in his whole life, he told me, he had wanted to know his own father. To talk with him man-to-man over a cup of coffee and to ask him simply how he did."

Damn Dr. Robert F. Campbell, I thought. Damn him for knowing the truth and telling it. I shut my eyes to wall up the tears there. I knew I was close to bursting. And I confess that I groped in Anna Ulmann's lap for her hand.

"Who then, I ask you, has known his own father?" Campbell had shifted his stance; his voice was rising in intensity if not in volume. "Who has seen his face in the moment of its nakedness? Who has heard his voice in the stillness of the night? And where, now, can we find the comfort of that strong arm, and the solace of that deep voice?... Where can we go that he will again lay his hand upon our troubled heads and bestow with strength the chance to rest, to lie down and to sleep? I only say to you now that James Henry Rumbough walks with his own father, who has waited for him along the ridge line. With his own father who had no time for him on this earth. With his own father whom he never knew until the old man greeted him at the gate and caught him in his arms."

Campbell sat down. To the surprise of the family and the dismay of his congregation, many of whom had hoped to hear hot coals shoveled on the high and mighty Rumboughs.

So far as I know, everything Campbell said was true of Jack Rumbough; even as a gruff and grizzled man he had longed for his father's voice. Even worse, everything Campbell had said was true for me as well. No man had ever replaced the father I had lost except, perhaps, Jack Rumbough. And so Campbell had said these things and sat down, leaving the church ringing with the sudden quiet.

Still, though, I sat frozen, managing through the ferocity with which I gripped Anna's hand and the companion pressure I now felt from Craven Johnson on the other side, to hold what felt like a river behind my eyelids.

"Are you all right, boy?" Craven whispered in my ear, his voice coarsened to sandpaper from years of cigars and his breath stinking from the same long habit.

I nodded. Not easily, I confess, feeling a sudden painful stiffness in my neck, but I nodded.

"You know where my office is. After the graveside service is over, you come down to my office. We've got something very important to see about. Come at ..."

My eyes were still closed, but I could feel his body shift as he pulled out his pocket watch. "Come at three o'clock and come sober." He must have looked across at Anna.

"He'll be there," she whispered.

CHAPTER SEVEN

As we left the church, my eyes stunned by the brightness of the sun, the first small miracle of that miraculous day occurred.

The Rumbough family was being ushered into long, black automobiles, of a type rarely seen in Asheville. All but Caddie and Johnny were fitted carefully by the funeral home attendants into the first two cars, and Caddie was in earnest discussion with the undertaker's assistant over the third.

After a moment, the attendant—suitably tall and dark and formal with a dark and formal beard—stepped over to Anna and me and requested with an almost European gallantry that we join the family in the third car. Anna looked at me for guidance; I looked across the lawn and sidewalk at Caddie. "Please," she mouthed silently, and I nodded.

Caddie was the youngest of the Rumbough daughters and, except for John, the youngest of Jack and Carrie's surviving children. Unlike the other girls, she was generally quiet and sweet; in her case, her sweetness was spiced with a sometimes wild-eyed belief in the imminent return of Christ. She lived sometimes partly, sometimes wholly in another world.

And so we got in, Anna Ulmann and I, with my former sister-in-law and former brother-in-law, seated with our backs to the driver and facing Caddie and Johnny. Anna poked me with her elbow and I made the introductions.

Caddie leaned over and patted Anna on the knee in the most familiar fashion. "Welcome, sister," she said. "If you are a friend of Stephen's, then I consider you a friend of mine."

And they chatted away for a few minutes in low voices, almost as if they were sisters. As they talked, I looked young Johnny Rumbough over closely. He couldn't be more than sixteen or seventeen, and he blushed under my examination.

"Mr. Robbins," he said, "I think Caddie has something she wants to tell you."

I shifted my gaze to his sister.

"Stephen," she said, her tone switching suddenly from friendly to more serious, "we don't have long before the cemetery, and I want to ask you something. Johnny's boarding school in Virginia has closed because of the war. Everybody assumed he'd come home and go to Asheville School, but Ed has announced that he is planning to send him down to work for you in Hot Springs to learn the hotel trade." I smiled at the boy, who was obviously nervous. "At first, I liked the idea a lot. I know Papa would have too. But then Johnny told me what Ed asked him to do. You tell it, Johnny."

"Mr. Robbins, my brother Edwin—"

"Thinks I am a bad man and is looking for any excuse to fire me."

He brightened immediately. "You mean you know?"

"But he doesn't know the rest, Johnny," Caddie said.

"He wants me to spy on you and find out anything you're doing that's illegal, so that as soon as the war's over, he can fire you." It came out all in a rush, like a confession.

"Or sooner," I said.

"Sooner?"

"I imagine dear brother Ed wouldn't mind getting rid of me a lot sooner than the end of the war, now that your father's not here to govern him."

"Are you doing anything illegal, Stephen?" Caddie asked.

I savored the question. "Caddie, we're keeping over two thousand German sailors on just over a hundred fenced-in acres. Housing, feeding, entertaining, and generally deluding them into thinking they're imprisoned when in reality they could all walk away most any day they chose to lean on the fence. I imagine we're doing so many things illegally that even Walter McBride hasn't been able to keep score."

"Papa would approve."

"Your papa would find the whole thing so immensely funny that he'd limp around all day laughing his ass off at us and at them. He had the gift."

"But apparently Ed does not." Anna's comment brought us back to reality.

"No," Caddie admitted, "my brother Edwin buttons up his vest very tightly. My question though, Stevie, is this. Will you take Johnny as long as you know he won't be coming as a spy?"

"Let him ask me, Caddie." I looked the pale, thin boy full in the face. "You have something to say, John?"

"Yes, sir. Would you take me on down at the Mountain Park and teach me the hotel trade?"

"Will your allegiance be to me and to the Park and not to anyone else?"

"Yes, sir."

"Then we know each other's minds. Come down on the train as soon as Ed turns you loose." And I shook his hand, this boy who reminded me now of his father.

Anna and I got out of the car first at Riverside Cemetery, leaving young John and Caddie to be escorted along with the rest of the "family." As we walked past the line of the cars toward the Rumbough crypt, Anna whispered to me a question. "Are you in danger ... of losing your job, I mean?"

"Now that Jack is dead, I figure I'm hanging by a thread," I admitted. "And I do mean hanging."

Riverside Cemetery lies on a huge, rolling flank of hill north of Asheville, running down toward the French Broad River from the affluent Montford neighborhood where the Rumboughs' Hopewell and other expensive homes had been built since the turn of the century. It contained poor and often nameless sections of graves down near the foot of the hill, the whole was segregated by race, and up at the top of it all were Asheville's finest families. The Major, in his anger at God for taking Miss Carrie, had caused to be built an elaborate tomb—not above ground like those of so many of Asheville's wealthy families, but dug into the side of the slope. We had brought Miss Carrie there herself four years before on a rainy April morning, and after her death, the Major had given an alcoholic metal smith in Asheville the job of decorating the outside of the tomb. The result: finely wrought brass hinges on the stone doors and as a door lock an elaborate letter "B" overlaid with the letter "R", uniting Miss Carrie's family name with that of Rumbough. All of this had to do with the Major's ongoing battle against fate and society. And no doubt all had been done by the Major without pausing to anticipate that he too would one day enter that dark tomb. Jack had never given much thought to his own mortality.

When we arrived at Riverside, mourners had begun to gather, standing in small groups along the curving gravel road in front of the tomb and among the stones that were scattered in seeming random fashion on the steep slope below. My own private sorrow, that had all but erupted while in the church, did not rise again as we watched the pallbearers, Craven among them, carry the casket carefully along the curved path to the open doors of this dark, implacable room under the earth. Nor was I sad as we listened to Campbell say a few forgotten words. It seemed to me that the major was already gone on to his next battle with fate, perhaps pausing to laugh at us for standing around wasting the time it took to bury him.

Unlike the dark night of the church service, this whole scene was rinsed in light, and it seemed to me that now we were all watching each other. The brothers and sisters were edgy and kept looking around as if to take stock of who was present and who not. Anna Ulmann stood beside me silently with one hand demurely tucked under my arm at the elbow, making no statement with her stance or action except that, mysteriously, she was there with me. She was, I was slowly realizing, the soul of ambiguity.

Our three o'clock appointment at Craven's office took even me by surprise. The reason: the presence of a slight, plainly dressed man of carefully nondescript features whose name was never revealed. The first thing that the Nameless Man did was ask that Craven leave for the duration of our interview, which he seemed relieved to do. I learned later that he and Anna had a delightful cup of tea at the Roosevelt Hotel while I was told the U. S. Government's version of the German presence in America.

Nameless Man worked, as he explained, for the War Department, and he was concerned with national security. His job, or so he told me, was to ensure that no ordinary American citizens within the borders of the country itself came to harm during the war.

I admitted to him my doubts as to whether any ordinary citizens were in danger and he asked me if I had ever heard of the Black Tom incident.

"Who?"

"Not *who,* Mr. Robbins, but *what.* Black Tom, New Jersey is a small unfortunately named community on the outskirts of Jersey City, very near Ellis Island. There has been a small army outpost there since the Civil War and a rather large munitions dump in recent years. Early on the morning of July 30th, last year, it suddenly blew up, killing two soldiers and two civilians."

"Why do I think that this has something to do with my Germans?"

"Because we know at least two of the men involved, and they were German citizens visiting the U.S. In other words, they were saboteurs, paid agents of the German Government. The explosion was large enough so that it cracked the foundation of the main processing building at Ellis Island and spattered the base of the Statue of Liberty with shrapnel."

"You're joking! Was this in the newspapers?"

"No, we kept it out of the press as much as possible because we felt strongly that the intent was to scare the U.S. badly enough so that we would stay out of the war. The President didn't want German spies helping make that decision."

"You mean the President of the United States?"

The faintest smile flickered across his pale face. "Yes, that's the President I'm referring to."

"And the German Imperial Band was being held at Ellis Island at the time?"

"Just so. And three of the luxury liners whose crews are now in your camp were docked in New York. Their crews were on shore leave during the period that Black Tom blew up."

"So you're telling me that there may well be a German spy among my German guests."

"More precisely, I'm telling you that there's almost certainly a loose network of agents and naval officers, any one of whom might have been involved in Black Tom. Odds are there is at least one trained agent of the German Government, who is in a position to receive orders directly from Germany either through the mail or through some third party, like a wife or other relative. Mr. Robbins, one of the reasons we selected Hot Springs in the first place is that there's nothing of any propaganda value to blow up."

"The post office."

"Excuse me?"

"I jokingly asked our token army officer just the other day what in hell a saboteur would blow up—our one-room post office?"

To his credit, the Nameless Man smiled at the irony. "I see your point. But what really concerns us is the chance that one or a group of German agents could escape at some point and make their way to a target of more significance. Or that the mail they're sending home could contain military intelligence—photographs, maps, descriptions—perhaps gathered by a third party."

I didn't mention Hans Ruser's theory that the war could be better fought inside the wire than out. Or that tensions would grow as the war went on.

"Mr. Robbins, Craven Johnson tells us that you are a very intelligent man. Can I ask you: is the security at Hot Springs tight or loose?"

"Loose enough to scare you."

"Is the outgoing mail being carefully monitored or not?"

"Not. … We have some school teachers censoring for obvious things, but they know very little German and they wouldn't know military intelligence if it crawled out of the envelope and bit 'em on the finger."

"Mr. Robbins, we are under pressure from certain authorities in the War Department to turn the Hot Springs Camp over to the army." He was watching me carefully. "There are those who don't believe that a civilian should be left in charge when so much is at stake."

"I can understand that," I said.

"But that's not all. There is also the question of whether or not you can be trusted with this responsibility."

I thought of Ed Rumbough. "Is that a local question or a national one?"

Again he smiled. "Local. Nobody in Washington has even the vaguest notion of who you are—or cares. No, I believe you went to church with one of your severest critics just this morning. However, it may help you to know that we place much more credence in the judgment of Mr. Johnson and in that of the late Major than we do in that of Edwin Rumbough. Even so, I'm compelled to ask you about one other issue that has been brought to my attention."

I fully expected him to ask me about the amount of alcohol I consumed on any given day, but he fooled me.

"Can you tell me why the elected sheriff of your own county has said repeatedly that you are completely incapable of your post?"

"He's my cousin, first of all, and he hates the sound of my name."

"Craven Johnson explained to me that he's your cousin, but I fail to see—"

"Five years ago, I shot a man who was attacking one of our flower girls at the Mountain Park. Shot him in the hotel dining room in front of about a hundred shocked guests."

"Shot him dead, I presume."

I nodded. "I assumed at the time from the way the woman reacted that he was her husband, but I had no idea until I was staring down at his body, wondering just how in hell we'd ever get the blood out of the carpet, who else he was."

"The woman's husband, and—?"

"Roy's brother. I hadn't seen him in ten years, and I wasn't even sure when I was standing there staring at him. But the fact remains; Nathan Robbins was Roy's brother."

The Nameless Man actually grinned, and it generated a flush of color in his pale cheek.

"What's so damn funny?"

"I'm sorry. Is this what they mean by a mountain feud?"

"Close enough. Roy made sure I stood trial, and tried to have me convicted. But people down there know me, and even though I have been a rough son-of-a-bitch at times, they knew I wasn't a patch on Roy and his brother."

"And you had a hundred witnesses."

"Exactly."

"You know, Mr. Robbins, I was going to ask if you thought you were up to running this internment camp, but now that I've gotten to know you, I think I have my answer."

"Meaning not a chance."

"Just the opposite. I think you'll do fine. Just make sure that no

Germans end up on the wrong side of the fence, especially none of the bad ones."

"You may have to blink at a few rules being bent."

"Break all the rules you like, Mr. Robbins. Take the law into your own hands. Just make sure that no reporters see the Hague Convention actually being violated and that there are no escapes. You do that, and everyone in our nation's capital will be happy, and you can afford to ignore Ed Rumbough and your sheriff."

There was more. Much more. Lists of suspects. Descriptions of individual family members that we were to watch for. A long, carefully typed list of things that had to be censored from the mail. And the whole time we were talking, I felt as though I myself had just been given a reprieve, allowed to stay inside my beautiful prison just a little longer.

CHAPTER EIGHT

THE result of it all was that Anna Ulmann and I missed the late train back to Hot Springs. Six o'clock that evening found us standing on a street corner in Pack Square, saying good night to Craven Johnson.

Craven recommended two things. "For my old friend Steve and my new friend Anna," he said. It was obvious to me that the old goat was smitten with his new friend, Anna. "I recommend dinner at the Sky Club up on the mountain." He pointed to a square, stone edifice three-fourths of the way up Beaucatcher Mountain. "It's private so you can have a very good drink with a very good meal. And you cannot pay except by giving them my name. In addition, I recommend a boarding house on Spruce Street named the Old Kentucky Home. At the boarding house, ask for Fred. He will drive you up the mountain to supper for the price of a drink." And he bowed to me and kissed Anna's hand, his old friend and his new, and then walked away.

Just that quickly, we were alone. Alone in a way that we hadn't been before. Alone without a schedule. Alone without the return trip to cut off the day for us and protect us from each other. Alone with only my envelope of papers and her hat box with which to defend ourselves.

"Should we take him up on his offer?" I asked Anna, wondering how she would handle having her day trip suddenly take on these new dimensions.

"Stephen," she said, suddenly nervous. "You do not have to spend the evening with me. You've been more than kind, just getting me to the funeral in one piece. I'm sure you have friends that you'd rather spend—"

"I can stand a little more of your company."

"No, really. I—"

"Before today, I had two friends in Asheville. You just had tea with the one that's left."

In retrospect, I think I feared being alone more than I feared her.

So we found the Old Kentucky Home, a five-minute walk from the square, with its pinched, puritanical proprietor, a woman named Wolfe who seemed to go out of her way to insure that Anna's room and mine were on opposite sides of her house. The house itself raw with the smell of ancient, blistered shellac and the faint tang of wood smoke and grease from the kitchen. And we found the proprietor's son Fred, a tall, lanky young man with the wildest shock of yellow hair. He stuttered maniacally as he yelled at us over the engine of his father's car, which he drove just as maniacally up the winding gravel roads to the Sky Club.

If this was the day of small miracles, dinner was the second. Apparently, it was the policy of the Sky Club that no money actually changed hands over one of its meals, probably because they made no secret of serving alcohol despite prohibition. We gave Craven's name at the door, and after that there were no prices on a menu, no mention of a bill, and no expectation of payment. We ordered mountain trout and a bottle of white wine that Anna recognized, a bottle from Italy with a name on it that I had never heard before. The waiter, stately and reserved, was obviously taken by Anna's self-assurance with the wine. I was relieved not to be tempted by something stronger.

As it was a Monday evening and the place almost empty, we sat at a table beside a high window, overlooking the small mountain city as the gas lights came winking on below.

After a glass and a silence that was almost comfortable, Anna Ulmann interrupted the memories swirling in my brain.

"I've made up my mind about you, Stephen Robbins," she said, with a smile, a real smile, flickering at the corners of her mouth. "You are not a man to be trusted."

"How so?"

"You're too hard on yourself. You claim to be busted up, mean, diffident and yet every single person in Hot Springs, North Carolina that I've asked for direction just points at you. You seem to be the compass."

"*Diffident?*" I asked.

She blushed slightly. "Too modest. Too shy. You act like you don't care when it's so obvious that you do."

"Let me pour you some more wine," I said, trying to avoid her eyes as I reached across the table.

"I believe you do care."

"Depends," I said. "Care about some things, yes, I will admit it. Don't give a damn about most others."

She didn't answer except to raise her eyebrows.

"I care about Prince and Dora," I said. "The people who work for me. Care about the Mountain Park."

"You love the Mountain Park," she corrected me.

I had to smile. "It's true," I said. "Every nail. Every board. Every brick."

"Is that all?"

"Maybe." I considered. "Maybe that's all I've got."

"You've got me," she said.

My glass was halfway to my mouth, my lips parted to meet the wine, and it took all the self-control I could manage to set my glass back on the table top without spilling it in my lap. "I'm sorry?"

"Maybe you've got me," she said.

My mind could not grasp what she meant, but I could hear my pulse pounding in my ears. I was saved by the waiter, who came just then with plates of salad greens, because I had no idea what to say to her.

As we began to eat, my eyes were drawn to her hands. There were those small, brown fingers with short clean nails, fingers ever so astute and ever so delicate. A gold ring on her right hand that looked like an open flower with small diamonds in the bowl of the blossom.

"Tell me about your former husband," I said to her after a bit. Trying to gain some distance from where she'd taken us.

"I lied to you about that," she said after a moment.

"What?"

She stared at me helplessly, mouth half-open to speak.

"Try the truth," I suggested. "Supposed to set you free."

"The truth is that I'm not divorced."

"Meaning that you're married."

"Meaning that I haven't lived with Dr. Anton Jurgens in over two years. I maintain my own household entirely separate from the man, but I've never been able to bring myself to force him into court. And meaning that even now, I'm afraid of him." She took a deep breath. "I hate even to say his name, I'm so afraid of him."

"Afraid because he mistreated you somehow? Abused you?"

"Yes. But not how you think. The abuse was kindly and soft-spoken and intelligent. But—"

"Kind and intelligent, but the sort of kindness that smothers you to death?"

She nodded violently, but then held out her hand to prevent me saying more. "That's it. That's enough. It's most of why I came south. Maybe even part of why I like you."

"What do you mean?

"You're not full of yourself. Not fat with self-interest. You're not—"

"Kind and intelligent?"

"Precisely."

I had to glance up to see that she was teasing.

"I don't trust anybody anymore," she said, suddenly serious again. "Not since my father died. "But for some strange reason, I relax around you. Even that first day when I met you at the depot, I didn't know you at all but it was as if you were a cool stream. As if you sucked the tension right out of the air."

"You thought I was the hired help, if you recall."

"I know, but when I started talking to you, I began to relax."

"Maybe that's not such a good—"

"See what I mean," she said. "Diffident."

Then there was the fish with its tender, white flesh. And the wine, cool and almost smoky against the fresh taste of the trout. Flashes of conversation that would have been impossible sober, impossible except there among the evening clouds, looking down over the remainder of humanity.

It was over dessert, an iced fruit something, that she asked the hard question, the one that burned into me like a hornet's sting. "Why are you so hard on yourself?" And if she had stopped there, perhaps I could have dodged it. But she didn't stop. "Why do you forgive everyone else so easily but not yourself?"

"I'll tell you the truth now," I said eventually. "To pay you back for earlier. But you better brace yourself. This is an ugly truth."

"Ugly to tell or ugly to hear?"

"Both, I imagine. Based on what it does to me to talk about it. When I was ten years old, my father took sick with pneumonia and died up home in Anderson Cove. February of 1885, black cold and a skiff of snow on the ground. One day he was working his full stint, nursing a cold with a ragged cough, but nothing to scare you. The next day he was in bed complaining that his chest hurt, and the day after he couldn't get up without help. That night, he was delirious, and my mother sent me for the doctor in Marshall."

"You were ten?"

I nodded.

"How far was it?"

"Six or seven miles there and the same back. On horseback. I rode up and over the Divide, down through Bearwallow Gap to the river. Across the bridge at Barnard and then down the Turnpike to Marshall."

"Didn't we go through Marshall this morning on the train?"

I nodded again. "Barnard and Marshall both. Problem is I got lost. The great problem of my life is I got lost in the snow and the dark when I came to the gap of the mountain. I went the wrong way for most of a mile and had to backtrack. And even then I was confused. Something no mountain boy should ever be. Something I should never have been, even on the darkest night. So it took me two hours longer than it should have.

"When I finally found the doctor's house, it was past midnight, and by the time I got the doctor back to the cove, it was dawn."

"What happened?"

"He died during the night. He managed to hold on 'til an hour or so before first light, the coldest part of the night, before he let go."

"You were just a boy."

"Doesn't matter. I failed him. So it seemed to me then. And so it seems to me now. It was years ago, but I'm still on that horse, scared to death, riding in the black dark and snow in my face."

"Two hours wouldn't have made a difference."

"Maybe. But I was just a kid, Anna, and for years after, I was convinced that everyone blamed me. My face goes numb just talking about it."

"But nobody really blamed—"

"I was the oldest son."

She paused, considering. "And so you've been taking care of people ever since."

"It seems so," I said, overcome then by the sadness of it all. "Maybe when I die, I can get off that horse, maybe the sun will rise."

She did something then. Rather than trying to say something where there was no place for words, she did something. Before the passive waiter standing by the door to the kitchen, and before God, she got up, placed her napkin carefully beside her plate, and walked around the table. She pulled me from my chair and hugged me. I was hot to sweating, at a loss for breath. And now it was she who felt like a stream of cool air.

Only later did she ask me to take her there, to Anderson Cove. So that she could take her photographs of real mountain people, living as they had always lived.

"You want to go there, even after the story I told you?"

"Even more so after the story you told me. For your sake as well as mine."

Although I shook my head no and she said no more, she had planted the seed and was content to let the thought take hold.

The rest of that evening runs together in my mind. I can't justify what happened. I wouldn't even try to justify it. Nor can I explain it except to say that I, at least, was in shock. From the funeral. From the memories of my father.

Nor am I sorry for what happened that night, in that awful boardinghouse.

As we drank our coffee, I said what seemed to me to be a next, obvious thing. "It will be hard," I said, as if admitting something unpleasant. "Hard for us to see each other in Hot Springs."

She looked at me quizzically.

"We're on either side of the fence. You live with Miss Jane Gentry, and I live with Hans Ruser."

She smiled. "Your fences aren't that high," she said.

Neither of us said anything to plan it. Neither of us whispered an intent or a desire. Neither of us made sure the other knew a precise location.

But after our wild ride back down Beaucatcher Mountain, Fred seemingly more drunk than either Anna or me; after stern directions and a churlish good-night from the mistress of the Old Kentucky Home; midnight found me creeping barefoot down a dimly lit upstairs hallway.

My eyes swam. The heavily varnished black floor was cold and treacherous with creaking boards. The plaster walls along which I crept were rough and scratchy to my bare arms. But I was half drunk and in search of that third miracle.

The door to her room was outlined in pale, wavering yellow. She opened it several inches just as I placed my hand on the china knob. The door opened far enough to yield her face, and I did the thing that now seems so obvious. I fit my face between the door and the jamb and I managed to find her lips with mine. Once. Again. And the second time there was a return pressure, a pressure and a softness.

I reached one hand through the crack in the door, but she caught it before I could touch her body. "I didn't bring anything to wear," she whispered dreamily.

"Thank God."

And she placed my hand on her hip. I could feel the smooth fabric of her dress, but it was loose, not tight; was slippery between my hand and her waist as if it were only wrapped around her. I pushed the door open with my shoulder and then was inside. She closed it behind me, the tongue of the latch clicking into its tiny receptacle sounding like metal thunder in the still house.

And so that night we fell into grace, neither of us suspecting even then just how fast and deep was the water in which we swam.

CHAPTER NINE

As I slept that night tossed in the stiff sheet and paper thin quilt—banked like a smoldering fire against Anna Ulmann—I went home again in my dreams.

I was a raven, black beak and wing with a stark black eye, floating north over the French Broad River Valley. Borne on a high swift current of wind, chill in the white night air. A river of air that chased after the water's run far below. I soared far above the river beneath, as high as the knifed ridges at my wing tips, and as my black head pivoted, my black eye saw diamond brightness where far below the gorge softened and widened to admit Spring Creek, and where before all had been the steep fastness of plunging ridge, now were fields, here a barn with its ghostly owl and there an orchard with its chattering wren.

In my raven mind, I had expected the valley, knew the country, but suddenly, unexpectedly, there was the silver glint of wire, barbed in the moonlight. Caught in the wire like birds in a snare were row upon row of long, narrow buildings, cut off suddenly by the straight line of the bridge street. Board fences and more wire, more wire, more wire, silver in my black eye as I soared, skimmed, rushed above.

Ah, there was the old hotel, what I knew, what I sought, but caught now in a giant nest of wire. It is my home, I croaked, not my home, my home, not my home. As I skimmed above the plunging roof, beating up against the river of wind, wing upon wing, stretching to see within and then ... and then ... my feathers, it seemed, were fingers. My black wings but pale arms. Again.

Imagine then that meanest boarding house bed and rough, iron-stiff sheets, with a thread-bare quilt thrown over us by our own careless and exhausted hands, surrounded by chalky, white-washed walls and rough pine floors varnished to scuffed blackness, the whole saturated with the sour odor of coal smoke from the fireplace and grease from the kitchen below ... an indifferent boarding house room. What was I to expect on waking? Disgust? Dismay? Fear?

I felt none of that. I felt dizzy. Even lying there, before anything other than my eyes moved inside their lids, I was dizzy. Wine and wing and something other than wine was spinning inside my head.

Anna was lying on her side facing me.

Her face was inches from my own, mashed into a perilously thin pillow. And I will confess that like Shakespeare's dark lady, she had her flaws. There were shadowy half-moons under her eyes and the slightest fleshiness under her chin that I had never noticed before. Her hair was thick and wild and all over her head, with a few iron gray strands woven into the profusion of lustrous raven's wing black.

But even in that harsh September light in that hard, cheap room, her face reached out and held me. Her eyes trembled beneath their paper thin lids as she dreamed. Her faint pulse ticked slowly in her temple beneath what seemed to me the most delicate sheath of skin. Even the tiniest scar on her cheekbone was all vulnerability and sadness. As I watched, she smiled in her sleep, her lips barely parted, and I glimpsed the glistening tip of her tongue.

Just then, she was herself and nothing more. She wasn't a desperate woman who feared her husband or a soft woman who meant to be hard or a Yankee lost in the Godforsaken South or a sophisticate or a spy or an artist. She was not any category in the wide world. But some creature that defied my science—her own wild, unremarked species.

We were sleepy on the streetcar ride down. Lazy and quiet in the chill, white September air, neither of us having been able to stomach the boarding house coffee, weak and cut with chicory.

Under the high, tiled dome of the Asheville train station, I bought our tickets from an agent whom I didn't know, a skinny, taciturn man who asked my name and when he'd heard it, asked me to see the baggage agent outside.

Anna motioned me on from the bench where she sat, utterly relaxed. Her very gesture seemed to say that she didn't intend to rise until the train was smoking on the siding.

Outside, I found the baggage agent laughing and talking with a short, plump, amazingly pink man in a somber suit. I told them both who I was.

"Mr. J. J. Hines," the pink man introduced himself, "of Hines and Sons Mortuary and Funeral Services. I am, of course, delighted to see you."

"Do we know each other?" I asked, immediately suspicious of anyone so pink and friendly.

"I'm sorry to say we don't, but any man of business knows the Mountain Park and has heard of its excellent proprietor. I am afraid, however, that we meet on a sad occasion."

"Major Rumbough's funeral?"

"Oh, no, although that too is an event to shake our world. No, I mean that I have been entrusted with the body of a young Hot Springs boy. A young recruit in the army who was killed in a training accident in Alabama. His body is on the way home, and I'm proud to say that Hines and Sons are commissioned by the army for the preparations. I thought I might impose on you to certify its delivery."

"Just what does that mean: *certify its delivery*?" My early morning lethargy was dissolving.

"In this case, it means to view the body briefly, to note its condition. To see it safely stowed on the train and then make sure it's unloaded in Hot Springs and sent to ..." Mr. J. J. Hines glanced at a folded sheaf of papers in his jacket pocket. "... the Hot Springs Post Office?" He looked at me questioningly.

"The post office is the only official building in town. It's that or one of the churches." I looked at the baggage agent, who stood patiently by. "*Certify its delivery*?" I asked again, still not sure just what I was being asked to do.

"Don't worry, Mr. Robbins, it's standard. If you or somebody else won't sign for it, then old J. J. here has to ride all the way down to Hot Springs and back."

He opened the door to the storage room, and J. J. Hines motioned me inside with what I was sure was the same grand gesture that he used to lure grief-stricken relatives into his parlor.

"But why do I have to see the body?"

"Because, Mr. Robbins, there have been instances wherein the family was not satisfied with the artistry of the embalmer. Never in the case of Hines and Sons, I'm sure, but in others. It's best if someone of integrity like yourself can testify to the condition of the body before signing the receipt."

I glanced at the baggage agent again, and he nodded.

The interior of the baggage room was lit by a single electric bulb hanging from the ceiling. The coffin was not prominent, rather it had been shoved to one side of the floor, and I could see that it was the cheapest of wooden boxes, joined out of pine boards. When I knelt beside Hines, I could smell his cologne, sickeningly sweet. He or one of his employees had left all but one of the nails pulled on top of the box, and with a deft movement, he was able to shift the lid, so I could look inside.

"Please step back," I said to him, "so I can see." More interested in removing his cologne than his shadow.

"Lord God," I said, "it's Robert Griffin. Why didn't you tell me it was Robert Griffin?"

"I'm terribly sorry, Mr. Robbins, but you didn't ask, and I never dreamed ... Is he related?"

"No, worse than that." Robert had worked in the stables at the Park for several years past. He had the most skillful hands and the quietest voice with horses of anyone I knew. He had sung his way through many a long night in the barns while the mares foaled, and he had always cried when we had to put down an animal. "O my Lord God," I whispered. Robert had not wanted to fight the Kaiser or anyone else, and it had taken me an hour one spring afternoon to explain why he'd been conscripted in the very first order.

"Hines!" I hissed. "Why does he look like that?"

"How do you mean?" He sounded insulted.

"Like he's been washed in flour." Robert's rich blond hair, slicked back over his head, was now darker than his pale skin. I stood up. "Like something scared him to death."

"We are all pale in death, Mr. Robbins," Hines said somberly.

"Yeah, well, it nearly gave me a heart attack. Can't you do something with all your ... artistry?

Hines brightened. "Of course!" More quickly than I could have imagined, he produced a tin from his pocket and unscrewed the lid.

"The mortician's friend," he said happily, and I could see that it was a rich, red rouge.

"No, you don't," I growled, grabbing his arm. And we actually tussled for a moment, tipping precariously over Robert Griffin's body. We broke apart and eyed each other warily, both of us panting, the stench of Hines' cologne all but choking me.

"I'll sign for him," I said. "Just nail down the lid and don't touch him. Let me take him home."

When the baggage agent and I emerged back into the light a moment later, I asked him: "How'd he die? Tell me that much in case his family asks."

"Papers said he fell out of a truck," he said. "And the one behind ran him over. ... Army don't take very good care of 'em, does it?"

"It's just the beginning," I replied, shaken. Robert had hated cars and trucks because they always spooked the horses. "Mark my words. He's just the beginning."

When I walked back into the waiting room, I saw Anna talking to a young woman who looked vaguely familiar. Long wavy hair that she had tried in vain to capture in a bun. Rusty hair above a pale, freckled face with an upturned nose.

"Stephen!" Anna said. "My God! You look like you've seen a ghost."

"Robert Griffin," I replied, more or less in a whisper. "I just saw little Robbie Griffin."

"Who?"

"Never mind, I'll explain on the train. Who is this?" I was trying to smile at Anna's companion, but I must have looked ghastly.

"I have rescued this young woman. The ticket agent was not going to honor the pass she bought in Richmond because it was dated for tomorrow, and she was trying to use your name in her cause. Using it in vain, I might add."

The young woman stood and half-bowed, half-curtsied, stuck her hand out and then withdrew it.

"It's all right, Colleen, he won't bite," Anna said.

"Colleen McManaway," I said, realizing at once who she must be.

She blushed to the very roots of her hair in response.

"You've come to marry your Georg."

"If you will allow me, sir," she replied, the edges of her diction roughed ever so slightly by her Irish.

"And why did you think that using my name would help get you to Hot Springs a day early?"

"Because, sir, my Georg tells me in his letter that you are the great man of the world. Greater than the mayor of New York."

Anna laughed. "My dear, he's never been to New York, but even so ..." She glanced at me. "... even so."

Colleen McManaway laughed a high, tinkling laugh and then sank down onto her bench again.

"Have you eaten, Colleen?" I asked.

"Oh, yes sir," she said. "The day before yesterday in Grand Central Station."

And so Anna and I boarded the train home, retracing our journey from the day before but with two souls in tow. Colleen McManaway fed on fried apple pies and then slept in a nest of baggage that Anna and I assembled in the last seat before the club car. Robert Griffin in his deeper sleep in the freight car, his rough, pine box wedged in between bags of lime and sacks of mail.

Anna and I finally had some coffee worth the name and hard rolls with butter. As we ate, I described for her Georg Mende's epic battle for his Colleen, and Robert Griffin's boyhood at the Mountain Park.

"So one comes home in life and one in death," she said finally. "And both come home under your broad wing. Perhaps you are a great man, Stephen Robbins, which, I admit, bothers me a great deal."

"Why? Not that I am, *but why?*"

"You know why. I have all my life fought back against authority, and since Dr. Jurgens, I have especially fought back against men. It's in my very blood to fight back." But she was smiling when she said it, and she touched my hand under the dining car table.

And so, I admit, it was a surprise—more than that, a shock even—when the train arrived in the Hot Springs station, and she suddenly left me. I know I should have expected it, but still I winced when Anna parted from me on the platform, so suddenly and so formally, as if she barely knew me. "Let me find you in a day or so," she had whispered, as the train slowed into the station.

Thus, I was fortunate that the next few hours turned into a whirlwind of seek and demand. I found several boys hanging around the depot to fetch a wagon and take Robert's body to the post office. As soon as they had the box loaded on the wagon, I sent one of the boys to find Prince Garner. He would know about Robert's family, and he would know how we should go about burying him. In the business of life and death, Prince's instincts were ever so fine.

Then I took Colleen McManaway in tow, with her pitifully small suitcase, and led her to the home of Thomas Frisbee on Spring Street. Like Mrs. Jane Gentry, Mrs. Frisbee took in boarders, but in a much smaller house and on a much smaller budget. I knew that if she had room for Colleen, Mrs. Frisbee would soon treat her like a daughter and help her find a job. And within an hour, and with few enough pleasantries on my part, Colleen was settled. She was to come to the Camp A gatehouse the next afternoon, and I promised her that she should see her Georg.

As I came back down through town, I met Prince at the corner of Bridge and Spring Streets, where he'd been waiting, having seen the coffin being unloaded onto saw horses on the post office porch.

"Who is it, hoss?"

"Robert Griffin."

"Yellow-haired Robbie, the stable boy?"

I nodded.

Prince shook his massive head sadly. "Good God almighty. They could've taken most any of 'em but they had no cause to kill Robbie Griffin."

"Prince, I'm scared of this. I admit it. I'm full of hate myself, and I expect his family to want blood."

"German blood?"

"Who else they gonna blame?"

"It was you put him on the train, hoss."

"Yeah, well, I thought of that. I should've sent him up home and told him to hide."

"I ain't saying you should blame yourself." He reached out to massage my shoulder. "I'm saying some of the sorry-ass mountain boys round here might want to remind you of it."

"Where's his family?"

"His mama's been dead for years. She worked at the Park before your time and lived with a man from down near the line. I don't know if they were ever church married, but I think his father's still alive. Man name of Harmon Griffin, if he's to be found."

"Can we find him in a day or so, before we have to bury Robbie?"

"Send your boy, Edgar Ramsey. He'll find him if he's above ground." He finally released my shoulder. "And Stevie, there's one other thing."

"Hmmm?"

"I been knowin' you for most of twenty years, and I'm sorry I said what I did about you puttin' him on the train. Truth is you've spent your whole life tryin' too hard to save people. Why you won't a preacher, makes no sense to me. But son, you can't save 'em all."

It wasn't Robbie Griffin's blood family who wanted revenge. Edgar Ramsey found Harmon Griffin much later that afternoon near Paint Rock, only five miles from town, but the man had no interest in seeing his son buried.

Not the blood family but rather his adopted family, the dozens of people in and around Hot Springs who had known him. Who had been favored by his smile or freshened by the sound of his voice, singing as he worked.

Prince and I sat by the body that afternoon, sat in the old, cane-bottomed chairs on the porch in front of the small frame building we used as a post office. Townspeople, many of them former employees of the Mountain Park, came by to sit for a while, and we told stories of Robert's famous gift with animals and his equally famous discomfort about people.

"Especially women," one of the former maids said to me as she passed by on the way to work at one of the boarding houses. "The sweetest, prettiest man you can imagine, and the one time I tried to tell him so, he blushed as pink as a posy and ran to hide in the barn."

"Did you find him?" I asked.

"Oh I went up and down the stalls, calling to him, promising him every sort of good time, but I couldn't lure him out no matter."

As afternoon wore into evening, people began to bring food and spread it out along the edge of the porch. A sliced ham, still steaming. Pots of beans and corn and cabbage. Several of the boys brought scraps of wood from Cap'n John Sanders' last building project and soon we had a fire in the street directly in front of the post office. As darkness came down from the high mountains, various men and boys brought more wood, and several added a fence rail or two for heat.

Unfortunately, wood was not all they brought. Several jars of white liquor and jugs of homemade brandy began to make the rounds on the outskirts of the crowd, and so I was grateful when the town's half-dozen preachers rose to stand on the porch one at a time to read a verse or say out a short benediction for Robert. Mostly, they had a peaceful influence, but there is no more competitive group of men than mountain preachers. They spur each other on, you see, to hellfire and damnation. So it was no surprise when one drunken excuse for a Methodist had to remain standing after his prayer to roundly curse Germany for stealing the soul of our own dear boy.

"Them Germanies done it," I heard shouted from the fringe of the crowd, beyond the revealing light of the fire. "Them damn Germanies inside that fence."

Prince rose up from his chair at this point and tried to carry us over the breech into the New Testament, describing his Father's house, with many mansions.

"What mansion is that, Prince? If God lets you and Robbins run the place, it'll be half-full of them damn Germanies too!" General merriment. But the laughter was growing meaner by the moment.

"It is a home for people of all stripe and kind," Prince tried, and for a moment they listened. "Mansions for the Jew and Gentile, for the Catholic and Protestant. A place where gentleness and kindness rule. No meanness. No meanness there, I say!"

Give them more blood and thunder, I thought, or you'll lose them.

A harsh voice yelled out from beside the post office itself, too close for my comfort. "Sit down, Nigger! And shut the hell up. Ain't you never heard of an eye for an eye?" The voice had the high, banjo twang of deep mountains. Mean and drunk.

Prince knew his time was up. He sat and leaned toward me. "See what you can do with 'em," he said. "They're startin' to sound like your people."

Before I stood, I leaned over to Jimmy Gentry, who was sitting on the edge of the porch, apparently enjoying the show. I shook Jimmy roughly to get his attention before whispering in his ear. "Find John Sanders now. Tell him to post every guard he's got and to load their pistols."

"But you said ..."

"That was before. Tonight, I'm saying to load their pistols. Now go." I kicked him for good measure and then I stood up.

"The Germans didn't kill Robbie Griffin." I shouted. "I did."

"What in God's name are you doing?" Prince hissed just loudly enough for me to hear.

A hush fell on the crowd, but I didn't lower my voice. I shouted out into the night. "The awful truth is that Robert fell off the back of a truck at Fort Henshaw, Alabama. When he fell, the truck next behind ran him over and broke his back."

"Then the damn army killed him!" It was a woman's voice from beyond the fire. "The damn army scripted him up and killed him!" The men weren't the only ones drinking.

"The army did kill him. But when his conscription notice came, Robbie Griffin came to me and asked me what to do. Me, Steve Robbins. He trusted me to tell him the right thing. But I didn't tell him to run. I didn't tell him to hide. I told him he had to serve, and I'll regret it to my dying day. I told him it was the honorable thing to do, and that when he came home he'd be a hero." I paused to catch my breath, and to listen to the spirit brewing in the crowd.

"Turns out I lied to him," I shouted. "Robbie Griffin came home today but he didn't live long enough to be a hero."

"Do you believe in hell, Robbins?" The drunken Methodist shouted.

"Oh, I believe in it, brother. I saw it today when I opened that casket in the Asheville train station. Hell is reserved for people like me, sure enough, but not for the likes of Robbie Griffin. He's gone on up the mountain today. I believe he whipped death today. ... Do you believe that, Edgar Ramsey?" Edgar was standing by the fire, warming from his trip to Paint Rock and back.

Edgar paused, and for a moment I wasn't sure he'd heard me. "Sure,

Mr. Robbins. I believe he whipped death's ass today." Quietly, with conviction.

"Prince asked me to preach a moment ago," I said, more quietly now. "After he and the others had used up all the best verses. But I believe I can recall a verse that even Prince Garner doesn't know. And I will line it out for you now, if you'll listen."

There was a long pause, and in the hot, flickering light, it seemed to me that much hung in the balance.

"Say it out, Mr. Robbins. We'll hear you." It was Edgar Ramsey again, the smallest and surely the bravest man there, around our grieving fire.

Death, be not proud, I began, quoting Donne straight and simple, saying it on to the end.

Though some have called thee Mighty and Dreadful.
For thou art not so;
For those whom thou think'st dost overthrow
Die not, poor Death, nor yet cans't thou kill me.
From Rest and Sleep, which but thy pictures be,
Much pleasure, then from thee much more must flow;
And soonest our best men with thee do go—
Rest of their bones and souls' deliver!
Thou'rt slave to fate, chance, kings, and desperate men,
And dost with poison, war, and sickness dwell;
And poppy or charms can make us sleep as well
And better than thy stroke. Why swell'st thou then?
One short sleep past, we wake eternally,
And Death shall be no more: Death, thou shalt die!

In the rushing stillness that followed, I could hear the crackling of hard timber as the fire gnawed on its resiny pine and coarse locust post. The breeze seemed to me to lift, whipping the fire, and then die away again, leaving a spreading warmth and perhaps peace.

"I ain't never heard that particular verse before," said an aged female voice close by the porch. "But it's a good un."

"It's in the New Testament," replied her friend. "One of them pistols from Paul."

We buried Robert Griffin the next day in the Oddfellows Cemetery above town. In a much appreciated gesture, the German Imperial Band led the way up the hill, playing as sad a death march as any of us had ever heard. And although Captain Robert Snyder never knew, his U.S. Army bridge-building funds eventually bought Robbie a bold, granite stone.

I confess that with all that to do and with being up most of the night walking the fence to be sure our more drunken neighbors had indeed gone away to sleep it off, I never once forgot about Anna Ulmann. Never ceased holding her in my mind, trying to make sense of her. Trying to feel my way through the dark. Hoping, as I walked, that she was peacefully sleeping. Sleeping as I had seen her sleep, deliciously relaxed and perhaps happy. Trying to grasp and hold onto the truth of her, even as the long night waned into dawn.

But I did forget about Colleen McManaway. Between the middle of one afternoon and the middle of the next, she dropped out of my mind as neatly as if she'd leaped from a bridge. And looking back, I suppose that my forgetting her was a sign of the state I was in. Treading water and exhausted.

So the next afternoon, after we'd laid Robbie Griffin in the soft ground on the slope under the hemlocks, and after John Sanders had gone home across the river to sleep and after the good citizens of Hot Springs had disappeared back into the stream of their lives, I sat down on the porch of the Park in a rocking chair and closed my eyes.

And departed this life. Gone utterly for what I suspect was a quarter hour, maybe more. Until I was jerked back unceremoniously by Walter McBride. "Stephen! Stephen Robbins!" It felt like he was yelling at me. My eyes swam. I wasn't dizzy like the morning before, but I was groggy with sleep.

"What! What is it?"

"You'll never believe it. You'll never believe what happened. She's actually here!"

"Who? Who's here?"

"Colleen McWhoever she is. What are we going to do now?"

"Wedding ... Honeymoon ... Bed." I was massaging my eyelids with the tips of my fingers, just to see if they would open.

"Stephen, I have to ... what are you doing?"

"Trying to stand up, damn it. My leg's asleep."

"Listen to me—I'm trying to warn you. You cannot marry these two off. I know you're fond of taking the law into your own hands, but there are grave problems here that you seem only too willing to ignore."

I was stamping my left foot on the boards of the porch, trying to get the painful tingling of new blood to subside. "Then why don't you tell me what they are."

"These two people are of different faiths. I don't like to presume on your ignorance, Stephen, but I must tell you that a Catholic and a Jew believe radically different things about the very frame of the world. Therein lies the problem, which is huge in this particular case. All of this is to be considered, along with the simple problem of who will marry them. So far as I know, you have neither a rabbi nor a priest at hand to do your bidding."

Both my feet had returned to something like normal, and I was standing upright now, eye-to-eye with Walter. He was literally pale with conviction. "Well, Reverend McBride, I had harbored ideas of your doing the honors, Presbyterianism lying somewhere in the district between Rome and Jerusalem, but the longer you talk, the less likely that seems. Prince will marry them. Prince will marry anybody who has the right feel."

"Then neither church will recognize the sanctity of the vows. And Colleen McManaway's father can have it annulled any time he so desires."

"The hell with Colleen McManaway's father. Listen, Walter, I don't know why this bothers you so much, and I may never know. But I do understand that Jews and Catholics stand at opposite ends of the lot on the issue of Jesus and that the churches themselves can be as deadly as any two institutions ever created. But behind all the fire and smoke, they both claim to believe in God. And they both believe in a God that expresses Himself on earth in the thousand various forms of love. We'll marry them all right. We'll marry them before God and let the churches run along behind."

And I limped off and left him standing there—our beautifully educated, remarkably sensitive, carefully thoughtful, scribe and minister— left him standing there looking painfully offended.

We married them that very night in the small candle-lit sanctuary of Prince's church. I had wanted to use the ballroom of the Mountain Park, but even John Sanders wondered about the advisability of "federal property." Cap'n John agreed to shepherd a few of Georg Mende's musician friends to the service, so that there might be music. Bird gesticulated wildly until she made us understand that we had to invite Anna Ulmann so there could be a photograph. Mrs. Frisbee was to stand up with Colleen and had agreed to have Georg spend this one night at her house, with one of our guards sitting on her front porch to prevent our Georg fleeing from his honeymoon bed.

We all gathered just before dark, in the waning light of the late-September day. And after Anna photographed the couple with Prince in front of the small, frame African church, we all went in. I waited by the door with Anna until everyone seemed to settle and then sat with her in the back row.

Prince preached from First Corinthians, in the candle light, to the dozen of us who were there. The passage you might expect, the passage that in part has been worn down by the stream of countless weddings. But so powerful was his deep, vibrant voice in the flickering, golden air, that the words seemed to hang in the light, a present spell against the looming bloodbath of the war and against our own smallness, our own selfishness.

Though I have the gift of prophesy, and understand all mysteries, and all knowledge; and though I have all faith, so that I could remove mountains, and have not love, I am nothing.

Those were the very first words the man said, after he stood up in front of Georg Mende and Colleen McManaway, who clung to each other in this strange land, before this huge black man with his voice like thunder rumbling on the mountain. Prince paused after this first offering and let the sound echo in the air, which flickered as though alive with candle light and emotion.

And though I bestow all my goods to feed the poor, and though I give my body to be burned, and have not love, it profiteth me nothing.

Love suffereth long, and is kind; love envieth not; love vaunteth not itself, is not puffed up.

Doth not behave itself unseemly, seeketh not her own, is not easily pro-

voked, thinketh no evil.

Rejoiceth not in iniquity, but rejoiceth in the truth;

Beareth all things, believeth all things, hopeth all things, endureth all things.

Prince paused and in the silent moment, let his eyes sweep over those assembled. German, Irish, African, Catholic, Baptist, Jewish— men and women brought together in this tiny mountain town by war. And for a moment, that war with all its gasping lust for blood seemed to loom over us, calling out our own hatreds and fears. But then Prince's voice began again, and the light seemed to return to the room, and we breathed again.

Love never faileth: but whether there be prophecies, they shall fail; whether there be tongues, they shall cease; whether there be knowledge, it shall vanish away. ... Love is all that remains.

Anna Ulmann and I sat there holding hands in Prince's tiny church, oblivious to the splintery wooden benches and the chill air, lost in the dream of a better world, a dream of stillness wherein two people might just love each other in the old and simple ways. Lost and, just for that flickering moment, safe.

CHAPTER TEN

THE fabric that we had so carefully woven, the quilt that we had sewn together of Germans and Americans, sophisticates and simple, mountain people, began to unravel. First, there was the pressure of Robbie Griffin's death, stretching and testing us, but that was only the beginning. Things began in earnest the next day, after we had buried Robbie and married Miss Colleen McManaway to her Georg.

I walked down to Mrs. Frisbee's boarding house that morning to check on the newlyweds. I found Georg's guard fast asleep on the parlor floor, while Mr. and Mrs. Mende were eating their breakfast. They had, it seemed to me, a sleepy radiance that had nothing whatsoever to do with either the cathedral or the synagogue, a drowsy stretching out like yawning cats.

I walked Georg back to Camp A, leaving the guard asleep, perhaps to assume Georg had escaped when he finally woke up. The morning was foggy still, the sunlight diffused through the mist that it was pulling out of creek and field. Neither of us bothered to speak as we walked along: Georg seemed lost in what must have been a reverie of long red hair and pale, freckled skin, the thought of which only served to remind me of Anna, perhaps still asleep up the hill at Sunnybank.

When we arrived at the gates, I saw the oddest sight. I sent Georg on in to join the roll call for officers and musicians being slowly assembled in front of the Mountain Park. Then I turned back to confront this strange vision.

A dusty figure sat sprawled in the road just by the Camp A gates. He—or she—sat against the fence with legs thrown out in a V shape into the road. Dirty brown pants and a coat that might have been any color at all. A sweat-stained hat with a string for a band was pulled down over the face, which in turn was pitched forward at an awkward angle, chin on chest. There was a pack and blanket roll tied up with a piece of rope clutched under one arm. And there was what appeared to be a dog.

A long mound of matted black fur lay beside the figure's leg with its head resting on the thigh. As I walked around its master, trying to gauge something of human age and sex, the dog's eyes followed me, pensive and intelligent, but it didn't move its head at all until I knelt in the road. Then, barely shifting, it pulled back its cracked, black lips to show me some surprisingly sharp teeth. I could hear the faintest growl deep in its throat.

"I see you," I said, gently. "I hear what you're saying."

"What in hell's wrong with that dog?" The guard behind me asked.

"Wants to warn me off," I whispered in reply. "Without waking up its master."

"What the hell kind of master sleeps in the road?"

I glanced up to see just who could be so ignorant. It was only one of the Gehagen boys. "Master who doesn't have any place else to sleep," I commented. "How long've they been here?"

"Was here when the sun come up this mornin'. Just like that. Ain't moved since we first seed 'em."

From where I squatted on my heels, I could see the long, brown beard beneath the front rim of the hat. Hair of the same tobacco juice color. He—for now I knew it to be a man—had stuffed both beard and hair into the front and back of his coat. Insulation, I thought, against the night air.

"You try to help him any?" I asked Gehagen conversationally.

"I ain't got close to him. Smells like piss."

Gehagen was right. From where I sat on my heels, the rancid odor of days upon days of sweat was almost unbearable, the musk of caked dirt, and beneath it all, the rankness of spilled urine. My gut suddenly told me that Gehagen and the other guards must have suspected he was dead. It wasn't the hobo's smell that stalled them; it was the stink of their own fear.

"He's not dead," I said, as I stood up. "He's only dreaming."

"Huh?"

"His hands are twitching." I pointed to where he'd hidden his hands in his coat pockets. "Sides, his dog'd be howling if he was dead. You and the boys bring that table out of the guardhouse. We'll use it for a litter."

He didn't wake when we carried him up to the Mountain Park. He didn't wake when we laid him gently onto a bed in the Wade Hampton cottage, the summer home beside the Mountain Park that had become our infirmary. He didn't wake when Pauline and I began carefully stripping off the layers of clothes stiff with dirt and, in too many places, dried blood.

The dog, whom I had petted and led along the way, barked once from under the bed, when the man's clothes began to drop to the floor. Even his dog's bark didn't wake him, though it must have done so many times on the road.

"It's funny, isn't it?" said Pauline, when we had him naked before us on the bed, still unconscious.

I glanced at the man's sex, shrunken to almost nothing in its nest of hair. "What's funny?"

"It's funny that his clothes, right down to this ..." She held the stained gray union suit we'd cut off of him at arm's length before dropping it on the pile of clothes. "...are filthy. And yet, he's as smooth and clean as a baby."

She was right; it was odd. He was emaciated to the point of starvation, and every rib in his body showed plain as he struggled to seize a raspy breath; but his skin was clean. As pale as bleached paper but clean. No wounds or boils or blisters as you'd expect from a man on the road, but whole.

The awful smell of him had followed his clothes down to the floor. I held my own breath, stuffed the entire wad of grimy, lousy clothes and busted boots into a coal bucket and carried them outside.

When I did, I saw John Sanders and three of his guards half-carrying two of the sailors from Camp B across the lower lawn toward us.

By day's end we had five of the Camp B sailors on cots in the Wade Hampton cottage, all with the same dramatic symptoms. Lacking a doctor of our own, we had telegraphed to the army hospital at Oteen. Because they all had the same mysterious fever, I had Walter McBride's school teachers nursing them with cold towels and long, cold draughts of water. We succeeded only in making them more comfortable, and as afternoon wore into evening, they became much worse. Two cases were delirious.

That night, when I realized I wouldn't be able to sleep, I walked along the river bank with Hans Ruser and after briefing him on the situation, went back to the infirmary. I found Bird still sitting up with our five sailors, all but one of whom was asleep. Bird was holding his hand and bathing his face with a cool rag. He stared at her with fever-bright eyes and muttered continuously under his breath in German. I patted her hunched back and went in to check on our hobo. I found him sitting up in his bed with his blankets pulled up around his waist, reading in Bird's fat Bible.

My surprise at seeing him in a conscious state must have registered, even in the dim lamplight of the room. "Good evening," he whispered pleasantly. "Do come in and sit down."

"I apologize," I said, "if I seem shocked. We were not at all certain—"

"That I would live?" He smiled. "Of course not." He spoke English with only the faintest trace of an accent, one that I couldn't place. "I apologize for being a burden to you in a time of stress. I sat down last night to rest, and now ..." He shrugged as if to say *here I am.*

"You passed out by the camp gate," I said. "We brought you and your dog in to shelter."

"So I am in Hot Springs," he said, almost as if relieved.

"Yes, inside the Hot Springs Internment Camp."

"I had hoped to come this far," he said. "I read about your glorious Mountain Park Hotel before the war, and I had always hoped to soak in your medicinal springs before I died."

"I'm afraid the springs are closed." I said automatically and immediately regretted it.

But he only smiled. "Of course they are. For the duration of the Great War, I imagine. Are you Master Stephen Robbins?"

"Yes, I am." The night, the room, the flickering light all seemed as surreal as the man himself. Somehow, it didn't surprise me that he knew my name.

"My name is Julius Christopher."

"Why have you come to us, Mr. Christopher? With all due respect, you are in no fit state to travel the roads, especially with colder weather coming on and no more than a dog to sleep with."

He didn't stifle the urge to laugh, but the laugh immediately transformed into the most frightening retching you can imagine. Deep, racking gasps that shook his entire frame, the rasping, grating noise of which brought tears to my eyes. I stumbled to his bedside to try to help him, but all I could do was hold the covers over him and offer him my handkerchief, which he gladly used to catch the debris from his throat.

"Good ... God," he struggled to say, after a final spitting up into the handkerchief. "Mr. Robbins, you are ... are as funny as they say, ... but you mustn't try to make me laugh."

"Don't worry," I whispered back. "You'd better stay here with us for a while." He'd scared me so badly that I was shaking. "You and your dog."

"Ah, the illustrious King James?" And for a moment, I thought he was referring to the Bible that had fallen to the floor during his fit.

I bent to pick it up and noticed that the dog's tail was wagging, thumping on the floor where he lay under Christopher's bed. "Your dog is named King James?"

"Of course," he whispered. "He has brought me all the way here from Canada. Can you imagine what I would do without him?" The dog raised his head, knowing full well he was being talked about. I thought for a moment that he looked to be more wolf than dog.

It was then, as the lamp in Wade Hampton's bedroom burned down to a last guttering flicker and then went out entirely, that he told me his story. Mr. Christopher was a Canadian American, who, though he was raised in Detroit, had volunteered to fight with the Canadian Army early in the war. He had enlisted with his cousin and they had been posted to the 48th Canadian Highlanders. He told me how they had been sent to a town with the odd name of Ypres in northern Belgium. In a voice hoarse from coughing, sometimes stopping just to breathe, he explained what had happened to him. After a while I noticed that Bird had come to stand in the doorway: hypnotized, like me, by his story.

"It was the wind. It seems so incredible in retrospect, Mr. Robbins, that something we loved, something we sought out on the hottest days, could have turned on us, could have become our enemy. Forrest and I were assigned to the radio unit at the captain's bunker, and our radio lines ran northwest to the French, south to the Englanders, and straight back behind us to our own artillery. It was late in the day. Twenty-second of April."

"1916? Last spring?"

"Oh, no. 1915. Long, long ago, it seems now. I say the 22nd of April because it was Forrest's birthday, and the next day. Well, you see, the next day he would be killed when we tried to make up for what happened. When we tried to take back what we'd lost.

"We were a hundred yards behind the trenches, hard up against the French. All day, they'd been moving troops in and out. Rotating the boys we were used to out of the line and bringing in the Colonials. Black men from North Africa. Turbans, bearded, marching along like toy soldiers with their uniforms so clean and their puttees wrapped as even as lines drawn in butter.

"Forrest and I sat for most of the day on top of the captain's bunker and watched the show. In the morning, we had to search for a break in the telephone wire back to our guns. Spent two or three hours following the line until we found the break in a little village cemetery where a stray artillery shell had fallen and tossed the graves all astray. Tossed up the stones as well as the bodies. And cut our line in two just as clean as scissors.

"So we repaired the break—took all of five minutes—and walked back home to the battalion. Then we had the day off, or so we thought. We were just about to make some tea, thinking it was too late in the day for any sort of attack, when the captain's orderly called us all up to the roof of the bunker to see the sight.

"It seems the wind had shifted, turned all the way around to blow out of the northeast, straight at us from the German lines. And there was this cloud of thick, yellow gas moving slowly toward us like some awful fate that we couldn't escape. Like a nightmare. Because, you see, we'd heard of mustard gas, been warned about it, but we'd never seen it. Never seen it before that day.

"I happened to glance over at the Colonials, and they were standing up above their trenches, pointing and laughing. 'Wonder if they think it's a sand storm?' Forrest says to me. 'They'd be more scared,' I said back to him, or something like that.

"We both knew that a mile behind us, a mile away, was a truck load of gas masks meant for the 48th Mountaineers; we knew because we'd been given the drawings to show us how to use them. Forrest took his drawing out and waved it in my face. 'We got the fucking instructions but not the masks,' he whispered to me, and we both began to laugh. We was hysterical, you see, and even though most of the unit was down in the trenches and had no idea what was happening up above, we could see plain as day the cloud coming toward us.

"I was praying, I will say, even as Forrest and I were laughing our bloody heads off, I was praying. And suddenly, like an act of God, the wind shifted. The breeze shifted ever so slightly, and funneled the gas straight down on the Colonials. Oh, don't get me wrong, it give us a caress as it went by. He paused to tap his bony chest and held up my bloody, crusted handkerchief. It give us a sweet caress and poured down over them poor Africans. And in what seemed like the blinking of your eye, they was screaming and coughing—you could hear the screaming, Mr. Robbins, from a hundred yards away.

"By then, the captain had pulled us all down into the bunker and was making us tie up wet handkerchiefs over our faces. But, you see, it was too late. Forrest and I and a few others had stood watching too long and taken a lung full. You felt as if the eyes was burning out of your head and as if you could never stop coughing 'til every bit of lung you owned was in your hands. We couldn't none of us draw a breath for an hour or so. I suspect you know what happened." He glanced at me in pity for having to hear his story.

I shook my head, no. I had always avoided the war news until that spring, when the war had come to me and I didn't need a newspaper.

"We didn't know it then, but the gas was heavier than air and settled down into the trenches where them poor African buggers were trying to hide; many of them died within a few minutes. The Germans put on their gas masks and walked right over them. Knocked a hole in our lines two miles wide just by taking an evening stroll. Walked most of the way to France, while Forrest and I were trying to stuff our eyes back in our faces, and the captain was calling anybody who'd listen on the bloody telephone."

"And the next day, you tried to take it back?"

"Of course we did. The generals were embarrassed and frightened of the gas. They had to save face, so they sent us over the top. Forrest was shot to pieces beside me precisely as if it mattered not at all, as if he'd never even existed. And we were driven straight back into the trenches where we started. Dead and dying."

"Were you wounded?" I couldn't help but look at his devastated body.

"On the 23rd? No. They had done for me the day before. Laughing and praying, I sucked in enough gas to melt my lungs. The Canadians sent me home, and I've been coming south ever since, looking for a warm place to lie down."

I took his bony hand in mine, afraid to squeeze, afraid of hurting him. "You've found it," I said. "If you can stand our Germans."

He smiled his strange and beatific smile. "Oh, I like them well enough," he said. "They've done me no more harm than I've done them, and now I can ask their forgiveness."

He was a strange man, wreathed in wiry hair and beard. Looked for all the world like a mountain man who'd stayed too long in the high, wild places with neither child nor woman to bring him down.

"Besides," he said, squeezing my hand now, with a surprising strength. "I believe you need me here."

"Why is that, Mr. Christopher?"

"Because the men in that other room are much sicker than you know," he whispered. "They have the typhoid fever, and you may not save them."

The army doctor, who arrived at the camp two days after the initial breakout of the disease, worked heroically with a team of nurses he imported from the army's hospital in Oteen. "Food and water," he kept telling me over and over, after his initial examination confirmed Julius Christopher's battlefield diagnosis. "It has to be something they put in their mouths and swallow. Find food and water that they have in common and you'll find the source."

This appallingly young man, Dr. Rudisill, immediately shoved us all out of the infirmary except Christopher, whom he seemed to accept as a natural part of things; and who in turn became the chief nurse. He sat up with the sick Germans long after the trained nurses fell asleep in their cots on the cottage porch. Dr. Rudisill had banished King James to the back porch as well, where Pauline's table scraps and several good brushings by one of the guards had produced a shiny black coat. Though Dr. Rudisill had put out King James, he allowed his master to stay on; and it was Christopher who would, when I tapped on his window late at night, tell me the truth of what was happening inside the cottage. He would, in the hoarse whisper that was his loudest voice, tell me who had improved, who had sunk lower under the fever; and on two occasions, who had died in the dark hours. It was Christopher who explained to me how Pauline and all her cooks must wash themselves and their utensils constantly. And it was Christopher who repeated what his patients had told him—the sailors in Camp B were scared to drink the water.

I received two telegrams from Cousin Roy Robbins during this period, each threatening an investigation, each having been rendered literate by the telegraph agent. The second was far more personal than the first, referring explicitly to me:

```
HIGH SHERIFF OFFICE MADISON COUNTY
News of epidemic spreading
Hot Springs residents in danger
Reports of prisoners rioting
Owners doubt your ability
Will replace you if need be Report immediately
```

I did report but not to Cousin Roy; my telegram went straight to Washington, addressed to William Smith, the name given to me by the Nameless Man the day we met in Craven Johnson's office. His reply was terse enough:

```
DEPARTMENT OF WAR WASH DC
Ignore the Sheriff Check the wells Find out who
```

I showed the reply to Prince, who immediately asked aloud the question that had been percolating in my brain since Bird handed me the folded telegram form. "What the hell does he mean—find out who?"

And hearing the question aloud let me say my answer. "He means somebody's poisoning the water in Camp B."

"The reservoir for B is—?"

"Outside the wire."

"Which means—?"

"Means you go find John Sanders while I pay a visit to the infirmary."

"Visit the sick?" Prince asked. "At a time like this?"

"Hell no," I replied. "Visit the one person in the whole place who seems to know what's going on."

There were now ten men crowded into the Wade Hampton cottage, even after we'd carried the two fatalities up to the Oddfellow's Cemetery. Ten, and only two of them well enough to sit out on the front porch during the warm afternoons.

I didn't have to knock on Christopher's bedroom window. He was standing just inside looking out. He raised the sash when I walked up.

"How are you holding up, Mr. Robbins?" He asked. "I know this is hard on you."

I didn't mention the fact that he himself looked little better than a corpse. "What would someone put in a water source to cause typhoid?" I asked him.

He stared at me for a moment, the perpetual smile fading from his face. "Shit!" he muttered.

"I know it seems impossible—"

"No," he replied, "I mean feces." His voice surprisingly strong. "Human excrement."

"How do you know—"

He cut me off. "Over there," And I understood him to mean in the war. "Over there, it took us months to figure it out, but it was always a case of the latrine being too close to the water supply. The two can't mix."

I heard a female voice, one of the nurses, call to him from the front of the cottage.

He turned to go, but then hesitated to reach out and grab my hand on the window sill. "Who in this heavenly place would do such a thing, Mr. Robbins?"

"I been wondering the same thing," I confessed, unable to meet his stern gaze. "And I'm afraid there's a long list."

That very afternoon John Sanders and I set up watch in the trees above the reservoir he had built on Spring Creek when Camp B was under construction. I sent Prince into town to begin his discreet asking around. Who'd been seen up above the reservoir? Who had been particularly vocal in hating the Germans? Who was adamant about the war? Prince, with his easy smile and pastor's manner, was the man for the job. Just as Cap'n John knew his reservoir and I knew the woods.

We found a spot in a stand of mountain laurel under a twisted jack pine, just above the squat stone tower that John and his masons had built as a catch basin, fed from above by a pipe that siphoned water from a bold spring directly into the reservoir. Before we found our spot, John showed me where someone had broken the lock off the iron cover to the reservoir itself. Hammered the lock with its hasp right out of the mortar into which it had been fastened. "Damn their eyes," he muttered. "Take half a day to put it back right." Before we climbed up above to watch, we lifted a dozen heavy rocks from the creek onto the lid of the reservoir, intending to slow down our saboteur, if indeed that's what we had.

And so we sat through the rest of the afternoon, on the increasingly cold ground, backs against the trunks of two convenient trees from which one of us could see the top of the reservoir and the other the pipe that fed it from the spring. I had brought my deer rifle and it leaned against the tree beside my shoulder.

Near dusk, after John, who had been smart enough to bring a coat, had nodded off, I thought I could hear someone approaching along the trail from town. I hissed at John, who slept on peacefully, ten feet away. I picked up several pine cones and on my second try bounced one off his hat. He started and glanced around suspiciously.

When he finally thought to look at me, I pointed toward the noise I heard on the trail. He nodded.

The noise came closer, and in the dusky dark, I could just make out a figure wearing an overcoat and carrying a bucket or something like it. The head and face were obscured by an army issue hat, like the ones we had given our own guards when the weather turned cool. The figure stepped off the trail below the reservoir and waded across the creek below the cistern. John began to edge down out of the laurel, surprisingly quiet for a town man. I crept behind him with my rifle, careful not to step on his heels and send us both crashing down the bank into the creek.

The shape of the figure below was obscured by the shadow of the stone reservoir itself now. But we could hear whoever it was attempting to push up the iron lid from below. One of the rocks we had weighted it down with rolled over the edge, bounced off the side and splashed into the creek. The figure stepped back in consternation, and John leaped from the side of the bank to grab him.

In trying not to trip John at the last minute, I slipped, and slid down the bank on my back, barely catching myself before falling into the icy, knee deep water. John grabbed the figure around the waist and wrestled him away from the reservoir; as he did, they both stumbled into the deeper water. Unfortunately, the mystery man still had his bucket in hand and swung it clumsily around, hitting John in the back. I staggered forward through the rushing water but couldn't fire the rifle for fear of hitting John, all three of us struggling to keep our balance on the slick creek bottom.

John cursed and spun away, turning the intruder loose. The dark man gathered himself and turned toward the creek bank and the trail to town. Just as he did so, I suddenly found my footing and was able to swing the rifle like a club. All my frustration and fear and anger must have come out in that one clean arc because when I caught him flush on top of the head, he staggered for only a step or two before collapsing on the creek bank.

"Son-of-a-bitch!" John shouted and waded to the bank, where he kicked the prostrate form in the ribs. He was stepping back for even better leverage and about to kick him again, when I grabbed his arm.

"John, wait. ... Wait! See who it is." I was shaking with cold; John perhaps with anger. "Then you can kick him to your heart's content."

"Bastard threw that bucket of shit all over me," John whined. And it sounded so funny that I started to laugh. There on the dark bank of Spring Creek, I laughed so hard that I had to sit down—and did so on the back of the man we'd caught. And just as I was about to regain some semblance of control, I would remember the sound of John's voice and cackle again.

"What in the damn hell is so funny about that?" he growled, but I could hear a snicker in his voice. He sat down beside me, two grown men laughing so hard it hurt.

After a moment, as John was wiping the tears from his eyes, he asked conversationally. "You reckon we killed him, Stevie? You bashing his brains out and all?"

And so, the two of us, soaked almost to the waist, bedraggled and cold, each took an arm and together dragged our saboteur onto the trail and back toward town. It was too dark by then under the trees to tell anything about him except that he was still breathing in ragged, shallow inhalations.

The first building we came to was at the back of the Dorland School. It was well after dark, but a three-quarters moon was up over the ridge, so we drug our man out of the trees and into the edge of the schoolhouse lawn where we could see. Without speaking, we rolled him over on his back and knelt on either side of him.

"Probably one of your damn relatives," John whispered, still gasping from the exertion of dragging him along.

"He's wearing one of your hats," I whispered back, and it was true. The blow from the rifle butt had ripped the crown of the army hat and smashed it down over his forehead.

"What's that black stuff all over his face?"

I reached out to touch the man's cheek and found it crusted. "Blood," I said. It was then my fingers found a pair of wire-rimmed spectacles, the lens broken out and the frames mashed down on the bridge of the man's nose. "Damn it!"

"What?"

"It's Walter McBride."

CHAPTER ELEVEN

THE coal oil lamps in Mrs. Jane Gentry's kitchen showed us that although Walter had lost a lot of blood, he was in no immediate danger.

Cap'n John went up the hill to fetch Prince Garner, the only other person I could think of who might be able to shed some light on why once we'd caught our culprit, he turned out to be one of our own. And not only one of our own but the least likely one of all, the Right Reverend one.

Mrs. Jane put water and coffee into her gallon-sized coffee pot, stoked the fire in the wood stove, and then went on out of the kitchen and about her business. I sat and stared at Walter where he lay on a daybed in the corner of the large room. I cleaned the blood off his face and ever so slowly pried the crushed hat off his head. His scalp was split just at the hairline where he'd fallen against a rock, and there was a huge welt across the top of his head where I'd hit him. For the life of me, I couldn't imagine what had brought this apparently gentle man to the point of—

"What are you thinking, Mr. Stephen Robbins?" The voice sent a current down my spine; it took me completely by surprise.

She was standing in the kitchen doorway, was Anna. Still dressed from the day but with the top few buttons of her frock comfortably undone, revealing the vulnerability of her throat.

"I am mystified," I admitted.

She stepped forward and around the kitchen table toward me. "Does that man in the corner have anything to do with it?"

I was distracted for a moment, just by her nearness. "That man in the corner is your friend Walter McBride. John Sanders and I carried him in just a few minutes ago."

She bent over Walter briefly and came back to stand beside me against the table, slipping her hand beneath my arm and pulling it ever so slightly against her side. "I know. Mrs. Gentry told me. What happened to him?"

"I knocked him in the head with the butt of my deer rifle." I was suddenly so tired that I couldn't manage to shield her from the truth.

I could sense her turn to study my face.

"We caught him getting ready to pour a bucket of filth into the reservoir up above Camp B."

"You mean—?"

I nodded. "It must be the cause of it."

"But why in the world? He's a minister."

"I don't know, Anna. I don't know!"

"Easy now ... easy." She was crooning close to my ear. Quieting me as you would a fractious horse. "Sit down and I'll pour you a cup of coffee." She went to the stove; the rich aroma of boiling coffee had filled the room, but I hadn't noticed it until she said the word. "Nobody's going to blame you for hitting him," she said from the stove.

"That's not what's worrying me. What's worrying me is who in the hell put him up to it."

She sat the cup down on Mrs. Jane's rough, oak table top in front of me. She'd added milk from the icebox and a spoonful of sugar from the crock. Exactly as I would have fixed it. I was so used to waiting on myself that it seemed like the kindest thing anyone had ever done for me. Just that and no more, and I was blinking to hide the feeling.

She was reaching out to touch my arm, still a nervous gesture for her, when the door all but slammed open and John led Prince in off the porch.

Prince took in the gathering at the table at a glance and smiled his ironical smile. "Where's the victim?"

I nodded toward the daybed and he dragged John straight over to the corner to examine Walter. Meaning, I suppose, to give Anna and me a moment to compose ourselves.

Prince bent over Walter, and after a moment, I could hear the Right Reverend groan in his torpor. "I believe the hat saved you, Stevie," Prince said. He straightened and turned toward the table.

"Don't you mean it saved Walter?" John said.

"No, saved Stevie. From having to face charges." He pointed John toward the coffee pot and sat down on the other side of Anna. "Stephen gets tried for murder now and again," he said to her happily. "Best when we can keep him out of court."

She glanced at me, and I held up one finger. "Only once," I said.

"Just once?" Prince asked. "I thought it was—"

"What are we going to do about Walter?" John sat down with a single cup of coffee, leaving Prince to serve himself and Anna.

The conversation drifted but only for a moment. Ever the practical one, John brought us back to the present problem. There was a pause as we all, even Anna, sipped the scalding coffee. "Does his wife know?" Prince asked.

I shook my head.

"I know her, Stephen," Anna said. "Sometimes she walks with me in the evening. I should go get her."

I nodded, and she went purposively for her hat and cloak. I knew that even though it was close to midnight it wouldn't take Anna long to bring the woman back from McBride's house a hundred yards away. But it would give Prince and me a chance to say whatever hard things needed saying. "Go with her, John," I said.

"But I just got—"

"I know. But I don't like her out alone this time of night."

He nodded and gulped his coffee, having needed the practical slant.

"And John ..."

"Hmmm?"

"Why don't you take that coat off and leave it on the porch?"

I pointed to my nose, and Prince laughed out loud.

When Anna and John had gone, Prince began to pull at the tangled knot of my thoughts.

"If he were convicted for this, it would be murder, wouldn't it?" He said carefully, as he pointed summarily at Walter.

I nodded. "If any sort of local jury would accept the notion that killing Germans in 1917 was murder."

"Any evidence?"

"The bucket he was carrying. I hung it in a tree up by the creek because it still had enough mess in it to tell the tale." I smiled. "And John's coat."

"But probably not enough ...?"

"To convict him? Oh, hell no. And even if it was ..." I let the end of the sentence hang in the air.

"You're not sure it would help the cause."

"How could it? Why give people ideas? Next thing you know, some vigilante'll be shooting at Hans Ruser from a tree across the river."

Prince stood and stared at Walter for a moment. "Why didn't you hit him just a little harder when you had the chance? Or sit on him in the creek for a while?"

"For a minister of God, you sure are a cold-blooded son-of-a-bitch."

He shrugged. "He killed them two German boys. One of 'em sixteen years old you told me. And it'd sure save us having to figure out what to do with him when he wakes up."

"Did it ever occur to you that if he died, Cousin Roy would be all over us? And besides, John Sanders is incapable of lying about it."

Prince smiled. "Imagine that. Almost seems like a moral flaw, don't it?"

"He has to wake up, Prince, to tell us who put him up to it."

"Maybe he just hated Germans." And after a moment. "Or maybe he just hated you." He had lowered his voice because we could hear Cap'n John and Anna on the back porch, along with a third set of footsteps.

They came in from the cold night air in a rush, John straight to the coffee pot, Anna to her chair between Prince and me, and Amanda McBride straight to kneel beside her husband's bed.

She was a slight, wispy sort of woman who had always seemed to me dreamy or just sad—very sad. One or the other and sometimes both. She was a mountain girl that had come to Dorland as a student, stayed to help with the younger children and met Walter when he came there as chaplain. That night, she had on a plain brown dress and stiff brogan shoes, something she'd pulled on her feet in a hurry when summoned. Her back was as taut as a strung bow where she bent over Walter, and I glanced at Anna to see if I could tell what they'd told her.

"Everything." Anna mouthed the word silently and pointed at John.

Cap'n John sat down again, having refilled his cup. "I told Mrs. McBride what happened, Steve. Told her why we were guarding the reservoir and how we came to fight with Walter. Told her that I thought he'd be all right, but that he couldn't go around trying to poison people."

"Not people." The voice was slight, whispery like paper rubbing together, but defiant.

"Ma'am?" I knew it had to be her.

"They ain't people." There was outright hatred in her voice. "Them in that camp. Only Germans."

Those of us at the table glanced at each other. I don't know why we were surprised to hear the words, but we were.

Anna went to her and carefully, kindly, led her to the table where she could sit in the light. Poured her a cup of coffee with a lot of milk and set it before her.

"They may seem like the enemy right now, Mrs. McBride, but part of my job is to make certain nothing happens to them."

She had lifted her mug with both hands to sip. She was shaking and it was a struggle to drink. When she lowered the cup, there was a frightening intensity in her eyes. They glittered with hatred. And when she spoke, she spoke directly to me. "Your job? You, a hotel manager and a drunk? You, who have no religion at all and no more sense of responsibility than ... than a dog barking in the street."

I felt Anna stiffen beside me.

I wondered aloud. "Whose job should it be, Mrs. McBride? Who should be the Inspector General of the Camp?"

She glanced about the table. "Why, look around you. He could've done it." She thrust her cup at John and part of her coffee spilled out on the table. "He could've done it if he weren't colored." Prince. "Or Mr. McBride. Mr. McBride was a fine teacher and a good man. Traveled the world and used to dealing with all kinds of people." She looked at Anna. "Don't you think any of these men would have made a better boss man than that thing there?" She sloshed her coffee at me. "But oh, I forgot. Mr. McBride told me all about how you hang all over him, Anna Ulmann, how you follow him around like a sick puppy. Of course, you think he's done a good job!"

"Good God, woman!" Prince interrupted her. "Are you trying to sit there and say that your husband thinks he should be the Inspector General of the Camp?"

She suddenly set her cup down and leaned forward toward Prince, ever so slyly, as if she were telling him a wonderful secret. "Of course he does. And what's more, so ... does ... the sheriff. He told Walter that once the army sees the truth about that thing there ..." She cut her eyes at me again. "The sheriff hisself'd recommend Walter for the job. What do you think of that, Mr. Nigger High-and-Mighty?" She leaned back in triumph.

We left Amanda McBride with her husband and went into the front parlor. The last of Mrs. Jane's boarders had gone up to their rooms, and the first floor of the house was slowly settling into a nighttime quietness. Whereas before our little jury had consisted of just two—Prince and myself—now there were four. And we were no closer to a verdict.

When we sat down in the parlor chairs, Anna and I together on the couch, Prince broke the silence first. "So now you know who's behind it all."

"Roy," I admitted. "And Ed behind him I expect."

"By Roy, you mean the sheriff?" Anna asked. We all nodded. "Your cousin?" she said to me. Again we nodded.

"But what do we do with the Right Reverend and his Missus?" I asked. "Any ideas?"

"Turn 'em all in," John Sanders said simply. "Walter, Roy, the whole bunch. Throw in that wife for an accomplice."

"Who do we turn 'em in to, John?" I asked.

"Well, hell," John said.

"I was in favor of burying the good Reverend under a rock somewhere," admitted Prince with a sigh, "but now that we've brought his wife into it ..."

Anna glanced at him in alarm.

"He's not serious," I assured her. "Never serious when he sounds serious."

"You have your own jail," she suggested. "I've seen it. Can't you just put him in it?"

"Could," I admitted with a smile. "Could put him in it, but not with Amanda running around town spreading rumors. And how long do you think it would be before we had both Cousin Roy and Ed Rumbough sitting in our laps?"

"Well," Prince looked at me. "You're the Inspector General. You got any bright ideas?"

"Banishment," I said.

"Banishment?"

"Exile. Walter McBride was a missionary before he came here, but his home church is in Princeton, New Jersey."

"And his family as well," Prince added. "I believe his mother is still alive."

"Well, then. We can't bury him for he's still alive. We can't turn him over to the High Sheriff as he's the one put him up to it. We've got to get them away from Roy and away from here. Roy will kill him, for getting caught if nothing else. I say we put him on the train along with his blushing bride. Send them both home to mother."

"Great idea," said John. "But how in the world do you—"

"Ever expect to get them on the train?" Anna interrupted to finish his sentence.

"I expect to discuss with them what course of action might be in their best interest."

"Oh, Stephen!" It was clear she thought I was out of my mind.

"And I think you better go on upstairs."

She glanced around our small circle.

"He's getting ready to scare hell out of one or both of them," Prince explained. "And he doesn't want you to see him at his most fiendish."

"Fiendish?" she asked.

Prince nodded happily.

When we walked back into the kitchen, Walter McBride was sitting up with his legs over the side of the daybed, half supported by Amanda, who sat beside him.

"Mrs. McBride," I said softly, "would you join Miss Ulmann and Mr. Sanders in the parlor? I need to speak to your husband for a few minutes."

She stood and stuck her chest out defiantly—most like a chicken who'd laid an egg. "I will not. I don't care to trust him with you two alone." Meaning Prince as well as me.

"Very well then. Stand aside and let me have a look at him."

"What?" She sputtered. But Prince had already pulled her to one side. He outweighed her by a hundred or so pounds and he barely even noticed her as he pulled her wispy form back from her husband.

I knelt in front of Walter, who, I have to admit, was even paler than usual. The cut on his forehead was crusted with dried blood, and his head looked slightly misshapen where I'd applied the rifle. His eyes, bloodshot now, seemed defenseless without his glasses.

"Stephen," he said, "I want you to know that—"

I had balanced myself carefully as I squatted down because I knew what I intended to do. And I did it then. Slapped him hard with my open hand. So hard that it stung me, and the sound was as satisfying a smack of flesh on flesh as you could wish.

"Oh, my Lord Jesus," moaned Amanda McBride.

"Walter, damn every degree you ever earned," I said to him in as slow and clear a tone as I could muster. "I don't want to hear what you have to say. I just need for you to listen. Hear me as clearly as you ever heard anyone in your life."

"Stephen, please. It will do me good to explain my—"

I slapped him again. And to the man's credit, he stood it. He saw it coming, and he didn't cower.

"Walter, damn it. Shut up and listen."

"Oh, help my soul!" Amanda wailed, and you could imagine half the boarders in the house suddenly sitting up in bed. It was then that Anna did something that endeared her to me. She stepped forward, from where she'd been watching in the doorway, and put her hand over Amanda McBride's mouth and very efficiently shut her up.

"Walter, do you know who I am?"

He stared at me. "My head hurts but my mind is ... You're Stephen Robbins, the Inspector Gen—"

"No, Walter, you're wrong. Very wrong. I'm little Stevie Robbins, the orphan boy from up on the mountain. And I grew up meaner than you could ever imagine. Look me in the eyes, Walter. For your wife's sake, you'd better look at me. I don't work for Ed Rumbough; I work for the War Department of the United States. And I work for them because they know I'll do anything short of burning down the Mountain Park to protect the pissant Americans from the scary Germans and the pissant Germans from the scary Americans—including that pig fucker Roy Robbins! Do you hear me now, Walter?"

I had him nodding, mesmerized. Even his wife had stopped struggling.

"I didn't get this job because I'm smart or cultured or kind, Walter, I got it because I don't give a damn. I got it because once those Germans came through that gate, they were mine. I don't care who they are or where they came from; they're mine; and you, Walter, killed two of them while they were under my care. Do you know how they died? Do you!"

My face was inches from his, and I could smell the salt sweat running down, mixed now with the rusty smell of his blood. He barely shook his head, no.

"They died of a fever so hot they mistook Julius Christopher for their own fathers. They died with their bellies and chests covered over with a bloody rash that hurt your eyes to see it. And they died a thousand miles from home crying for help. I didn't see you at their funerals, Walter. Were you at their funerals?" I drew my hand back to strike him again, but this time he flinched away from me.

"You really want my job, Walter? You want it now that you know what's required?"

He shook his head, desperate now.

"I got this job, Walter, because I'm the one man in this room who seriously considered taking you down to the river and drowning you so your body would float off to Tennessee and I wouldn't have to think about you anymore. ... Do you believe me, Walter?"

He barely nodded, just enough so that I could see his chin bob.

It was enough.

"But for the sake of the two women in this room, Walter, I don't care to do that. For their sake, not yours, we're going to put you and Amanda on a train in a few hours. Train going north. With two tickets to Princeton. And then I'm going to telegraph the War Department and tell them who you are. And if I were you, Walter ... you hear me, Walter! If I were you, I'd never come back here again, not while there's a war on. Because if you do come back, my boss in Washington will let me deal with you any way I want to."

Our problem then was two-fold. One was simply getting a bag packed for both of them and depositing them safely on the train north without letting either out of our sight for seven hours. The second problem was keeping them more-or-less out of sight just in case Cousin Roy was hiding in the bushes. It took all hands, including Anna, who volunteered to help Amanda McBride pack two bags for travel, while John Sanders went stoically along to ensure that she didn't run for help.

Finally when we had both Mister and Missus along with their bags safely back in Mrs. Jane's kitchen, I escorted Anna into the parlor and politely ordered her upstairs.

"You think you can scare me the way you scared Walter?" She was teasing, but we were both so tired that it seemed as if we were floating across the parlor rug in a daze.

"Not now. Not since you've seen all my tricks."

"Tell me then ..." We'd reached the foot of the stairs just behind the front door. She leaned back against the banister and, as the whole front of the house was dark and quiet, pulled me against her. We seemed to float there for a moment, isolated in time and in the dark, sweet foyer. "Tell me," she whispered, "how much of what you said to him was true?"

"To Walter?"

She nodded, the side of her head rubbing against my rough cheek.

"Most of it was more or less true."

"Did you really think of drowning him?"

"Oh, hell no. But ..."

"But what?"

"If I could get my hands on Cousin Roy, that might be a different story."

She nodded again. She'd heard and seen enough to understand.

"Come upstairs with me," she whispered. "You could sleep for a little while." The world seemed to turn upside down, and gravity pulled me toward the stairs and the bedroom above. A room that I had imagined constantly but had not seen since she'd moved into it.

"Mrs. Jane," I muttered, half asleep even as we leaned deliciously together. "She would take my hide off in strips if ..."

She tugged at my arm, and I could feel myself leaning like a tree in the wind, very heavy wind, but even then, I stopped myself. "Once they're on that train," I whispered, "you can take me anywhere you want."

"Promise." she said. "Promise and I'll let you go."

The morning train came and went on time at 7:30. Prince, who had been the barber on that run for years, boarded with his "dear friends," Walter and Amanda McBride, to ride with them as far as Richmond. John went home, finally, to sleep.

I made my way from the depot ever so slowly back to Camp A. As the guard on duty was letting me in, I glanced across the lawn to the early morning assembly of the Mountain Park inmates, six-hundred sleepy officers standing in rows on the lawn where the ninth hole of our golf course had been. Guarded by another fifteen local men who had just come on duty, they as sluggish and sleepy as the men they guarded, and all of them—guards and prisoners alike—were happily oblivious to the drama that had taken place in town the night before. The officers standing in ranks were rosy with sleep and hungry for their breakfast.

"Is where it all started," I mumbled through a yawn.

"Sir?" the guard asked.

I shook my head. I had been thinking of Julius Christopher, the hobo who'd first said the word typhoid to me, who'd been the first to recognize what fury was upon us. And without speaking further, I shook the guard's hand and set out toward the Wade Hampton cottage, intending to thank the man who'd warned me before I went up those stairs to the third floor and found my own bed inside the wire.

When I rounded the far corner of the Mountain Park and approached the front of the cottage, I saw on the porch Dr. Rudisill packing both his travel bag and his medical kit. His nurses were busy carrying the bedding from the front room out into the open air and throwing it onto a cart, presumably to be taken away to be burned.

"Are you abandoning us, doctor?" I called out as I walked up.

He shook his head. "No, Mr. Robbins, it seems we're done. All the sailors except the two we lost are past the crisis. It'll take them a week or so to get their strength back, and Mrs. Randall ..." He nodded toward one of the nurses from Asheville. "... has agreed to stay on until they're back on their feet, but my work is done."

"So in all this we lost only two," I said with genuine wonder.

And for the first time, he looked up from his work to actually acknowledge my presence. "You don't know, do you?"

"Know what?"

"The rest of the Germans all lived." He was as casual as if announcing the breakfast menu. "The old man in back died last night just after dark."

"Damn your soul," I said.

He shrugged and continued packing. In one leap I was on the porch, pushing past the nurses who were carrying out armloads of soiled sheets and blankets, through the front room and down the short hallway to Wade Hampton's bedroom. There I found Julius Christopher laid out very prim and straight on the bed. Someone had pulled his thin woolen blanket neatly up to his waist and combed out his long hair and beard. His hands were folded together over his sunken chest, still and at rest. His face had shrunk into the recesses of his skull pulling his lips back from the few teeth he had left. Still though, I could have sworn that the smile remained. The smile that suggested he saw beyond what we see to something brighter.

A figure sitting beyond the bed stood up and handed me a folded sheet of paper. It was Bird, and I understood immediately that she had been with him, and that it was she who had cared for him after he'd died.

I nodded my thanks to her, for once as mute as she, the tears blushing up in my eyes.

The note was written in a strange, old-fashioned script, the hand shaky and a little difficult. "Thank you, dear friend," it said. "I am one who believes we must serve our enemies, and it was you who carried me in the gate."

CHAPTER TWELVE

THE week that followed brought the first days of October. In the mountains, October can be religious in its intensity. The night air brushes out a rich palette of color over the hills, such that even the thickest human creature must pause in wonder.

When we buried Julius Christopher, the mountains and valleys were agleam like burnished metal in the clear sunlight. King James adopted me after Christopher's death, and his constant, curious presence at my knee only reminded me of just how many men we had buried in the few short months since the Germans' arrival. When the wind-borne clouds obscured the sun that October as they often did, the mountains took on a brooding, rusty tone, and I could sense their great age. In the autumn of 1917, as in most years, the months of August and September had seen the harvest into the barn, and all of life began to slow down in October.

That year, the barns were bursting, and the calves strong enough to bear the coming cold long before the first frosts dropped out of the sky. The townsfolk had begun to burn wood in their fireplaces as well as their cook stoves, so that the night air in Hot Springs was musky with wood smoke. Farmers were picking their last apples, and cider making had begun in earnest.

Cows walked more slowly now to milking; even the frisky bell cow in the Mountain Park herd paused to graze on her way in of an evening. Birds were flocking together in the smoky, agate-colored sky, preparing for their longest journey south. Every night now gave a concert of hoarse voices, as packs of hunting dogs roamed the higher ridges after fox and coon. Conscription had thinned the ranks of the hunters, but the dogs ran still, chased by the old men and young boys who were left, wearing the overalls, work-worn boots and stained slouch hats left behind by sons and brothers now hunting in a different uniform.

And sometimes, the leaner, tougher hunters brought in the giants they had stalked and killed up high. Edgar Ramsey and his cousin, with the help of a mule-drawn wagon, brought the biggest bear of that season—over five hundred pounds—through the front gate of the Mountain Park. Even dead, the beast was a shock to the Germans who gathered around in admiration, one young sailor poking it with a stick and then running.

As we watched the Germans marvel at his bear, many holding their noses at its rank odor, Edgar told me the story in his offhand, laconic way. "Traced him into Harmon's Den late last night," he said, staring at the ground. "The dogs pushed him up hard against a cliff. Strangest thing, Mr. Robbins, was I didn't want to shoot him. First time in my life I ever hung fire over a creature, but he seemed as old and tired as the hills, and if he hadn't set about killin' the dogs, I believe I'd a walked away. But he pinned two of 'em against the rocks and raked 'em, so I run in close and shot him."

I looked down at Edgar and could sense his sadness, strange in so tough a man. I knew there was something else. But he didn't speak, not until he and his cousin climbed back on the wagon seat. "I aim to leave this bear on your back porch," he said to me with a grin. "It's a present. Post office says I got to go fight this Kaiser fellow, and I don't know exactly when I'll have a chance to kill another'n."

And so Pauline taught some of the German officers to eat bear steak—after she'd boiled and fried it—and I nailed the hide to the gray, weathered planks of the barn just across the creek from the back of the hotel. Nailed it there to winter-cure. As I drove the nails through the thick, hoary paws, I knew that if Edgar Ramsey didn't come back, I might find a way to hate the Germans myself.

And thus, the fury of summer retreated ever so slowly before the reflection of fall. And the leaves of a thousand trees floated down into the river.

Each moment of that particular autumn seemed painfully precious to me, as if unique in my history. Perhaps it was the light. Since Anna had begun teaching me to see through her camera, to judge what quality and quantity of light would be admitted to a plate during the exposure, I had begun to look at the world differently. I began to see almost everything as made of various shades and textures, even as the days grew shorter and the sun crept further into the corner of the sky.

As the days shortened, life itself went to ground. Sap ran down from the trees, and animals of every sort searched out the burrows and dens in which they would survive what was coming. Mountain people followed the ancient course they had learned from the land—stuffing corn cribs and root cellars, bringing stock down out of high meadows into fenced pastures, and in the first really cold snap, killing their hogs and rubbing strong salt into the hams that they would hang in meat houses to cure, stoutly built against the stray wolf that winter would bring.

As life in the mountains around us slowed, the Germans seemed to exist in a backwards running time and place. They became more active as the air grew colder, and a team of officers began to build a village on the bank of the river behind the hotel. Using driftwood, of which there was a God's plenty, scrap from John Sanders' projects, and lumber they purchased from a local sawmill, they began construction on "New Heidelberg," a built-to-scale village of ornate playhouses and chalets, the center piece of which was a small chapel with a tall steeple and cross-shaped windows over the door and altar.

One October afternoon, John Sanders took me on a tour, and we watched a team of younger officers tack flattened tin cans onto the roof of this chapel, giving it a patchwork sort of elegance. For the life of me, I could not gauge the tenor of this alpine village growing up before our eyes: it was so carefully crafted and yet a sort of fairy land made up of half-sized and quarter-sized playhouses. John and I stopped at the heavy table that seemed to be at the center of the village, where a man who introduced himself as Captain Schlimbech, explained that he was an architect and builder. Schlimbech showed us drawings of incredible geometric complexity, including one chalet with an octagonal tower that was intended for Commodore Ruser.

"We Germans must be busy," he explained to John and me in formal, precise English. "The Commodore says we will survive our captivity better here than any place else, and so we try to make ourselves at home. We try to make our own little town." He nodded toward the river, as he scratched King James behind the ears. "We try to build a life out of what the water leaves behind and what we may buy with our wages."

"Do you build such so you can remember what home is like?" John asked.

Captian Schlimbech smiled. "No, we build this so we can remember what we are like. It is not always easy to recall who you are. Am I right, Commandant?"

I nodded and smiled. *More right than you know,* I thought.

As John and I walked back up to the Park, he puffing away on his pipe, I suggested he might help the village along with lumber and tools. "Nails too," I said, "if there are any to be had."

"Are you suggesting that I give the property of the United States government away for free to German nationals?" He asked. And for once, I thought I caught an ironic gleam in his eyes.

"I'm suggesting that if playhouses make them happy and keep them settled behind the wire, then they can build to their heart's content. They can build a circus back there for all I care, just so long as none of them are building a boat to cross the river." John laughed and so did I. Little did we know that a month later the Germans would start work on a carousel.

As we walked back up the street that the Germans had so carefully raked into perfection, I saw Hans Ruser, sitting in state in a large wicker chair beneath a basswood tree.

I parted ways with John, who had his autumn appointment to clean the Mountain Park furnace, and I walked over to the Commodore, King James at my heels. "May I join you?" I asked and started to sit down on the grass.

"No, no Stephen. Here we are in public and you must not sit below me." He called out in German to several sailors who were helping an officer on his chalet. They hurried up the street and returned with a chair like the one Ruser sat in. They placed it several feet away and beside his at an angle, so we could look out at the world together. King James stared for a moment and then went to lie against the bole of the tree, between two of its great roots.

"Thank you," he said, when I sat. "For solving the mystery of the typhoid." He said it in a very loud and stern voice, completely unlike the quiet, reasoned tone I was used to. No one in sight spoke English, at least as far as I knew, and I realized that Ruser and I were performing a little drama for the officers and men around us.

"The typhoid epidemic never should have happened," I said clearly back, trying to emulate his serious tone. "And those men should never have died."

He waved his hand dismissively and said in a slightly more normal voice. "If you follow the sea, Herr Robbins, you will soon understand that men have the unfortunate habit of dying." He paused. "Even the men under your command."

I nodded.

"But it is something else that I wish to discuss with you. Something that soon will be urgent."

"Winter coats?" I said, guessing at his meaning. The two men who had brought my chair were in their shirt sleeves on that windy October day.

Ruser smiled at me, forgetting for a moment his role as Commodore. "Just so. Hats and gloves if such a thing were possible."

"I'm working on it," I admitted. "The problem, of course, is that the War Department seems to think that such garments should go to our own army first."

"Ahh. Well then."

"I won't give up. Why should one man freeze while another is warm? Do we need two thousand coats?"

"No, no. The officers are well-provided for in one fashion or another. But the men. Perhaps a thousand coats. Hats of any kind at all. Gloves we can do without."

There was a momentary pause while Siegfried Sonnach walked by with another young officer. Ruser nodded gravely to Siegfried's enthusiastic greetings and spoke to him in German.

After the young men had passed, I asked him the question I'd been meditating, still in a staged voice, but lower, more confidential. "Why do you think they build, Commodore, your men I mean. Captain Schlimbech says that it helps them remember who they are."

"Certainly that is so," he said, quieter himself, perhaps satisfied that we had staged what formality was required. "But you and I also know that it is the work of our senior officers to keep as many of the men occupied as possible. Give the German an impossible task and he will be busy forever. That is a saying in our service."

"So keeping busy keeps the peace?"

"Yes. For now. And what a few of us old men know that the younger do not is that war, particularly this war, is ravenous. It will eat countless towns and villages like the one we build here. Only those towns are real, and the fire and smoke will consume them and their people down to ashes and dust. So perhaps this ... this fairy tale that we build will be a small tonic."

"Medicine for a sick world?"

"Just so."

Another pause. A sudden breeze surged and the brown leaves rattled down around us. King James growled once, and a squirrel scattered back up the tree. I thought of Robert Snyder, our own private maniac, and of the young warriors that Ruser and his officers sought to pacify. "Who will write the history, Commodore? Whose story will this be when all is said and done?"

He looked across at me appraisingly. Like me, he was a bookish man, always wanting something to read. "Why, the great historians will write the story of the great men," he said. "Do not be naïve about that. The crown princes, the statesmen, the generals. And a few, very few, heroes to represent the truths we proclaim after the war." He smiled. "Even this place, Stephen, will have its ... what? ... at the bottom of the page?"

"Footnote?"

"Thank you. Even your little camp will have its footnote, but a very short one. With not room enough for your name or mine. But here is the thing my young friend. The history in books is not the history that matters. For that history will not tell of women and children. It will not tell of the two who died of typhoid." He pointed at the Wade Hampton cottage just fifty feet away. "It will not tell of the boy you buried, the boy you loved."

"Robbie Griffin."

"Your Robert Griffin. It will not say the story of the little girl who always waves to me from the other side of the fence as she walks home

from school. Each day she waves, and it is her war because the guards
tell me that her father was among the first from this town to go to your
army. If he dies, it will be the thing that signs her life. This is her war
and she doesn't even know it."

"Is it your war?"

"Oh yes. Though I hate it, it is still my war. And though you would
hide from it too, my friend, it has come to you. It has found you even
here, in your North Carolina. Although the history books of the great
men will never tell it, the war is inside us. And so we build to deny it."

A few days had passed since the midnight trial and early morning
banishment of the McBrides. I had neither seen nor heard from Anna,
so I wrote a note to say what I hoped to say to her in person. To say
that I would take her to Anderson Cove. Any time she liked, but soon.
Soon.

I admit I dreaded going up home, but something about the deaths
that had come upon us in late summer, something in what Ruser and
even Schlimbech had said, something in the air itself—dusty with dry
leaves and wood smoke—crept inside my mind. I wanted to go back
to Anderson Cove in order to remember who *I* was, in order to gulp
down my own cup of tonic before the war destroyed me.

And Anna Ulmann? Was I not afraid that whatever she heard or
saw in Anderson Cove would frighten her away? The answer was certainly yes. Or at least, on a purely rational level, I should have been
afraid because Anderson Cove, where my family lived, was at least fifty
years back in time. It had been almost ten years since I had been home.
It existed in a place before automobiles, before the telegram or telephone, before trolley cars or electricity or plumbing. In the winter it
was bitter cold and in the night it was pitch dark. And so it was truly
the life that Anna Ulmann thought she wanted to photograph, but I
was certain that she had no clue just how dark, how cold, how rough
the place—and the people—could be. And if it appalled her, this place
and people that made me, would it alter her opinion of me? Could she
accept me as I was—as dark, as cold, as mean as well water in a splin-
tered bucket, drawn on a mid-winter night? Anna knew that I had
been involved in the death of Bird's husband, but she didn't know that
I had gunned the poor, desperate man down with Jack Rumbough's

goose gun. And she didn't know that many of my own family blamed me still for having killed my own cousin.

My *mind* said that she need not know just how harsh a man I could be.

And yet, somehow, my *heart* wasn't afraid.

So I wrote her the note inviting her to travel to Anderson Cove to take photographs of mountain people as they once were, in the timeless state of nature. To leave as soon as she was able, before the weather got any colder. And I gave the note to Bird to deliver.

Anna brought back her own answer.

The next afternoon as I walked up to the side porch that led directly to the offices, I saw her camera standing tall on its three legs. Anna herself was at the counter in what had been Walter's office, with a note she'd written before her, talking to the Dorland teacher who was standing in as accountant.

"Just how long do you think he'll be, Miss Worley? Take a guess."

"Oh, I don't like to guess, especially with Mr. Robbins. This time of year, he's as unpredictable as the weather."

"Fair and cloudy all in one day?"

"All in one hour, that's him." She was smiling, was our Miss Worley, until precisely the moment she looked up and saw me. "Or should I say that's him standing right behind you?"

She turned. And we smiled. And it seemed like clouds lifted. I'm not sure how to describe it, but when her closed face opened, there was a sudden solstice inside of me. I shifted from living within myself to living again in the world. King James did the oddest thing; he began to bark happily, the first such noise I'd ever heard from him. The room grew lighter.

"What in the world?" she said, kneeling down to pet him. He immediately began to lick her face. "Stephen Robbins with a dog."

"He belonged to Julius Christopher," I said. "And he seems to have chosen me."

"Of course he has. He knows you need him." She addressed the dog as if he understood exactly what she was saying.

Even as she played with King James, she reached into her pocket and handed me a note. I walked out onto the porch to read it.

Dear Sir,
You have taken so long to offer up the riches of your fabled
Highlands that I can only believe you have been testing me.
I hope that now you begin to see my true worth.
And that we will delay no longer.
Your Yankee,
Anna

I carefully folded the paper and placed it in my inside jacket pocket. When she walked out onto the porch, King James dancing around her feet, I picked up her camera.

"Let's go," I said.

"To Anderson Cove?"

I nodded.

And she laughed her deep, throaty laugh. "As tempted as I am," she said. "I have assumed that we might stay several days."

I nodded.

"And for your sake, you will want me to prepare some sort of bag. Not a trunk and not a huge, great suitcase, but a valise, I promise a valise. I would like to be better prepared than the last time we got on the train together."

Ostensibly, she had come that day to photograph New Heidelberg under construction and to talk with an officer named Thierbach she'd heard of who was also a photographer. So we walked around the east wing of the Park and past the swimming pool and bathhouse, me studying how to balance the weight of the huge box camera over my shoulder, the tripod legs thrust comically out in front of me. We set up the camera in front of one of the dozen finished cottages: a replica, she said, of a Black Forest Lodge. We exposed one plate, with the "owner" of the house standing proudly on its front porch holding his cat. A cat which King James chose to ignore.

While she talked to Thierbach, who turned out to be a serious photographer, I strolled the two hundred feet from one end of New Heidelberg to the other. Received the silent and quite pleasant bows of the officers and men at work there; bowed in return as they had taught me by example to do, thinking of how the next great rise in the French Broad River would wash all their work away and how they worked on anyway.

When I came back to Captain Schlimbech's table, I discovered that together, he and Anna had sketched out something of a laboratory, wherein she and Thierbach could develop their own photographic plates rather than shipping them to Raleigh. And together, they asked if Schlimbech could have such a laboratory built in the basement of the Mountain Park, if we could order the chemicals for them to use. If ... if ... if. ... And I said back just as seriously, just as playfully: Maybe ... perhaps ... yes, of course.

Then, as if by mutual agreement, Anna and I wandered off beyond the German chapel, the roof of which was now completely covered with flattened tin cans scavenged from the hotel kitchen and tobacco tins saved by the pipe smokers. Together, we drifted into the trees along the river bank. I was intensely aware that it was the first time we'd really been alone together since our trip to Asheville, and I had to fight the urge every few steps to touch some part of her. Her elbow, her hand, her shoulder.

We came closer to the point of land where Spring Creek flowed from our left into the broad stretch of the river on our right. There in the shallows of the confluence stood a blue heron: tall and perfectly regal. The yellow spear of its beak was poised over the meeting of the waters, its black mask flowing back into long headdress feathers, its yellow eye piercing as it twisted its long neck to regard us. To regard us but for a moment before turning back to gaze into the swirling mirror of the waters.

I stepped behind Anna and placed my hands on her shoulders. "I want you to hear something," I said. "Something you can only hear one place on earth."

"I don't hear well," she admitted. "You may have to describe it to me."

"Oh, you'll hear it. It's subtle, but you'll hear it. Now, close your eyes and I'll take you to the spot."

"Can I trust you at all?" She was smiling, I knew.

"Just this once. Shut your eyes, Anna." I touched her face to be sure her eyes were closed and then guided her between trees, instructing her to pick up her feet in the loose sand. Half-pushed her to a spot between Spring Creek and the French Broad, although closer to the creek. To the one spot where in her left ear she would be able to hear the whispering of the creek and in her right the deep, hollow booming of the river. Water to her right and to her left: water all around, and as the breeze picked up in the trees, water seeming above and below her. "Leave your eyes closed," I whispered. "Relax your shoulders, let your neck go soft. ... Just listen."

Water flutes and water drums, water horns and water bells. And all was a ceaseless, living symphony.

"Will you stand just behind me?" she asked. "And shut your eyes too? I want you to hear it with me."

I was already just behind her and I had already shut my eyes. I was there with her, in the midst of that hollow room made of water, inside the flowing away song that water makes.

And despite all the ragged pressures of our hectic world, despite the fact that we were standing within the wire of a prison camp, I leaned forward and rested my forehead against the back of her neck, so that the sound of water vibrated from her body into mine and back again.

"What do you hear?" She whispered dreamily after a moment.

"The inside of water," I whispered back. "Your blood pulsing in your neck."

"Can you hear what I'm thinking?"

"I can feel what you're thinking."

She raised her arms straight out from her shoulders, pointing out, as if to touch both stream and river; I stepped forward just at the same time and slid my arms around her waist; she leaning her head back to me and the thick brush of her hair against my lips. "I hear the inside of water and it feels like it's running through us all the way to the ocean."

As we walked back through the trees toward the wagon gate, she asked me suddenly, almost as if playing a game, what I would like most in the world. Catching me just enough off guard, so that I blurted it out, the haunting desire that had run through my mind the two long and sleepless nights previous.

"I want to sleep with you."

She laughed. "Now, that's what I call a gracious proposal."

"I mean it. You asked. I'm tired to death, and at midnight the lone-liest man God ever made. And ..." I suddenly realized I was almost shaking.

"And you miss me."

"Unfortunately, I do."

"And you just want to sleep?" It was a moment before I realized she was teasing.

"I want a world of things. But more than any other thing, I want to fall asleep and wake up with you. To roll over and discover you're there. And to wonder gently whether to roll toward or away from you. And to let my tired, old body decide which."

"Not so old," she said. Staring into my face.

"Hummm?"

"Body's not so old. If my memory serves ... I would hope it would roll toward me."

"It's rolling toward you right now."

"Just where will we do this sleeping, Mr. Robbins? Sunnybank? You wouldn't come upstairs with me the other night when I all but begged you."

I pointed back the way we'd come—toward the Mountain Park. "Suite 305-306, with a fire in the fireplace. A glass of something strong."

She hesitated for a moment. "I'm not sure I can spend the night there, Stephen, though I've imagined it more than once. Something about being inside the fence ..." I'm sure she could see the disappoint-ment on my face. "But what about a nap?"

"What?" I could feel the smile tickling my lips. We were standing in the middle of the wagon path, staring into each other's eyes.

"A nap. You know. Neither one of us sleeps at night. Which sick-ness, by the way, I caught from you. And there is all the long day to be had. In your rooms that float up in the sky. With wine and cheese and a bed. Surely to God you have a bed. No clock to wake us ... a nap."

"How about now?"

She reached across and pulled the pocket watch from my vest. "It's nearly two o'clock," she said. "So I say tomorrow. There's a lot more of tomorrow than there is of today."

CHAPTER THIRTEEN

AFTER Anna passed through the wagon gate to return to Sunnybank, I took myself back the way we'd come, around the flank of the Mountain Park and into Camp A.

I collected Anna's camera from New Heidelberg and took it with me up to 305-306. Where, stripped to my waist, I did something I had never done before. I tried to look at my rooms as I imagined a woman might, a woman who craved order. And then, in my own offhand way, I sat about straightening and cleaning.

After a few hours, I heard Bird's characteristic rap on the door: the slightest three taps that she used for fear of waking me from sleep. Often, she knocked so quietly that it didn't fetch me whether I slept or no. This time I answered the door while holding a book, the last of several I was returning to the shelf. She took the book, a slim, forest-green volume, out of my hand and replaced it with a note from Siegfried. While she carried the book into the bedroom, I read his reminder that I had promised to dine with the German officers that night. Thursday, the one night of the week they were allowed a ration of beef. I knew what Siegfried did not; it was to be a stew simmered with potatoes, onions, and carrots in a heavy stock, with for once no cabbage. Easily the best meal of the week. So, despite Bird's sly, curious bobs and grins at my straightening up, I wasted no time in pushing her out so I could dress for dinner.

We sat, Siegfried as translator and I, at what had been the head table in the hotel dining room. The table was one that had survived from before the war, covered with a heavy cloth to protect it from imagined German atrocities. The chairs, however, had been stored in the basement and replaced by rough benches. The hotel china had been carefully boxed for the duration and replaced as well by thick, white crockery shipped to us by the Department of Labor. The stew was rich and strong. Pauline told me later that she'd sliced some venison into each huge pot for flavor. The conversation ranged from the differences between German and American cooking even to the war itself. Ruser and several of the more senior officers listened gravely, until suddenly, the Commodore interrupted one of his junior officers to address me directly.

"Herr Robbins, do you know what they have done with our ships?" This, again, was his official person, his voice deep and stern.

I must have given him an especially blank look.

"The great luxury liners of the Hamburg-Amerika fleet!" He motioned to the man on his left, a dour old captain, who threw a folded newspaper on the table. "*Imperator, Bismarck,* and even *Vaterland*—do you know what has happened to them?" I could almost smell the sudden tension; I had forgotten just how afraid most of these men were of Ruser.

I picked up the newspaper. "Surely they haven't been scuttled."

"Worse. They have been stripped and recommissioned as troop ships. The most elegant ships in the world used to haul ignorant American soldiers packed in like cattle."

"Commodore Ruser, do you object to their being used in the war effort?" I had found the article in *The New York Times* and was reading quickly even as I listened.

"Pah! The so-called Great War has nothing to do with me or with my ships." I could sense a new source of tension now; several of Ruser's junior officers leaned forward as if to disagree, but the cagy old man went on, and I had the sense that his true feelings were emerging despite their attention. "It is as if you seized the most beautiful, most stylish woman from the streets of New York and ripped her clothing from her body. Dressed her in sacks and made of her a whore to your army so that their filth would cover her inside and out. This war is a mere passing nightmare; we will wake in a few years. But these ships were built to last forever."

"Herr Robbins." It was the old captain next to Ruser who now spoke but with such emotion that he immediately lapsed into German. Siegfried translated, "We find it that we must inform you. We intend to write a formal letter. A letter of outrage and protest to the International Red Cross at the Swiss Consulate. We believe the destruction of our ships is a criminal act, and that someone must pay for the damages."

I nodded solemnly and assured Ruser that I would see their letter delivered. "Which of these ships have you commanded, Commodore?" I pointed to a series of photographs in the *Times*.

He drew himself up such that he took on a certain majesty, even seated on a pine bench with a prisoner's bowl and spoon before him. "I have commanded them all, sir, and in every ocean of the world."

As we walked out of the dining room, I overheard a young officer with the tell-tale saber scar say loudly enough to be heard that the old man was a fool. "To say that the war has no meaning is to be a traitor. It is for the Kaiser; it is for the Father—"

He was cut off by the companion he was speaking to. A companion who pulled Saber Scar back from me and from the older officers. The companion? Siegfried Sonnach.

After seeing the German officers into their rooms for the night, I wandered outside—too restless even for my nightly rambles up and down the halls. That there was war in our own ranks—between Ed Rumbough, Cousin Roy and me—I had taken for granted from the beginning. They were far more of a threat to me than all the Germans put together. But what I'd heard and felt that night in the dining room suddenly reminded me of Ruser's earlier warning—that the Germans were also a nation unto themselves. It seemed certain that they had their own wars, carried on in secret; and they only turned a peaceful, passive face to their sleepy guards. Was I supposed to protect them from each other as well as from us—whoever the hell "us" was? Ruser hadn't told me that, or at least not said it out loud.

When I came back inside the Park close to midnight, I discovered John Sanders in his room with the door cracked open. When I looked in, I saw him sitting at his small work desk, sketching something on paper. I could see the stem of his pipe sticking up out of the coffee can he used for an ash tray, and despite an open window, the room was thick with the aroma of smoke.

"I thought you went home hours ago," I said softly. "Hearth and home and all that."

"More peaceful over here." He looked up and actually grinned at his own admission. "... than it is across the river." His wife was a large and very stern woman—with a long list to be held up against most any man.

"What's that you're drawing?"

"New water system," he said. He motioned me over to his desk. "It's for *after the war*, when we get out of the prison business." He used the sharp tip of his pencil to trace the flow of fresh water from a new reservoir across the river. "All gravity," he said. "And you'll even have water pressure on the third floor."

"You reckon there'll be an after the war, John?"

"Oh yes." He picked up his pipe and stuck it cold between his teeth. There was a strict policy against smoking in the hotel, and he wouldn't light it until I left. "Soon as enough young men get themselves killed," he said around clenched teeth, "us old farts can get back to our lives."

I liked him at that moment, sketching a practical, ordered future even as the present sought to burn us up alive.

It was perhaps four in the morning before I slept; even reading in the novel Bird had tossed on my bed didn't dull my mind to sleep. But when I did sleep, I had the most intense dream, a dream that is fresh to this day.

I am standing alone at night on the lower lawn. I know that it is before the war because there are golf links where inmate huts will soon be built. It must be late because the Mountain Park behind me is quiet, with only a few lights showing on the ground floor. The town sleeps, still and remote, and all around me is the essence of simplicity. I know who I am and where I am, and there is peace.

But something large and threatening looms upstream; it is just beyond my sight and coming closer down the river. I can feel the shadow it casts over my valley as first the stars and then the sliver of crescent moon are blocked out of the sky.

And then it comes into sight, filling the entire riverbed and dwarfing the trees on either bank, sailing slowly and majestically down toward me. Even in the dark, I can see the monstrously high bow adorned with the ornate scroll work and gilded lettering of German craftsmen. From either side hang anchors as large as any house in Hot Springs, and from the three great funnel stacks billows smoke gray and black into the night sky. I smell coal burning.

It is Vaterland.

The ship grinds the bridge under its bow as if the whole structure were made of tin cans. Before our tiny town, it slowly comes to a halt in the midnight river and with a thundering rattle of chain, one monstrous anchor drops onto the lower lawn of the Mountain Park, crushing trees and embedding itself deeply into the soft soil.

Though I cannot see him, I know Commodore Hans Ruser has by celestial navigation driven his master ship onto the very banks of our once broad river, has driven the spike of imperial culture into the heart of our lost and timeless little place.

I am aware of myself now on the deck of the great ship, the largest in the world, looking down onto the roof of the Mountain Park, looking down on what had once seemed my refuge, dwarfed now in German smoke and steel. When I turn back to the huge expanse of deck, I see a couple walking toward me, a woman slight and dark on the arm of a much taller man, expansive and elegant, a trim mustache.

They walk toward me without flinching, aware of my presence but utterly contemptuous of me in this new and dangerous world. What I am—hill-born, narrow, ignorant—is almost beneath their ridicule. They pause for a brief moment, and turn in an eerie sort of promenade. When they do, the woman looks longingly over her shoulder at me, and I realize that it's her. It's Anna. But the force of the man's personality and the bulk of his body turn her away.

He points, and following the line of his arm, I see a mountain of luggage that he apparently means for me to remove. He pulls her farther and farther away. Toward some stately place that I cannot follow. I am left before the luggage, put firmly in my place.

I am alone again on the lower lawn. The worst part seems over, but when I look up in relief, the ship is still there as if it will always be there, huge and carnal.

The dream was so real that when I woke in a sweat, I actually stumbled out onto the balcony to see if my horizons were the same, to be sure that the Park hadn't been dwarfed by a gargantuan luxury liner from the Hamburg-Amerika. The night had worn on in peace, however, the velvet sky had spun in place above, and the sun was coming. Never did the cold air breathe so well as it did right there, chasing that dream.

I pulled off the night clothes in which I'd slept and dropped them into the laundry hamper, grateful for the sudden coolness against my skin. The fire in the fireplace had burned down, but the room was slowly gathering light through the windows. I visited the bathroom and washed my teeth before crawling back into bed to outline my body against the cooling sheets, luxuriating in the feel of thigh and groin, chest and face against the cool linen. I, at least, was real to the touch and could lapse again into a doze.

What woke me the second time was the slightest shifting in the balance of my bed. I opened my eyes slowly against the brightness that wasn't there before. Anna was sitting on the side of my bed, looking thin and composed. She reached out with one gloved hand and ran her fingers through my hair, unable to resist the urge to repair the night's damage.

"I hope it's true," she said, quietly, evenly.

"Hope what's true?"

"I hope it's true that you want me here. That you invited me. And I hope it's true that this evening when I leave, you won't regret me."

I shook my head barely *no.* Meaning no regrets. And I pushed my covers down slightly, to my bare waist, I suppose to invite her on. To nap. I closed my eyes. To give her time and space. To think about the fact that she was there. And that, praise God, she was not a dream.

When I opened them again after a few moments, she had stoked the fire and was standing beside the bed, divested of hat, jacket, and gloves. She was unbuttoning her dress slowly, pausing once to stretch and yawn. *How early in the day it must be.* She laid her dress neatly over the arm of my fireside chair. And removed next an exotic corset, full and even frilly, pausing to stretch again as she pushed it up and off her arms. Then stooped to lower and step out of the last bit of cloth that covered her. I shut my eyes again. *So much light.*

The first few, flustered moments, during which all we did was try to touch each other everywhere all at once. Stretching out now but against each other so that more and more of each touched more and more of the other such that our bodies could find peace and release. As if we were competing with the dawn, we burned into each other with a wild ferocity. And there was a blinding lightness such as I'd never known before.

I think that we were both so in love with the idea of sleeping together that we tried. We attempted sleep. But couldn't help ourselves with nuzzling and occasionally biting. And talking. *Forever she and I talking.*

"Last night," I said. Speaking out loud into the deep, luxurious mat of her hair. "Last night, I had the strangest dream. Disturbing and strange."

"Dreamed of me, didn't you?"

"Well, yes, actually. But there was much more than just that." I told her about the ship that had sailed impossibly down the French Broad and anchored in the middle of the valley. Split the world in half. About the smoke spoiling the midnight sky. About being on the deck so high above even the hotel. The luggage. "And then your father pinned your arm with his and whirled you away as if you were far too good for the likes of me. You looked back once but—"

"It wasn't my father." She'd brought me up short with the ice in her voice. She pulled away from me to sit up in bed.

"But he was big and impressive and dressed like the most expensive gentleman you could imagine. He must have—"

"He wasn't my father, Stephen. My father was a small, happy little man who loved to walk down the street in carpet slippers. I wasn't a little girl, was I, Stephen, in your dream I mean?"

"No," I admitted. "A bold woman."

"Not so bold if I was with him."

"Who? If not your father, who?"

"My husband, the man who owns me."

"One human being doesn't *own* another, Anna."

"That's easy for you to say," she cried. "You've never met him."

"Dr. Jurgens," I whispered. "Freudian analyst."

"Freudian analyst. Journalist. Advisor to great men. Friend of my father's for long years past."

"Why are you so afraid of him?"

She looked long and hard at me, considering. Now we were both sitting up in bed, she with the blankets pulled up to her shoulders. "You really expect me to answer that, don't you?"

I nodded.

"Because I saw him in his professional capacity after my father died, trying to work through the loss, and he chose me out of all his patients to marry. Because once he married me, he continued to treat me like someone to be handled with kid gloves. Because he ..."

"Because ...?" I whispered, ever so gently.

"Because when I said I couldn't stand it anymore, that I had to have my own life, he tried to lock me up in the house and keep me like ..."

"A prisoner?"

She nodded, her eyes clenched shut, the tears beading at their corners. "Like a crazy woman."

"No wonder you hate the fence."

She nodded, hard, trying not to cry out.

"I'm sorry, Anna, to be such a fool."

She shook her head, no, still with her eyes driven shut.

"I'm sorry not to have paid better attention. Not to have listened better to all you've said." I reached out and pulled her to me. Even though for a long moment, she stiffened as if to push away, I pulled her to me and down under the covers where I could hold her while she sobbed.

After a time, when she had rolled over to face me, I whispered to her. Whispered that she needn't be afraid any more. That she was in a new and different world.

"Oh, Stephen, what if he gets down off that train one day."

"Why then I'll kill him," I whispered reassuringly. Into the endless, whorled depths of her ear.

She sighed. "That's so sweet. But Stephen, you can't kill him."

"Why not?"

"Because he's rich," she whispered and shortly after fell asleep. Smiling, she was, and in my arms. Gently sleeping.

When I woke, she was sitting in the old, overstuffed chair by the fire with my dressing gown wrapped loosely around her. Reading the novel that I had tried to trick myself to sleep with the night before.

I watched her comfortably as my mind slowly swam up into consciousness. So the *Vaterland* of my dream wasn't a ship but a man, I thought. Well, let him come on. Let him pay a visit to my country and we would see who carried the goddamn luggage. She was smiling at me, having noticed I was awake.

"It's hard to believe that Christian Reid is a man," she said. And for a moment, I was very confused as to who was whom, until I remembered that Christian Reid had written the book she was reading.

"She's not." I said. "Christian Reid is a pen name for a woman named Frances Something-or-Other. She wrote most of that book while she was staying at the old Warm Springs Hotel, the building that stood here before the Mountain Park."

"*The Land of the Sky*?" She was making fun of the title.

"I was only trying to put myself to sleep with it."

"Oh, it's not that bad. And what she has to say about men is exactly right." She got up to hand me a water glass half-full of wine.

"And just what does she have to say, Miss Ulmann, about my kind?"

She sat back down and traced a few lines in the book. "*Sylvia has gone as far as she can go—has said all that a woman can say.* And still this ... this Charley is too dense to realize what she's trying to say."

"Is she telling us that men don't listen?"

"I'm glad you're not as dense as Charley." She smiled.

I had been sitting in bed as I sipped my wine. As I got up, I set my glass on the floor, so that I could kneel in front of her.

"Just what are you doing?" she said languidly.

"I mean to be the very first," I said. "Miss Anna Ulmann, I mean to be the pattern of a man who listens. Who watches and thinks and reads the signs. I would like to go to school on listening with you as my teacher."

"What do you expect to learn?"

"All the great God's plenty that you know, or at least as much as you're willing to whisper in my ear."

That afternoon, we learned to drink wine in bed. We learned to read poetry aloud in bed. We learned to meditate—no, that's not quite right; she tried to teach me to meditate by counting my breaths—in bed. She told me about the power of depth psychology and the knowledge to be gained from analysis of one's own mind—in bed. The empty wine bottle sat on the mantle, the fire guttered down to ashes, and the room filled to its brim with rich, creamy afternoon light.

We were lying on our sides facing each other: content, I suppose you would say. And content is a word. But it was richer than that. Sated. Smiling. Not asleep, but sleepy relaxed like a dog and a cat who are old friends, lying in the sun. Whose paws barely touch.

"There is this one other thing I'd like you to teach me," I said. "And I suspect it is like listening in that it involves paying attention. Taking care."

"What's that?" She was purring more than speaking.

"To give to you what you give to me."

She opened her eyes wide. "You mean physically?"

I nodded.

"You want to ...?"

"Yes, please." If it's possible to hang your head while lying down, mine was hanging. I couldn't have said it, but I loved Anna Ulmann. And this was one way in which I had failed her.

She laughed. I swear. Laughed! "Oh, I want more than that," she said.

"More?"

"More difficult." The humor was still in her voice as she reached out to touch my face.

"What then?"

"That we go there together, woven."

"Like music."

"Yes, like the music at that place ..." She was touching me somewhere else now. "You showed me where the creek flows into the river."

"The confluence."

"What I really want you to give me," she whispered, "is some wicked *confluence*."

CHAPTER FOURTEEN

It was around five o'clock, I suspect, when we finally began to stir. When the evening shadows had begun to invade our world, she grew quiet, and I asked if we should go. She nodded, said that she'd feel better if she was at the dinner table at Sunnybank on time. She wanted us to be unhurried, unflustered.

And so we dressed, putting on a slightly distant mood with our clothes, mourning perhaps, the end of the day. When we were fully dressed except for her hat and gloves, she sat down suddenly in one of the fireside chairs. "Stephen, you said you would listen to me. Earlier, when you were kneeling, you said so. Will you listen now?"

"With all my heart." I sat down opposite her without speaking further. Letting her find her own pace.

"I think that if I love you, I have to share your world whether I want to or not."

I nodded. Only nodded. But my mind was swirling because of the word she had used.

"And as much as I'd like for it to be, Anderson Cove is not really your world."

I nodded again. "This is," I said. Swinging my head around to indicate the Mountain Park.

"You remember the man you were talking to the first time I ever visited you here?"

I must have looked blank.

"You said he was the sheriff and that he had a gun under his coat."

A storm of darkness exploded inside my head. "Oh, God no," I whispered.

"I have seen him, Stephen. I walk in the evenings, on out the road beyond Sunnybank, walk 'til I'm tired and then turn back. Sometimes, I cut through the back streets and walk up to the back of the house through the school. Two different nights when I came back along the streets, I met that man. And Stephen ...?"

"Tell me."

"One night I saw him walking along talking to one of your Germans."

"After dark, you saw him with one of the internees?"

She nodded.

"Did you recognize him?"

"A blond man who looked like he was very impressed with himself."

My stomach had already begun to sink, but my mouth kept talking, to fill up the space while I thought. "Did he address you in English?"

She was nodding. "Yes, as a matter of fact. Perfect English and not much of an accent."

"You saw Siegfried Sonnach talking with Roy Robbins? ... What time of night?

"Nine o'clock maybe. Late ... Stephen, are you all right?"

"Yes, ... well, no. No, there's a whole new layer to this knot that I hadn't even imagined. I have a new set of problems."

"You might say we have a new set of problems."

"We? That's sweet, Anna, but you're not—"

"No, Stephen. I mean that when I saw them together, they saw me. I passed them on that little street behind Sunnybank, and the blond boy spoke to me and called me by name. And when he did, the other man, the sheriff, stopped him to ask who I was. I kept right on going, but I could hear them standing behind me talking. Laughing at me."

I couldn't say anything. My mind was racing and cursing at the same time.

"Stephen, I'm sorry to have upset you. Should I have told you all this?"

"Good God, yes. My being upset doesn't signify. What matters is what in the hell are the two of them up to together? Why didn't you tell me sooner?"

"Because some of the Germans seem to have the run of the town, coming and going, working for local people. Until Amanda McBride said what she said the other night, I didn't imagine it mattered."

"Everything matters," I muttered.

"What?"

"In this world—the world of the fence and the Germans—every-damnthing matters. Everything is supposed to be still and quiet and yet every time you look up, it's in motion."

Later, as we were walking with King James slowly up the lower lawn toward the camp gate, she whispered questions she'd obviously been fretting over. "Does this mean we can't go to Anderson Cove?"

"No," I said. "Now that Roy has his eye on you, you have to go. But Anna ..."

"Yes?"

"You'll have to go without me. I can't leave with—"

"Stephen, I don't want to ..."

"Listen to me. You'll be safe there. And I can't leave with the two of them hatching some sort of plot."

As we walked along in the cool evening air, we became friends again. Not so close as when we were comfortably asleep like some mid-winter country couple, but friends nonetheless. Once again in tandem. Once more with a rhythm.

We walked arm-in-arm out the gate onto Bridge Street. She, having said what she was troubled to say, seemed relaxed and happy, asking me questions about Anderson Cove. How many people lived there? Were they all related to me? How did they make a living? And King James played his game, galloping on his long legs after first a cat and then a squirrel as though the world was made all of cats and squirrels.

When we reached the corner of Bridge and Spring Street, she paused.

"Why don't we part ways here?" I asked. "I will step back into the shadows and watch to be sure you are safe on the porch at Sunnybank. I need to know you're safe."

"Thank you," she said ever so simply.

"No, I should thank you. I never thought I'd hear myself say it, but I'm actually glad you're going up home."

She squeezed my arm and walked on, and I watched, my heart

stretching out to follow and protect her, while my mind raced back to the camp. To Siegfried and the question of how he was strolling around outside the wire after dark.

As I walked back down Bridge Street, I saw ahead of me a tall, distinguished figure that could only be one man in Hot Springs—Prince. I called out to him and he turned.

"You always lurkin' about, ain't you?" he asked, when I had caught up to him.

"Lurking about is my job." I patted his broad back affectionately. "Same token, I might say that it's kind of late in the day for an elderly man like you to be out in the streets."

"Well, I was on my way to fetch you. You got a couple of hours to eat supper up at Rutland?" Rutland, the mansion on the hill that looked like a gigantic Victorian gingerbread house.

"The big house? Why would I want to eat supper up there; I was hoping you were going to invite me to your house."

"Same difference. Dora's cooking."

I looked up at him in surprise.

"Johnny Rumbough showed up at the train station this afternoon with a trunk that's bigger'n he is, lookin' as lost as a kitten. One of the boys found me, and when I walked down to greet him properly, he asked where he was to go. I figured you didn't want him stayin' inside the fence, so I took him up to Rutland. Now, he claims he's to report to you."

"Sounds to me like you been playing nursemaid all afternoon."

"I don't mind Johnny. The minute she heard he was home, Dora went racin' up to the house to open up some rooms and start fixin' supper. He's spent the whole afternoon sayin' yes ma'am and no ma'am and tryin' to carry her groceries from one end of the kitchen to the other. She's near bout adopted him by now."

"Adopted him?"

"You talkin' about a fifty-four year old woman who never had any children. Her momma been dead ten years August. She's tired of lookin' at me, and she'll take any family she can get. So if you don't come up with somethin' for little Johnny to do, I'll be stuck reminding him to wipe his nose twenty-four hours a day."

"Oh, I've got plenty for him to do."

We had started up the long drive to Rutland and Miss Carrie's chapel. From below, we still couldn't see either structure, but I could feel them both, particularly the massive house with its four-story tower, looming over us.

"Listen, Prince, I need to tell you something before we get there. Something I want you to think about."

He stopped and leaned back against the rock wall that kept the long, steep yard from tumbling into the drive where we stood. Crossed his arms and waited.

"You reckon Roy Robbins is possessed of Satan?" I asked him.

He shook his head. "No. Cording to my physics, he'd a had to a been human first, so Satan could possess him. Here's what I think. I think he might be Satan, particularly after what he did to that Starnes girl up at Mars Hill."

"What did he ...? Never mind. I can guess. Anna says she's seen him twice in the last week, both times at night and both times out behind Dorland School with one of our Germans."

"Oh hell," he said.

"Yes, hell. Is there any way to find out what he's up to? Where he's staying if he's down here at night? Who's he's bought off?"

"Let me think about it," he said. And then he paused, continuing to stare down at his shoes. "Stevie," he finally muttered, "all this makes me wonder about our boy, Johnny. Did it ever occur to you that—?"

"Ed sent him down here to spy on us?"

"No, that Ed sent him down here to spy on you. I'm just a shufflin' old Negro to Ed."

"It didn't just occur to me. Caddie had Johnny confess as much at the funeral."

"And you still said he could come?"

"Hell, Prince, he was honest about it. And he is his father's son."

"Yeah, well, so is Ed his father's son. That don't necessarily make me feel any better."

"Prince Garner, it is given to us to train this youth up in the way that he should go, to shape him as a slender reed. To finish his education in the ways of the world, so that he might walk as a man among men."

And he laughed. Started to respond, but then just shook his head and laughed. And we didn't stop laughing as we walked around Miss Carrie's tattered boxwood maze and up the front steps of Rutland.

Dora Garner had set the smaller of two tables in the dining room for two, but I told her that I wouldn't stay unless she and Prince ate at the table with Johnny and me. She would not allow King James into the dining room, but gave him some gravy and chicken skin in the kitchen.

While Dora lectured the dog about his manners, Prince and I placed two more settings of the fine china she had unpacked for Johnny. Then she served us fried chicken and collard greens, mashed potatoes, and fresh wheat bread, a meal almost unheard of even that early in the war. An apple pie from the trees behind Rutland. The moment we sat down and the dishes began their rounds, I knew this was special to her.

Johnny had put on a tie for dinner, and Prince and I were seeking to rise to the occasion.

We took turns praising the meal, lavishly, for she had outdone herself. Johnny, to his credit, asked Dora and Prince to call him "just plain Johnny," while he deferred to me as Mr. Robbins.

At one point, he asked me how Miss Ulmann did, and I saw Dora glance at him in surprise. I knew Prince was grinning his Mexican bandit grin.

"She is quite well, thank you, Johnny, and will be glad to know you have arrived."

He turned to Dora. "I met Miss Ulmann at father's funeral. That was one part that I didn't tell you about this afternoon. Mr. Robbins and Miss Ulmann rode to the cemetery with Caddie and me."

"What's she like, the camera woman?" Dora asked Johnny, as if I wasn't there.

"She was very nice. She and Caddie chatted away as if they'd known each other forever."

Since Caddie was famous for being simple-minded and was the only white sister who had actually accepted Dora into the family, this caused Dora to smile in turn at me, some ever-so-slight sign of approval from one woman of another. "I'd like to meet her," she whispered.

"Couldn't we all have dinner here one night?" Johnny asked me.

"I would like that very much and so, I think, would she. The day after tomorrow, she is going up to Highlands so she can take photographs of the old mountain ways. I promised her that she could go, but she'll be back in a week. As soon as she gets back, we can all sit down together."

"What will be my job, Mr. Robbins? In the camp, I mean?" Johnny asked.

"Nothing dangerous, I hope." Dora spoke for the first time above a whisper.

"Nothing so dangerous that he can't get himself out of it if he needs to."

I could tell my answer didn't satisfy Dora, but Johnny liked it. "Mr. Robbins," he replied happily. "Does it help you to know I read German?"

For a man who prides himself on not being caught off guard, this was at least the second time that day when someone had more than surprised me. And I must have shown it because Prince laughed out loud.

Laughed and then said, "He's been prayin' for your arrival, boy, and didn't even know it."

"You mean that you read it but don't speak it?" I asked.

"I learned to read it at boarding school, but I've never heard it spoken enough so that I could pronounce it."

"That doesn't matter; you'll hear a lot of it in the next few weeks."

We began the next morning, Johnny and I, with a long walking tour of both A and B. I introduced him to prisoners as well as guards, the mighty low as well as the high and mighty. I introduced him to architect Schlimbech at New Heidelberg and to a group of seamen in the "Y" who were weaving intricate floor mats to sell. He was especially interested in the bridge construction and drew a sketch of the new pillars and beams that were already in place. I watched him tease a smile out of guard John Goforth at the wagon gate and listen ever so attentively to John Sanders as Captain John explained the guard rotation on the fences and in the Mountain Park.

After our grand tour of Camp A, Johnny and I met Prince on the porch of the old hotel. When we paused to breathe the fresh air, Prince asked me a question that cut straight into my conscience.

"You sure you want to be gone just now, when the devil himself is runnin' around loose outside the fence?"

I paused, trying to formulate a clear answer, when it was all still so confused in my own mind.

"Who's the devil himself?" Johnny asked.

"The devil himself is the High Sheriff of Madison County," Prince answered. "Related to Mr. Robbins here."

"Sheriff Roy Robbins?" Johnny asked.

"The very man, the original snake in the grass." Prince made a slithering motion with his hand, to illustrate his point.

"He's in cohoots with my brother, Ed."

Prince looked at me. "You know that?"

I nodded. "Been knowing it for a while. Question is, how do you stop the sheriff when the sheriff is the law?"

"And you plannin' to be gone?" Prince shook his head in dismay.

"Only for the day, damn it. I was going for a week 'til I heard about Roy." I glanced at Johnny Rumbough, who was soaking all this up. If we were going to trust him, now was the time. "When Anna told me about Siegfried, she also said that Roy noticed her. Asked Siegfried who she was."

Prince studied my face for a long slow moment, barely blinking.

"Am I wrong for wanting to protect her?" I said suddenly. "Wanting to protect her even more than all of them?" I waved my arm out toward Camp B, where the Germans were spending the day, exercising and studying French.

"He loves her," Johnny Rumbough said helpfully.

"What do you know?" I said to him. "You're only seventeen."

"Some things are kind of obvious."

"Brother Stevie," Prince finally spoke. "I been prayin' for something good to happen to you for a long time. And now that somethin' good has come along in the form of Miss Ulmann, we'd damn well better take care of her. ... Sides, I got some ideas of my own about Cousin Roy."

We parted ways with Prince on Bridge Street, he to go on about his town business, Johnny and I to tour Camp B. Once we were inside the gate, I led him to the bench in the stand of hemlocks near where the Imperial Band had played its concert. I told him how I had wept when

I heard of his father's death.

"What was he like, my father?"

"Didn't you know him?"

"Not well. I was always in Asheville with my mother or away at school. When I did see him, he liked to punch me in the stomach and slip me a ten dollar bill. For years, I only thought of him when I smelled cigar smoke."

I smiled; old Jack Rumbough had loved his Cubans. "Your father is a large subject, Johnny. He was sly and he was funny and he was very, very powerful. Not in a political way, though he had that kind of influence too. He was powerful in a personal way; when you were with him, you automatically began to dress like him, walk and talk like him. And I guess you know by now that women loved him."

"Miss Dora is my sister, isn't she?"

"Your half sister, but Caddie is the only one who'll admit it."

"My other sisters pretend I don't exist either sometimes." And then after a moment: "You too, huh?"

He was so sincere I had to smile at him. "Not really, I only have a history with one of them, and now I'm happy to say that whole weeks go by and it doesn't even occur to me to think about her."

"Mr. Robbins, now that I know you a little bit, can I tell you one thing I do know about my father?" He paused as he petted King James. "My father admired you. He told me last summer that he hoped I would grow up to be more like you than Ed or Harry."

"Did he tell you I was a drunk?"

"Yes. But he also said you'd stop drinking the minute you had your hands in something that mattered to you."

I had to laugh, in part at the memory of the boy's father, in part at his bluntness. "You know, little brother, I may have found the thing he was talking about, that thing that matters."

"Miss Ulmann?"

I didn't speak but I didn't have to. I smiled and he knew.

"Johnny, I do have a job for you, and though I don't think it's dangerous, it is important. In a few minutes, when we walk out of these trees, we're going to find an officer named Siegfried Sonnach. He's young and energetic and very entertaining. Prides himself on his English and on his ability to keep his finger on every pulse in both camps. He is the self-proclaimed liaison between us and the internees, and so far most of the German officers have been willing to accept him as their translator."

"Why are you telling me all this about him?"

"Because I'm going to ask him to take you under his wing for the next week or so. I'm going to tell him that you are to become my assistant and that I want him to teach you the ins and outs of the camp." Johnny nodded. "And I'm going to tell him that I want him to teach you elementary German."

"But I already know—"

"I know you do, but I want you to play dumb, at least when it comes to the language. I want you to listen when he assumes you don't understand, and I want you to read every scrap of paper that crosses his path."

I could tell he was excited. "You want me to spy on him."

"Yes, but very slowly and very carefully. More than anything else, I just want you to pay attention. I need to know what is going on in Siegfried Sonnach's mind. And if I'm gone from the town and from the camps, even for a day, I think he may be a lot more careless than he would be otherwise."

"Is he dangerous?"

I had to stop and think about that one. "I honestly don't know," I admitted. "But I'm certain that he won't lay a finger on you inside the wire. Not when he knows he'd have to answer to me. And I don't want you outside the wire with him under any circumstances."

"I understand."

When I introduced Johnny to Siegfried, he was almost beside himself with joy to meet and to know his new, young colleague. And when I drew him aside, near the gatehouse, to explain that I was trusting him to be Johnny's mentor, he almost glowed. "Young John, you have not a way to know this, but the entire camp runs almost as the out-flowing of this man's will. He is—"

"Yeah, yeah. Listen, Siegfried. I also want you to teach him as much German as you can right away. You've told me over and over that you are the linguist of the world. Now is your chance to prove it."

"How long do I have?"

"As long as this war lasts."

"It will not take nearly so long. In three weeks, he will speak as a native of the Fatherland. He will become German."

"That reminds me. Don't start by teaching him all the curse words."

As we parted, Siegfried bowed and, for my benefit, taught Johnny the "correct" pronunciation of *auf weidershen*. "It will be my honor both to know you and to teach you," he said to Johnny. "A friend of Stephen's is to be a friend of mine."

That afternoon, I sent Bird up to Sunnybank with a note, asking if Johnny and I might join Miss Jane and Anna for tea. High tea at four o'clock that afternoon, a habit that Anna had slowly impressed on Miss Jane, teaching her to make strong English tea and, even more amazing, teaching Miss Jane to stop working long enough to sit down and enjoy it.

When we arrived just before four, Jane had set a table for us in her front parlor beside the fireplace. Tea was already steeping, and there were cookies and small slices of cake on a tray. From the porch, I could see Jane and Anna sitting and talking quietly, so quietly that I almost hated to knock on the door and disturb them.

When I did, Anna jumped up and gave Johnny a brief hug and led him to the table. She introduced Johnny to Jane who smiled her beatific smile. "Oh, I remember little Johnny Rumbough," she said. "Seen him for years being carried about the town. Not so little any more though, is he? Better part of a man now."

Anna beamed at him, and Johnny blushed under all the attention; King James collapsed next to the fireplace, where Jane had lit a small blaze against the afternoon chill.

"Miss Jane was just saying to me that in addition to taking photographs while I'm in Highlands, I should ask your aunts and uncles to sing some of the old songs."

"Jane should know who to ask, but what she didn't tell you is that the most famous voice in the hills is her own."

Jane smiled benignly.

"Sing a piece of something for Anna and Johnny," I encouraged her.

"What would you favor, dear?" she asked Anna.

"Oh, I don't even know. Let Stephen pick." Anna busied herself for a moment with the tea pot, and Johnny helped her add sugar to mine and milk to his and Miss Jane's.

"Sing 'King Henry,' Jane. It's coming on Halloween, and we need a winter fright."

"And so you think it's fit for young ears?" She asked and nodded at Johnny.

"He'll be fine. He's been away to school."

The summer before, the famous British musicologist Cecil Sharp had traveled through the southern mountains carefully recording the ancient ballads that had survived in our shadowy land. What very few people know is that once Sharp heard Jane Gentry sing, he went no farther than Sunnybank for several weeks because ... well, because of what followed.

Miss Jane stood up at her tea table: plump, perhaps even dowdy, her skin stained to the color of tea by her part Cherokee blood. Then she opened her mouth and at once a high quavering tone emerged that dropped you off into a deeper, darker time, a time of kings and witches and ghosts, a time when death followed love as surely as winter chases fall. And Miss Jane Gentry was no longer there, nor her parlor nor her guests; only the lilting tones of the ballad existed—and the ancient, smoke-stained halls of a British castle, lost on a storm-tossed moor.

> *King Henry's huntsmen followed him*
> *To make them burly cheer*
> *When loud the wind was heard to sound*
> *And earthquake rocked the floor.*
>
> *And darkness covered all the hall,*
> *Where they sat down at their meat*
> *The grey dogs, howling, left their food*
> *And crept to Henry's feet.*
>
> *And louder howled the rising wind*
> *And burst op' the fastened door*
> *And there came a grisly ghost*
> *A stamping on the floor.*
>
> *Her head hit the roof tree of the house*
> *Her middle you could not span*
> *Each frightened huntsman fled the hall*
> *And left King Henry sore.*

Her teeth were like the tether stakes
Her nose like club or mell
And nothing less she seemed to be
Than a fiend come straight from hell.

Some meat, some meat
Young Henry, some meat you give to me
Go kill your horse, King Henry
And bring him here to me.

He's gone and slain his berry brown steed
Though it made his heart full sore
For she's eaten up both flesh and bone
Left naught but hide and hair.

More meat, more meat
Young Henry, more meat you give to me
Go kill your dogs, King Henry
And bring them here to me.

And when he's slain his good grey dogs
It made his heart full sore
For she's eaten up both flesh and bone
Left naught but hide and hair.

More meat, more meat
Young Henry, more meat you give to me
Go fell your goshawks King Henry
And bring them here to me.

And when he's slain his gay goshawks
It made his heart full sore
For she's eaten up both skin and bone
Left naught but feathers there.

Some drink some drink
Now Henry, some drink you give to me
Oh, sew you up your horse's hide
And bring a drink to me.

And up he's sewn the bloody hide
And a pipe of wine put in

And she drank it up, all in one draught
Left never a drop there in.

A bed, a bed, young Henry
A bed you'll make for me
Oh, you must pull the heather green
And make it soft for me.

And pulled has he the heather green
And made for her a bed
And taken has he his gay mantle
And over it has spread.

Take off your clothes young Henry
And lie down by my side
Now swear, now swear you, Henry
To take me for your bride.

Oh, God forbid, said Henry
That ever the like betide
That ever a fiend clumb up from hell
Would stretch out by my side.

Jane paused for a long moment, looked at each of us dramatically and then sang, even more slowly.

When the night was gone and the day was come
And the sun shown through the hall
The fairest lady that e'er was seen
Lay 'tween him and the wall.

I've met many a gentle knight, said she
That gave me such a fill
But never before was a courteous knight
Who gave me all my will.

Jane paused again, to salt home the effect; and then, eyes twinkling, she nodded at Johnny. "According to my Grandma Hicks, 'King Henry' is over three hundred years old. But the lesson is as fresh as morning milk. And if you're ever not sure what it is that we women want, just ask yon Stevie Robbins, and he'll explain it in terms you can understand."

Then Anna laughed her throaty laugh, and it was that sound, I realized, that I meant to protect. The mood, the tenor, the spontaneous happiness of just her laughing.

We left not long after. I kissed Jane on the cheek and thanked her for "King Henry." And as Anna shook my hand with high, mock-courtesy, she said, "I will see you early in the morning, Mr. Robbins, without fail?"

"Without fail." I bowed to her, which seemed the only natural thing to do.

We parted ways that evening on the porch at Rutland, young Johnny Rumbough and I, with one last question. One last question in what suddenly seemed a day full of questions. "Do you think that Siegfried Sonnach is a German...?"

"Saboteur?" I asked.

He nodded.

"I confess," I said, "I find it hard to believe that a spy could ever make his way out of a story book and into the streets of Hot Springs, North Carolina. But our Siegfried is not the clown that he appears to be. He may well be dangerous, and that's why all I want you to do is watch. Watch and listen and smile and keep King James with you at all times."

"But he's your—"

"Oh, I know he's my dog. Or says he is. But I don't want to take him on the train tomorrow. And I'd feel better if there was somebody here to take care of him." And even better if he's here to take care of you, I thought. I was rubbing the King's head as I said what I said and thought what I thought, and I could have sworn he understood both. He licked my face full in the mouth and then looked expectantly at Johnny.

When the screen door had slammed behind the two of them, I turned and sat down on the steps, expecting Prince to come outside to have his say. Which he did, sitting down heavily beside me and leaning back against the railing.

"What did you mean earlier today when you said you had your own plans for Roy?" I spoke low so as not to be heard in the house.

"I mean for every Negro in Hot Springs to be watching for the man morning, noon, and night. Especially at night. And if he's still out there, we'll find him. You know why we'll find him?"

"'Cause you see better in the dark?"

"Kiss my brown ass. 'Cause we're used to seeing without being seen. 'Cause we're used to knowin' what the white man's up to without him ever even suspectin' we're alongside him."

"What you gonna do with him if you find him?"

He leaned over to pat my shoulder. "We're gonna box that bastard up and save him for you," he rumbled. "'Cause *you* the Inspector General."

CHAPTER FIFTEEN

IF our previous journey to Asheville had seemed unconventional, the journey that Anna and I made to Barnard, where I intended to turn her over to my uncle, was truly out-of-place, out-of-time.

The brief train trip upstream to Barnard was unusually quiet for the two of us. She went through the box of glass plates that she had brought, touching each tentatively by the edges through its dark paper wrapping, pulling out and showing me one that was cracked. I opened our window and tossed the faulty sheet of glass against the rock bluff that was streaming past, where it exploded into shards of light.

My Uncle Walter met us with the mule-drawn wagon that I had promised Anna, and the look on her face told me that she'd assumed I was joking when I mentioned it to her. Walter was going to take Anna up to my mother's and return her in a week, hopefully with a crate full of exposed glass plates. After I had made the introductions—Walter removing his hat and bowing his head in antique fashion—the three of us loaded Anna's camera and her other baggage into the wagon. Walter went into the store for a twist of chewing tobacco, giving Anna and me a last moment.

She watched as I walked around to the mule's head and let the creature look at me. She, the mule, was perhaps fifteen hands high. Leggy but well-fed. And as with so many mules, she had that deep, inquisitive gaze in her wet, chocolate eyes. She kept flicking her ears forward to me as I spoke to her and backward to keep track of Anna.

"Walk around to her head," I said, "so she can see you. Let her sniff your hand."

169

"What's its name?" Anna asked as she stepped tentatively around the mule's head.

"*Her* name is Janey ... according to Walter. And she could probably take you straight to Walter's barn if you sat on the seat and asked her nicely."

Janey was lipping my fingers experimentally to see if she liked the taste, and I knew that in a minute she'd start on my coat sleeve. Anna patted her neck tentatively.

"I believe she's satisfied with you," I said. "You can climb on now."

I gave her a long hug, more than a week's worth by most counts, and helped her up onto the wagon seat. While we waited on Walter, I told her how, when I was a boy, my mother had sent me down the other side of the mountain to Hot Springs, down Puncheon Camp Branch to sell a basket of eggs at the hotel. She'd sent me on a mule, like the one that was to take her up home, intending me to be back before dark, and the mule had put his foot wrong on a steep bank and thrown me. I had the basket on the crook of my arm and when I was thrown had managed to break every single egg with my elbow except one.

"What did you do with the one that was left?" she asked.

"Threw it at the mule," I admitted.

She waved as the wagon rocked and creaked across the bridge, and I was left to myself while I waited for the return train. As I dozed in the sun, I half dreamed, half imagined what she would see when she first crested the ridge and looked down into Anderson Cove. Down into the seven hundred acre ocean of home, blue green and rusty brown in the slant afternoon light.

I had not been home in almost ten years. The Mountain Park was my excuse for not visiting, but in reality, I didn't know that I would be welcome outside the bonds of my mother and sisters.

I hadn't been home, but I could see Anderson Cove as clear as midday in my mind. Most of the dozen cabins and houses would still show a trace of dinner time smoke at the chimneys. The fields would be a wrinkled patchwork of color—greens, tans and speckled browns—with the lazy curves of Anderson Branch snaking down the middle of the valley. The largest structures Anna would see would be the barns, larger even than the mill; in my mind, I counted the three large horse and cattle barns that I remembered. She would see herds of beef cattle and sheep but wouldn't see the half-dozen brands of people, interlaced and interrelated: Caldwells, Waldrups, Worleys, some few Fortners and Buckners, a very few Robbinses, as well as the Andersons from whom the valley took its name. Anderson—my mother's maiden name.

And across the valley, she would see the slight rise where my father was buried. The wind overhead and a raven circling in the high breeze.

It was late afternoon when I arrived back at the depot, but Johnny Rumbough was standing expectantly, watching the passenger cars to see who emerged. When he saw me step down, he rushed down the platform, his breath whistling in his throat. Even then, his boarding school manners didn't desert him, and he paused to say good afternoon before grabbing my arm to rush me down the steps.

I made him slow down long enough to tell me there was an emergency. That I was needed at the Mountain Park, that he was sure all hell was about to break loose, that John Sanders and Prince Garner were both on their way to the Park to meet me, that thank God I was back. As we walked the hundred yards down Bridge Street toward the Camp A gatehouse, I made Johnny talk even more slowly as he began explaining.

"He's gone," he kept saying over and over while I tried to interrupt him. "He's gone."

Finally I grabbed him by the shoulders to shut him up. "Who? Who's gone?"

"Siegfried. Siegfried is gone."

"You mean he's escaped?"

"No. Well, maybe. I don't know. He was gone at morning roll call and we haven't found him yet."

"Are the Germans in Camp A or Camp B? Never mind, I can see for myself." For we had just walked up the incline to the railroad tracks, and I could see over into the camps. Camp B, the sailor's camp, was deserted, and the Mountain Park and its grounds were full of men involved in every kind of activity available to them.

I stifled the urge to run; I didn't want to give away just how disturbing was the thought of Siegfried coming and going as he pleased. "Where are Cap'n John and Prince?" I asked Johnny.

"They're up at the Mountain Park in the office. We're supposed to meet them ..."

They were there, standing at the counter in the outer office of the Park, these men who each day were becoming my brothers. John Sanders, his cold pipe clenched between his teeth. Prince Garner, his portly form and bandit's smile. Even the dog, standing at the ready, his tail barely wagging, his eyes—the most intelligent in the room—watching my face.

"Is Siegfried still missing?"

"Oh yes," John said.

One of the censors who worked in the inner office, a young Dorland teacher from Burnsville, wandered out of the inner office, took one look at my face and retreated back inside.

"Then listen to me. Johnny, take King James and walk the Camp A fence starting out at the corner closest to town. Every few yards, shake the wire down along the ground to make sure it hasn't been cut somewhere. Especially at the posts. It wouldn't take much to cut a piece loose to fold back and then hook it back over a nail so nobody'd notice."

He started out of the room.

"Oh, and start by working your way along the railroad tracks first; most of that stretch is in the trees."

He started out again.

"And for God's sake, if you find the place he's going in and out, just leave it be and come get us. I want to see the ground."

Johnny looked blank.

"Tracks and such," Cap'n John explained. "The boss is a hunter."

The boy nodded and was gone.

"What are we gonna do?" Prince asked. "Other than pray?"

"We're going to turn Siegfried Sonnach's room inside out. Best chance we'll have."

There were luxury suites in the Mountain Park, several in fact along the outside of the west wing on both the second and third floors, but those had been reserved for the senior officers. Originally, Siegfried had been given a standard guest room on the second floor, to be shared with a roommate. But once he'd made his case as a translator, we'd agreed to move him into a smaller, single room next to Hans Ruser's suite. We'd agreed in part because he'd argued that he would be a constant help to the Commodore in dealing with us Americans. It struck

me, however, as we climbed the stairs to the second floor, that once
he'd settled into his new quarters, he'd had almost nothing to do with
Ruser or Ruser with him.

Our first shock was that when John turned the handle of Siegfried's
room to open the door and walk in, he ran the bowl of his pipe into
solid wood and nearly skewered his head. "What the hell?" he muttered, rattling the door.

"Door has a lock, John," Prince said, trying to hide his grin.

"Yeah, but where the hell did Siegfried get a key?" I was too concerned to laugh at the blood on Sanders' lip.

John pulled the master set of keys I'd given him out of a deep pocket and tried several before he found one that worked.

The room had been part of a set of servants' quarters before the war,
and it was the plainest of rooms. A single, narrow bed under the window. A washstand with a battered metal bowl. A scarred chest of drawers
against the left-hand wall. And on the right, a closed door that I knew
led into a small water closet, containing a toilet and a miniature sink.
Two simple chairs with woven seats faced the bed as though three or
four men might have sat together talking, their heads close together.

After a moment's consultation, I put John to work on the chest of
drawers, Prince on the bed, and I started in the water closet. "We're
going to put it back," I warned them. "Just as close as we possibly can.
We may not want him to know we've been here."

There was nothing in the bathroom except a packet of the rough
brown paper we gave the Germans for simple sanitation. And two
surprisingly thick towels with the hotel's monogram—something he
could only have found by plundering through the locked closets on the
first floor where they'd been stored for the duration.

John was the first to strike pay dirt. In the bottom drawer of Siegfried's chest under his meager clothes, he found three mason jars of
homemade white liquor and five boxes of cigars. The ornate labels on
the boxes proclaimed them to be the property of Commodore Hans
Ruser of *Vaterland*. Ruser had either given Siegfried this treasure trove
or he had stolen them, and I was sure I knew which. The jars of liquor, however, puzzled me for a moment until I remembered Cousin
Roy Robbins, famous for busting stills and confiscating liquor all over
Madison County.

Prince paused from his careful examination of Siegfried's bed long enough to open one jar and dip in a finger. "Bobby Shelton made this," he said after a thoughtful pause and a second dip of his finger. "I'd know it anywhere."

"Bobby Shelton ain't selling his wares to no German," John commented.

I glanced at John. "Roy gave it to him."

"Roy *Robbins*?"

I nodded.

"I was afraid you'd say that," he said and began to put the cigars and liquor back where he'd found them.

As he worked, I watched Prince fish around inside the bedraggled mattress on Siegfried's bed. He found a slit on the side next to the wall that was only held together by a few pins. After a minute of running his hand inside the mattress itself, he handed me a sheaf of letters, some handwritten, some typed, all in German. I ran my eye down each of the mystifying pages in turn, and the only thing that emerged was the name of Hans Ruser. Even though they all seemed to be addressed to "Herr Sonnach," Ruser's name appeared again and again. "We'll need Johnny," I said, "before we can put these back."

When we were almost done, I sent John Sanders to find Johnny and had Prince pull the chest out from the wall and search behind it. While he did, I ran my fingers along all the woodwork, the door frames and the molding at the bottom of the walls. Stuffed behind the molding over the door into the hallway, I found one last sheet of paper, folded into a thin strip and slipped into a crack that felt as if it had been widened with a knife.

I stepped into the better light close to the window and unfolded the piece of paper, a full sheet torn from a lined pad, obviously something that Siegfried had meant to save.

It was a letter with no salutation and no signature. A brief note written in pencil in more-or-less straight block letters.

I have talk to the owner. He does not care about Russer. Go ahead with yur plan. And kep in mind that if something happens to S. Robbins along with Russer, it is better for us. We will fix it for you after.

"What does that mean?" Prince asked. He was reading over my shoulder.

"Means Roy should've stayed in school past the fifth grade," I said.

"Not that. I mean the part about *if something happens to ... along with Ruser?*"

"Means that Siegfried has permission to take care of me along the way."

"Bastard! Why would he keep such a thing?"

"'Cause he's smart enough to think he might need some protection from Roy after he kills Ruser."

In the end, Johnny's sketchy reading of the letters we'd found in Siegfried's mattress only confirmed what we'd already learned. Correspondents in Germany found Ruser's happy holiday in the mountains an insult to the Kaiser. And the typed sheets, unsigned except with a set of initials, made it clear that if something were to happen to Ruser, other officers in the camp might then help the German war effort by leading escapes into the American countryside thereby keeping American troops at home.

While we'd been searching Siegfried's room, King James had led Johnny Rumbough to Siegfried's own, homemade gate, secreted away as was so much of his life, under our very noses. Johnny took me to a spot in the trees below Rutland, halfway between the open and public corner of the fence near the depot and the wagon gate behind the Park. It was one of the few places close to town where the fence was hidden from view in a thick stand of hemlocks. It was dark green and cool inside the aromatic shadow of the trees, and I could see the faint trail in the needles where someone—I had to believe Siegfried—had snuck under the low boughs of the trees and out of sight. Looking through the fence in the dim light, I could also see where someone had placed a line of flat stones across Spring Creek so that with care you could run or walk across without getting wet.

As we crept up to the section of the fence where Johnny had left the wire pulled back, I reached out to stop him. "Hold the King's collar," I said and give me a few minutes just to look." And then I did what perhaps I do best: stop and breathe deeply, letting my mind go blank, so I would see what was actually there rather than what I wanted or expected. Years of hunting had taught me to stop dead still when my heart was pounding.

I knelt in the hemlock needles a foot back from the hole in the wire. When I leaned close to the ground, the rich smell of black dirt and rotting needles washed over my face. Just under the fence and on either side, traffic had worn away the leaves and needles to a layer of deep, loamy soil. There were parts of foot prints blended with scuffle marks and even what looked like three evenly spaced small holes where someone had poked his fingers into the dirt to steady himself as he ducked through the wire.

"Regular highway, ain't it?" Johnny whispered.

"*Isn't* it," I corrected him, my nose three or four inches from the ground. "You ain't old enough to abuse the language."

"I'm old enough to have found this."

"When you found it, did you give in to the temptation to duck through it?"

"No, but I wanted to."

I stood up with a grunt and peered through to the other side. The one thing that still bothered me was there. Along the creek bank were the clear prints of at least two men. One wearing slick-soled brogans, perhaps, and the other a set of worn-down dress shoes, the heels almost non-existent. Roy and Siegfried, seemed to me, even though I didn't want to trip over the wrong assumption. But mixed in with both was a smaller set of footprints, and those were barefooted. A child or a small woman. The fact that the feet were bare this late in the year said that it was a child, but still, there was Roy's nasty way with women.

"What do you see?" Johnny whispered.

I pointed. "Two men," I said. "One of whom goes in and out regularly. A child or a small woman. Probably a child, who is probably a messenger of some kind, or maybe a guide to lead the man from inside the fence somewhere. And then, last of all, Siegfried's back home."

"What?"

"Look just inside the wire. There's one print on top of the others. Set deep at the toes where he's leaning to come under the wire. Which way's it pointing?"

"In?"

I nodded. Come home to kill Ruser, I thought, or me. "Run get the

guard from the wagon gate," I said. "No, wait, don't go out into the
open. Cut through the trees by the wire and bring him back the same
way. Leave King James with me."

And he was off, all but laughing, thinking no doubt that chasing
spies and prisoners around beat hell out of going to school. What he
didn't know was just how ugly this was all going to be.

In a few minutes, he brought back James Goforth.

"You a deer hunter at all, Jamie?" I asked him.

He nodded, as taciturn as ever.

"Show him," I said to Johnny, who then pointed out the slit in the
wire, and the multitude of tracks between the fence and Spring Creek.

"You want to get paid some overtime?" I asked Goforth.

He nodded and almost smiled.

"Your pistol loaded?"

He pulled several shells out of his pocket and exhibited them in the
palm of one calloused hand.

"Where would you watch this spot from if you didn't want anybody to know you were here?" Any deer hunter would give the obvious answer.

Which he did by looking up into the thick tangle of branches over
our heads. He pointed to a thick limb to one side of the fence post,
shielded from the far side of the creek and the Park but with a clear
view of the wire.

"That'll do," I said. "I just want you to watch the other side, and if
somebody from over there wants to come in, let 'em go right on by. But
don't let anybody slip out, even in the middle of the night."

"What's the bullets for?"

"In case somebody from inside wants out enough to fight you."

He put the bullets back in his pocket and nodded. I stopped him
when he turned toward the tree however.

"One other thing, Jamie ... if the sheriff shows up, you let him be.
Don't even let him see you."

"He gonna be a goin' in or a goin' out?"

"Who the hell knows?"

At that point, I had Johnny find John Sanders and Prince and bring
them up to 305-306. Served them out apple brandy from an earth-
enware jug, which made Prince a happy man though John ignored

his cup and Johnny could only sip. I let Johnny tell them about the fence, as my mind was still racing, ranging in tighter and tighter circles around what had to be the only logical conclusion.

After Johnny was done, and all three looked to me for the next step, I served it up for them. "I think Siegfried will show back up at evening roll call. And if anybody calls him on it, he'll just claim he was here all along, and we just missed him this morning. Then, if we seem satisfied, Siegfried and probably one or two others are going to try to kill Hans Ruser, probably tonight."

"Why tonight?" John asked.

"I think night is their only real chance. And given all the going in and out, along with the fact that I'm now back to bear the blame for it, I think they'll try tonight and not run the risk of waiting."

"I'm too damn old for this," Prince said reflectively. "You know that, don't you?"

"Too old or too fat?"

"Both."

"What do we do next?" John asked, ever the practical one. "Why don't we just grab Sonnach at roll call and throw him in the gaol? Hell with him."

I thought of the young, saber-scarred officer I'd heard criticizing Ruser. "Because he has accomplices."

"Who?"

"Friends. The young wolves who are dying to go to war and are stuck here in this backwater while their friends are getting blown up all over Europe. We grab Siegfried, who may be the only sensible one, and God knows what they'll try."

"So what do we do?"

"I hate to say it, but Siegfried is probably back inside the wire and watching us. We need to act as ignorant as possible."

Prince nodded. "Should be easy."

"I'm going to stroll down to New Heidelberg to visit with Ruser. I'm going to invite him to use my rooms for tonight, so that we can set a little trap in his. John, you find yourself the quietest man you've got so that tonight the two of you can watch Siegfried's door."

"And if he comes out?"

"If he goes anywhere other than into Ruser's room, follow him. See where he goes, what he does. Give him enough rope to hang himself, but if he starts to leave the Park, grab him before his hand turns the door knob."

"What about me?" Johnny asked.

"You're going to visit your sister Dora."

"What!"

"You're going to sit in the parlor at Rutland with Dora and King James."

"But...!"

"You heard me. Go on; you can pout later."

As I walked down from the back of the Mountain Park into the fairy tale village of New Heidelberg, it was as if none of what we suspected could possibly be true. Julius Christopher's dog, now attached to me, was free in the autumn air: chasing leaves, running ahead to drink from the swimming pool, sniffing at a pet cat one of the Germans had installed in his chalet. The air was as crisp and clean as air could be, dyeing the last leaves on the trees the deep rust and gold of old fall. Why, I kept thinking, when the world is this beautiful? Why had I not gone to Anderson Cove with her? I could be there with her now. Rolled up against her in a feather bed, listening to the cry of a screech owl hunting mice in the barnyard. And here I was, ignoring my own wide world, so I could try to save one German sailor from murdering another in his sleep.

The Commodore served me tea. We sat in two strong, ingeniously made chairs, constructed by seamen out of driftwood and rope, and drank strong, black German tea. And as I talked, he listened quietly, stroking his carefully trimmed white beard.

"Of course," he said finally in his slow, careful English. "Siegfried Sonnach is an agent provocateur. And I would imagine, although we are not informed of this, an officer in the German navy. If he has orders to destroy me, he would not hesitate."

"If you don't mind my saying so, Commodore, you don't seem very upset."

Ruser shrugged. "Germany is a complex land, Stephen, with a long, harsh history. I have not spent much time in the Fatherland these last forty years, and I am not surprised to be considered expendable. The other thing that you should know is that if you do not catch up little Siegfried tonight, then I will have him killed tomorrow." He must have seen the look on my face, but he only shrugged again. "It will happen so quickly and quietly, that you will only have his body to deal with. His body and perhaps one or two of the others."

So complete was his composure that I found myself both unsettled and reassured at the same time. "Is there anything that we can do to make you more comfortable during your stay in my quarters?" I finally asked.

He chuckled. "Could you arrange for my wife to spend the night with me there, Stephen?"

"Your wife! I didn't know she was in Hot Springs."

"Oh, no. She is in a small cottage in New York. Brooklyn, New York. She came to me when *Vaterland* was impounded, and it was in our house there that the authorities eventually came to arrest me."

"What is her name?"

"Sophia. She is Italian. ... Haven't you ever been in love, Stephen?" I confess that I blushed.

"And is our current trouble keeping you from the woman you love, your Anna?... I have seen you together walking."

"I'd be with her now," I said, "if it weren't for our current troubles."

"Then we are both prisoners, aren't we. I am seventy-three years old, Stephen, and I had forgotten what physical passion is for these many years. So many years spent alone and on the ocean. But I have not seen Sophia since your army came and took me away in the spring. Since then, I have dreams of her that cause me to ... wonder. Do you dream of your Anna, Stephen, that we take you away from her?"

"I find myself dreaming of her even as I walk across the yard from the hotel to your little house. The wind makes me dream of her. The light as the sun sets."

"Again, we are brothers." He stood. "Even though I am much the older brother. And we must agree that we will live through this darkness, so we may sleep once again with Sophia and Anna."

And so it was that Siegfried reappeared at evening roll call. Fresh and rosy and joking with the guards as well as the other prisoners. So it was that he waved to me across the lawn, as one would a long-lost friend. And so it was that when Siegfried was safely in his room, Commodore Hans Ruser and his lieutenant, an elderly officer who spoke no English, were led quietly up to 305-306, and Prince Garner and I slipped into Ruser's room. Prince took his station in a chair behind the door of Ruser's bedroom, and I lay down in his bed. Beside me I cradled the goose gun, the eight-gauge shotgun that had been my favorite bargaining tool with drovers for a dozen summers, the same gun with which I had shot down Nathan Robbins in the Mountain Park dining room years before. Jack Rumbough first called it the goose gun because it was a relic from the days of turn-of-the-century wildfowl shooting on the river.

"Why do you get the bed, and I have to sit up in this damn chair?" Prince's stage whisper sounded like a muffled drum, deep and resonant.

"So if somebody gets shot, it won't be you," I said, trying to find a comfortable niche on the hard mattress. "Besides, if you lie down, you'll fall sound asleep."

"You ain't keeping me awake just by denying me the bed." I could hear his chair groan as he leaned it back against the wall.

"Rest your eyes then. But for God's sake, don't snore."

His breathing was already regular, almost deep enough for sleep before he spoke again. "Since it's just you and me, Stevie, will you answer me one question?"

"Just one?"

"Are you in love with this woman?"

"Who?"

"Who, my ass. ... *Who* Ann Ulmann."

"Anna. *Anna* Ulmann."

"Yeah, well." His chair creaked again as his big frame shifted. "Is you or ain't you?"

"Why does everybody keep saying that? How am I supposed to know?"

"You're too old to be as stupid as you act, Stevie. Damn near as old as me. So try this on—some Kaiser-quotin' maniac with sword cuts all over his face shoots you tonight, who you gonna be thinkin' about afore you die?"

"Woodrow Wilson?"

He grinned. I could tell even in the dark. "You got a Woodrow all right. Between your legs. And I say it's because of this ... what's her name again?"

"Who?"

"Ann, Anna. I say you're in love with her."

I rolled over, trying to get comfortable where I could face the door. "I will admit this much. I'm lying here cold sober. That sip of brandy this afternoon was the first hard drink I've had in weeks. Cold sober and I don't want to die. First time in years and years that I don't care to die."

"Well, maybe you're not so stupid after all. But what's angel Anna gonna do if you up and shoot somebody tonight? You think she could stand Roy haulin' your ass off to jail."

"I hope so."

"But what if she can't? What if the sight of you with a shotgun in your hands scares her to death and she runs back to the big city with her tail between her legs?"

"Then I'd be back to ..."

"Back to what?"

"Back to the way it was before."

"Well, ... shit on that. If it comes down to it, Stevie ..."

"Yeah."

"If it comes down to it, you best let me shoot 'em. I got my old army pistol right here in my coat pocket."

"That's awful sweet, brother, but you're a man of God. You're not supposed to shoot people."

"Hell you say. You remember the Spanish-American War?"

I sat up in Ruser's bed to look at Prince. "You fought in the Spanish-American War?"

"No, but I was in the army. I didn't get to go 'cause they had me in the stockade."

Prince dozed for a while and then stood beside his chair to stretch out his legs and back while I dozed for a few moments. We waited for hours upon hours. And then, just as I had begun to give up entirely, we heard the door leading to the hallway creak open.

We held our breaths. Prince crouched behind the half-open door, and I froze, lying on my side with the covers pulled up to my neck.

My back was cramping, the bug bite on my ankle was itching like fire, but I was afraid to so much as move, let alone try to breathe like I was asleep. "Let them come all the way in," I murmured to myself, mouthing the words I'd repeated over and over to Prince. "Let them come all the way in before you slam the door." The blood thundered in my ears.

Then, time bent fluidly into a faster tempo. The door eased open, shielding Prince from view, and two silent forms ghosted into the room: the first carried a pillow from the empty bed in the front room, the second floated up to stand soundlessly beside him. Before I had a chance to even frame the thought, Prince slammed shut the door so loudly that the window behind me shivered in its frame.

All noise.

Prince shouting like a band of angels as he pistol whips the man closest to him. The other form leaps at me with a wavering scream, his arm rising up above his head and slamming down at me. Thinking for the briefest moment that he is trying to hit me and drawing back just as I'm hearing the thunk of a heavy knife driving into the mattress beside me, pinning me under the covers. Twisting around and firing off the goose gun, shooting at him through the blanket. Somehow pushing up to my knees and swinging the gun at his reeling form. The satisfying crunch of the barrel cracking into the side of his head. Gasping breath.

He was down, my attacker, and I stepped on him as I moved forward toward Prince, who was lighting the lamp on Ruser's table. Adjusting the wick so that the sudden light grew strong and stable. "Mine had a knife too," he whispered. "I kicked it under the bed." His man was lying on his face where he'd fallen, groaning.

"Roll him over," I said suddenly. "Let's talk to the bastard."

Prince rolled his man over, and there was his familiar face. Long, thin, saber-scarred: the angry, young officer from the dining room. I kicked him in the ribs. "See this," I shouted at the man, waving the shotgun in front of him and then shoving the end of the barrel hard against his chest. "Who else is involved?"

"*Nein*," he whispered. "No *Eng-leesh. Nein!*"

"Put your foot on his chest," I said to Prince. And then shoved the barrel of the shotgun squarely between his thighs, hard so it would hurt him and so he could feel the hot barrel against his privates. "Who the hell put you up to this?" I hissed. His eyes swelled white and glassy, and sweat poured off his face. He shook his head furiously from side to side, banging it against the floor. I shoved the barrel even harder against his groin and fired off the second barrel into the floor. "Siegfried! Siegfried! Siegfried!" he screamed, and fainted, certain he'd been shot to pieces.

The next few hours happened, as I meant them to, very quickly. Siegfried had sprinted out of his room at the first sound of gunfire. John and one of the Gaither boys had tackled him in the hallway. Just like the football the Germans had been practicing, according to John. I had them gag him and take him straight to the gaol in Camp B. Neither of our assassins was badly hurt: merely bruised, bloody, humiliated, and one had to change his pants. I put them in the charge of Robert Snyder and the most sadistic guard we had, loading all four on the morning train south to Fort Oglethorpe, Georgia and a much tougher camp run by a regular army brigadier.

When the train was pulling away, Prince laid his meat-heavy hand on my shoulder. "I think you should come on up to Rutland for supper next week. Bring Miss Ann."

"What day of the week is it? I asked absently. "It's Anna."

"It's Friday, October the somethin' or other. You need me to tell you the year?"

"No, but I would like to come up to Rutland for supper. Anna damn it is her name and she'll be back next week. Maybe for one night out of all this spinning nightmare, we can sit down and not think ..."

"Not think about what, hoss?"

"Death and dying," I said.

CHAPTER SIXTEEN

I visited Siegfried the next morning, and by then I knew what day it was. It was October the 24th, 1917.

After I had thanked damn near everybody I could think of to thank. After I had given myself time to regain my sense of balance and of reason. Even then, when I came to Bridge Street and the camp gates, intending to walk across the road to the gaol that we'd built for just such an eventuality, even then I wasn't sure just what to do with him.

I knew that if we put him on a train to Fort Oglethorpe like the others that he'd escape before he ever got to the Georgia line. I knew that if we tried to keep him behind bars for long, that he'd either win over his guards or, even worse, Roy would find him. To release him or kill him, who knew? I did know that somehow he was mine—thing of glittering darkness though he was—and that somehow I had to figure out how to dispose of him.

As Gehagen let me out through the gate of Camp A, I suddenly turned on him. "Foster," I called out directly into his shocked face.

"I ain't Foster," he said, shrinking from me.

"No, you're Andy. But don't you have a brother named Foster?"

"Yeah," he said sullenly. "He's the deaf 'un."

"Didn't we give him a job?"

"Yeah, but it won't the smartest thing you ever done. He's stone deaf I tell you."

"Where's his station?"

"Up by the kitchen and the barn where he can't get in no trouble. He can't take on no important job like me." The man actually swelled as he patted his chest.

"Is he on duty today? Up by the kitchen?"

Andy Gehagen nodded.

I patted him on the back as he let me out the gate. "You do have an important task here, Andy. Guardian of the Gate."

"Damn right. And don't you forget it, neither."

"Don't worry."

That morning, Cap'n John had posted two guards at the gaol, one to warn off the other Germans, curious beyond curious to know who we'd jailed and why. Inside, there was one lone man, playing solitaire on a rough-hewn table. I told him to lock me in the cell with Siegfried and to go fetch Foster Gehagen. "Bring him back here with you," I said. "And note his station because you're going to keep it for the rest of the day."

"Foster's kinda deaf, boss."

"He's more than kind of deaf," I said kindly back to him, for he'd meant what he'd said kindly. "That's why he's perfect for this job."

"You be all right in there with that man? He's been singing and talking most of the night."

I pulled the long, heavy hunting knife out of my coat pocket to show him, the knife that had very nearly been stabbed into my stomach rather than Ruser's mattress.

"You aim to cut him with that?" He was clearly intrigued by the idea.

"No, but I aim to be right here when you get back, ready to be let out again."

There was a chair for me inside the cell: an old patched up dining room chair from the Mountain Park. There was also enough sunlight through the barred window to show me his form resting on the cot. Siegfried was lying down, but he sat up in his bunk as soon as he heard the bolt being drawn on the door. Sat up and leaned back against the wall when I came in. I don't know why I thought I would catch him off guard by visiting him in his cell. Certainly, I had never seen him speechless before and he wasn't speechless then.

"Stephen, my brother, it is such a joy to see you. I cannot believe that you have allowed them to keep me in this place, but now that you see what it is here, I am certain that you will—"

I held up my hand to silence him. "I'm the one who put you here, Siegfried."

"Oh, but there has been a mistake then. And you've come to set it right. By what rights, dear Stephen, would you choose to do such a thing? I am certain that the Hague Convention forbids the use of solitude to ..." I held up my hand again for silence, but this time he chose to ignore me. "To punish poor unfortunate prisoners, men who—"

I picked up the metal chamber pot that sat beside the door and flung it at him. Unfortunately, it was empty, but it still made an impressive *CLANG* when it hit the wall beside his head, crumpled slightly and fell onto the cot beside him.

"The Hague Convention does expressly forbid solitary confinement except for punishments of an extreme nature. And *you*, Siegfried, you qualify. By the rights invested in me by this ..." And I leaned forward to hold up the hunting knife that had almost done me in. "I was waiting in Commodore Ruser's room when your two assassins came to kill him, one of whom named you as their leader. By the contraband letters in your mattress. For the life of me I can't figure out why I don't just turn you back out and let Ruser have you."

"He would kill me."

"Exactly," I said quietly.

I could hear sounds from the outer room, the return of my two guards, one of whom would be able to hear us if we continued to shout at each other.

"Dear Stephen," Siegfried's tone was soothing, almost hypnotic. "I only wanted to remind my German brothers that they are men. Hans Ruser is a tired, old man, a relic from another age. This is a young man's century and a young man's war. And certainly, I never dreamed you would manage to get into harm's way. Someone as valuable, as ..."

As his voice droned quietly, inevitably on, it suddenly occurred to me exactly what Siegfried Sonnach was. A serpent. He was a copperhead just after it has shed last year's skin, and the sun gleaming off its new head and body with an eerie golden beauty. And like a copperhead in spring, you know full well you should kill it for it has a head swollen with poison. You should cut off that head, but its beauty is hypnotic.

"If I had any sense at all, Siegfried," I interrupted the spinning, winding flow of his voice. "If I had any sense, I would kill you tonight and bury you under the Mountain Park. I have a feeling the world would be a much safer place, especially for me."

He did pause for a moment. "Oh, but my brother. There are two reasons why you cannot simply cut my throat. First, I know you and you do not have the necessary evil. Your outside is hard, but you will not kill me unless I force you to, and after today, I will be careful not to force you."

"Assuming you're right. Assuming I'm soft in the middle, what's the second reason?"

"If something were to happen to me, the High Sheriff of this place will come to find me. He will come to make certain that I was not abused or, how do you say, done away with."

"I saw the letter he wrote you," I replied.

"Letter?"

"Stuffed into the crack in your door frame. He was giving you permission to do away with me."

He studied me carefully to see just how much I might know. To see just how far he could trust my ignorance.

"Here's what *you* don't know, *Herr* Sonnach," I said in the face of his questioning stare. "I've known Roy Robbins since he was six years old. He is a nocturnal creature, doing his business after dark in the back roads of this county. He would never even bother to dig up your body, let alone investigate your death. He only cares about what he's paid to care about and the next woman he can find to prey on."

"He is sworn to—"

"Don't even say it! You are a fool, Siegfried. You are the only person alive who could tie him to what you just tried to do. And as of this morning, you are caught in a thick web. Roy will come for you sooner or later, and whatever he does to you will be worse than Hans Ruser could even imagine." I stood to go. "Why should I even bother to protect you?"

"Because," he said, with a curious, twisting smile. "Because he hates you more than he hates me."

I turned to look back at him, even with my hand on the door.

"Because you shot his brother dead many years ago. He only wants to use me; he wants to destroy you."

"He tell you that?"

"Not in just these words, no. He has not so many words. But everything he does says it. I think, dear Stephen, that you and I had better protect each other. And besides, to protect me is to do your duty, and you always do your duty, I think." He shrugged. "Just like me."

I rattled the door, the signal that I wanted to be let out. "You better hope you're right," I said to him. "For your own sake, you better hope you're right."

I left Foster Gehagen in charge of the gaol. Wrote out on a piece of paper just how I wanted him to treat Siegfried. He could eat, he could exercise, but under no circumstances did I want him talking to anyone. His talking was as dangerous a thing as I could imagine, its own kind of weapon.

When the sleepy guard let me out of the gate, I hesitated. Walked halfway across Bridge Street toward the Camp A gatehouse, the gate that would take me back to the Mountain Park, and perhaps, to rest.

When I stopped in the middle of the road, I experienced a sudden rush, an overwhelming sense of what I had felt so often as a child and young man. Simply, it was the pull of the long road. I felt that I could walk fifty yards to the skeleton of Robert Snyder's half-finished bridge, cross the thin ribbon of steel girders and onto the Turnpike. Then north or south, simply turn suddenly and instinctively one way or the other and be gone by morning. Disappear completely out of the lives of the Germans and of the people in Hot Springs whose destinies were knitted into mine. Perhaps leaving a torn place in the fabric of their lives, perhaps not.

I could catch a ride in an old mule-drawn market cart and be in Knoxville in a day. Nashville, Jackson, New Orleans. Be on a ship to South America in a week, where the birds were such that I had never seen nor could imagine.

I, who had never even seen the ocean, felt the pull of the tide.

I stood in the middle of the high crown of that twisty, worn gravel strip we called a street, and the dirty road seemed to rush past me like waist-deep, muddy water, fast, pulling me uncontrollably in its current, away and away.

And it felt like a choice: between life known and unknown, seen and unseen. My stomach ached and my heart swelled in my chest, so that I thought it must surely choke me.

And I knew, I *knew* what heart sickness had so invaded my chest, what kept me anchored there against the pull of the current. It was simple enough; I loved her. She had seen and felt the core of me, run her hands through the inside of me. She had tasted on my tongue the grief of my own dead child, had breathed in my sleeping breath all my hatred and fear. And still she didn't look away. Still her mind sought mine through the aperture of her eyes.

And knowing all she knew of me, she still loved. Though the words still tied up her tongue, she loved me. Free to flee, she stood still. Smiling even.

And I loved her. In light and sleepless dark, I would need the knowledge and knowing of her. Simply to keep on living.

Even with the ghost of her husband still to be dealt with, hovering fat and rich in the beyond of her mind. Even poised on the far side of some prison wire, half with me and half gone from me. Even so, I knew that if she remained just within and just beyond my reach for ten or fifty or a hundred years, I couldn't choose to stop loving her. There are connections beyond choice.

When I visited with the Commodore that afternoon in his New Heidelburg chalet, I refused his offer of tea and served him instead apple brandy, made by my friends the Ramseys. There was a sturdy little blaze in his meticulously constructed brick stove, and from a pot on top Ruser served King James a bowl of something that looked like mush but smelled like bacon. Whatever it was, the King happily lapped it up.

After we had sipped our brandy appreciatively for a few minutes, he said evenly, "So two are gone and one remains."

I nodded. "Two gone to Fort Oglethorpe, not gone from this world."

He chuckled. "I never thought you capable of executing them. You should have let me take care of that. ... But then perhaps you are saving young Sonnach for something especially gruesome."

It was my turn to laugh. "No, no. I'm saving Herr Sonnach because I don't yet know what to do with him. He is the dangerous one, I think."

Ruser nodded, sipping his brandy. And as he bent his face appreciatively over his cup, I could see etched there all his seventy-plus years.
The long journey that must have been his life, staring into a thousand
moons and a thousand suns.

"What is that ribbon, Commodore?" I asked, seeking for his sake
to change the subject. "The ribbon in your lapel?"

He touched with his forefinger the faded ribbon I referred to,
mostly gray now, descended from the black and white it must once
have been. He always seemed to wear it, so I thought it signified something he was proud of.

"It is, you might say, the order of the Fatherland. It is an honor,
with it came a medal for distinguished ..."

"Service?" I guessed.

"No," he smiled. "We Germans assume service. It is for bravery. The
medal is an iron cross, like the infamous ones in your war posters."

"How did you earn it?" I asked, hoping still to take him far away
from his cold mountain prison, if only in his memory.

"When I was a young man, Stephen, I was in the Imperial Navy.
This is a secret that I am telling you because I have never admitted it
to your authorities. A young officer struggling to find his advancement.
And during our war with France in 1871 I saved a man from drowning.
Simply because I was there blockaded in port and I could swim. It could
have been any man." He shrugged. "The sea makes no distinction between one and another, and I did not know until I had brought him up
to the boat that he was my enemy, my opponent in the service, another
young officer who also happened to be a prince of the royal family."

"But you were brave, nonetheless," I insisted, "whoever he was."

Ruser laughed, enjoying the brandy and the story. "If he had just
been a fool then I would not have my ribbon, but he was a prince as
well as a fool. And so I am rewarded." Again he paused, seeming to
reflect as he sipped, and again I was struck by his age, his frailty even.
"I wear it still, Stephen, to remind me that in those few moments, I
found myself truly to be a man. No matter who he was, I was the man
I wanted to be."

We sipped our brandy in quiet for a few more minutes, the stove's
warmth comfortable around us. He was savoring his memories, it
seemed to me, this fine, imperial old man, who the world would call a

prisoner, or worse, a Hun. King James was curled by the glowing stove, content as well, and courting sleep.

"If we lock the gates, Commodore, perhaps we may yet keep the war at bay."

He smiled. "I wish it were so," he said. "But I think we both know differently. War is what men do when they are afraid. War is what we do to mask the fear. And even here, in your little mountain valley, inside the beautiful village you have allowed us to build, even here there is fear."

"But—"

"My men fear your mountain people, the ones who stare through the wire with empty, hollow eyes. Your mountain people fear my men with our marching and singing. Even here, the fear is lurking, is it not?"

"Yes," I said. As it was all there was to say.

CHAPTER SEVENTEEN

THE night before she came back from Anderson Cove, I dreamed that I met Anna by moonlight, at the torn fence under the hemlocks.

Inside a fragrant church of hemlocks. And that I reached to her through the fence—and she to me. And we held our faces up to the same small tear in the mesh of wire and kissed passionately. Our lips ... our tongues ... in hemlock darkness, pressed into mutual being despite the metallic, dew-bright fence. I could taste the salt of her tongue pulsing against my lips and the passage of the spirit as it flowed back and forth between us. A spirit that was neither she nor I but both of us conspired.

Was it frustrating that still there was icy wire between us; was it a nightmare? Perhaps. But then who is to say whether it was even a dream?

I don't remember the morning of the following day, Halloween 1917, except that I met Anna at the station and walked her up to Sunnybank. Her dress was torn and dusty from her week up home, her shoes worn nearly off her feet. But her face was brown and full of life, and when I invited her to dinner at Rutland that night, how excited we both were at the simple thought of a meal together.

I don't remember the afternoon either. My memory again strikes a chord that evening as I sat on the rock wall above the driveway that curved up the hill to Rutland. Anna had asked me to meet her there so we could walk up to supper together.

And as my memory stirs, it recalls the spangles of sunlight filtered through the trees along Spring Creek and surprising warmth for an evening at the very end of October. It recalls a sense of a hot meal eagerly anticipated. A meal outside the fence, with people that I liked and even loved. There was, I'm sure, a few minutes of restlessness because Anna was later than the time she'd suggested, and King James was up and down the drive in his eternal squirrel games. Even a momentary shadow of fear, since Cousin Roy was a very real goblin and nowhere to be found.

But the shadow disappeared when I saw her walk quickly across the street below and hurry up the drive. Determined, intense, her slight dark form that already seemed so familiar. When she looked up and saw me, she slowed, and when I smiled, she laughed breathlessly. "I'm sorry I'm late. Did I worry you?" She called up to me.

"No," I lied. And held out to her two bottles of Spanish wine that I had saved since the summer season of 1916, rich and so deep in tone they were almost purple.

"Are we celebrating?" She stood below me in the driveway, looking up, full of spirit and expectation.

"We are."

"And what are we celebrating?"

"That we have survived. That the Mountain Park still stands. That of all moments out of the flood of time, we're here in this one."

She stepped forward and touched my knee with one tapping forefinger. I was sitting still on the rock wall and she standing on the side of the road below me.

"Are you sure you're all right? Prince Garner stopped by to see me this afternoon and told me just a little of what happened."

"Son-of-a—"

"No, he was very sweet. He wanted me to know that you'd almost been killed. He wanted me to understand."

"I'm sure he did. But I don't want him to scare you to death."

She stepped back and bowed her head, the very picture of stubbornness. "Listen to me," she said. Shaking her head from side to side. "The thing that finally destroyed any chance I had of a relationship with my husband—my husband the mighty Dr. Jurgens—was that he insisted on treating me like a child. Not a woman but a sick, frightened child. And the more he treated me that way, the more sick and scared I became." She looked up and hit me twice on the thigh with her fist. "And when you set about trying to protect me from the truth, I start to get scared. I start to feel like I'm living back in that castle on 62nd Street."

"What are you saying?" I whispered.

"I'm saying that you cannot make me go back there."

"I don't *want* you to go back there. Of all the things in this world, I—"

"Then treat me like a woman." Slowly her hand relaxed from a fist to fingers again. She rested it on my knee. "That's all," she said, much more softly. "Just treat me like a grown woman and don't try to hide all the scary things from me."

"Do you promise you won't leave?" I said suddenly. It was what I had sworn to myself I wouldn't say. But the words were out of my mouth like a breath, before I could stop them.

Even now, years later, I remember the raucous cries that interrupted the silence between us. A blue jay in the trees above was yelling at us, singing and whistling, even in the heart of the fall.

"Will you promise me that if I do, you'll come after me?"

"Yes," I said. "I would have to do that."

"Then it doesn't matter if I leave, does it?"

There was another long pause, as we both searched for strength. "He's mocking us," I said. I pointed up at the flashing blue wings, where the jay strutted from limb to limb. "For being so serious. For being so harsh on such a soft afternoon."

She looked up, searching in my face for some sign that only she might recognize.

"I won't ask you to promise," I whispered. "Not yet anyway."

She nodded and her lips curled ever-so-slightly into a soft, ironic, hopeful, playful, perhaps even faithful, smile. "Maybe not yet is all I need."

"Then we should celebrate. Just this day and no other." I handed her the bottles and jumped down to stand beside her. "A long time ago, an old mountain man wrote a very elegant argument that the world belongs to the living. That we must make our own laws new and live complete to this day. I think we should take his advice."

"And who might that old mountain man be?"

"He was a tall, red-headed mountain man named Jefferson. And if he were alive today, he would say that we shouldn't waste time fearing what might happen."

She smiled again, that sudden light. "I won't be afraid if you won't."

We each carried a bottle and held hands as we walked, laughing at each other like children. We turned up the stone steps to the front yard and walked quietly through the boxwood maze planted just after the Civil War by Carrie Rumbough.

We walked up to the porch of the ornate Victorian house. And on that porch stood an apparition! Anna didn't understand why I actually staggered because at the head of the steps stood Major Jack Rumbough. My heart raced until the Major spoke, and I understood with a gasp that it was Johnny Rumbough in some elaborate costume, his hair whitened and a long, white mustache hanging down on either side of his mouth. His body was draped in one of his father's suits, that hung on him as though he were a scarecrow.

"Gaw-damn you, Stevie Robbins! Where the hell you been?" He was trying desperately to approximate the gravelly drawl of his father.

"I been doing your damn work for you, you old goat. While you been sitting up here at the big house, drinking your whisky."

"Damn right!" Johnny drawled, his voice breaking abruptly in mid-sentence. "It's best you know your place and keep to it."

I jumped up the steps and grabbed young Johnny by the shoulders; his father's suit swallowed him up, especially through the chest and arms. "What in the hell are you doing?" I said to him. "You very nearly gave me a heart attack."

"It's Halloween. You're supposed to dress up. Where's your costume?"

"He's disguised as a gentleman." Anna said as she reached the porch beside us. "I'm surprised you even recognize him."

We went in and joined Dora Garner in the kitchen. All five of us— Prince, Johnny, Anna, and I along with Dora—talked as Dora cooked. I uncorked the first bottle of wine; and Prince, Anna, and I enjoyed a brim-full glass as Johnny and even Dora sipped to keep us company. The wind picked up outside as we talked; you could hear it bend and wrap around the sides of the house as we sat warm and content in the kitchen. We carried the food into the dining room together, laughing and talking as we went. She had baked a wild turkey, shot several days before by a boy in town, with cornbread dressing and sweet potatoes from the cellar; with fresh loaf bread, steaming as the knife broke through the crust; with peeled apples baked in a glass dish, swimming in their own juice, spiced with cinnamon and cloves. The smell alone would have reduced us to slavering dogs, and the wind's howl through the darkness added to the sense of the special moment: warm, spicy, absolutely preferred and suspended in time.

Prince blessed the food and we ate, laughing and talkative. Dora sat between Prince and Johnny, and Johnny especially paid her court, asking her questions and complimenting most every bite of food he took. At one point, she took advantage of a moment's silence to ask a question that seemed to both honor and threaten us all at the same time. In her soft voice, barely to be heard at all above the wail of the wind and the crackle of the fire on the hearth, she said. "What would you change? Each of you, what would you change?"

"About tonight?" Anna asked. "I would change nothing at all."

"No," Dora said. "What would you change about this wicked old world we live in? If you could change anything, what would it be?" I glanced at Prince; he was gazing in mild shock at his supposedly shy wife.

"I would wish there was no color between us," Johnny said suddenly. "I know that you are my sister," he said directly to Dora. And you are a much better sister than most of the ones I've got … cranky old bitches." I realized that we were well into the second bottle of wine, and Johnny had been sipping along quite steadily.

"You shouldn't call them that." Dora whispered to Johnny, although it was fully evident from the tone of her voice that she agreed with him. "Besides, look at this." And then she did the most extraordinary thing for those of us who knew her: she pulled up the sleeve of her blouse and held out the underside of her arm, placing her hand and wrist on the table beside Johnny's. In the flickering lamplight the tone and pigment of their skin was indistinguishable.

We all stared with a sort of suspended fascination until the mood was broken by Prince's loud guffaw. "Who you reckon is the Nee-gro?" Prince said to the world, but gently, gently.

Dora sat back. "What would you wish?" She said to Anna.

After what had just happened, I fully expected Anna to at least hesitate, but she answered without pause. "Oh, that I could live in this beautiful house with all of you and forget about this awful war. And there would be no fuss about who was what in relation to whom. No locks on the doors and no anger or jealousy."

I glanced at Prince; he winked at me. I think we both still expected Dora to gasp at this, for she knew by now that somewhere out in the big world Anna had a husband. But Dora didn't gasp; she only nodded at Anna and reached to pat her hand. Both women, I realized, were tipsy.

"And what would you wish for?" Dora was looking straight at me, almost it seemed to challenge me.

Obviously, I had known the question was coming. But three glasses of wine had stolen my habits from me, and when I reached for the prepared answer, it wasn't there. My mind was blank. But my mouth, I discovered, was busy as usual. "I would wish that one year from tonight we would all be here again. One year older, with a few more scars, but sitting right here, with the light inside and the wind out."

I glanced around the table. Prince was regarding me strangely; I wasn't sure why. Johnny was smiling absently; he was now chewing vaguely on his costume mustache. Anna had what seemed to me a reflective, perhaps even a sad smile. And Dora whispered aloud to me as she had to Johnny, straight across the table. "You do love her, don't you?" Meaning, I knew, Anna.

"Of course I do."

"Well, Jesus does make a miracle," she said. "Even in a man of stone."

And suddenly, the power of her glance shifted, away from me, from my mind, and on to the only other one at the table. To Prince, her husband. "What would you wish for, old man?"

"That you'd quit scaring the shit out of people when we have 'em over for supper," he said, and we all laughed, even as Johnny began to droop toward his plate.

After we'd eaten, I led Anna up the three flights of stairs to show her the tower. Prince had stoutly refused our help with the dishes, sending us pointedly on our way. When we had climbed the last, narrow passage into the tower room, we both stopped in amazement.

For the wind lived in the tower.

The windows on all four sides were open, a sure sign that Johnny had been up there, and the wind—with the moonlight and the sweeping tide of night sounds—flew unimpeded through that small, square room. I hadn't thought to bring even a candle, so suddenly we were alone with the moonlight, the rushing past of Spring Creek far below, the ominous river of the wind as it poured through the trees all around us. And the tower itself seemed to move when the wind gusted, the floor and walls to bend as a tree would bend, to keep from breaking. We were inside the night, and it was a night that lived and breathed and flew above the countryside.

And suddenly, from the trees near the chapel, there was the long, quavering cry that seemed to give voice itself to the night.

Anna leaned against me. "What in ...!"

I put my arms protectively around her, holding her as she sought me. "It's just a barred owl," I whispered. "Calling for its mate."

The screaming cry came again, this time from behind the house.

"But it sounds like—"

"I know, but it's just an owl. And the fact that it's calling at all means it's safe."

"Means we're safe?" All of her warmth against me.

"Means the night sky is safe. And that's exactly where we are, seems to me."

"In the sky?"

I nodded into her hair.

And so we stood for a time out of time—breathing in deep, regular rhythms and flying in the night wind.

It took us quite a while to work our way back down those three flights of stairs, trying to simultaneously negotiate the steps and keep our arms around each other. The farther down into the house we descended, the less the wind seemed to buoy us up and the more we sank into the weight of our bodies.

We found Prince and Dora in the kitchen, she now sitting at the table, watching as he finished washing the last of the fine Rumbough china we had used for dinner. Anna sank down at the table beside Dora.

"Now I have a question for you." She spoke with an obscure brightness that seemed left over from the tower and the wind.

"What is it, honey?" Dora replied.

"I think I know how you and Prince met. What I want to know is when you decided you should marry the man."

"Oh, my word! I'm not sure I can tell all that. He'll have to help me." She nodded at Prince, who turned to lean back against the sink, drying his hands on a dish towel.

"Tell what?" Prince asked. "I'm not sure I can say that you ever decided you should marry me. Your daddy decided that."

Dora had not taken her eyes off Anna. "It was the night that he … that we. …" Prince laughed out loud. "No, not that night, you old fool. Not the night he's thinking about. It was the night we went to the springs."

"The what?"

"Do you know why this is called Hot Springs?"

Anna shook her head, no, wanting to hear Dora tell it.

"Hot mineral springs bubble up in the river, right across from the hotel. And they pipe the water up into the bathhouse. Stevie has shown you the bathhouse, surely?"

"Only the outside, not what it's like inside."

"Well, then he's not the man I thought he was. I'll tell you why I say that. One night after we'd been going around together for a while, Mister Prince Fancy-Pants talked me into walking over by the river. And when we came along beside the bathhouse, he pulls a great, huge key out of his pocket, showing off, and he leads me over to the door. I pulled and pulled back on his arm; I knew we'd get in endless trouble, but nothing would do but he had to show me the baths. Well, he got me inside and bolted the door behind us and led me around where all the rich hotel guests would go to soak their ailments. All the time, he was whispering how lovely I was and how I was as good as any rich, white woman from any old New York or Chicago.

"Directly he got me over by the dressing rooms and got his big arms around me and kissed me, which was all I ever thought he was up to in the first place, but then he told me we were going to dip ourselves in the healing waters. I was scared half to death and excited all the same time cause, like you, I'd never even seen the inside of that place before. I told him I couldn't swim, and he told me it won't that deep. I told him I was afraid somebody'd see us and he minded me how he'd bolted the door. I told him I couldn't be havin' any little babies, and he told me you couldn't get pregnant from no hot mineral water he'd ever heard of.

"Well, you know what happened after that. Prince Garner could talk the devil out of his horns if he'd a mind to. I was out of my clothes before I was even done thinkin' about it, an' so was he. And he carried me down the steps into that water. And it was the softest, warmest thing you can imagine. I just let him hold me so I floated. And after a while in those nice, hot waters, you couldn't have pried my arms off from around his neck with a crowbar."

"I had to make her get out and get dressed." Prince's voice sounded harsh and dry after Dora's, even leavened as it was with humor. "She'd be in there yet."

"After that you had to marry him?" Anna asked, enthralled.

"He was my hero after that," Dora admitted. She glanced up at Prince, smiling through the tears in her eyes. "And he ain't failed me more'n a couple a hundred times since."

Anna and Dora walked to the front door of Rutland arm-in-arm, while Prince and I held back for a moment, and I told him how and where I'd left Siegfried. Then when I stood to follow Anna, he said something else. "You know that old woman told that story as much for you as for Ann, don't you?"

"Why for me?"

"Because it is sinfully obvious that when it comes to making love to a woman, your sorry ass needs all the help it can get."

When I hugged Miss Dora good night and found Anna on the walkway in front of the house, she held two large, folded towels in her arms.

And so it was that we took the short cut down from the Rutland driveway, across the railroad tracks to the footlog, and over to the wagon gate, where a sleepy-eyed Goforth brought me the key from its hiding place in the tree. From there we walked the wide arc around the back of the Mountain Park, partly in the trees, along well-worn paths, past the infirmary, past the edge of New Heidelburg, abandoned in the moonlight, until we came to the river. We didn't bother to be secretive; as we came in sight of a guard, I would half-wave, half-salute, and each in his turn would wave or nod. We came to the back of the bath-house, a long, brick structure that held sixteen marble baths laid well before the turn of the century. The moon was near-enough full so that we were walking in an open, silvery light for much of the way, almost as if in a pleasant dream, enjoying the wind and the now faint, far-away cry of the owls, calling out as if they spoke a language we shared.

I led Anna over by the river and lifted the lid so she could dip her hand down into the cistern that collected the water as it bubbled up from the bottom of the stream.

"My God, it's hot!"

"Over a hundred degrees year round," I whispered, feeling for a moment more like a tour guide than a lover.

I unlocked the iron padlock on the back door, not with the large, ornate key that Dora claimed Prince carried in his pocket, but with a small, modern pass key. We stepped through into the humid darkness. I stood on tiptoe to slide home the rusty dead bolt at the top of the door to close the passage against any curious intruder. The heavy security bolt had been there forever; I was certain it was the same thick bar that Prince had thrust home so many years before.

While my arms were over my head and my body stretched to its full height, I heard the whispery fall of the towels and felt Anna's arms slip around my waist. Then the full, soft weight of her head against my back between my shoulder blades. "It's warm in here," she whispered.

I turned inside the circle of her arms so I could return the languid pressure of her body, pulling her against me. "Sometimes I miss you terribly," I admitted into the wonderfully thick tangle of her hair. "Sometimes, when it's even for a day, just a day or two, I miss the smell and touch of you. ... I confess it."

"Confess away," she said into my chest. "It's good for the soul."

I led her down the dark corridor, barely lit by slivers of moonlight through the boarded up windows, and into the first dressing room we came to. As if by unspoken agreement, we stepped into the same five-by-five foot cubicle. In the bare sprinkles of moonlight from the hallway, I could sense more than see her begin to undress, as I stepped on through the other door and reached down into the pool.

The water was there, just as it has always been there, hot and luxurious against my hand. I stepped back and began to undress as well, hurrying to catch up with her. I could already feel my body straining toward hers, as I bent to push off my suit pants. Even though my pulse was pounding in my ears, I could hear the rustle of her underthings sliding along her limbs.

She was faster than I. As I stood straight and bare, her naked arms were around me. Our skin against skin was all the known world.

"Aren't you afraid ... after that story?" I whispered.

"Afraid?" Her lips were deliciously muffled, tickling my chest.

"Afraid that if you go in the water, you'll know you want to marry me?" The moment the words emerged, I felt a spark of panic, as if even the thought of marriage would spook her, this woman who came and went so in secret.

"I won't be afraid if you won't," she said. For the second time that night.

And so I bent within the circle of her arms to pick her up. Anna Ulmann, this ever so slight, ever so powerful woman. I knew she hated to be picked up, hated to have her feet even off the floor. Even so, I lifted her up and turned, my bare feet whispering now on the polished planks and then splashing down the marble steps into the hot, mineral-laden water.

I stood with my legs wide, my left arm under her knees, my right under her shoulders, barely supporting her as she floated easily. Her body just beneath the surface, her head above water at my shoulder, where I could hear her breathing soften again into a deep, regular pattern after the initial gasp at the moist, penetrating heat.

I shut my eyes, holding her.

I realized as I held her that it had been weeks since the day we had spent together in 305-306. And now, my utter abandoned fondness for her body was almost heart-rending in its intensity. When I touched her, it was as if the fire in my stomach rushed out through my arms to flicker into her, the flame of me conducted by the hot, lapping water into the flame of her. My eyes shut in the pitchy darkness, it felt to me that we were two ignited creatures, barely contained by our skins, and where we touched, we melted into one another, such that light flowed back and forth between us in gentle waves, such that now one extremity—me—and then the other—her—was illuminated by alternating waves of light.

"Baptism," I whispered, somewhere, perhaps only in our minds.

For once, when we kissed, time slowed rather than evaporated. For once, our lips, tongues, teeth, made a kind of languorous reflection. For once, our lips spoke not by hurrying past, but by lingering in the moment. And it seemed that even as our mouths moved, our lips slippery, that time stopped, and that kiss—as our bodies flared—lasted forever. And I suppose it did, for it lasts still.

Anna Ulmann: the only sure passage I have ever known out of darkness into light.

CHAPTER EIGHTEEN

THE first days of November brought *The New York Times*.

The eyes of the world came in the form of a rather snappy dresser, a cocky, middle-aged man who had managed to turn a severe polio limp into a strut, a reporter with the unlikely name of Lawrence Edmond Rosenstern. Larry Rosenstern.

He was preceded by rumors of his presence and rumors of rumors. He was in New Heidelberg questioning the architect Schliembeck. He was in Camp B on a journalist's pass, asking questions about the gaol and the man imprisoned there. He was in town, talking to citizens, asking them what they thought about the way the United States Government was coddling German prisoners while their own boys were being gassed to death overseas.

And he was looking for a photographer, a New Yorker whom he knew to be in town. This rumor from one of the censors in the Mountain Park office, who'd talked to the man on the street. He was looking for a photographer to take the photographs to accompany his Sunday feature on German nationals; the woman who, with the help of the Germans, was developing photographic plates in the basement of the Mountain Park.

Even with his limp, Lawrence Rosenstern was as quick as the will-o-the-wisp. I missed him in Camp B, I missed him at the Hot Springs Post Office, I missed him in New Heidelberg. I finally caught up with him in the first-floor hallway of the Mountain Park after having followed the hearsay of him through both camps and the town. I was on the way back to John Sanders' office when I saw a stranger talking eagerly with a middle-aged seaman named Edwin Kussner. Kussner was a seaman third-class from one of the liners, to whom I'd given permission to paint a mural on the large oaken panel opposite the first floor ballroom.

I was rushing down the hall on the way back to John's office when I realized what I was seeing and hearing. This strange, crooked figure dressed in finely tailored clothes was questioning Kussner intently. I slowed to listen. "Why is it that the officers are housed in a luxury hotel while you enlisted men stay in quarters made of tarpaper and tacks?"

Edwin stared at him with a look of pure puzzlement. "It is because they are the officers and we are the men," he said patiently, as if to a child. I stepped back into a doorway, as was always my instinct.

"But that is exactly my point. You are men. Why should you live in shacks when they live like the Vanderbilts? And the food? There are meat rations being observed across the country, and these officers of yours eat like kings."

Edwin stared at him expectantly: waiting, I imagine, for a question.

"Why do you think that is? Do they bribe the camp guards? This … this Robbins—have they managed to get to him?"

"Ah, Herr Robbins. He is the man who lets me paint." Edwin half-turned from Rosenstern and gazed longingly at the mural behind him. It was of a farm scene, perhaps ten by twenty feet, a great, living-and-breathing farm scene that could have been anywhere in Madison County except that the large barn in the center of the mural had a thatched roof. Behind the barn, walking toward us was the figure of a farmer with a scythe over his shoulder. Somehow I had known it was Edwin's father, perhaps because the tired, slouching walk of a laborer at day's end had reminded me so hauntingly of my own father. Jules Robbins, coming down from his upper fields.

"I don't give a damn about the painting!" Rosenstern's voice had taken on a strident tone that didn't go well with his fake British accent. "I want to know why our nation's enemies are being housed at government expense in such obviously luxurious quarters. I'm certain that someone must have been bought off, and it stands to reason that it's this Robbins who has—"

I interrupted him by stepping out of the shadows and addressing Edwin Kussner. "More color," I said to him. "Your father is carrying a scythe," I pointed. "So it must be late summer or fall, so there should be more color."

Edwin held out his palette, and I pointed to the russet and vermilion, the yellow-gold, and the orange he'd streaked together on one side.

"Such as it is now," Edwin said, waving at his painting. "Awe...?"

"Autumn. Which is the season of blood, all the colors are mixed from blood and sun. Red and gold."

He turned happily back to the wall and began to add strokes of the reddish gold to his horizon, assuming that since I had materialized, he was free of the reporter.

"And who, might I ask, are you?" Rosenstern said, his voice friendly, his pad and pencil poised.

"I'm on staff here," I said. "I work in the office."

"Your name?"

"I'd rather not say if you're going to quote me."

He perked up, smelling a lead. "I'm very interested in why the German officers are being treated like royalty. Can you tell me anything about the man in charge? This ..." He glanced at his notes for a first name. "This Steve Robbins?" I motioned with my head that we should move down the hall out of earshot of Edwin. "Do you think it's possible that Robbins has been bribed by the officers to provide them with better care?"

I noticed that Lawrence Rosenstern's necktie had the faintest touch of pink in the weave that set off the blue and black pattern. "Stevie Robbins is a drunk," I whispered. "I'm not sure he knows where he is half the time. And he lets some of the Germans, like Kussner back there, have their run of the place."

Rosenstern stepped back and stared hard at me, trying to see my face in the dim light of the hallway. "I would find what you say hard to believe if I hadn't already interviewed the sheriff." He glanced down at his notes again.

"The Honorable Roy Robbins?" I asked. Ironically, out of the corner of my eye, I could see Pauline, Roy's legal wife, walking down the hall toward us, a stained apron wrapped around her waist and her arms white with flour to the elbow.

"Yes, Sheriff Robbins. And he said that this other Robbins, this Steve, is an alcoholic and a degenerate who is incapable of running a one-horse parade, let alone a prison camp."

"Did he say that Steve Robbins had killed someone before?" It was part of Roy's standard litany.

Rosenstern was still studying his notes. "Actually, yes he did. ... And

I always make it my policy ..." Pauline stopped to listen, crossing her impressive arms across her impressive chest.

"Now, that Roy Robbins is a fine man." I winked at Pauline. "He's a little near-sighted, but all in all, he's a stout, upright, pillar of the church. Been known to take in little orphans off the side of the road. Solace widows in their grief."

"Not at all like his cousin? Someone told me that Steve Robbins is the sheriff's cousin."

"Not at all like. But you better be careful who you talk to. Stephen Robbins has an ugly streak o'justice in him."

Rosenstern wrote furiously even as Pauline snorted out loud, unable to contain herself any longer. "He's also standing in front of you, and he's full of shit. Be sure you put that in there."

"If you're so concerned," Rosenstern said later, after he'd gotten through stamping his one good foot in anger about our first interview. "If you're so concerned that I tell the truth about all of this, why don't you just tell me what the truth is?"

"There are a whole flock of truths that have come here to roost since we strung the fence. The one that matters most outside our 'little world,' as you call it, is that the Germans are being treated civilly. The 'bloody shacks,' as you insist on calling them ..." I waved my arm toward Camp B. "... are well heated, and they each have a wash house attached. All two thousand, three-hundred plus of our internees are fed three full meals a day at an approximate cost to the U.S. Government of fifty cents per man per day."

"But isn't it true that you haven't observed wheatless Tuesdays and meatless Thursdays like the poor citizens of our great—"

I held up my hand to stop him before he got wound up; sometimes his questions were paragraphs long. "In the beginning, no, we didn't. We had government barrels of beef that would have rotted at the depot if they hadn't been eaten. But ever since that cartoon appeared in the Asheville paper, the one portraying Hans Ruser as a great, fat German hog, we haven't served a scrap of bread or a shred of meat on ration days."

"But still, Mr. Robbins, aren't they better fed than most of the citizens of this region?"

I gazed at him in frustration. "*Lawrence*, is that what you go by?"

"Larry, my friends call me Larry."

"Larry, most of the good citizens of this region are hard-scrabble farmers. In a good year, more lambs survive than are eaten by wolves and wild dogs. Your milk cow bears a calf in spring and stays fresh for another year. Your corn and wheat survive hail and flood and fire and drought. You're able to butcher two hogs come the first hard frost rather than one or, more likely, none at all. You make more things out of corn than God himself ever imagined, including the liquor that addles your brains and keeps you sane. That's a good year."

"What's a bad year?"

"A bad year fills up the cemeteries between November and March. Children and old people before their time."

He wasn't writing but he was staring intently into my face. I think he was honestly trying to understand.

"What I mean to say is that if we didn't feed the Germans better than some of the people around here, we'd have the International Red Cross raising hell in your newspaper, and I'd have been replaced weeks ago."

"Are you saying that you have to—"

"I'm saying that there are two things at stake here. Right here in Hot Springs, North Carolina, the end of the known world if you're from Manhattan, New York City. One has to do with the reality of the war. Before the war in Europe is done, there will be thousands of American prisoners whom we hope—we hope, mind you—are treated humanely. The Kaiser reads your newspaper, Larry. And if he thought we treated these noncombatants badly, American prisoners of war would suffer. Hell to pay ten times over."

"You said there were two things."

"There is common decency."

"What?"

"Common, human decency. The way that one human being should treat another. Even in times of war."

"Are you telling me that you think of these Germans as human? Human in the same way that you and I are? Have you not read the reports of the atrocities from overseas?"

Again, he had me. Sitting in the front office of the Mountain Park, he was the picture of the sculpted gentleman. Every hair, every thread in place. The clothes on his back, I was certain, having cost more than every stitch of cloth I owned. It was only when he stood and tried to walk that his body betrayed him. And caused one to think that the same twistedness that marked his legs might also evidence itself in his thoughts. I didn't know what to say to him, so out of desperation, I tried the simple truth. "I don't believe the reports of the atrocities that I read in the papers, Larry. Even your paper. I don't believe that the man who is painting that mural in the hallway is very different from me except in his loneliness, and most nights we are not different in that. And I think that simple kindness—kindness, nothing more—has to be reborn in the world. Somewhere. Here perhaps." I had said more than I meant to, more than I even knew there was to say.

He looked at me strangely. "My God," he said. "The sheriff is right. You are utterly unsuited for this job." He stood and with a few subtle adjustments, pulled his crooked body straight. "You should be running an orphanage or a church school. Not an internment camp for enemy aliens."

He spun impressively on his withered heel to make his exit, but before he did, he paused for one more sally. "There is one more way in which you can help me, Mr. Robbins."

I nodded glumly.

"I am in search of Mrs. Anna Jurgens. I am charged with ascertaining her well-being by her husband, and I also seek her services as a photographer."

"Not her name," I said. I stood up, feeling the muscles in my forearms twitch.

"Excuse me?"

"That's not the name she chooses to use. She goes by Ulmann. Anna Ulmann."

"Well, that may be her fancy of the moment, but I would like to see and talk with her. Her husband is quite worried about her status in ..."

"This wilderness?"

"Something like that."

"She's staying at the Sunnybank Boarding House, Mrs. Jane Gentry, proprietor."

"Thank you. I may be able to offer her some work that will benefit her career when she returns to the city. With your permission, I would like to have her execute a series of photographs of the internees themselves."

He hadn't really said it as a question but I nodded anyway.

"If she will be safe inside the fence. I imagine some of your Germans can be quite dangerous."

I nodded again, and as I did, I nearly choked. On the words that I wanted to say to the sanctimonious bastard. That perhaps she wouldn't return to the city. That perhaps there was a better life here—even inside an internment camp—than in New York licking her husband's polished shoes. I merely nodded, feeling the heat rise in my neck and face.

It was only two nights before that we had swum together in the springs. The very springs that gave the place its name, its essence. And she seemed to live still in the texture of my skin, the play of my fingers and my hands, my naked mind as it rubbed against the fabric of the world. The boundary of my mind was mixed inextricably with hers, and the invasion of this hopfrog man from the North was already an insult to me, both because he so misunderstood what we were trying to do and because he seemed such a threat to her. So the next morning, I walked out of the Mountain Park, intending to range out into the world in search of her, to watch her work for *The New York Times*, if indeed that was what Rosenstern had arranged.

As I walked out the gate into Bridge Street that chilly morning, I saw a clump of townspeople gathered at the corner of the Camp B fence where the board stockade ended and the wire began. They were watching some event inside the camp with evident interest.

"What the hell is it?" I called out to the guard who was manning the gatehouse, even though I suspected I knew already.

"That newspaper feller," he said back. "Got that Yankee woman over there takin pictures for him."

The seconds it took me to cross the street and be admitted to Camp B seemed to stretch out with a vivid slowness.

I stepped through and could see clearly that Anna had her camera set up thirty feet from the gaol, focused on its slapped-together roughness. The bars on the windows were perfectly obvious from her perspective as well as the board-and-batten bunk houses beyond that housed the crewmen. Anna was bent to her work, her head secreted beneath the cloth that protected the back of her camera. Larry Rosenstern was strutting, limping in a tight circle behind her.

"Damn it to hell," I thought. And must have said it perfectly clearly because the guard, one Jimmy Thomas with whom we'd replaced

Gehagen, stepped toward me in concern.

"Anything wrong, Cap?" he asked.

"That! That is wrong," I called out. "That is about as wrong as anything I've ever seen in my life." But I was already moving. Walking with too-hurried strides across the hundred feet that separated me from the camera, from Anna and Rosenstern.

I know what it's like to feel space and time bend. To feel reality twist inside you. Larry Rosenstern had gone unerringly to the spot I least wanted reported in his newspaper, and I was that angry. But even with this spurting sense of righteous indignation, I knew I couldn't drag little Larry to the gate and throw him bodily out into the street. I knew that if I hurt him in any way, I'd pay. I'd pay in print, black ink on the page.

My face was ablaze when I walked up to the two of them. "Lawrence," I nodded to him. I was trying desperately to be pleasant, assuming, I'm sure, the most grotesque of appearances. "Miss Ulmann, may I speak with you for a moment?"

She lifted the cloth from her head and slowly straightened. There was something in this motion that should have warned me. She turned, and the look on her face said clearly that she didn't intend to recognize me in any private capacity. "Excuse me?" she said.

"May I speak to you for a moment?"

"I'm engaged on an assignment just now, Mr. Robbins." Her tone cut like a butcher slicing.

Rosenstern chuckled. I could feel a professional and geographical partnership between the two tighten against me: photographer and writer, New Yorkers both.

"Perhaps after you've finished your work here, you might spare me a few minutes." I hadn't spent years waiting hand-and-foot on some of the wealthiest gentry on the East Coast without developing a certain servile urbanity of my own. I was seething like a kettle on a hot stove, but I knew how to pretend.

"Perhaps," she said, glancing at Rosenstern. "I am committed to Mr. Rosenstern for the duration of the day, but if time permits, I will call at the Mountain Park when we are finished."

"Thank you, Miss Ulmann," I think I said. I'm certain that I turned on my heel and walked away. I felt like I'd been gutted.

I walked back to the Park, but I couldn't force myself inside. It was late morning by then, so I stopped at the front porch that faced the gatehouse. From nearly fifty yards away, I could see the gatehouse itself, and the path that led from there up to the Park. Or rather I could have seen it if I had let myself watch. Instead, I sat in the one rocking chair left on that porch and I faced to the east, away from the fence and the gate. It was cold that day, and as I watched the cloud shadows play catch over the mountains on the other side of the river, I let the wind slowly chill my skin and then my blood and then my bones. I wanted some peace before I saw her. I wanted some distance from my anger before she came. If she came.

I burrowed down inside my coat as I gazed at the cloud-strewn mountains, steep flanks of trees that turned the color of cold steel as the sun spun lower in the sky.

"I do not appreciate you offering to interrupt me when it was obvious that I was working."

I had felt her approach but did not let myself look up until she spoke. "But—"

"Excuse me. I'm not finished. Not only did you interrupt me, but to do so in such a high-handed, I'm the Lord of the Manor sort of way—it makes me absolutely furious. Just because—"

"Anna!"

"Don't you dare interrupt me again; you've already done that enough today. Lawrence Rosenstern is a widely respected journalist from *The New York Times*. Do you have any idea what that means? Could you have any clue at all living in this ... this place? And for Larry Rosenstern to ask me to carry out an assignment for the *Times*, so that my friends in New York will see that I haven't lost my mind or fallen off the face of the earth, and for you ... you ... to get in my way is beyond belief!"

"I was trying to help you—"

"Help me what? Just because some things have passed between us, Stephen Robbins, does not mean that we have that kind of relationship. You were just trying to protect yourself and this great, hulking monstrosity that you love so damn much!" She kicked the door of the

Park so hard that it rattled in its frame.

I stood and held out my arms to her in vain, as if to somehow help and stop her at the same time. "You're right," I admitted, growling in frustration. "I was trying to protect myself. And all this. If Rosenstern prints a story that implies some of the Germans are being mistreated and the International Red Cross raises hell, I'll lose my job, and Ruser's Germans will be shipped out to that hellhole, Fort Oglethorpe, in Georgia. I don't care if it looks like a country club, but the first thing I saw was you taking a picture of the gaol, for Christ's sake. And—"

"Why in hell do you have one, if you don't want a picture taken of it?" She was in tears now: pure, unadulterated frustration and anger. "You're not in charge of the whole world, you know. You can't control what reporters write and what photographers pose. You can't run *The New York Times* from a rocking chair in North Carolina! Not even you!"

"There's something else."

"What?" She nearly screamed.

"I wanted to protect you from your husband. He said he was here on behalf of your husband."

She groaned out loud. "Of course he did. He thought all he had to do was intone the name—Dr. Anton Jurgens—and you'd fall on your face in fear."

"I nearly hit him with a chair instead."

She groaned again.

"Are you all right?" I whispered.

"I think I broke my damn toe," she muttered, "and it's your fault."

I made her come in, cursing under her breath all the way. And I made her ride the slow, creaking elevator up to the third floor. Once inside 305-306, I poured her a generous water glass of red wine, precisely the way she'd described Italian gentlemen drinking it before the war.

I threw several lighted matches into the fireplace to get a flame and then knelt before her as she half-lay in my easy chair. I slowly unlaced and pulled off her shoe; then I reached up under her skirts feeling up her leg for the top of her long stocking, which top I didn't reach until half-way up her thigh.

"Just what exactly are you doing?" she asked. "I warn you, I'm in no mood."

"First aid," I replied. "Massage the point of injury."

"Well then ..." She placed her other foot against my hip for leverage. "Massage away, but if you hurt me, I'll kick, you know I will."

I tapped the end of each toe in turn, including her lovely big toe, and she neither kicked me nor rose up out of the chair in pain. Her toe wasn't broken, and I began ever so gently to massage the bottom of her foot with both thumbs.

"Anna?"

"Hmmmm?" I noticed her glass was empty, and I got up to pour her another half-glass.

"What are you really trying to tell me about New York?" I began to massage her foot again.

"That ... that does feel good, don't stop. ... I'm trying to tell you that for years I have wanted nothing more or less than to be an artist. ... You're tickling me. ... to be an honest-to-God artist with the camera and to exhibit my work at the 291 Studio and to walk down the street in Greenwich Village wearing a cape and have people who know stop their friends to point me out. To smile enigmatically at younger, oh-so-naïve women who want to be me, to know who I know and to have done the work that I have done. ... Ouch, don't press so hard. ... Do you know who Alfred Stieglitz is?"

"Sure. ..."

She giggled. "Who is he?"

"Artist?"

"You're guessing."

"Brilliant ... ah ... painter?"

"You poor, benighted ..." She was dreamy with wine and the simple pleasure of someone rubbing her tired feet.

"Country bastard?"

"Precisely. Listen. You will need to know this when you come to see me in New York. Alfred Stieglitz is the very photographer of the world. The man can do anything with a camera: portraiture, cityscape, abstract composition—"

"But can he do natural and compelling portraits in the documentary style?"

"Like me?"

"Like you."

"Unfortunately, yes he can. Early in his career, he did a series of such in Italy and Spain." She waved her arm for dramatic effect. *Italian*

Mason, Bellagio, 1887. Say it with me: *Bee-laa-geee-o!*"

"Beats hell out of *Backwoods Stump Jumper, Anderson Cove, 1917,*" I admitted. "You want some more wine? It, at least, is Italian."

She opened her eyes to stare balefully at her glass. "What happened to my other wine?"

"You drank it."

"No, I mean the wine after the first wine."

"You just threw it all over the room while you were waving your arm about."

She shut her eyes comfortably again, leaned her head back. "Yes."

"Yes, you want some more wine?"

"Yes. And yes, I think you must also minister to my other foot. I think I may have injured it as well."

I poured her wine. "Hurt both feet while you were kicking the monstrosity?"

Her eyes popped open, and she blushed ever so faintly. "I didn't say that."

"I'm sure you didn't. I was distraught at the time myself."

"I know you love this old place."

"I do, but tell me about Steinmeyer." I began to unlace her other shoe.

"Who?"

"Alfred Stee ... meyer?"

"Stieglitz. Alfred Stieglitz is the dean of American photographers. My teacher, Clarence White, bows when Stieglitz sweeps past on the street with his cape swirling out behind him. Did you know that my hands ... here, hold my glass." She held her hands before my face in a rather artificial pose, but even so I was struck yet again by their simple beauty. Small, brown, compact—and elegant. "My hands were photographed by the great Alfred Stieglitz. Before this current woman, this Georgia O'Keeffe creature, showed up, my hands were the ones in front of Stieglitz's lens."

"Tennessee?"

She giggled. "No, fool, *Georgia.* O'Keeffe. Some artistic woman with a paint brush."

"And you want to go back and break the paint brush over her head?"

She sipped from her glass meditatively as I removed her other shoe and stocking, began ever so gently to massage the foot. "No. No, she's safe from me. I want to be the artist, not the model." She handed me her glass again and sat up as if to strike a serious pose. "Kind sir, I intend to take the photographs that will define our generation. I want to do great work that will earn me the respect of the New York *aristoi*— New York and all it means." She slumped and took the glass back. "Am I being a fool, Stephen?"

"No, you are a supremely talented woman. I believe you must go where you need to go and do what you need to do to use your gift. I'll carry your camera for you."

"Will you follow me to New York?"

"Do they have hotels in New York?"

"Of course they do. Hotels that need you desperately."

I had to laugh. Both at her, so utterly serious, and at myself for being so foolish.

"I hate to ask an obvious practical question, but what about your husband?"

She lifted her head from the back of the chair again. "I don't know. You promised me you'd kill him, remember?"

"That would solve it," I admitted.

"Maybe that's another reason why you need to come to New York. ..." She pushed at me with her foot. "Why are you laughing?"

"Because I can't imagine anything or anybody in New York that would admit to needing somebody like me."

"Don't be so sure," she said quietly. She slowly raised both her bare feet and placed them against my chest, letting her dress fall back to pool in her lap. I was so mesmerized by the intensity of her stare that I was only vaguely aware of the erotic abandonment of her pose. Thus, we were frozen for a long moment more, suspended in silence as we stared into each other's tired and fiery eyes. *Suppliant Man before Woman Acquiescent,* a tableau carnal. Or spiritual. Or both.

"Oh, damn!" she said suddenly. "What time is it?"

I fumbled at my watch chain, suddenly aware again of this world and of how much my knees ached from kneeling on the hard floor. "It's almost six."

"Damn it!" she exclaimed. "I'm sorry. I'm sorry, Stephen, but ... where's my other shoe? ... Thanks. I'm supposed to host Rosenstern to dinner at Sunnybank. And I'm about to be late for my own little dinner party. ... Can you lace up that one?... Yes, please. Start at the bottom."

She paused long enough at the door to put her hand on my shoulder. "Look, I'm sorry about what happened earlier. I know I'm simpleminded about New York, but I also know that I need you desperately. Please forgive me?"

I nodded, still half stunned by the sudden whirlwind of sound and motion, light-headed from having stood so suddenly.

She was out and gone, but as I reached the doorway to look after her, she turned and ran back down the hall to me. Again reached out to place her hand affectionately against my chest. "Can you trust me about Rosenstern and the photographs and the *Times*?" she asked breathlessly. "Trust me to help you?"

"Yes," I whispered, once again arrested by the dark glimmer of her eyes. "Yes. ... Maybe. ... Yes. ... Yes." The word continued to echo in my mind after it ceased on my tongue.

But she was gone again.

For me, the next two days were like watching a play; although at the time I wasn't sure whether comedy or tragedy. I watched Rosenstern interview guards and townspeople, internees and staff. I even arranged an interview with Ruser, so the two could talk for a while undisturbed by the other Germans. Even more dramatic than Rosenstern, however, was Anna, who set up her camera and took photographs in both camps, framing the best and worst of life inside the fence. Panoramas of the officers lounging in front of the Park, playing tennis on the courts they had resurfaced, and reading in their New Heidelberg bungalows. But she also photographed the tarpaper barracks in Camp B and the crude infirmary we'd set up in the Wade Hampton cottage. She even asked permission to take a photograph inside the gaol and winked at me when I politely refused.

The morning of the day that Rosenstern was to leave, I received a note from Anna asking me to come to Sunnybank to help her pack the photographic plates he had requested. And there in Jane Gentry's parlor, I helped her slide eight solid glass plates into their center slots in a metal carrying case. Then she held up the first plate out of a second stack. "Camp B," she named it, "Siegfried Sonnach staring out of the window of his cell." Then she wrapped a rag around the plate and tapped it lightly on the edge of the table. When she removed the rag, I could see a web of minute cracks in the plate. She repeated the process with more plates: Camp B barracks and mess halls, as well as one of a Camp B privy. And then helped me slide each ever so carefully into the outside slots in the same metal box.

"The privy?"

"It is disgusting, Stephen. When I suggested to Rosenstern that it would make a powerful image to show just how truly degrading were the conditions here, he declared me an imagistic genius."

"*Imagistic* is it?"

She nodded. "Of course he held his embroidered handkerchief over his nose the whole time I was exposing the plate. Do you have an embroidered handkerchief, Stephen?"

"Not on me. Listen, Anna, I know I said I'd trust you, but why are we ...?"

"Sending him home with the evidence of your horrors?"

I nodded.

"Because by the time this box arrives in New York, there won't be anything left of the Camp B exposures except cracked and broken glass. If I'm really lucky, he'll be able to see enough of the images or at least read the labels to know that I tried my best to give him what he wanted, but all he'll have to work with are images of German officers playing cards and enjoying their stay at one of America's premier resorts." She slammed the lid of the box shut, and I could hear the reassuring tinkle of at least one plate breaking.

"Rosenstern's right about at least one thing."

"What's that?"

"You're an imagistic genius. I could kiss you."

"You could and probably should, but ..."

I stepped toward her.

"... not here and not now. I want you to carry this box down to the station for me, and say a very pleasant good-bye to the respected Mr. Rosenstern."

"I don't mind carrying the box, Anna, but—"

"He can still write anything he wants about you and the camp, once he's back in New York, and you can't do anything about it."

I nodded grimly. "I know."

She was so pleased with her work that she all but skipped down the terraced steps to the sidewalk and nearly stuck her arm through mine before thinking better of it. "Be careful," she whispered as we walked through the waiting room of the depot. "It will look painfully deliberate if you drop the box, and then I'll have to scream at you."

Rosenstern was standing on the station platform, leaning against one of the posts that held up the porch roof. He was wearing perhaps the prettiest suit I'd seen him in yet, and he had added an ornate walking stick to his ensemble for the trip. As we walked up, he reached out with the stick to tap ever so lightly the box cradled in my arms. "And does this crate contain the fruits of your labors, my dear?" he said to Anna, successfully ignoring me.

"Yes, Larry. And I want to thank you again for the opportunity. While my work has been widely exhibited, it has never appeared in a major newspaper."

He gave what must pass for a cocktail party laugh in New York and motioned with his stick for me to carry the box onto the train. "No, not the box car, Mr. Robbins. The passenger car, seat 19 beside my luggage. I want to be certain that the contents of that box make it safely back to civilization."

I set the metal box down carefully on the floor beside three matching suitcases sewn out of dark, brown leather. There was no question whose they were, even though the initials tooled into the side of each were too ornate to be deciphered.

"What in hell's that?" asked the conductor. A fat, happy Irishman I'd known as he'd ridden the Knoxville to Richmond for years.

"A box full of glass photographic plates."

"Mary, Mother o'Jesus, should I put 'em someplace safe?"

"No!" I whispered. "As far as I'm concerned, you can even give it a kick when you go by, so long as he's not looking." I motioned with my head out the window where Rosenstern was speaking animatedly with Anna.

As I walked back the length of the car, I passed one open window, through which I could hear Rosenstern's excited voice. I eased into the seat beside the window, nodding to a plain, country woman with her sleeping baby who sat opposite. She was vaguely familiar, but I was already focusing on the conversation outside the window.

"... but my dear, your talent is entirely wasted in this awful place. I know that you are a skilled documentarian, but just how many plates of rickety children and bleary-eyed grandfathers can you make?" I risked a brief glance out the window; I could see Rosenstern's head—crisp and oiled, delineated on this day with a blood-red bow tie to contrast his coal-black suit. He held Anna's hand in both of his, pleading almost. I confess, my midsection gave a lurch. Jealous nausea on an empty stomach.

"Yes, but why New York? What is there for a documentarian in New York?" Anna was, I could sense, leading him more than a little. Interviewing the interviewer.

"My dear, there is that esteemed man, your husband. Haven't you kept away long enough to make whatever point you were making in leaving? I'm certain that the good Dr. Jurgens has missed you enough by now to give you whatever it is you might want when you return."

"It might come as a great shock to you, Larry, but I have no intention of living with the good doctor ever again."

There was a significant pause before Rosenstern again seized the initiative. "Even better. My girl, half the photographers on the *Times* are overseas, either in the army or covering the situation in Europe. For the first time in its history, *The New York Times* is considering hiring professional women to fill its august ranks. Once my editor sees the work you've done on this project, you could have a job working directly with—"

"Scuse me, ain't you Stevie Robbins?"

I jerked. The woman across the aisle was whispering to me, trying to get my attention without waking her baby.

I smiled at her and nodded.

"Margaret Goforth. I used to sell flowers at the Park back before the war," she whispered. "You'as always kind to us girls, maids and such." She nodded happily at the memory. "Used to buy all the flowers us girls had left at the end of the day."

I was trying desperately to both hear her whisper and overhear the conversation outside.

"What you a doin' on the train?" The flower woman asked.

"I'm trying to decide whether to strangle a man," I stage-whispered back, and pointed out the window.

She braced herself against the seat and half-stood to peer past me at Rosenstern and Anna, all without disturbing the baby.

"Don't blame you," she whispered. "Him sparkin' on your woman like that."

I spun around in time to see Rosenstern lean forward over his stick to plant an oily kiss on Anna's cheek. I could feel a fire building in my neck and head, my skin burning with embarrassment and anger. I hunched down in the seat so I could lean closer to the window.

"May I tell my editor that you are interested?" Rosenstern asked. There was again a pause; did she nod? Rosenstern again: "I wonder just how soon you could be in New York?"

"Soon enough," Anna replied ambiguously. "But you had better board—these steps are dangerous when the train is moving."

I stood up to leave, and my head swam.

"Don't you worry, Mr. Robbins," my flower woman said. "He ain't a stitch on a man like you." And she laughed silently to herself, utterly pleased.

I managed to step down the platform and even to help Rosenstern tactfully up the steps. "Thank you, Robbins," he said evenly, and blew Anna a kiss from the top of the steps.

"What are you scowling about?" Anna asked, as the train carried him away. "He's gone."

"Just how soon is *soon enough*?" I muttered.

"You've been spying again." She laughed and turned to stare into my face. "Stephen Baird Robbins, can you even possibly be jealous?"

I nodded. "I wanted to crack that pretty, damn walking stick over his head."

She reached out and ever-so-briefly touched my face. "What in the world makes you think that Lawrence Rosenstern has any use at all for a woman other than to take his photographs for him?"

"Oh."

"Besides, *soon enough* might have as much to do with you as it does me."

CHAPTER NINETEEN

WINTER in the mountains.

In Western North Carolina, winter turns the world gray and brown. White? In a storm, yes, with snow and ice, but for the most part, the river turns a rock-quarry gray and all the woods the color of bark and crumbling leaf. The air is ghostly with wood smoke and rich with the pungent odor of rotting leaves. The fluid of yellow sunlight seeps into the corners of the sky, the green sap sinks down into the ground, and what life is left in between—even human life—dies back into a shadow of its summer self.

In the camp itself, even the supreme rank of German ingenuity slowed to a crawl. Despite the thunderous meals cooked by Pauline, D.C., and their staff, despite the cord upon cord of cured oak and maple consumed by the boilers under the Park and the stoves of Camp B, life seemed pinched and cold; even the Germans found countless reasons to retreat indoors.

Hans Ruser's engineer had the River Bridge all but finished by the first of November, leaving that bantam rooster Robert Snyder to take all the credit in the countless telegrams he insisted on sending to Washington and Raleigh. As a result, even the men on the bridge crews were now back in their barracks, loathe to emerge except at mealtime.

During the first weeks of November, yet another typhoid epidemic invaded Camp A, the infirmary was suddenly flooded with sick officers, and four more bodies were carried by wagon through the smoky air to the Oddfellow's Cemetery above town. I was immediately in a panic, certain that Roy Robbins had again found a way to infect our lives inside the fence, until the day that John Sanders came to me with what he'd discovered. What had poisoned us was not human—not

Roy—but rather a malignancy of lead pipes, a tangle of leaky plumbing behind the second-floor walls that allowed sewage to seep into a water storage basin below. The epidemic died back, along with the rumors of sabotage and my own certainty that cousin Roy was lurking.

Although Roy seemed to have retreated, the war had not. It seemed that the Great War itself had finally emerged from the newspapers and reached a bony hand into the hidden places of our mountain world. On November 17th, Lawrence Rosenstern's perfectly benign article about the camp appeared in *The New York Times* graced with Anna's photographs. One day later, when we saw the paper for the first time, I also received a telegram from Washington, D.C. The plain, unadorned scrap of paper that would cross the length and breadth of North America in the years to follow. Hundreds of thousands of silent electronic impulses that would produce tens of thousands of silent, screeching pieces of brown paper.

```
WAR DEPART WASHINGTON DC
We regret to inform you
of the death of Corporal Edgar Ramsey
Killed in action in Belgium Novem 6 1917
The Secretary extends his sympathy
for the loss of your son
```

Weeks later, I would learn that Edgar, all one hundred and thirty pounds of him, had been killed trying to rescue two other soldiers pinned down by a German machine gun. By virtue of nightfall, they had survived; by virtue of his offhand courage, he had died, and his body was not to be returned.

It was Robert Snyder who explained that Edgar must have listed me not only as his next-of-kin but even as his own father on his enlistment papers. I wished that it might be so; no man more sure in the woods than Edgar Ramsey, no man finer of heart. In the stillness of a November night, I carried the War Department telegram out to the barn and impaled it on one of the nails that fastened Edgar's great bear skin to the iron-cold planks. It seemed to me as I stood beside the barn in a shower of frigid moonlight that we none of us know just who is our child, our child of the spirit or even of the blood. None of us, when humbled, can deny the stinking boy drawing in the dirt street with a stick, or the lonely girl being whipped by her mother just for talking to him.

I wept there in the moonlight, cold twisting into the marrow of my bones, and I wished for Anna. For Anna, who had the eyes to see and the ears to hear what beauty was left in the world. I longed to say something about Edgar to someone who would understand; I longed to feel the touch of living, caring hands. But she was not there; she was asleep, a half-mile away at Sunnybank. And the barn, the great matted hide of Edgar's bear, the telegram fluttering in the icy wind—were all more real by night than she.

The next afternoon I walked there, between the cold dinner we served at noon and the hot supper Pauline planned for evening. I went in my winter loneliness up to Sunnybank, and we stepped out, she and I, walking up the old road along Spring Creek, her gloved hand tucked calmly, tightly into the crook of my arm, burrowing there for simple warmth, I imagined, as well as affection.

We talked, as we most always did. I told her about Edgar Ramsey: his slouching, shambling gait that came from a thousand nights of running through the woods; his crooked, tobacco stained teeth; his prematurely thinning hair. "But his heart was bright," I kept saying. "His heart was young."

"And now he's dead," she said quietly, as we walked. "For no reason at all except that there are crazed old men who want to rule the world. ... Stephen, do you think there's a God?"

We kept walking. But I confess our pace slowed: slowed as her question—as old as a fire for warmth and meat torn from the bone—chewed its way into my mind. "When my father died," I said quietly, "I knew there had to be. I knew there was a God because there had to be someone on the other side of the river to gather him up. But for Edgar to leave here, leave everything he knew, to be carried a thousand miles away, and die staring into a strange sky ... what light?... what God is there in that?"

We walked on, and because her face was lifted—toward the sky, yes, and toward the trees that loomed around us on either side of the road—I lifted my face as well. Lifted my eyes into the frozen ranks of the trees, majestic even in the silence of winter.

"I think there's a God in the trees," she said simply.

"The standing people," I replied.

"Hmmm?"

"The Cherokee call trees the standing people. We are the walking people, and they are the standing people. First cousins, I expect."

"They are like us." She smiled. "I've often thought it. They blossom in the spring, when the sun finds them; they sing all summer with the birds, and then when the frosts come down again, they shrink back into themselves. They shudder and shake, and try to hide from the cold."

"Anna Ulmann," I said in mock surprise. "You *are* a mountain girl."

"Am I then?"

"You sound like it today. Do you know your trees, the ones you're talking about? Dogwood from oak?"

"I know that's a Shagbark Hickory." She waved at a tall, straight behemoth towering over a stand of dogwoods. "Of all the ones you've told me, that's the one I remember. And since he's lost his leaves, you see his coat all the more plain." She pointed at a different, much smaller tree, almost lost in the dense woods beside the road, a tree the smooth, gray trunk of which was rippled, as if with tendon or muscle. "But that's the one I wonder about. I know you've told me, and I know it's something hard, but what ...?"

"Ironwood. My dad always said it was because it *looked* strong."

"Reminds me of you," she said and looked down, almost as if she was embarrassed. She pulled me back toward the smooth, frozen dirt of the road.

"Reminds you of my sterling character?"

"Oh, no," she said. "Some other part of you that ... I remember at night."

Suddenly, it struck me what she meant, and I could feel my face heat up, even in the cold November air.

"Isn't Mrs. Jane gone from home today?" I asked.

"Do you mean is there any reason why we shouldn't visit in my room for this afternoon? Light a fire in that little fireplace?"

"Take a nap?" I said hopefully.

She laughed out loud. "Mrs. Jane is gone to see her daughter in

Marshall, or so she told me at breakfast. No, I cannot think for the life of me why we shouldn't have a nap by the fire."

But as warm an idea as that nap might be, all the more gloriously warm as we walked back along the road toward town, it was not to be. There was an even colder reality waiting for us along a back street behind Sunnybank. A reality that we couldn't avoid.

We climbed the set of stone steps behind the Gehagens' barn up to the lane that ran through the Dorland School. It was a shortcut that would lead us directly to the back porch of Sunnybank and up the kitchen stairs to the nest we craved. As we walked behind the largest building on campus, classrooms on the first floor and dormitories above, a small, frantic woman dashed out from the dark shadows of the porch and stopped in the street before us.

She was there so suddenly and unexpectedly, that both Anna and I drew up in surprise. Some worldly visitor would have said she looked like something out of Dickens: her dress so threadbare that in places it was more like a brown stain on her skin than cloth and thread; her skin so pale that it was almost blue; her hair tied back with strips of rag into a stingy bun. She was thin to the point of emaciation, which made her swollen belly painfully evident.

"You ain't rememberin' me, Mr. Robbins," she said to the ground, her head bowed submissively. "But I used to work fur you afore the war." I followed her eyes down to the ground and saw that her brogan shoes were tied round with rags, which meant that the soles were worn through to the ground.

"Look up so I can see your face," I said as gently as I could. "No need to hang your head down."

She looked up obediently, and her face was pale and sharp like most of the rest of her, with a stray dash of stark brown freckles thrown across her nose, freckles that matched her dull, brown eyes.

"Jonsy?" I said to her. "Used to work as a maid?"

She nodded and curtsied, as we had taught her to do when addressed by a guest of the hotel.

"Jonsy Wright, isn't it?"

And just for a moment, she grinned, as she must have done when a child at play, before her face learned the lines of fatigue and fear. "Yes, sir. My daddy's Bill Wright, the smithy on Spring Creek."

"This is Miss Anna Ulmann, Jonsy, who is visiting us from New York."

"Oh, yessir. I done seen her awalkin' in the afternoons. How'do, Miss Ulmann." She curtsied again; and, although I never saw her do it before or since, so did Anna.

"Miss Wright, it is a pleasure to meet you," she said.

Jonsy Wright was shivering in the gray cold. "Come into the kitchen at Sunnybank, Jonsy, and tell us how you do." And between the two of us, Anna and I led this frighteningly cold woman up to the back porch.

Anna made tea at Jane Gentry's stove, even popping open the stove door to feed a few sticks of oak into the fire, a skill I never would have imagined in her. As she did, Jonsy sat primly at the table and told me about her father and mother, about how she'd found work as a maid at Dorland, about her one brother who had escaped going to the penitentiary by joining the army and about her sister who'd married well in Tennessee. She was a graceful story teller, direct and precise.

"Might you be married also, Jonsy?" I said, again as gently as I could, with her stomach pushing her back from the table.

"Oh, no sir. Looks like I ought to be, I know. That's why I can't go up home this winter like I do. I ain't got no husband to father this baby, and I'm afraid they won't keep me at the school for I'm become a bad example to the girls."

"Do you need work, Jonsy? You'd might come over to the camp and let us find you something to do inside the Mountain Park where it's warm." I thought I could see tears beginning to glisten, even though, like most mountain women, she was unlikely to let a man see her cry.

"Oh, Lord, Mr. Robbins, I need work awful bad, but what am I to do when it comes around spring and this baby ripens? I can't help you none then."

"No, but by then you'll have earned enough credit that it will be our turn to help you. I can't say for sure, but I bet Pauline would like to have some good help in the kitchen, and when your baby comes along, she'll like as not want to help you raise it."

Anna set mugs of steaming tea on the old scarred table, napkins and spoons and sugar; and her serving distracted me for a moment so that I didn't see Jonsy begin to cry. But when I looked back at her face, there were slow, silent tears sliding through her freckles, and her lips were trembling.

"I don't know that Mrs. Robbins would want me in her kitchen, sir," she whispered.

"You mean Pauline? Why in the world not?"

"She might not care for this baby so much neither, once she seen it."

My mind circled the obvious. "Is Roy Robbins the father of your child, Jonsy?" And I hated myself as I said it, for the question came out of me with the sound of Old Testament prophesy, dire and deliberate, packed with all the pent-up emotion I stocked for the man.

Jonsy nodded miserably, and Anna dragged her chair to the girl's side, giving me a warning look as she did so.

"He came here and hid out with you while he spied on the camp, did he? Over there in the basement of the schoolhouse?"

"Yessir, but I promise afore God that I didn't know he was a spyin'. I thought he just wanted me for myself." She had stopped crying, and the stern courage of a mountain woman was in her countenance again. And in her words. "I was fool enough to think he liked how I did for him. Fixin' up leftovers and warmin' his bed for him."

I thought suddenly of the small, bare footprints I'd seen in the Spring Creek mud just outside the hole Siegfried had cut in the fence. "Did Roy ever ask you to carry messages to one of the Germans, Jonsy?"

She nodded, suddenly happy to be of help. "A real, pretty blond-headed boy. Sweet-talkin'. Roy wanted me to carry him some pistols once, but I wouldn't do that."

"Did he beat you, Jonsy?"

Anna looked up in surprise, not knowing Roy's reputation as I did.

"Well, you know he did," Jonsy replied matter-of-factly. "Right reg'lar. But I thought he'd quit beatin' on me when he seen I was car-ryin' this baby." She glanced up at Anna. "I'm sorry for you to have to hear this, Miss Ulmann. For you ain't from around here like me and Mr. Robbins. But some mountain men'll beat a woman like we was mules or dogs or somethin'. But they won't nary touch a woman once she's bearin'."

Anna was close to tears now and nodding.

"What did he say when you told him you were to have his child?" I asked, knowing full well what she would say.

"Oh, he cussed at me and threw me up agin' the wall as if to hit me, but he stopped short of that. Then he hissed at me like an old snake and said the baby weren't his'n. Told me to keep my mouth shut, and he'd send along some money if it was a boy." She turned to Anna. "It's all right, Miss. Don't cry. You see, the sheriff was afraid a me once he knew I was spectin'. He knew if he hurt me after that, then Mr. Robbins would kill him."

I looked up in surprise. Jonsy Wright was nodding reassuringly at Anna, who was staring at me in some kind of shock. "You mean ... my Mr. Robbins?" Anna nodded at me.

"Yep, that old sheriff is determined to run ... your Mr. Robbins out of his job, even if he has to tear up the German camp to do it, but even so, he's still afraid after all these years."

"Afraid of Stephen?"

Jonsy nodded happily. "For he beat him so bad when he was a boy."

I nodded at Anna. And ever so gently, borrowed Jonsy's phrase to explain. "Right regular," I said. "Because he seemed to need it so much."

Anna nodded. "Apparently so."

Mrs. Jane Gentry found us that evening, still together within the warm circle of her kitchen. And rather than take Jonsy inside the fence and inside the Park, we agreed that she was to move her few, ragged belongings into Sunnybank, where she could help Mrs. Jane, and Anna could keep an eye on her.

And so we sat together 'til supper time, while Mrs. Jane peeled and sliced apples for a pie. "You need never fear Pauline," I reassured Jonsy at one point, as I was replaying our conversation over in my mind. "She's more likely to adopt you for a sister than anything else."

Mrs. Jane nodded from the stove. "There'll be a bond betwixt the two of you now, since you have that son-of-a-bitch in common."

But Mrs. Jane also knew what I did—knew what Anna did not. That by taking in Jonsy Wright, they were placing the household in peril. The countless mountain girls that Roy had forced himself on in the years prior to the war—all of them poor and ignorant enough to derive some hope from him—had all disappeared in one way or another. They had gone back up home to their families and been absorbed into the warp and woof of life in an isolated cove, or they had left with a one-way train ticket north, or in one or two cases, they had simply died. In childbirth.

By taking her in, Mrs. Jane knew that she, and probably Anna as well, were placing themselves in Roy's path. Living in the same house with a secret he didn't want known. And, I suspect she also knew that they were aligning themselves with me, the man he despised most in the world. For all these reasons, I wanted to move Jonsy into the camp and put her to work inside the Park, but neither Anna nor Mrs. Jane would hear of it. For some reason, they thought they could take better care of her than I could.

I found Anna the next day in the basement, deep in the bowels of the Mountain Park, where the German photographer Thierbach, had helped her create a laboratory in a cold storage room where there were long tables and a sink. She had a German assistant that Ruser and Schlimbech had assigned to her, but she sent him out when I knocked on the door.

The room itself was always chilly that winter, and because it was not well ventilated, smelled sour from the chemicals she used to transfer the images from her glass plates to specially prepared paper. And while she was working, it was spooky dark, lit only by red light bulbs she had ordered from Raleigh—bulbs that had arrived on the train wrapped in a cocoon of shredded paper in a specially padded box.

I had tried to help her several times before, thinking there would be some intimacy working alone together in the sealed room. But Anna Ulmann was all business in her laboratory. Not only would she not let me touch her; she would not let me mix the chemicals. Nor would she let me handle the plates before she had brought out the images through a series of chemical washes.

Only after she had prints on paper would she hand me a plate to lean on an old hotel towel to dry, and even then, she had to lecture me over and over about how to touch and handle the precious glass. The paper prints she would clip to a long line over our heads where they would hang suspended while they dried. She, who could be careless in so many things, was an absolute perfectionist about the process by which her precious glass plates became photographic images on paper. Several times before, she had made me leave the laboratory, saying bluntly that my presence there distracted her when she should be focused on her work.

That day, however, the day after the disturbing confessions of Jonsy Wright, she did let me stay inside the sealed door with her, allowing me to watch while she worked. Eventually, she did something unprecedented in our relationship. She helped me mount one particular glass plate into a metal platform that the Germans had made for her and shine a bright light through the plate onto a sheet of specially prepared paper.

Then I sat with her standing at my shoulder, her chemical-stained hand resting at the base of my neck while I carefully swished the paper in a shallow metal dish half-full with a clear, pungent chemical bath. "When you think it's just at the right stage, then set the tray down and I'll pull the print out with the tongs," she whispered. "You know this face better than anyone alive, and you'll know when it's just right."

Even as she said it, I couldn't imagine just what it was that we were about to see—or who. But then I could perceive the vague outline of the door of my mother's house, the frame of the porch roof and the floor, and I knew what would emerge. What was frozen inside the mechanics of Anna's art. And then, there it was, my mother's face, outlined severely against the inky background of the open door. I stared, suddenly unable to blink, as she pulled back slightly on my shoulder to keep me from sticking my face all the way into the tray.

"Easy, easy," she whispered. "It'll burn you. Just watch, watch the lines of her face, the smallest detail will tell you when to stop."

And she was right, exactly so. Just at the moment when I could feel the tears well up in my eyes because what I saw was so painfully her, my own dear mother, her face there before me swimming on the table, I set the tray down. None too gently, I confess, because my hands were shaking, my forearms burning from the tension.

She ever so deftly used the tongs—on permanent loan from the kitchen—to capture the curling paper. Even with one hand still resting at the base of my neck, she was as sure-handed as a surgeon, and then her touch was gone too as she used both hands to clip the edge of the print to the line above.

I slumped with my eyes closed, the image of my mother's face lingering on the inside of my closed lids, knowing that if I opened my eyes, she would disappear again.

Then I felt both of Anna's hands on my shoulders and the weight of her body as she leaned against me. "You did very well," she said quietly against the back of my head. "For your first time, you were almost delicate."

I could feel the skin on my hands burning. "Except that I spilled half the wash when I threw the dish down."

She smiled; I could feel her smile against my hair. "Everybody does that," she said. "Why do you think my hands are so ugly?"

I shook my head. "Not ugly," I said. Those same hands were rubbing at my shoulders, trying to find and release the frozen knots that I carried there. "Never ugly."

"Stephen?"

"Hmmm?"

"Would it help to tell me about Bird's husband?"

I had begun to relax, the world was dark and close, and for some reason it didn't seem like a strange question.

"Help me?"

"Yes. Or help me. I'd like to know just how or why."

"Nathan Robbins was his name. He was a dirt farmer. One hog in a good year. Perhaps one milk cow in all his miserable existence."

"Isn't her name Shelton?"

"Bird?"

She nodded, her chin rubbing against my head, so that suddenly I wanted badly to turn around and into her. But I knew she wanted me to talk, to tell it first.

"Is. Bird Shelton. I don't believe she ever married him in a church."

"And she worked at the Park?"

"Yes. As a flower girl. But she was so cheerful, so full of sound and smiling all the time, that she began to help out by serving in the dining room at dinner. And I'm sure took home leftover food. Kept herself and Nathan from starving probably."

"And he attacked her."

"Oh, he meant to kill her. Came after her in the dining room with a corn knife, a long, curved knife we use to chop corn stalks down to make fodder. He had knocked her down and was standing over her with the knife raised when I shot him." I could feel the terrible tension returning to my back and creeping up into my shoulders. "I wasn't drunk," I said. "Even though they said I was at the trial."

"If you were drunk, you couldn't have saved her, now could you?" she said. Spoke out loud what I had whispered to myself a thousand times. "But why, Stephen?" Anna went on. "Why would he attack her? She's the most gentle creature on earth."

"She was then, too. Gentle, I mean. But he was proud. Proud like all the Robbins, and stubborn. And it tore him apart to know that every day he was eating somebody's handout. Some leftover meat and potatoes that had sat on somebody else's plate first. And even worse, that it was his wife that was bringing home the food rather than the other way around."

"Had you ever seen him before?"

"I had seen him when I was a kid, years before up home, but not so I remembered. And I'd warned him away from the Park once when he was drunk out behind the kitchen, yelling for Bird to come home and do for him. But the strange thing was I never realized who he was until he was lying on the floor in the dining room, bleeding all over creation. Never knew."

"Never knew that he was Bird's husband?"

"No, that was plain enough. Never realized that the husband she kept warning us about was Nathan Robbins, Roy's brother."

"Oh, Stephen ... I'm so—"

"Make a hell of a story in New York, wouldn't it? Cousins shooting down cousins, a feudin' in them thar hills."

"New Yorkers are not especially kind," she admitted. "Imagine Larry Rosenstern—"

"New York can go fuck itself on a hoe handle," I said.

And bless her, she laughed. Laughed out loud and couldn't stop laughing. When she finally did stop, there, in the acid darkness of her laboratory, she wrapped her arms around me, and finally, finally I turned on the stool, away from the burning images of my mother, of Bird, of the searing blast of the shotgun, of the blood—turned away from all that and leaned into her.

Thus, it was the very next day that I brought that same shotgun, the well-worn Remington that Jack Rumbough had called the goose gun, up to Sunnybank. It was an afternoon beautiful the way early autumn is beautiful, even though we were well into November by then, with sunlight as warm as the golden leaves still clinging to the maples. On that gorgeous afternoon, I taught Miss Anna Ulmann of Fifth Avenue, New York to load, aim, and fire a shotgun.

"What a romantic gift," she said teasingly, when it became evident that I meant her to keep it loaded beside her bed.

"Romantic enough," I said, for once as serious as I knew how to be. "If it keeps you safe from what's out there in the dark."

CHAPTER TWENTY

THE golden days of mid-November did not last. And when they had disappeared downstream, cold and ice followed. The late-November air itself seemed denser, harsher; the nights seemed to consume the days; and soon we ate all but the mid-day meal by lamplight.

The world inside the fence was troubled by the growing cold and dark. The usually regimented Germans grew restless as the days grew shorter, forcing them inside, and I spent more and more of my time keeping peace inside the wire. I missed Anna cruelly, and the world seemed to draw in on itself. The nights were bitter cold for that time of year; Spring Creek froze solid, and thick ice formed along the edges of the river everywhere except where the hot springs bubbled up from below.

Out of the depths of those nights and the frigid darkness of that season came the devil, scratching in the frozen dirt and ravenous for our blood.

In the middle of a Sunday night, the Sunday before Thanksgiving, Bird woke me from a restless doze. I had read myself to fitful sleep while still lying on top of the covers in my clothes with my robe pulled over me. Even so, it felt entirely odd that someone was inside my rooms, standing beside my bed, shaking me furiously.

I pushed up off the bed as though pulling myself out of a deep hole, and even as I struggled to stand, Bird rushed to the chifforobe and fished in its depths for the goose gun. When I realized what she was looking for, I waved her off and retrieved the major's pistol from a desk drawer, the gun that I had cleaned and loaded after giving the shotgun to Anna.

Even half asleep, I could all but smell her fear. Something truly ugly was going on, and without thinking, I poured .32 caliber shells into my coat pocket.

Despite her twisted torso, Bird's legs were just fine, and I had to run to keep up with her as she lifted her ancient nightgown about her knees and sprinted down the third-floor hall and into the stairwell. I broke open the cylinder of the pistol and checked the load as we tore down the stairs.

When we reached the first floor, we turned right toward the back of the strangely silent hotel, and she led me through a side door into the kitchen. Through the kitchen proper and into the small back apartment that had been assigned to D. C. Peinart. Bird pushed the door open before me and then turned away as if to shield herself from what was inside.

The room was a shambles. D. C.'s small table lay on its side against the far wall, half obscuring a shattered exterior window. Cold air from outside was flooding into the room in waves. One chair stood upright and undisturbed but the other was smashed to pieces. D. C.'s bed was also thrown onto its side, and I could see the man's bare feet sticking out from behind it as he apparently lay between the bed and the wall. I could hear him moaning.

But I was wrong. D. C. Peinart was not lying behind his bed; he was kneeling over the mostly naked body of Pauline Robbins. He was moaning as he wiped gently at her face and neck with a handkerchief, rocking on his knees and whispering to her in a singsong pigeon of German and English.

I pulled him carefully to one side and knelt beside her. Pauline's face had been brutally battered, and part of her hair was pulled from the scalp on the side of her head, but she was breathing evenly. Her skin had a sickly green cast in the faint electric light. I lifted the shirt D. C. had laid over her chest just enough to see that one long bruise ran from beneath her ear over her strangely sunken collar bone and almost to her breast. She was wearing a robe that was mostly knotted beneath her body, D. C.'s robe I assumed, and nothing else.

I lifted first one strong forearm and then the other to the light, and it was just as I expected. The knuckles on her right hand were badly bruised and her little finger broken. And in her left hand was clutched the wire ear piece from a pair of eyeglasses. Her skin was disturbingly cool to the touch, and I pulled the blanket from the bed over her.

I stood and lifted D. C. bodily to his feet. When I did, I could see that his face was streaked with dried blood and that he had tied what looked like an apron around his forehead. "Did you see Roy at all?" I asked him. He continued to stare past me and mutter to Pauline. I shook him like a doll, resisting the urge to slap him. "D. C.! Did you see who did this?"

He stared at me vacantly for a moment before answering. "No. He struck me as I came in at the door. Just as I saw the wreck of our room, he struck me on the head." Even D. C.'s teeth were black where the blood had run from his forehead down into his mouth.

Holding him up by the collar, I walked him into the kitchen. Bird was standing there, and in the interim had gone to her room for her own apron as well as her coat and shoes. And I knew without asking that she'd stuck her butcher knife into her apron pocket, ready as she always was for what next.

"You actually see Roy?" I asked her.

She shook her torso and head, no.

"How long ago you think he was here?"

She pointed down at the floor just inside the door where a clock lay on its face. I picked it up—a beautifully ornate mantle clock—and could see that it had stopped at ten-thirty. Stopped when it had been flung to the floor. My own watch was upstairs, but I knew it was much later.

I tried to sit D. C., who was still moaning to himself, down in a chair, but the minute I released him, he went straight back to Pauline.

Bird looked at me and cut her eyes at the doorway behind me.

"No, she'll live," I replied. "Looks like she fought him off or D. C. came in just in time. Or both. You run get as many guards off the fence as you can find quickly. We've got to move them in case he decides to come back and finish up."

While she was gone, I racked my brain for the place I could hide them. Hide them long enough for me to find Roy. And when I thought I might have the place, my mind immediately leaped forward to what had drawn Roy away in the first place. There had to be something or he would have taken D. C. with him. Taken him, or at the very least, killed him on the spot. I knew Cousin Roy only too well, and I knew there had to be something else.

When we got to the gatehouse with Pauline and D. C., I got my first clue as to what it was.

We had made a stretcher for Pauline from the slats out of D. C.'s bed and padded it with his blankets. After binding her one arm—I was certain her collar bone at least was broken—tightly against her side, I helped a team of guards carry her out to the gate, with Bird and D. C. to steady the stretcher. At first, I thought to hide them at Sunnybank, under Mrs. Jane's broad wing, but Jonsy and Anna were there. It had to be somewhere else, but where?

When we got to the Camp A gatehouse, however, the guard from B crossed the street to pull me aside. "You send the sheriff over here to collect that prisoner?" he whispered, obviously worried.

"Hell no," I stuttered. "Is he in there?" I motioned for the stretcher bearers to wait, and they laid Pauline down on the guardhouse table.

"Come and gone," admitted the guard, whose name I couldn't think of. "Took that tow-headed man who was in the jail with him."

"Sit tight for a few minutes," I said to Bird. And to the guards, "Don't let anybody near her." Meaning Pauline.

I ran across the street, through the gate and as fast as I could to the gaol fifty yards away. The outside door was standing wide open. Gehagen was lying in the front room groaning. I jumped over him and found Siegfried's cell door thrown open as well, with a piece of folded paper stuck into a seam between the planks. I held the paper up to the lantern in the front room long enough to see that it was a warrant for Siegfried's arrest on a charge of attempted murder.

"You all right?" I wrote quickly on Gehagen's slate, the board he used to communicate with.

He was sitting up, leaning against the wall. He nodded and held up his own revolver and motioned at his head, meaning to say that he'd been pistol-whipped.

"You and everybody else," I said to him as I took the gun out of his hand. "I may need this before the night's over, Foster," I said. "And I'm sorry. I wouldn't have left you in Roy's way if I'd had any idea."

Of course he didn't understand what I was saying, but he smiled weakly and motioned for me to go on.

I sent the guards with Pauline and D. C. up the hill to Rutland, away from the main part of town. I sent Bird to wake Prince and take him to meet them: Prince to take charge and guard the house. I ran myself to Sunnybank, ran as the wind tossed with a lonely cry in the tree tops. As my mind swirled in Roy's wake, I remembered that he knew Anna had seen him with Siegfried, making Anna a witness to his crimes. And the thought of a bruised and battered Roy Robbins in the same house with Anna took my breath away.

The house itself was dark and quiet as I hurried up the terraces from the street to the front porch, so I ran around back and pounded on the kitchen door. I knew Mrs. Jane's room was at the back near the kitchen and that I'd have to rouse her to move Anna and Jonsy Wright. The thin, wavering light of a lamp appeared in the kitchen windows, and suddenly she was at the door.

Even though slightly stunned with sleep and more than a little frowzy in her great, quilted robe, Jane grasped the urgency of the situation the minute I told her that Roy Robbins was on the loose and perhaps looking to harm Anna. "You need to get 'em both out of here," she whispered, loudly enough to be heard in the parlor.

"I know. I mean to take them up to Rutland and post the camp guards 'til I can find Roy. But you've got to—" She was already gone up the stairs, and I could hear her knocking first on one door and then another.

Jane must have made an impression because in just a few minutes, both Anna and Jonsy came down the steps together. Jonsy looking tired and drawn, but Anna leading her along.

I tried not to stare openly into Anna's face as I told them to throw on their coats. "It's cold as a well digger's ass," I said. "And we're going out the front door and up by Prince's house to Rutland."

"But why in the middle of—" Jonsy began sleepily but Anna hushed her.

"No, you should both know. The sheriff took Siegfried out of the camp jail and left a warrant for attempted murder." I looked straight at Anna. "He knows you saw him talking to Siegfried beforehand, and if he means to shut Siegfried up, he'll come for you next. Now hurry, damn it! And bring the shotgun!" I called up the steps after Anna.

While they scattered for coats and hats, Jane came clumping back down the steps, having added her heavy brogan shoes to the robe. I held out Gehagen's pistol to her. "You better keep this just in case," I said.

She gave a short, hard laugh. "I got a lot more gun than that little pissant," she said. "Sides, you better carry that and more. Make Roy's night to kill you along the way."

"No doubt it would."

She enveloped me in a huge hug. "Get them two little women outta here," she said. "If old Roy does show up, I'll fire off a warning shot."

I led Anna and Jonsy out the front door, not wanting to meet Roy in the shadows out back; then down the front steps into the street. As we climbed the steep hill behind Rutland, all three of us breathing hard in the frigid air, Anna pulled at my arm so she could whisper in my ear.

"Stephen, is Jonsy really in danger?"

"Not nearly as much as you are," I explained in a gasping whisper of my own. "Roy hates me, and he'd love to hurt you just to get at me. Plus, Siegfried ties him to an attempted murder, and you saw him with Siegfried." I pulled her to a stop beside me for a brief instant, to let Jonsy get a little ahead of us.

"He caught Pauline in D.C.'s room tonight and beat her senseless. All of which says his blood is up. ... I'm taking both of you to Rutland, where I've already sent Pauline and D. C. Prince should be there by now and enough guards to hold." We were in the back gate at Rutland by then, our breath smoking in the still air, and Jonsy was already knocking on the door. "Please God, just stay put," I whispered fiercely to Anna, my face inches from hers. "I think you'll be safe here until I get back."

"What do you mean, *get back*?" she said, just as fiercely.

"I mean I've got to try to save Siegfried if he's not already dead."

"You're going after Roy?"

"I don't have a choice. Siegfried's a dead man otherwise, and I've already lost seven of 'em."

"Seven Germans?"

I nodded dumbly. "Not to mention Robbie Griffin and Julius Christopher."

"Then I'm going with you," said an unexpected voice from the porch.

Johnny Rumbough stepped down from the shadows. "You know my brother probably put him up to this, and we owe it to you to—"

"You owe it to me to finish growing up," I said to him quickly, even cruelly.

"I am grown up. Grown up enough to help."

"Not with Roy, you're not," I said. "I need you to take care of Anna ..." I almost said, and Jonsy, but decided to stop with the truth. I glanced around for Anna, hoping she had gone inside.

It was a frozen moment, with Johnny staring at me, all the raging frustration of being seventeen racing across his face. "I'm sorry, Johnny," I said, "but I'm responsible for you too."

I walked around the house and down through the yard past the boxwood maze. I meant to go straight through town past the camps and to the French Broad Bridge. Somewhere between here and there, Roy was waiting for me; and if not waiting, then he was across the river, and I'd have to chase him down the Turnpike toward Marshall and the county jail.

But before I reached the steps at the foot of the yard, I got my next surprise. Anna stepped out from behind the boxwood hedge with King James at her heel and fell into place beside me, struggling to match my gait and carry the shotgun.

"Where in the hell do you think you're going?" I asked out loud, too aggravated to hide my fear.

"With you," she said.

I wheeled on her. "Hell you say. What in our past relations makes you think I will let you chase through the dark with—"

"Damn you, Stephen," she stopped me cold. "I have to. I can't sit in the house any longer. I just can't. Maybe our past relations are about to be future relations, but they won't be if you go out and get yourself killed."

"You'd rather get killed with me?" I'm not sure I meant to say exactly that, but the words were suddenly there.

She nodded furiously. "Better that than be locked up alone." She took a deep breath and waved the shotgun at me. "Besides, you need me to protect you."

I tried; I honestly tried not to laugh. Not at her. But at the both of us. Standing in the middle of the road in the middle of the winter night waving guns at each other. And still flirting. King James barked at me, laughing along in his own dogged way.

"What the hell is so funny about that?" she asked, trying to keep a straight face.

"Just about every damn thing I can think of," I said, still laughing. And started walking down the dark drive, feeling her, hearing her laugh in reply as she walked beside me.

"Just tell me one thing," I said when we reached Bridge Street. "If he comes after you, will you shoot him?"

"I think so," she said.

"Don't think. For my sake, just aim and pull the trigger."

We didn't have to go far, Anna and I. When we came to the end of Bridge Street at the river, we faced Robert Snyder's new bridge, constructed with War Department steel. We could see a mysterious, solitary figure halfway across in the dim moonlight, standing beside one of the upright steel beams that provided structural support to the span. As we came out onto the planks of the bridge floor, perhaps fifty feet away, I could barely make out that it was Siegfried, more by his blond hair than anything else.

I stopped Anna with my hand on her arm and called out to him to come to us. In what seemed like a dream, he jerked his arms up and down against the post and they rattled.

"What—?" Anna began.

"He's handcuffed," I interrupted her.

"Mustn't we save him?"

"Fish don't save the bait, Anna."

For a long moment, all time seemed to stop, with only the river flowing by twenty feet below us. With only my beloved river to remind me that the world had not just stopped in place. The rushing, sluicing sound of the water passing beneath and above us the scudding clouds that passed, obscuring the moon. We were all trapped in place together: Siegfried by his handcuffs, Anna by her fierce independence, Roy—wherever he was—by his legion of demons, and even me, trapped by having brought them all together. Trapped inside the wire of our own high fence.

"Please stay here," I whispered calmly to Anna.

I walked forward, my shoe heels echoing as they struck the decking, and for once, Anna actually did what I asked. I knew Roy had to be somewhere, and yet there seemed to be no place on the vacant bridge where he could hide. King James stalked beside me, growling for no apparent reason at Siegfried. I wondered why Siegfried did not speak; he didn't appear to be gagged and yet ... When I was about three feet away, I put the pistol I'd been carrying at the ready into my own pocket, so that I could try to free Siegfried.

And at that perfect moment, my cousin Roy, my mother's brother's son, stepped out from behind Siegfried and the beam and struck me flush between the eyes with the long-barreled pistol in his fist.

I could feel that I was down, writhing on the wooden planks, and in the sudden, raw shock, I was convinced I'd been shot. I could hear the King barking savagely, standing over me, but I was blinded by thick blood, and during the first, exploding seconds could do nothing but wipe savagely at my face, trying to clear my eyes.

Then I heard a vicious explosion just behind me, followed by a hoarse, animal grunt, and then something like a building or a ship fell onto me, crushing me, drowning me down in a scarlet flood.

After some long moment of being unable to breathe, I could feel the mysterious weight being rolled off me. I was ever so slowly regaining some sense of my own body, my own form; lying on my back against the cold, stiff planks of ... a bridge ... our French Broad bridge. And someone was gently wiping water ... or blood ... from around my eyes and my mouth. My mouth was gaping open like a fish's, full of the rusty taste of blood and gasping in the cold air. Just for a moment I felt the warm breath of some other and then a hard-soft pressure against my straining lips. I paused; in the middle of that nightmare, something had pressed its lips against my shattered face.

I would believe later that I never totally lost awareness during those few fractured and violent moments, for it seemed to me that I had sensation throughout. Had some sense, however scrambled, of being struck down; of King James' stout defense, of Anna's double-barreled blast that struck Roy in the stomach; and of his harsh grunt before he collapsed, nearly suffocating me. Of my long moment spent drowning in his gushing blood mingled with my own, while Anna fumbled for the keys in Roy's torn coat pocket and uncuffed Siegfried from the bridge. Of King James licking at the blood on my face. And the most telling sensation of all: Anna's anguished kiss.

The two of them, Siegfried Sonnach and Anna Ulmann, helped me to sit up, and I gained some dizzy sense of consciousness as I tried to push on up to my feet. "*Mein Got*, Stephen, what do we do?"

Out of some broken set of dreams, I answered. "Leave the gun," I whispered. "They'll know it's mine. We will walk ... through the middle of town ... and up the hill to Rutland." I was swallowing warm, salty blood even as I tried to string the sentences together. "You will have to help me walk for a ways 'til I can get my feet ..." They didn't understand yet; we weren't moving. "Goddamn it, there's a crowd coming. Go! Go now!"

And so we went, the two of them supporting me between them, my feet dragging though I strained to lift them.

There were two parallel streams in that long, shambling walk back to Rutland. One was the external night time world that I could barely testify to: first the camp fences and then the fuzzy buildings of the town. The physical sense of shuffling down the frozen dirt street as the dog dashed silently ahead and then back to walk beside us before racing ahead again. The sense of being propped up on one side by Siegfried, his teeth chattering in the cold; and on the other by Anna, whose bobbing, determined head came just to my shoulder. Though I had wiped away most of the blood with my shirt, my vision was still blurry from the swelling, so that the outside world through which we stumbled seemed far less real than the roaring inside my head.

A tide of pain, deep and throbbing, rose beneath the burning needles in my face. A tide that I knew probably meant a concussion, shock and maybe loss of consciousness. And I knew that I had to fight it off long enough to think. Long enough to finish the job I'd been given only a few hours before when Bird dragged me out of bed—or was it months ago when Major Rumbough had put me in charge of the camp.

"Go faster, damn it," I whispered hoarsely when we reached the drive at the foot of the hill.

"But your face," Anna began. "It will—"

"Hell with my face!" My lips, even my gums, felt thick, and I could feel gaps in my teeth. "Drag me up the hill if you have to but hurry!" And they broke into a tottering, lurching jog, the cold air stinging my broken face and the blood pounding in my head.

But I was awake. The pain helped me think. I could feed on the pain to keep myself awake long enough to slowly untie the knot in my mind. *Somebody would stand trial for Roy ... Ed Rumbough would see to that ... One of the three of us would face a judge ... and a mean-ass Madison County jury ... Siegfried would hang ... just for being German ... Anna, oh God, would ... I couldn't think it ... for being a woman shooting a man ... I would hang just ... I would not hang ... not so likely to hang if ... my face hurts so damn bad ... I don't care if I hang.*

"What you say?" Siegfried cried out. We were laboring up the steps into the front yard.

Don't care if I hang ... I said inside my raging head, shoving the pain back with each ragged breath.

We got as far as the front steps, where they both all but fell, exhausted from half-carrying me; nothing in Anna's months of walking or Siegfried's incarceration had prepared them for this. The King was barking at the door, calling out for help.

I sat on the steps between them, gulping deep, wheezing breath after deep, wheezing breath, and when a uniformed figure swam vaguely into sight before me—I only had the use of one eye by then—I told him to get me Johnny Rumbough.

And when he came, a much larger figure came with him. Pauline, I guessed from the lopsided appearance, one arm strapped to her chest.

I tried to keep my face intentionally away from Anna throughout the harrowing walk back to Rutland, and now I turned away from Johnny. Even so, I heard him grunt when he caught a glimpse.

"Listen, Johnny," I said to him, as carefully and clearly as I could. "We don't have much time. You too, Pauline. Roy has been shot dead." I tried to speak slowly because I knew I was hard to understand. "We got to get Pauline and D. C. out of here tonight. Far away as possible. Pauline, the back way to Paint Rock on the Tennessee line. Catch the train north. Johnny here'll go with you as far as Knoxville."

"I'm not running away from my home," Pauline said clearly.

"Lean over here," I said to her furiously, spitting blood onto her bare feet. And when she did, I growled into her hair. "If you don't get

D. C. out of here tonight, you and him both will be testifying at a murder trial. Don't be a fool, just go." I let that sink in. I could feel the shift in her body as she rested her one good hand on my back.

She straightened up, heaved a huge sigh, and started up the steps. And so out of my mind. If Pauline was determined to go to save her little man, then go they would.

Anna was pulling at my arm. I could sense she wanted to take me inside, but not yet I kept thinking. "Not yet," I more-or-less said to her. But drag me inside they did: Prince and Dora and Anna. Laid me on the couch in the front room and started on me with warm towels. And oh, my Lord God, it hurt. And I cursing at them until finally Anna made out what I was saying. "Not yet, damn it! If you keep on doctoring, I'll pass out. Get me Prince!"

"Prince is right here, Stephen."

"Prince, damn it!"

"I'm right here, Stevie. You don't have to yell."

"Is Siegfried still—?

"He's in the kitchen. Shaking like a leaf."

"Roy's dead. Gut shot. Sieg—"

"Siegfried?"

"Was in his custody. First suspect. You got to get him out of here tonight." There was a long pause. A pause that surprised me; surely to God Prince could see ...

"Where must he go? How?" Anna's voice.

"Prince can take him south. Get him on the train at Stackhouse or Barnard, not Marshall. But south toward the coast. Hell, Florida. Anybody can disappear in Florida, or leave the country."

"You sure about this, Stevie. You took a hell of a whack on the head."

"He didn't shoot him, Prince. You hear me; he didn't shoot him, but they'll hang him for it."

The room seemed lighter; Prince must have gone to the kitchen.

"Anna?"

"I'm here, Stephen."

"Please lean close. I know it's awful, but I have to whisper." I could feel her breath against my battered face. "You better go too."

"What!"

"I will ... have to stand trial ... for Roy. I will. But even so ... you better go too. New York." The scarlet tide of pain was rising, tearing through me, and I hated the words New York, New York, New York.

"I'm not leaving you like this," she said clearly. "Can you hear me, Stephen. The rest can go, but I'm not leaving. ... What are you trying to say?"

"New York!" I all but shouted, half rising off the couch. Hating myself for bleeding, for bleeding on her hair, her shoulder, her arm. "Promise me ... you'll go. They won't hang ... they won't hang me for Roy, but you must go."

"Are you sure? Stephen, are you sure?"

I was nodding. My bloody head, my straining neck. My whole body was nodding at her.

"Stephen? I'm not leaving. Do you hear me say I'm not leaving you?" Her voice, her very breath, were so close.

I hear you, I tried to say. *Please, oh please,* I tried to say, as I sank finally, inexorably beneath the flood.

CHAPTER TWENTY-ONE

I spent most of the next month in an eight-by-eight foot basement cell in the old Buncombe County jail, that ugly, squat building that stood for years on the edge of the public square in Asheville. Cold, miserable, cramped quarters for a man used to gazing out at the world from the balcony of a third-floor hotel suite.

Occasionally in life, one is given an irony so appropriate, so just, that it has a gorgeous quality all its own. Roy Robbins' deputies laughed off Anna's first, desperate confession when they came around to Rutland to arrest me. Shoved her out of the way and led me roughly out to the wagon they came in even though I was barely conscious and couldn't put one foot coherently in front of the other. Later, when she tried again to speak to the state's attorney in Asheville, he showed her the door without even bothering to take her statement. Ed Rumbough had discovered in Roy's murder the chance to get rid of me once and for all, and nobody under his influence was going to listen to her claims that she had shot Roy instead of me. I learned to pray that winter simply by praying that her protests would continue to fall on deaf ears, and my prayers were answered.

There was no Thanksgiving that I can attest to, as my first week in jail was spent with my face wrapped in bandages, even my eyes padded and swathed in cotton. The alcoholic Dr. Hugh McGuire who anointed and re-sewed and bandaged me up took some delight in explaining that even in the pitch black dark on the river bridge, Roy had struck me a telling blow: the long barrel of that pistol crushing my nose and cracking the bone just behind my upper lip while the butt of the pistol clipped the side of my face and knocked out two teeth. The sight on the end of the barrel was what had sliced through my cheek to the bone, and what's worse, I had been carelessly stitched up in Marshall while I waited to be moved to Asheville.

So it was McGuire who first tried to put my face back together, two days after Roy had wrecked it. "Wonder you could see to shoot him," he added, as he took another turn around my head with the bandage roll.

How had Siegfried stood it? I wondered to myself, as I lay at night, shivering under my thin blanket, my bandages only just allowing me to breathe. How had someone as mercurial as Siegfried stood days upon days in the gaol at Hot Springs when I was about to crawl out of my skin after only a few in the Asheville jail? And in the dark, middle watches of the night, I even began to wonder just who had the right to fence in another human being, no matter what the charge or what the war.

The only visitor I was allowed that first week was Prince Garner, Prince among men, who talked his way into seeing me on the Sunday after Thanksgiving. My face was still swathed in bandages, although by this time McGuire had uncovered my eyes, and I could at least see Prince as I talked to him.

"How bad is it?" Was the first thing I asked him.

"Your face?" They wouldn't give the man a chair, so he was sitting beside me on my lousy cot.

"No, I can feel that part. I mean how bad is the trial likely to be."

"Well, seems to me things could be worse."

"How?"

"Well, maybe if you had every single one of the Rumboughs screaming after your blood. Way it is now, Ed and the sisters have everybody in Asheville convinced that Roy was a Baptist deacon in pursuit of his duty, and that you have always been a sorry-ass drunk."

"So, how could it be worse?"

"Miss Caddie, the crazy one, is a'prayin' for you day and night, and calling her brother, let me see, the *Toad of Perdition*. I think that was the latest thing I heard."

"Toad of Perdition. You have to admire a crazy woman like Caddie."

"Yes, you do. But more to the point, the littlest one, our boy Johnny, ain't crazy, and he is convinced of your innocence."

"Innocence?"

"Well, he's convinced that if you did shoot Roy, it was just what was required at the time."

"Why am I being tried here and not up home?"

"Ed took care of that."

"Shit!"

"Yeah, well. We been a'knowin' that. Now listen to me, Stevie." Prince put his massive, brotherly arm around me. "Here directly, they gonna run me outa here, and there's two things I need to tell you."

"Yeah?"

"One is, you in the men's jail."

"So?"

"So Miss Anna's been trying to get in to see you. Every day since they brought you down. But for the last few years, they've kept the men down here and the women up on the second floor of the court house. Jailer says no women allowed down here even to visit. It's non-sense of course, but she wants you to know that she's done ever'thing she can to see you."

"You said there were two things?"

"She's hooked Craven Johnson."

"How do you mean?"

"I mean she went straight into the lion's den and talked Craven Johnson into defending you despite Ed Rumbough. Today or tomor-row, one or t'other, you should see old Craven coming along to save your ass. And you and I both know that if he's willing to thumb his nose at Ed and take your case, then maybe you got a chance."

"But still ..."

"Still what?"

"You've got to get Anna out of here. Even with Craven like a thun-dering bull, I'm still scared shitless we'll lose. I don't trust an Asheville jury with a newspaper in their hands, and I don't want Anna sitting in the courtroom when they hand down a verdict. I couldn't stand that. ... You hear me, Prince?"

"I hear you, but I don't think—"

"She can stay down in Hot Springs with Mrs. Jane. She can ..." I had to swallow before I could bring myself to say it. "She can go home to New York 'til it's over. I mean it. You've got to tell her—for my sake."

True to Prince's prediction, Craven Johnson came early the next morning. Carrying his battered briefcase, wearing an equally battered suit, and of all things, a sky-blue bowtie. When the guard unlocked my cell door this time, he carried in a chair for whoever was to follow, leading me to expect a celebrity—leading me to expect Craven.

He didn't look like an oil painting of himself that cold November morning. He had an elegant Homburg mashed onto his head and was smoking an ugly, black cigar.

"Greetings from the land of the living," he said as he settled himself into the jailer's chair. "From what I can see of your face, you look like hell."

"Thanks, Craven. I have always appreciated your fondness for the truth."

"Good. Cause you're about to get a dose of it."

"Let me go first then, before you start the lecture. Why are you even here? You're not known for taking on lost causes."

Craven held up three large, tobacco-stained fingers. "One, working for Ed Rumbough is not like working for his father. I'm tired of taking orders from the boy. That's one. Two is your little Anna Sweet Thing. Took me to lunch at the Roosevelt Hotel and told me in no uncertain terms that in standing trial you were just doing your duty as a Christian gentleman."

"I doubt she used those words."

"Actually, she did say gentleman several times, which caused me to have to ask her if we were talking about the same Stevie Robbins. Yes, she says, Stephen Baird Robbins, the only man worth the title she had met in North Carolina thus far, except that perhaps I might be the second." Craven took the cigar out of his mouth long enough to laugh. "I asked her who was going to pay this gentleman, meaning myself. And she allowed that your friends would pay me, including her. You got any friends, Stevie?"

"Least one. At least her."

"Ah, well, yes you do. More than you suspect, probably. Half the people in Madison County think you're the Second Coming for sending Roy on to his just reward, Miss Anna Ulmann wants to pay your legal fees, and then there's number three. Which may just be the reason why I decided to take on your desperate cause."

"Number three?"

"John Calhoun Rumbough. Baby of the family and about to be his brother's sworn enemy."

"Not Johnny!"

"None other."

"You got to protect him from himself, Craven."

"Now, that's funny. That's exactly to the word what he said about you. The thing you don't know, Stevie, is that he's carrying around a heavy burden about what happened that night. As it turns out, he had seen his brother in Asheville, and under what I imagine was some goading from Ed, bragged about how the two of you had saved Hans Ruser from the murderous plot of the crafty German saboteurs, whom Ed and Roy were then convinced you were harboring from the law."

"Johnny's no fool."

"Of course he's not; father's son. I can even imagine that Ed and Roy had you pegged for an accomplice or some such. At any rate, Johnny blames himself for having given Ed what he needed to ruin you. He even blames himself for Roy's death, or rather I should say, for your being charged with it. Tell me Stevie, why does Johnny Rumbough think you didn't do it, when the whole world knows you did?"

Craven was a past master of the sudden, unexpected question during cross-examination. I winked outrageously in reply. "I can't imagine why he thinks that."

Craven stared. "Are your injuries affecting you, or did you just wink at me?"

I winked again. My injuries were affecting me; my face hurt every time I even shifted on the cot.

"That means you didn't shoot him. Shit on you, Stevie. Who did?"

I winked again.

"That means your German boy shot him. With your shotgun."

I nodded ever so slightly. "Craven, I can't imagine that anybody stands to gain from hanging a German national for shooting Roy Robbins."

"Who, I grant you, desperately needed killing."

"Roy's been looking for someone to pull a trigger on him for most of the last twenty years."

"Well, there are some people who actually believe that we don't have much to gain from frying you either. You thought about that?"

"What do you mean, *frying*?"

"Son, the great state of North Carolina has been using the electric chair since 1910. Where the hell have you been! They don't aim to hang you. They aim to fry you."

"Don't have to fry me. I was scared for my life, Craven. Just look at me."

"Self-defense, is it? Well, I thought of that too. ... You happen to know where I might find a witness or two?"

"Long gone, or so I hope. Nobody else was there."

"Sure, there wasn't." I thought for a moment he would ask about Anna, but for reasons of his own, he moved on. "You're cutting this pretty damn fine, Stevie. I'm gonna have to put you on the stand. And you're gonna have to keep that sarcastic sense of humor of yours in check long enough to tell your story. And we're gonna have to come up with a reason you followed Roy and his prisoner in the first place. ... And one more thing."

"Yes."

"I'll get this into court as soon as ever I can, but the jury needs to see you as the victim of a truly ugly beating. You look perfect just the way you are, so try not to heal too much between now and the trial."

"I'll do my best."

Craven stood to go but then turned after knocking on the door to be let out. From the door he threw me an envelope from his brief case. I saw that it was addressed to me from Hans Ruser and that Craven hadn't bothered to hide the fact that he'd opened it. The guard opened the door, and Craven paused to interrupt me as I was about to examine the envelope. "The bodies are starting to come back from France, Stephen. A dozen boys from Asheville already, and the town's in a black, damn mood. What you and Miss Anna ain't calculated is if we lose this thing, and it looks like you were protecting the German, I may not be able to save you."

I nodded. I didn't know what to say to make either one of us feel any better.

The envelope contained Hans Ruser's iron cross, the one he'd been awarded for bravery. It was folded carefully into a sheet of plain paper, on which nothing was written. As nothing needed to be.

In the cold, squalid days that followed, they posted a guard on the street outside the foreshortened window to my cell, and they kept everyone out except Craven. Apparently Ed Rumbough's influence extended far enough into the local sheriff's department to make my life as uncomfortable as possible and to keep even brother Prince away from me.

Despite Ed's influence, however, Craven was able to circulate anecdotes of Roy's famous cruelty; stories about his disregard for the laws he was sworn to uphold began to appear in the Asheville papers. And perhaps best of all, my trial for murder was scheduled to begin on Monday, December 11th and my face was still a fright.

It was the night before that I dreamed of her. In the first days of those weeks in jail, I had savored any warm thought of her, memories of the hours we'd spent together, especially those hours when we'd managed to forget the war, managed to ignore the presence of the fence all around us, and managed to live inside the smaller circle of who we were together.

But as my wounds began to heal, and I began to gain back some strength, the erotic memories of our too few days and nights drilled into me like fire. I missed her voice, her throaty laugh, her spirit, but most of all at night, I longed for her touch. Would I ever again feel the absorbing warmth of her naked skin abandoned against mine? Dying didn't scare me; never touching her again terrified me.

I dreamed that I was ... *lying asleep on my cot in my cell, but somehow it was neither so narrow nor so hard as usual. And blankets—glorious, thick, woolen blankets—so that I slept warm and secure. A pervading sense of safety as well as warmth, almost as if the world was locked out rather than me locked in. As I lay there, luxuriating in the hot, scratchy wool against my skin, I suddenly realized that a beautiful, black-haired woman was in bed with me. My whole body was stiff and warm, turned on my side toward this happy creature. Then her bare foot, just that and nothing more, her bare toes were caressing the top of my foot, and it was the most sensual experience. And I knew they were Anna's toes, Anna's foot and all of her there beneath the blankets she had brought. I didn't think I could bear any more of her than that alone, but then when I reached out toward her, my hand brushed her hip. The naked swelling from her waist rising up to the elegant curve of her hip, all within the heat of our wonderful blankets, and when I rested my curved palm on her hip, her skin glowing golden even in the dark. And my body yearned toward hers, straining through my skin to be inside her skin.*

I moved in my sleep toward her, every nerve ending extended in urgent crying need, and ... I fell off the cot and onto the stone floor of my cell.

I confess that I lay there shaking. In waking, my heart cracked open, and I had no spirit left with which to drag my body back into that narrow, empty, black hole of a bed. Nor could I stop weeping for a long time into the night.

Craven brought me a clean, white shirt and one of my own wool suit jackets to wear. He had McGuire change my bandages on the very morning of, and in changing them, leave only the protective wrap over my nose, revealing the nasty, inflamed scar that extended onto my forehead above and down through my lip below.

When the Buncombe County deputies led me handcuffed into the courtroom proper, I had the briefest opportunity to look back over the crowd. And, hope raging against hope, I saw Anna sitting only several rows back, looking pale and drawn, between Prince and Johnny Rumbough. I thrilled to the fact that she was there and hated it for what she was about to hear. The room was already packed, the crowd restless and perhaps even angry. The whole thing felt out of control and threatening, but then Craven was in the room and seated beside me.

He leaned over and whispered to me in his gravelly voice, bathing me in the stink of stale smoke. "Relax, Stevie. I been here a thousand times. All that's going to happen today is culling through the jury and our first waltz with our wee, small District Attorney, Mr. Adler. He is going to tell their version ..." It struck me that Craven Johnson was nervous. "... and then he is going to abuse you with his witnesses. Then we are going to abuse Roy with some of our own witnesses. It will be great fun, and it'll be Wednesday at least before you're on. Try to relax and—"

"Jesus, Craven," I whispered. "You forget that I've done this before."

He smiled and leaned back in his chair.

"Sometimes, Craven, you scare the shit out of me."

His grin broadened, and he visibly relaxed.

It took five days. One day longer than Craven predicted. And the first two days were ugly—uglier by far than Craven had predicted. The prosecution put two former employees of the Mountain Park on the stand: one of whom was happy to say that I had spit on her while drunk and the other who had been in the dining room the night I killed Nathan Robbins.

The first witness, a former maid, admitted to Craven in cross-examination that she had been fired for theft, casting some doubt on the veracity of her testimony. The second, a retired waiter, didn't seem to understand that by describing in gory detail the night I had gunned down Roy's brother he made me sound nothing short of a blood-thirsty gunman, who made his rounds armed with a sawed-off shotgun. He was happy to explain that I had only been saving Bird's life by shooting her common-law husband, but by that point, the damage was done.

The one time I glanced back during this testimony, I saw that Anna had left the courtroom, and I immediately began to worry about what she must be feeling.

Jonsy Wright was by far the most entertaining witness either for or against Roy's character. She was so distressingly pregnant that the judge offered her a cushion to sit on in the rock-hard witness chair. She described how Roy had been in contact with certain of the German internees and had even had her deliver messages to one of them, a "pretty, yellow-haired boy." When Craven asked her what she meant when she said Roy had a "heavy hand," she managed to somehow say with a rueful grin that the deceased "liked to hit me onct-in-a-while and to grab me round the neck while we was, you know, havin' relations such that it was awful hard to figure just what he liked best about it anyway."

The judge couldn't hear Adler's objection because the laughter in the courtroom was so loud. Several men on the jury were as moved by Jonsy's plain, unadorned account as I had been when she first told it in the kitchen at Sunnybank. Perhaps it was then, in that flow of laughter, that the silent tide began to turn.

Anna was in the courtroom for most of the first three days, and I became practiced at inventing excuses to turn and catch a glimpse of her. After the third day, however, she disappeared and Jonsy with her. By that point, I was relieved, knowing that we were nearing the judgment.

On Wednesday, Ed Rumbough actually testified, which neither Craven nor I expected despite the fact that his name was on the list. Stiff and serene in his wealth, his mustache waxed to perfection, Ed swore under oath that I was protecting German saboteurs, establishing my motive for killing Roy and helping Siegfried escape. Craven challenged most everything he said as hearsay, but the judge smiled warmly on Ed and denied Craven, proving yet one more time what mere money can do.

Only Johnny's competing testimony and his confession that it was he who had told his older brother about the attempt on Ruser's life eased some of the effect of Ed's dark and impassioned accusations.

I took the stand on Thursday afternoon just after Johnny, took the stand knowing that at best the odds were even—for and against us. As I was sworn in, I searched the crowd in vain for Anna, trying to remind myself that I was the one who'd kept sending her messages by both Craven and Prince to leave, including a scrawled note passed back to her on the first day of the trial. I kept telling myself that she was gone for all the right reasons, even as I swore to tell the truth, the whole truth, and nothing but the truth, so help me God. Which I intended to do, more-or-less. Except for two small details: who was on the bridge at the end and who pulled the trigger.

As I searched the courtroom, I noticed a small, nondescript man sitting in the next-to-last row. A man who was obscurely familiar but whom I couldn't place despite the nagging thought that he was somehow important. It was when I began to tell my story, slowly and patiently with Craven's guidance, that I remembered the Nameless Man. The agent from the War Department who had lectured me about German agents in Craven's law office, months before. What the hell, I thought; he's here to see just how much damage I've caused and to see me pay for it.

But shortly thereafter, I wound my way more deeply into the story of that haunted night, and the vision of the courtroom before me became less real, less immediate than the story I was telling. The version, most of which was literally and verifiably true, that Craven and I had rehearsed until I was sick of the croaking of my own voice. I added only one true detail that I, myself, had no memory of. At Rutland that night, before Roy's deputies had come with their wagon, Anna had told me that as I lay at Roy's feet on the bridge, moaning and calling out, Roy had kicked King James out of the way and pointed the long-barreled Colt straight at my head. And laughed. She was certain he'd intended to fire. And I was certain as well. I had never heard Roy Robbins laugh, never in forty years.

Even under oath, it was easy to lie and say that I had fired up from the deck of the bridge into Roy's body. I think it was so easy simply because I had imagined doing so every day since he had died. Imagined it until it had become emotionally real. And even secretly satisfying.

My story told, the cross examination was a quick and surreal anticlimax. Little Mr. Adler, advocate for the state, wouldn't meet my eyes, and after a few questions, I realized he couldn't bring himself to look at the scar, which I'm sure flamed out against skin as white as new paper. When he told the judge he had no more questions and sat suddenly down, there was a long, hushed pause and then a kind of collective exhalation from the crowd. The cold, dark winter sky seemed to penetrate even the oaken heat of the courtroom, and we were adjourned.

That night, the Nameless Man came to visit me in my cell. Unlike the earlier visitation by Anna, this was not a dream. I admit I was shocked: I had seen no one but Craven within those walls for days.

He handed me a thick object wrapped in paper and then sat in Craven's chair, or so I had come to call it. I unwrapped what turned out to be a cigar as he propped back against the wall. "Congratulations," he said.

"Whatever for?" I asked, remembering some bare evidence of his sense of humor.

"I think you dodged the bullet on this one." He fished in his vest pocket and tossed me a book of matches.

"You been hobnobbing with the jury?" It took me several matches to light the cigar. It had been so long, and my fingers were so cold.

"No, but they trust Craven Johnson, and by the end of that story you told today, they trusted you."

"I hope you're right." The taste of smoke in my mouth and against my parched throat was simply glorious. Sinfully glorious. "What are you doing here?" I asked. "I figure I've generated all kinds of bad publicity and scared any thinking citizens half out of their minds."

He smiled. "Oh, we haven't got so many thinking citizens as you might imagine. And after talking to your attorney and watching you in court today, I know you didn't kill the sheriff."

"And so ...?"

"And so I'm glad that Siegfried Sonnach isn't standing trial for murder instead of you. *That* is the publicity that would soil the britches of the unsuspecting populace. And I'll tell you a little secret, something that may help make up for all you've been through."

I waited expectantly, my mind racing.

"Siegfried Sonnach is already out of the country. That son-of-a-bitch is no longer any of my concern or yours. So I really don't care who shot your sheriff."

"Out of the country?" I could hear the disbelief in my own voice.

"Cuba, probably South America by now. Trying to get back to Germany, I suspect. Or out of the war entirely to find himself a rich widow."

"I won't miss him," I said, although for a brief moment, I suspected it wasn't true.

"No, I imagine not. Besides, there is something else I want to talk to you about."

"After all this?"

"Once you get out of here, after you take some time and get your strength back, I'm going to offer you a job."

I stared at him in disbelief. "The War Department got some hotels that need managing?"

He laughed, the Nameless Man actually laughed. "You might say that. You have amazing luck, Mr. Robbins. When I first heard from Lawyer Johnson about your dilemma and when I read the papers on the train down here, I fully expected your luck had run out. But I think you'll walk away from all this. Probably tomorrow morning." He stood and regarded me with what was almost a friendly glance. "And as strange as this may sound, your country needs you. Not here; not after this. ... New York maybe. You ever been to New York, Mr. Robbins?"

"I've never even seen the ocean," I said.

CHAPTER TWENTY-TWO

IT was most like a great church awash in waves of light.

Of course I had heard about Grand Central Station, New York. A wounded soldier on the train, a boy who had seen England and France, still compared Grand Central Station to the hub of the world. The place where all tracks eventually led. And standing there, in the middle of the vast lobby, with the light pouring in through the high windows, I believed. I dropped my valise on the pink marble floor and turned in a circle, staring open-mouthed at the towering ceiling far above me.

I had slept on the train during the night, and I stopped in a washroom in the tunnel beneath the station to wash my face and teeth and put on a tie. The valet in the washroom, whose mahogany skin reminded me of Prince, had refused my tip, assuming from my face that I was a veteran.

When he did so, I returned for one more glimpse into the cloudy mirror. The scar was long and jagged, but it had faded from a constant application of Bird's onion juice, so that now it was only a thin line that ran diagonally across my face. My nose was only slightly crooked, and I had baked my whole head to a uniform nut brown in the spring sunshine. "I think I look pretty damn good, all things considered," I commented to the valet.

"Oh, yessir," he said, and I heard in his voice that he was a Southerner.

I handed him the quarter again. "I got this in North Carolina, not France," I said, pointing to my nose. "Our own little sector of the war."

He examined my face critically. "Hell of a place, that North Carolina."

I am frightened, so frightened. By what's happening to me and by what's happening to you. I had read her letter over and over in the four months since the trial. The letter she had written to me on the evening of the third day, after Ed Rumbough's deadly testimony. The letter she'd given to Prince and that he'd passed to me at supper the night after I was released by the jury. The letter that I'd carried in every suit of clothes I'd worn since. For months folded and refolded. Read and reread.

Stephen Dear,

I am frightened, so frightened. By what's happening to me and by what's happening to you. I sat today and listened to Edward Rumbough testifying how you had protected Siegfried and betrayed your country. And the whole time, I thought that it shoul be me on trial for my life, not you. In the beginning, I begged Prince to help me convince someone, anyone, that I had killed that awful man. But he refused because you had asked him to.

He refused and then the changes began.

What kind of perverse fate would let you die now? And would it be my fault if you did? After today, when even Mr. Johnson seemed defeated by Edward Rumbough, I am terrified.

You have asked me to leave. Over and over, almost as if you knew.

So now I think I must leave. I think I must go and take Jonsy away as well, for she is about to give birth, here now, in the middle of all this death.

How long ago in the summer I tried not to love you. But how could I know, Stephen, what it would all mean? I don't know yet how to pray, but I promise you that I will learn. Every day.

Your Anna

It had taken me a long time to imagine how she could blame herself for the choices I had made. I left Asheville on the first of April after all the Germans had been relocated to Fort Oglethorpe in Georgia; Hans Ruser and his senior officers had been removed while I was still in prison. Using Siegfried's escape as their trump card, the army had finally taken over ownership of the Germans and decided within weeks that Hot Springs was entirely too soft a berth for the Hun. The more Americans who were killed overseas, the more anger there was against anything German.

In April of 1918, after all our efforts, it was announced that the camp was to be closed, and I was without a job. Edmund Rumbough had finally gotten rid of me, but only after the War Department shut him down entirely and the Mountain Park was left a wartime ghost town. King James and I walked the streets of New Heidelburg alone, he with his squirrels, and both of us remembering the men who had built such beautiful patterns out of almost nothing at all.

I left King James with Prince and Dora in Hot Springs. I went first as far east as Wilmington, North Carolina, where I found some slow peace in a boarding house near the ocean. I had watched the waves hour upon hour, and in the slowness of their measured time, I came to understand her sense of responsibility, her need to blame herself. From my own dim memories of the trial, I understood her fear. But still I wondered what changes she was talking about. A change inside her mind, a diminution of her love? Despite all my irrational fear, I was certain that our hearts had never betrayed us, and so I couldn't understand what had finally taken her away.

Her letter was all I had. I had written and telegraphed to her in New York, at the address she had given me; I had written a dozen times from Hot Springs, and one long, rambling letter from the salt air of Wilmington. Letters that stitched together the past, the very precarious present, and what I hoped of the future. And no answer. Nothing to say what she thought or felt. Nothing to say she was even in New York.

"How can I get to 1000 Fifth Avenue?" I asked a policeman who was standing near the giant clock in the middle of the lobby.

He looked at me quizzically, with a grin on his face. I repeated the question, and he shook his head at me and shrugged.

Then the valet from the washroom appeared beside me, wearing a coat now over his uniform. "He don't understand you, boss. You in New York City now and no Irish cop gonna grab onto what a cracker like you n'me tryin' to say." He nodded and smiled at the policeman, who laughed at both of us. "Come on. I'll start you."

He led me by the arm as we walked toward the huge doors. "You see that there floor?" he asked.

I nodded. "Pink marble isn't it?"

"Pink marble out of Tennessee. That's down there bout where you're from, ain't it?"

I was still nodding as he led me out to the wide street and down to the corner. "What's wrong, boss?"

"I've never seen so many people in my life," I admitted. "Not on a sidewalk at any rate."

"You should'a seen it afore the war. Most empty now."

He led me across the street to the far corner. On the way, we stepped over tracks just like those that bisected the main streets in Asheville. "Streetcar runs by here ever' 30 minutes. Going north." He pointed and laughed. "No, that way. You get on it and ride 'til you see Central Park. That'll be trees and ponds and such on your left hand. First stop after you start seein' woods, you get off. Make damn sure you get off or you'll end up so far uptown you'll never get back. Then all you gotta do is look at the numbers on the doors. Think you can member that?"

I grinned at him. "I'm not quite as stupid as I look," I said. "And thank you!" I called out to his broad, laughing back as he disappeared into the crowd.

Riding the streetcar down the wide, frantically busy street in New York only served to remind me of the first time she and I had visited Asheville for the Major's funeral. The streetcar ride from the train station by the river up to Pack Square, and the ride back down the day after, when we had become lovers and the earth had tilted on its axis. As it tilted still.

But what if she wasn't there? What if the house at 1000 Fifth Avenue was boarded up or rented out? I had an address given to me by the Nameless Man, an address to which he wanted me to report, but I hadn't really come to New York to find him. Her rather. Always her. And I'd traveled a hell of a long way to face an empty door and my own crashing heart.

The brass number 1000 was scribed above an ornate stone entry way. I stood for a moment and focused on trying to control my breathing. It wouldn't do to be gasping for air if she should happen to answer. ... I knocked.

The door swung open suddenly, impetuously. "Would you be him?"

A tall, thin woman with her hair pulled back in a loose bun, wiping her hands on her apron.

"Well, I guess—"

"Come on then. I'll take you into the front room. It's there that she does the portraits." Her face was pockmarked by some past flirtation with smallpox, but her voice had all of Ireland in it.

She spun on her heel and I followed her, closing the door behind me, not sure just what else to do.

"Are you an artist fellow?" she asked conversationally. "She does mostly artists and writers and editors and such like. I don't know why editors, as they don't create nothin'. And the one thing she loves like Mary and Joseph is the creatin' of things." She turned back in the wide, rich hallway to examine me more closely. "And just what is it that you do?"

"I tell stories," I muttered in surprise. And then more boldly. "I'm a story teller from—"

"Well, a writer it is then. You must be that Sherwood Anderson fellow. Rumor has it he's as ugly as—" She flashed a gap-toothed smile over her shoulder. "Sorry. It was the ..."

"Scar?"

"To be sure, the scar. And a fine scar it is. Plus that funny gray patch in your hair. But never you fear; she'll be lovin' that. She has the very eye of the world for beauty in strange places." She turned suddenly off the hall and into a large sitting room whose windows opened onto Central Park. Her camera, oh my dear God, her camera stood on its battle-scarred tripod in the center of the room, facing a large easy chair before a wonderful, deep bay window. "Don't you worry now, Mr. Anderson, she will think you just the finest thing with your lovely face."

"Where must I sit, Miss ...?"

"Mattie. Actually Miss Maitlen McCall, but you must call me Mattie. You must sit where they all sit to have their portraits done. The throne I call it. And you must have a drink or a cigarette, whichever makes you feel to home. That's her style, you know, to make these important people feel at home, and then to catch them most natural."

"Will she come along soon, your mistress?"

"Oh, yes, she's very prompt. It's only that she hasn't felt at all well since ..." She looked critically at me. "Lately, she hasn't been her usual self, and I do worry when she works so hard, but you must do just as she tells you and give her not a moment's worry."

"I don't mean to worry her at all if I can help it."

That earned a smile from Mattie McCall. "It's a drink, then, you'll want?"

I sat in the chair. It was firmer than first it appeared. Caused the subject to tip forward, actually, toward the camera. "I need a drink," I admitted. "Would you pour me something strong into a cup of hot tea?"

"A man after my own heart with his dram in his tea. The kettle's on so it won't be a minute. And she'll follow soon, once I tell her you're here."

I studied the room while Miss Maitlen McCall put liquor into a tea cup. The walls were covered with book shelves and the shelves stacked with books. Her father's, I imagined. And in the breaks between the shelves, she'd hung photographs, one of which I recognized.

When Mattie came back with my steaming cup, I was standing before an image from Anderson Cove, the photograph of my mother in her porch rocker. Suddenly, I was back there once again, in that isolated mountain valley.

"You've found her favorite of all then," said Mattie as she handed me a fine china cup on a fine china saucer. "It's the place she says she'll go back to some day. Some place down there ..."

"In North Carolina," I whispered.

"So it is. In them mountains they have there. ... Now, you listen, Mr. Anderson. When she comes in, you must sit and be natural. Look at her and smile, as if you've known her a thousand years. That way, she'll have your portrait before you know it."

"Thank you, Mattie." I hesitated. "Is she all right, your mistress? Before, you seemed to say that she'd ... been ill perhaps."

"You seem a nice enough man, you do. And I will tell you what I tell you so that you'll be patient with her today. She was to have a baby, you see. And she has lost it."

"Oh, my God."

"Yes, we were enjoying the thought of it, as women are like to do." She must have seen the stricken look on my face. "But still, it was early enough, so that she didn't suffer except in her heart. But oh, it cut her something cruel. She is the strong woman of the world, but it was weeks before she got out of her bed. So you, sir, must be gentle with her."

"Gentle," I repeated.

"Then Mary and Joseph and Patrick be with you," she said and left the room.

And I did sit, after a few minutes. Sat forward in the chair Mattie called a throne and sipped my tea, so strong that it would have brought tears to my eyes if they weren't there already.

And so it was that I sat so still, breathing in the musky glories of the liquor and tea, as she came into the room. Anna Ulmann. As she came forward to stand beside her camera and so to consider the light. The light as it emanated from her subject. She looked ever so much like herself. Pale and worn, but still the woman who carried my whole heart in her hand.

"Oh my," she whispered. "You're not Sherwood Anderson."

"No. No, I'm not." All I could think of to say.

She leaned over and pulled the cloth attached to her camera around her head and studied, I suppose, the strange man who'd come there in my skin. I looked down and then squarely back into the aperture, smiling as bravely as I could, as the tears began to trickle down my crooked face.

She stood after a moment, one hand massaging her lower back in a gesture I'd never seen before. "You are a far more beautiful man than any Sherwood Anderson," she said. About to cry herself. Fighting back her tears like any mountain woman. "Far more beautiful than any man I know except one."

"Who would he be, this beautiful man?"

"Oh, someone I knew down in Carolina. In a pure state of nature and ever so long ago."

"Might I be him, this man?"

"Yes, you might," she admitted. And so we stared into the current of each other's eyes, she standing and me sitting on the edge of her overstuffed chair.

"Why didn't you write to this man of yours? He ached to hear from you." I heard the words more than said them.

She looked suddenly down at the carpet beneath her feet, the river of light between our eyes broken. "I lost his baby," she whispered. "I never meant to. And I was so ashamed when it happened. I was scared that it would break his heart." She looked up suddenly, and the river flowed again. "Your heart. Tear your heart in two to know what we'd lost."

"I never knew until today," I whispered. "Or I'd have been here the first moment."

"I know," she cried. "I know. I wanted to be sure, and so I waited. And then she was gone. How could I write then and tell you? Or not tell you? I so feared what you would think of me. The sadness lingers still. Even into spring."

I sat my cup carefully on the arm of the chair. Stood slowly to face her. "Perhaps I could help," I said softly. "I am ever your servant."

"And I yours," she said. "Though I know I've never been very good at it."

"You saved my life at the bridge," I said slowly. "You save it still."

"I am a divorced woman," she said. "That much I have done. A divorced woman trying to make her way in the world." She fell silent.

"Does that mean you want me to leave? Go back?"

She studied my face critically as if to make a photograph. Memorizing, I thought; she is memorizing my face before she sends me away.

"No. I think you had better stay," she said with the tiniest flicker of a smile, the smile that was my heart's balm. "Stephen Baird Robbins."

"Where must I stay, Anna?"

"Why, here. With me." And then, almost as an afterthought. "For a time anyway."

"Until I die?"

She nodded and began to laugh. The months falling away from her so that she seemed to stand again in the garden behind Sunnybank, laughing in the honeyed light.

Acknowledgments

A Short Time to Stay to Stay Here is a work of fiction inspired by historical events. We owe a debt to Jacqueline Burgin Painter for capturing these events in *The German Invasion of Western North Carolina*. Many thanks to the staff of the North Carolina Collection at the University of North Carolina for contributing historical details from their fabled riches.

You will find more historical information and photos as well as discussion questions at **www.ashortitmetostayhere.com.** This book was designed in a style similar to novels published in the time period when it is set.

Many thanks to Doris Betts, John Ehle, Vicki Lane, Jake Mills, Robert Morgan, and Elizabeth Spencer for their kind words. Thanks to Robin Sheedy, Ranier Blaesius, Todd Bailey, and David Strange for their close readings. Special gratitude to the people of Madison County just for being who they are.

Much appreciation to the team at Ingalls Publishing for believing in *A Short Time to Stay Here*. Bob and Barbara Ingalls along with Judith Geary. Thanks for your true love of literature.

A heartfelt thank you to my wife and family, who contributed much during the making of this book.

TERRY ROBERTS was born in Asheville and raised near Weaverville, North Carolina. His father, Lee, to whom this novel is dedicated, was born in Anderson Cove, as was Lee's mother, Belva Anderson Roberts. All told, Terry Roberts' ancestors have lived and farmed in Madison County since the 1700s. The Director of the National Paideia Center, Roberts is a graduate of UNC-Asheville, Duke University, and UNC-Chapel Hill.

For more of the story behind the story, visit the author's website:
http://imap.ashorttimetostayhere.com

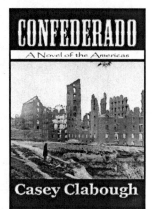

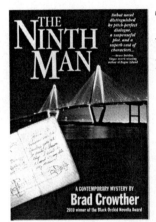

THE NINTH MAN
by Brad Crowther
ISBN: 978-1932158922

Contemporary mystery tied to the Southern past

In 1864, the Confederate submarine, *H. L Hunley*, vanished in Charleston, SC harbor. When Russ Berard's father, a Hunley enthusiast, learns of the diary of a Yankee spy on board the sub that night, he is murdered. Berard, a Rhode Island police detective, returns home to Charleston to investigate his father's death and is confronted by a descendant of the spy, determined to keep the diary secret, and by an old friend planning a Hunley reality show. But why is the diary of a Yankee spy, the Hunley's ninth crew member, worth killing for so many years later? Finding the answers takes Russ on a journey through the history of Charleston as well as his own past.

Brad Crowther is winner of the 2010 Black Orchid Novella Award presented jointly by The Wolfe Pack and *Alfred Hitchcock Mystery Magazine*

"Debut novel distinguished by pitch-perfect dialogue, a suspenseful plot, and a superb cast of characters ..."
—Bruce DeSilva, Edgar Award-winning author of *Rogue Island*

Action-packed blend of history, mystery, romance, and suspense."
—Vincent H. O'Neil, Malice Award-winning author of **Death Troupe**

"Blends a fast-paced story with a fascinating historical puzzle. ... keen insight into what still matters for people who cannot— or perhaps will not—let go of the past."
—Albert A. Bell, Jr. Award-winning author of *Corpus Conundrum*, & the Pliny series of historical mysteries